THE TURNING OF THE TIDE

Liz Shakespeare

LETTERBOX BOOKS

First published 2010
by
Letterbox Books
Littleham
Bideford
Devon
EX39 5HW
Reprinted 2013

www.lizshakespeare.co.uk

ISBN 978-0-9516879-2-5

Printed and bound by SRP Ltd, Exeter

ACKNOWLEDGEMENTS

I would like to thank Shirley Cowling, Alison Harding and Nora Bendle for their support and encouragement; Peter Christie for answering my numerous questions on local history; Kate Cryan for her careful reading; and my son Ben for working so hard for me and never complaining.

I am also grateful to the staff at the North Devon Local Studies Library and Record Office; the staff at the Devon Record Office; the volunteers at the Bideford and District Community Archive; The Wellcome Library in London for access to the papers of the Ackland and Littlewood families (MSS.5410-5419 and MSS.7205-7216) donated by Dr M.J. Littlewood; Caroline Jones for permission to reproduce the photograph of Clovelly on page 48; and the Westward Ho! History Group for allowing me to reproduce the photograph on page 307.

Birth certificate of Thomas Burman, 1863, Bideford Union Workhouse

Birth certificate of William Burman, 1867, Bideford Union Workhouse

Extract from census return, 1871, Bideford Union Workhouse, showing Selina, Thomas and William Burman. (The National Archives, RG10/2201/76)

October 1871

Chapter One

Selina pushed her watery porridge to one side and raised herself a few inches above the bench; she could just see over the heads of the other inmates to the children's tables on the far side of the dining room. She had to take care; if she stood right up the Mistress, Mrs Eastman, would shout at her. There. It *was* Thomas whose cough was crowing out above the rest. He was sitting with his head down, and was not eating his gruel. Will was sitting next to him, his head almost reaching Thomas's shoulder. You could see they were brothers from the shape of their closely-shaved heads. Selina always told them to sit together when they could, to hold hands and try to keep warm, and they did, but their faces rarely registered affection. Like all the Workhouse children they were subdued, always sad but rarely crying once they were past the frenzied grief at being separated from their mothers. Thomas coughed again, his shoulders shaking with the effort. She had known it was him. She had learnt over the last few years to identify Thomas and Will's cries, coughs and the rare giggles from those of the other children, whether she heard them from across the dining room or from the other side of the high wall that divided the exercise yards.

She picked up her spoon again and whispered to the woman next to her on the bench.

"Ann, how many days be it now 'til Sunday?"

On alternate Sundays the mothers were allowed to spend a short time with their children.

Ann Champion thought for a moment. "'Tis Friday today. Two days 'til Sunday. Be it him coughing?" She craned her neck to see the boys' table. "My William's eaten all his bread. He's always hungry. I shall give him mine, Sunday."

"He gets a cough every winter, Thomas does. But 'tis early for winter i'n't it?"

"'Tis October now. That idn't winter, not really."

Ann's face crumpled suddenly and she started to cry silently, hugging herself and rocking. Her younger son George had died a few weeks ago, just twelve months old. Selina took her hand.

"There, come now, it don't do no good. It saved him the pain of being parted from you in this world. He never knew sorrow."

Images flashed before her eyes of her boys screaming and trying to cling on to her as the Mistress pulled them from her, first one, then the other, when they were weaned at two years old.

She swallowed the last of her gruel with some water to wash it down. She heard Thomas's cough again, hard and dry, ringing out amongst the other coughs, the subdued mumbling and the intermittent shrieks from the idiot Elizabeth Gregory. October. That would mean that Will must be four years old or close to it, and Thomas nearly seven. Neither had ever been outside the Workhouse walls.

All of a sudden the Master strode between the tables and grabbed a small girl by the arm. He lifted her high off the bench and, dropping her to her feet, proceeded to slap her bare legs ten, twelve times, the slaps reverberating around the silent room. The other children started to whimper and Selina held her breath until he yelled,

"Stop snivellin', the lot of you or you'll be served the same!" and marched back to his table at the end of the room. The small girl clambered quickly back on to her bench and buried her face in her arms to hide her sobs.

"Poor little chiel. Who was it?" Selina whispered to Ann.

Ann peered over, keeping one eye on Mr Eastman who was now taking his son Percy on to his lap. "I think 'twas Mary Bale, one of that little orphaned family from Abbotsham. Her was licking out her bowl, I saw her."

Gradually the room settled back into the hum of subdued voices and coughing. Ann nudged Selina. "Don't do that. 'Twill sting when you'm working."

Selina looked down at her hands. Her fingertip was raw and bleeding where she had torn the nail off with her teeth. She hid them under her apron but Harriet Braddon saw her and leaned over, smiling and whispering rude comments.

The children were given the order to stand and all the women watched as they filed out for their lessons, knowing they would not see them again until the evening, as they took their lunch in the schoolroom. Thomas sought out Selina's face and gave a sad little smile when she surreptitiously blew him a kiss. Since he had turned seven, he spent only three hours in the schoolroom and had to work for the remainder of the day. The men, most of them elderly, shambled out next and then the women were given their orders. As the others went out, table by table, Selina held on to Fanny Mock to prevent her following, for they were working together in the dining room along with Ann and the imbecile known as Mad Mary. Ann took Mary down to the men's end and Selina told Fanny to pick up the plates and bowls. She had to be told every time and Selina often wondered whether she was being deliberately difficult. She was always slow because she wiped her finger round the porridge bowls if there was a smear left, a habit which made Selina feel sick even if she was still hungry too. When all the things were cleared away to the kitchen they got their buckets and brushes and started scrubbing down the tables and benches. The carbolic and the hot water were stinging their cracked hands but they had to scrub and scrub although the deal couldn't have been any whiter, for if they finished too quickly Mrs Eastman would make them start again. Selina noticed that Elizabeth had peed on her bench again and made sure Fanny did that one because she never noticed the difference between water and pee so it didn't turn her stomach. Then they cleared back the tables and started on the floor.

Selina had scrubbed many floors in her twenty-four years, but none as big as that one. As she sat back on her heels it stretched out at such a length it could have been her whole life in front of her, and Ann and Mad Mary so far away it scarcely seemed possible that they could meet. She sighed and turned around to work backwards across the room until they met in the middle. Her hands were as calloused as any blacksmith's but somehow her knees could never get accustomed to that stone floor. Each time she shuffled backwards it felt as though she was kneeling on a bed of red hot needles. Her back ached so much she thought it would snap like a dead stick, yet her bones were not old. Twenty-four isn't old, not really, she thought. Fanny was crying and Selina had to urge her to move on otherwise she would keep scrubbing the same patch. She kept her eye on the pillars, for each pillar they reached meant fresh buckets of water, and that meant she could get up off her knees to fetch them. But just as she had scrubbed level with the first pillar, out came the Master across the clean floor and stood so close she had to take care not to splash his boots and the dirty black of his trousers. She could smell him, that male smell of sweat and hair oil and she felt her hands starting to shake. She kept scrubbing, trying to look from the corners of her eyes to see if she had missed a speck of dried porridge or a crumb that he would find fault with. Still he stood and still she scrubbed, trying now to see what Fanny was doing, for if Fanny had missed a bit that was her fault as well and they would both have to go back to start again. At last he shouted and she jumped because that shout had been so long coming.

"Selina Burman, be there two mump-heads working here? Go fill your bucket and be quick about it. The Mistress wants the windows cleaned as well before dinner." And he kicked the bucket over before walking off, his nailed boots ringing like gunshots on the hard floor.

It was as much as she could do to get up and fetch the water. However, it did mean a breath of air, a minute out in the yard away from the carbolic. She made Fanny pump while she held the buckets so she could look up past the high walls to the sky. It was grey and the darker grey clouds moved quickly across it as if away to a better place. Fanny was still crying, thick snot dribbling down into her open mouth and a few strands of her greying hair sticking to it. Selina gave her a hug, taking care to avoid her face and Fanny hung on to her as if her life depended on it and sobbed even harder. They stood there for a full minute, two small figures in the empty yard with the high walls all around.

Selina had been scrubbing the floor twice a day for over a year. Before that it had been the laundry for several years and before that it was picking oakum. The oakum was the worst. The Master always set the mothers of bastard children to pick oakum when they first came in and they had to pick away at those hard bits of rope until their fingers bled. The work was hated so much, they were sure to leave as soon as someone came asking for a maid, however rough that person might be. Of course the Master hoped they would soon set themselves up and come back for the child. Selina wasn't the only one who came back with another in her belly instead. And once they had had two he never let them leave. Not without taking the children with them and there were few who could do that and survive.

The thing she dreaded most when scrubbing that floor was having someone come through the door behind her. She was not supposed to look around so would have to stay on her knees with her bottom sticking up in its grey and white stripes and her workhouse cap on her head and she knew that Fanny looked just the same, so for anyone looking on they were two of a kind. She hated the thought that the person would not be able to tell her and Fanny apart. And that led her on to think that perhaps there was no real difference between them. She cried to think of it and had to stop and blow her nose on her apron, hoping Mrs Eastman wouldn't see. Was her hair as coarse and wiry as Fanny's? Did she smell as bad as her? Were her teeth as black and rotten? Harriet Braddon had a scrap of broken looking-glass which she kept hidden under her pillow and she stared into it before she went to sleep. Once she had passed it to Selina who had flinched to see the pale, pinched face and the startled eyes looking back at her, but she hadn't thought to look at her teeth. Fanny was as daft as a brush now, but she hadn't always been like that, for she had once been up in London working in a big hotel and who was to say it wasn't the Workhouse that had addled her brains? No one would ever employ her now; she would never leave the Workhouse. During those hours when the water slopped from the buckets, the brushes went scratch, scratch on the hard floors and the smell of the carbolic filled Selina's head, and she knew that after dinner she'd have to start over again even though there'd only be a few specks of dirt, she often wished she were dead because what use was she to anyone? If it hadn't been for her boys she would have found a way to end her life even though it would have been a sin.

Harriet Braddon used to say,

"Take 'em. Just take your boys and go."

Harriet had done so, many times. She'd just tell the Mistress she was discharging herself and little Emily and as soon as they had done her papers, off she would go into Bideford town. She used to be away for a month or two, but the times got shorter as the years went on and now it was often only a week before she came back in. Ann had said that was because Harriet was getting older and the men didn't like her so much. She'd come back even thinner than she went out, often with a black eye or two and once with her arm broken. And she'd be quieter for a while, but it wouldn't last.

The things she used to say. Selina blushed to think of them. About the men she met, and how they looked. And what they did. A lot of the women laughed and then she would tell more, becoming louder and ruder until she would start to shout that she hated this place and then she'd cry and once she threw her cup across the room. When the Mistress heard her, she would be shut her up on her own, and her fortnightly visits with Emily would be stopped for a while. That was what kept them going, all the women with children. If they couldn't see their children for ten minutes once a fortnight and give them a cuddle when no one was looking, then what was there to live for?

Selina had asked Harriet once what she should do if she

took the boys and left. It was after her youngest son had been taken from her and she'd hear his crying at dinner and at night her arms were so empty she felt as if a part of her had been cut away. Harriet laughed at her but told her where to go and what to do until her words brought back the memories that gave Selina bad dreams at night. Nevertheless she had tried to imagine herself saying and doing those things that Harriet told her. But she couldn't. Even for the sake of having her boys with her she couldn't do it. There were some who did turn to sin, she knew that. Some never returned and it was never known what became of them, except for one who set herself up with a room and found some gloving work. Her story was told with envy for she had achieved what so many craved for. But Selina knew that those who went were acquainted with Bideford and the names of the streets Harriet told of and some had a sister or a mother who would help them for a few days. So she stayed put. She had almost given up hoping for something better. And if she thought at all of the future it was to a time when her boys would be grown and found a position, then she would be free to leave too, with only herself to care for. She wondered whether Fanny once thought of leaving. But none of them knew what Fanny really thought.

She didn't mind cleaning the windows. Fanny held the stepladder while Selina climbed slowly up with the bucket and the cloths, her arm aching with the weight of the heavy bucket while she kept her balance with her other hand. As she wiped the soapy cloth over the glass, she left until last a little round spy hole near her face and then wiped that bit clear of soap first so that she could look out all the time she was cleaning. Inside the Workhouse all she ever saw were walls. High walls to keep her in and stop her seeing into the children's yard. The lower windows whitewashed to stop anyone looking out, except in the master and mistress's rooms as their windows were used to spy on the inmates in the yards. But from the stepladder there was a view. She could see roofs and chimneys, lots of chimneys like at home in Clovelly only not so steeply ranged one above the other. And beyond the chimneys she could see fields and a farm, a long way off. She didn't know where the farm was. She wondered whether it was the one she had known at Woolsery though probably it was too close for that. Even so it was wonderful to see those chimneys and the farm and the fields. There was a tree with a few leaves still on it, moving in the breeze. And smoke from the chimneys which meant that there were people there, outside the walls. When she climbed down the ladder the memory of what she had seen stayed with her, almost until it was time to clean the windows again.

In the afternoon they scrubbed the floor again and Fanny went into one of her moods, sitting on the floor and rocking and moaning, "No, no, no!" Selina did her best to bring her round, first coaxing then shouting and finally slapping her, until she turned suddenly with some sense in her eyes amongst the tears for once and said,

"Don't 'ee know better than to serve a poor old woman like that? I'd have given *you* orders once!"

She was a strange one, was Fanny Mock. She went back to her rocking and crying and nothing Selina did made any difference. The Mistress heard the noise and came strutting across the wooden floor. She held a cane in her hand and she kept poking Fanny in the ribs.

"Get up, get up and work or I'll have 'ee put away in a dark room. No light, Fanny Mock, and no food!" until Fanny saw sense and picked up her brush again. By then Mad Mary had started up at the other end of the room, standing up and shouting out unholy words one after the other, but she hushed when Mrs Eastman waved the cane in her face.

When they finished the floor they were sent with all the other women to the yard for an hour before supper. Selina crouched with Ann against the wall in the cold drizzly rain. They usually sought out each other's company. Sometimes they talked but not often, for what was there to say? Sometimes Ann cried when she thought of George and Selina held her, but it was hard to think of words to cheer her. She knew that they had sinned, both of them, and there was no changing that now, but it seemed hard that their children suffered for their wrongdoing.

They filed back into the dining room again and took their plates of bread and cheese and mugs of water back to their seats. The bread looked a bit softer than was customary and the cube of cheese was a little bigger and Selina was so hungry she felt she could have eaten it in one swallow. They waited while the elderly paupers came in, collected their plates and hobbled to their tables. Then the children came. There was Will and he was staring around with a worried look, searching the faces of the women. He nearly tripped over the boy in front and quickly put his head down and his hands behind his back like the rest for fear the master would notice him. Selina knew he was looking for her and she was so busy staring at him while he stood in line for his supper, hoping he'd look once more, that it was a while before she thought to look for Thomas. He wasn't there. She leaned to one side to see the end of the line until Harriet Braddon dug her in the ribs with her elbow. The children with their close-cut hair and Workhouse clothes looked alike, save for their height, but even so she could pick out her boys at a glance. Thomas wasn't there. Again and again she searched the line of downcast heads, hoping that as the children shuffled forwards in their heavy boots, Thomas would appear from behind a bigger boy or even come through the door, beaten and sobbing after some wrongdoing. But before long they were all at their places, prayers were being said and the benches scraping on the stone floor as everyone sat down. Ann whispered to her.

"Selina, leave off chewing your fingers and eat your cheese. What's troubling you, maid?"

"It's Thomas. He idn't here."

"I hadn't missed'n. I was watching my William." She looked across the room. "It may be he's in the infirmary. He coughed bad at breakfast, mind. 'Twill be better for him if he's there. For if that idn't the way of it, he may be locked away for being wicked."

13

It comforted Selina to think that Thomas might be in the infirmary, but now she worried that he was sick, and maybe alone. She ate her bread and cheese, forcing it down, and watched Will across the room as he ate his. He looked so small, just a baby without Thomas at his side.

Harriet Braddon had overheard their whisperings and that started her off.

"Us mothers should be told if our children are sick. Go on maid, ask the Mistress where he's to, you've a right to know."

Her voice rose and Selina whispered frantically, pleading with her to stop. But she would not be quiet and finally marched up to Mr and Mrs Eastman and spoke loud enough for the whole room to hear.

"Please ma'am, us wants to know where's Thomas Burman. His mother's that worrited about him and it ain't right."

Every head in the room seemed to turn towards Selina, and she hunched down on the bench and pulled her apron over her face. It was the Master's attention she feared most.

"It's no concern of *hers* where the boy is, he's in my charge. And d'you think I can mind the whereabouts of every pauper child when there are so many? Sit back down now Harriet Braddon or it'll be the worse for you."

She couldn't sleep that night. She was forced to share a bed with Fanny Mock for there were always more women than beds, and her nerves were so on edge that everything irritated her: the bitter cold; the scratching of the blanket on her cheek; Fanny's foul breath in her face; the hard lumps and sharp ends of straw in the mattress; the snores and mumbling and scratching from so many women shut up close in one room. She thought of Thomas, his little face that always seemed so sad and worried, more like an old man of shrunken stature than a boy of seven years.

It was all her fault. Her fault that her sons had never known what it was to have the freedom to run and play at will, had never had a home or good food or a loving family round them. How innocent she had been when Joseph Andrew had stood so close to her in the barn at Stroxworthy and whispered those cherished words! It was so long ago, yet she could almost imagine him to be with her now and feel his gentle, caressing hands. How warm he had felt when he pressed up against her, his hair smelling of fresh air and wood smoke, his hands so strong and persistent. When she found she was expecting, she had imagined that they would marry, that they would live on the farm and she would take care of the calves and the hens and have many more children. But his parents said she was not good enough for him. She had been sent home to Clovelly and for two days her father had raged at her for the shame she had brought on the family and for imagining that he would be able to support her, before turning her out to find her way to the Workhouse in Bideford. She did not know whether Joseph Andrew knew what had become of her. No doubt he was married now, with children he owned to be his. He would never think of her now.

She would not have dared to resist the other, the one that was Will's father. He had taken her from the Workhouse as if from charity and she had thought herself lucky to be chosen. He had said he needed a hard-working girl as a general servant to help his wife and had taken her from the Workhouse in a straw-filled cart as if she was a ewe or a heifer. It had hurt her to leave Thomas behind but she had hoped that she would soon earn enough to remove him from the 'House and support him. She pictured again the farmhouse that she had tried to banish from her memory and remembered the constant fear as she moved about it, performing her duties, trying to keep close to the other servants or within earshot of his wife. But time and again it would happen, in an outhouse where she had been sent on an errand or in a distant bedroom which she had been forced to clean alone. She would hear his heavy footsteps, then the hated laugh and coarse words, smell the sweat and the pungent detested hair oil as his rough hands pulled at her clothes and threw her against a wall or on the floor. She never looked at him but remembered the texture of roughly plastered walls as her face was repeatedly pushed against them, the dust that she saw collected around the legs of beds as she turned her face away from the pounding figure that pinned her to the floor. When her condition had become noticeable he had hit her in front of his wife and called her a slut and a whore then driven her back to the Workhouse in the cart.

The lumps in the mattress pressed against her hip bone. She turned away from Fanny and tried to find a more comfortable position. She had never seen the dormitory where the boys slept, as the mothers were not allowed to enter it even for cleaning, but she had often been comforted from thinking of it as it had been described to her, and of her boys lying there asleep. Now she did not know where Thomas was. Eventually she pushed back the blanket and crawled to the end of the bed, taking care not to unsettle those in beds close up against hers. The floor was cold under her bare feet as she felt her way to the bucket at the end of the room, held her breath against the stench and passed water. As she crawled back into bed, Fanny opened her eyes and murmured,

"You'll be out one day, maid, you will," then reached for her hand. Selina felt her eyes fill with tears and she clutched Fanny's calloused hand, although she knew that Fanny rarely talked sense and probably meant something else altogether. How would she ever get out? She wouldn't be allowed to leave two children behind even if she wanted to and no one would employ her, unless to make use of her like the last time.

The next day passed in the same manner as the last. Thomas was not at breakfast, nor at dinner. Will no longer looked for her as he came into the room but she could see where the tears had washed his face clean. But that night no sooner were all in bed and the candles put out than the door opened and Mrs Eastman appeared, looking even more ill-tempered than usual. Several women sat up in bed in surprise at her unexpected arrival and Mad Mary shrieked,

"Don't let her take me away!"

"You, the Clovelly maid, Selina Burman, you'm wanted in the infirmary." Selina must have looked at her stupidly because she shouted,

"Get up woman, that's your name, i'n't it? The doctor wants you there, though for why I can't figure."

Selina struggled out of bed then stood there in her bare feet.

"Hurry up, he's not to be kept waiting. Put on your boots and a blanket over your nightgown."

She did as she was told and followed without waiting to lace her boots. She followed Mrs Eastman down the steep, dark stairs, through the doors that were unlocked and locked again behind her, and across the cold yard illuminated by a thin moon. They came to a room and she hesitated on the threshold. She clasped her hands together to stop them shaking and looked down in confusion when she saw a dark figure standing by a bed.

"You are the mother of Thomas Burman?" Although the man's voice was abrupt there was no unkindness in it. Mrs Eastman said,

"She is, Dr Ackland, and should be asleep in her bed at this time."

"It is only right that a mother should be with her child when it is sick." He spoke more sharply to the matron than to Selina. "What is your name?"

She raised her eyes a little and saw shiny black shoes and the hem of a dark coat. It was with some difficulty that she managed to answer him.

"Well, Selina, come here and see your son."

She saw the shoes move round to the other side of the bed.

"Confound it, there is never a chair to be found in this place. Here, be seated on the bed and take his hand. Mrs Eastman, he needs a pillow for his head. As I know you will tell me you have none, will you please fold a blanket so that his head may be raised."

For the first time she realised that Thomas was in the bed and in an instant was beside him. He appeared even paler than usual and his breath came with some effort. His eyes were half-open and she saw that he knew her as she took his hand and stroked his dear head. She did not realise that the man was addressing her.

"Is she capable of understanding?"

"She is, Sir, providing you speak slowly."

He sat down on the bed opposite Selina so that their faces were level. She flinched at the proximity of the broad bearded face but she saw that his expression was kind before quickly looking down again.

"Selina, your son is very ill. He has a grave infection of the chest which is causing him to cough very badly. I have given him linseed to ease the congestion and he would benefit from your presence."

She dared to glance at him again as his meaning became apparent.

"Can I stay with 'n, Sir?"

"Yes, I wish you to stay with him until the outcome is clear." Mrs Eastman tutted and stamped her feet impatiently.

"Can I stay with 'n all night, Sir?"

"Yes, I wish you to stay with him tonight and tomorrow also if that is necessary. Is that clear, Mrs Eastman?"

"Well, if her's staying up I shall send the nurse to bed. It don't need two to care for them in here."

"Do as you wish. Now Selina, I shall be back tomorrow to see how the young patient is. Good night."

She gazed at Thomas again and stroked his face and when she came to her senses enough to look around, she and Thomas were alone but for three shadowy breathing shapes in adjacent beds.

That night was one that she would never forget. To spend a whole night with her son, to sing him the little songs he had liked as a baby, to stroke him and hold him up in her arms when the cough troubled him, to lie on the bed and sleep with him for a while as they had slept in his first two years – these were pleasures which she had never dared to hope for again.

She told him that one day they would leave that place, they would go home to Clovelly where people were kind and the walls were there to keep people dry rather than keep them in, and there were trees and cliffs and sea across which you could see to the very edge. She told him of the little houses people lived in, with doors through which they came and went as they pleased, and of the soft bread of which there was nearly as much as one wanted to eat, and of the fish which tasted so good. It seemed he understood, for he gazed at her as if she was telling him of heaven, and it seemed to her that she was.

When he slept she left his side now and then to walk around the room. There were three old women on the other beds. Two slept uneasily and she was unable to recognise their faces in the candlelight but she saw the third to be old Mrs Evans whom she had not seen for many months. She held the candle up so that the old woman might see her face and reminded her of her name but the old woman mumbled and blinked vacantly without looking at Selina, her face tiny and withered within her huge bonnet. In the corner of the room, behind a wooden screen, a young woman who had just been delivered of a girl was anxious for reassurance, having been brought to the Workhouse shortly before the birth. Selina sat on her bed for many minutes while they looked at the tiny creature and stroked her still damp hair. The young mother told Selina that the child's father had gone away to work but would return for her, and Selina wished her well with her hopes for the future.

As the sky began to lighten Thomas took a turn for the worse. His breaths came fast and short and it seemed to Selina that they pained him though he did not cry out but stared at her with fear in his eyes. She held his hand and stroked his face, telling him over and over that he would soon be better. It seemed as if the morning would never come as she sat there listening to each breath and cough and the sighs of the old women who had begun to wake. At last the nurse, Mary Jones, came in and bustled around making things appear safe again. She said that Thomas was very ill but she made him more comfortable and he seemed to sleep. She was kind to Selina and allowed her to stay. She even brought a mug of tea and a piece of bread so that she would not have to go away for breakfast.

It was only when the doctor came and told her that the end was near that Selina began to realise that his sleep was one from which he would not wake. The doctor made Thomas comfortable and then sat with her for a short time and asked her many questions about her life and how she came to be in the Workhouse. She still could not look at his face for he was looking intently into hers, and she answered his questions with many "Yes, Sir"s and "No, Sir"s. He asked her such questions that she would not have been able to answer at all if her sorrow and confusion had not overcome her sense of shame. He stayed with her until Thomas passed away.

It was not until that night, in her bed, that she wept. She wept until her stomach ached and her blanket was sodden and she could barely draw breath, and she thought that she would never stop weeping, seeing Thomas in her imagining and knowing that she would never stroke his sweet face again. Ann and Harriet and others held her and wept with her, joining their sorrow with hers as they all cried for their children, those from whom they were parted and those whom they would never hold in their arms again.

REGISTRATION DISTRICT   Bideford

1871.....DEATH in the Sub-district of.....Bideford.....in the .....County of Devon

No.	1 When and where died	2 Name and surname	3 Sex	4 Age	5 Occupation	6 Cause of death	7 Signature, description and residence of informant	8 When registered	9 Signature of registrar
412	Thirtieth October 1871 Union Workhouse Bideford	Thomas Burman	Male	7 years	Son of Arthur Burman, Domestic Servant	Acute Pneumonia — Certified	Mary Jones — Present at the death — Union Workhouse — Bideford —	Twenty fifth October 1871	James Lee, Registrar

Death certificate of Thomas Burman, 1871, Bideford Union Workhouse

Dr W.H. Ackland
(Wellcome Library, London)

Chapter Two

Dr Ackland walked out of the Workhouse in a less decisive manner than was usual for him. He nodded at the boy in Workhouse garb who was holding his horse, then mounted and rode off, leaving the boy staring after him, disappointed that the usual currant bun had not been handed down from the saddlebag.

He let the horse walk down Meddon Street and hesitated when he reached the junction. He did not feel ready to go home to Bridgeland Street yet. There had been another case of smallpox that he must report to the Local Board. There was a child in Landcross who was still suffering from a fever; would it not be prudent to fit in a visit? The thought of the ride to Landcross was inviting. He urged the horse into a steady trot and let his thoughts drift back to the Workhouse. It was fortunate that he was not often asked to cover for Dr Pridham as a visit to that place put him in an ill humour for the rest of the day. He should try to put the matter behind him. A child had died; a mother was left bereft like so many other unfortunates. To be sure there had been injustice, but was it not ever thus? But to be in that abominable place through no fault of her own, separated from her other child and without her family to comfort her! He kicked his horse into a canter on the grass verge that ran between the road and the broad river glistening in the late afternoon sun. And why was she there? Because of a man who, instead of employing a good, respectable girl as a servant, finds some poor drab in the Workhouse, pays her a few pence, uses her to satisfy his own depraved appetites and discards her back in the Workhouse when she is carrying his bastard. The Doctor lashed out at a low branch with his whip, making his horse shy. Who was that man? The girl had been innocent, he felt sure of that. He remembered the downcast eyes, the calloused hands with nails bitten to the quick which writhed with embarrassment in her lap as she responded to his searching questions. There were many who would have denied him a response, given him that challenging stare which said, "And what business be it of yours?" He was familiar with that look from the more debased of the women he visited, both in the Workhouse and out of it.

Selina Burman was not one of those. She was modest, respectful, suffering no doubt from a persistent melancholia as did so many in that place, but with some quality that he found hard to define. A small kernel of optimism perhaps, an ability, however smothered, to look out beyond her present situation. There was some hope of redemption for her. But not while she remained in the Workhouse. He slowed his horse to a walk as a carriage approached and he raised his top hat with a flourish to the coachman from Hallsannery, on his way, no doubt, to meet the London train.

In some cities there were now training colleges for Workhouse girls of good character, establishments set up by beneficiaries so that the inmates might learn the skills of good servants and obtain suitable positions. But Selina Burman would not, of course, be acceptable even if such a place existed in Bideford. She had been mother to not one but two illegitimate children and it seemed from what she said that she had been a willing victim the first time. It was foolish of him even to consider that she might be saved.

He let his eyes wander over the myriad russets and bronzes of the beech trees that clung to the steep slopes above the road. It was a fine autumn; several sharp frosts had turned the leaves before they had started to fall. He must bring the family out to see them, either here or perhaps out on the Yeo Vale Road where they could partake of a picnic in Parkham woods. That unfortunate child in the Workhouse had died without ever seeing such sights.

If only he could remove her from the Workhouse, find her a position where she would be secure and give her poor remaining son a chance of a better life. But who would take her on? Of all the professed Christians in the town, there were none he could name who would open their homes to one who would be perceived as a Jezebel. The fear of censure and loss of respectability would be too great. An idea occurred to him. But such a girl would not be appropriate for his own household. Yet they would soon be in need of a housemaid and if he was correct about her potential... He slowed and soothed his horse as they approached the railway workings. The ringing of iron on steel rang out and echoed across the wide river valley, traversed now by a modern iron railway bridge. He imagined all the men at work beyond the high embankment, navvies many of them, a rough lot brought in by the score and upsetting the neighbourhoods where they crowded together, eight or ten men in one house. The railway would be open all the way to Torrington next year. It would be curious to ride here and see trains steaming past where all had once been tranquil.

If they took the girl in, they would demonstrate to the town that even respectable households could help those most in need. He would need to explain the matter to Sophia. Their home and its efficient management were of the utmost importance to her as was only right, and she was very careful in her choice of servants. Immorality in any form was abhorrent to her, admirable of course, but she naturally lacked the knowledge and understanding that close contact with poverty brings. She was unaware that many young girls were debased not through any inherent evil but simply through living in overcrowded conditions, boys and girls thrown together without shame or privacy, then frequently sent out to situations where a lack of supervision allowed them to mix freely with members of the opposite sex. Sophia did not understand the fine distinction between immoral and unfortunate. Selina Burman, certainly, was unfortunate. Sophia would be doubtful of course, but she valued his good judgement. And had he not transformed *her* life?

It was with an unusually abstracted air that he turned his horse towards the thatched cottages that gathered next to the diminutive Landcross church.

Extract from census return, 1871, Bridgeland Street, Bideford.
(*The National Archives, RG10/2200/74*)

Sophia Ackland passed the plate of bread and butter to her youngest daughter, Lucy, while raising her eyebrows at four-year-old Hugh who had made an interesting connection between the raspberry jam he was spreading on his bread and a noise he had learnt to make with his mouth.

"One more piece, darling, before you go on to cake. Kingsley dear, pass me the sugar, would you? Jane, he'll have his elbow in that jam in a minute."

Jane, the nursemaid, swiftly moved around the table and took the bowl of jam out of Hugh's way, then poured some more milk for the children from a large blue and white jug. She was an attractive girl with dark hair coiled expertly under her cap and her neat figure well set off by her black dress and white apron. She was quiet and sensible in her manner and had been quick to learn Sophia's ways, so that now the children knew they could expect the same firm kindness from both. Sophia regretted that two adults were necessary to supervise tea but, with five children aged between four and eleven still at home, it was essential if bad manners and spoiled clothes were not to result. Perhaps in another year or so Jane would be able to manage on her own and Sophia would be able to have a quiet hour in the drawing room. There were many unread books awaiting her there.

She sat back for a moment and observed the dining room: the decorative mirror over the mantelshelf, the sideboard with its display of blue and white china reflecting the gaslight, the very fine rug - Mary had made a good job of beating it. It pleased her that the children were growing up with beautiful things around them. She encouraged them to be attentive and observant and they would surely grow up to be adults of fine sensibilities. The words of Mr Keats came to her unbidden: "Beauty is truth; truth, beauty," and she felt them to be true. Her gaze moved on to her family, Kingsley looking so grown up and serious now and the three girls so pretty in their identical dresses, and Hugh – she frowned at him and he put down his teaspoon which he had been rattling against his cup.

She knew she was a good mother. When she had been

forced so suddenly and unexpectedly to find a situation as governess all those years ago, her only previous experience with children had been with her younger sisters; she had been fortunate in being sent to the Reverend Bazeley's family which was a well-ordered and loving household and she had quickly learnt by example. She had seen other households of which she did not approve at all, where the children were looked after entirely by servants and were only presented to the parents for a few minutes each day, the mother usually being preoccupied with socialising. Certainly she had little time for that sort of thing, especially as she was now responsible for teaching her five younger children, as well as a proportion of their physical care. They had employed a governess at one time, after Hugh was born, but she had proved to be poorly educated and almost coarse in her manners and had been quickly dismissed. She felt blessed with the way her life had blossomed, although she had not been prepared for how *tiring* it would be to have seven children in ten years.

"Mother, you did say that Emily must finish her piano exercises after tea, did you not? Because she says she does not have to."

"Emily, you know you must and you can do yours afterwards Mary. I shall be reading to Lucy and Hugh but I will listen out for you."

At a sudden sound from the hall and the familiar "Hello there!" all five children leapt up from the tea table and rushed out to throw themselves at their father, a daily indulgence that was permitted provided that there was no quarrelling. While the deep male voice added to the commotion with as much enthusiasm as the children's, Sophia quickly made a fresh cup of tea with the pot brought right on cue by Mary, and then put some more coals on the fire and picked up her husband's slippers so that within a minute, having greeted her affectionately – she never knew quite what he was going to say or with what degree of enthusiasm he would kiss her, which embarrassed her somewhat – he was seated at the table, beslippered and stirring his tea.

The children chattered to their father and he gave them all his attention, reacting with humour to their anecdotes and questioning them on the day's studies. He allowed the younger ones to relate what they had learnt but questioned his son Kingsley more closely, for he was anxious that the boy, still being taught at home by his mother at the age of eleven, was not making adequate progress. Sophia watched her husband. He was passionate about his work and he found it difficult to leave the cares of the day behind when he arrived home. They were never, of course, discussed in front of the children but he often confided in her later in the evening: the story of a family stricken by more than their fair share of tragedy; a death which could have been prevented by earlier advice. She always did her best to sympathise or reassure. It was difficult tonight to know what response would be necessary. It had not been an easy day, she could see that, but there was also an air of enthusiasm or determination about him. As if in answer to her thoughts he clapped his hands together as the children were finishing their ham and declared,

"Now, my darlings, a swift bedtime tonight, if you please, for I have a plan I wish to discuss with your mother!"

When all the children were settled and dinner was served for her husband, Sophia dismissed Mary and sat opposite her husband at the long table. Dr Ackland started his soup and launched straight into his story.

"Well, my sweetness, I think I may have found a replacement for Mary without you having the nuisance of enquiring and interviewing. Allow me to relate the story to you. I have been to the Workhouse again today as Dr Pridham is away. Unfortunately I have lost the child."

He dropped his soup spoon and banged his fist on the table. Sophia rose, shocked to see the anger in his face.

"Seven years old and he had seen nothing but those cursed

walls! No woodlands or pleasant green places! No childish pleasures, no laughter, no love or affection! Just the harsh regimentation of that abominable place and unkind words and fear - that is all he knew in his short miserable life!" Sophia laid her arm around his shoulder, soothing him as she would the children. He clasped her hand tightly. "My dear, I apologise. This matter has unsettled me more than I had realised."

Seeing that he was calmer she returned to her seat, in trepidation of what might to be to follow. She felt a pang of guilt that her thoughts were focussed more on the impact on their own family of what he might have to say, than on the plight of these others.

"He has a brother, a child of three or four who will also end his short unhappy life in the Workhouse unless he is lucky enough to survive the starvation rations and the icy draughts in winter. His mother is a poor harmless soul who was abused twice – her abusers walk free and she is incarcerated, unable even to give comfort to her children! My dear, you should have seen her gratitude when I gave instructions for her to stay with her dying boy! But I have a plan. She is a quiet girl who has never given any trouble in the House – I have enquired on that. She comes from a Clovelly family whom I had occasion to visit when they lived and worked on Lundy some years ago, my fees being paid by the Reverend Heaven. The father is a common labourer, but an honest man who does not partake excessively of drink. She is very different from the majority of young women in that place who have become horrifically debased by their past circumstances and in many cases also by faults of character."

He folded his arms on the table.

"My dear, if we were to employ her here as housemaid, it might be that her parents could take her remaining son and give him some love and a better diet. She could send them her wages to support him. And what an example it would set! Perhaps others in the town might follow our lead and give an opportunity to some of the young girls who have never seen past the walls of the Workhouse."

He started again on his soup, with more relish this time. Sophia stared at him. Her objections to the proposed plan were so numerous she hardly knew where to start.

"She will not have had any training."

"She has had posts in the past as a farm servant. I know they would have been rough households, but I believe she would be willing to learn. If there is one thing the Workhouse does produce, it is a submissive temperament, at least in those who have not become degraded. Your presence here would have a beneficial, civilising effect on her – it would be the making of her! In addition to giving her poor remaining son a chance."

Sophia felt her throat drying and tightening. "What would we say to the children? Am I right in thinking she has a son but no husband? They would ask questions! They are far too young to be told the truth. I *cannot* let them gain knowledge of such immorality."

Her husband reached across the table and patted it gently, a habit of affection he had developed as he could not reach her hand.

"Come now, my sweetness, that is easily solved. It will be simple to tell them the husband had died, just a small untruth which will only serve to make them more aware of their own blessings. The girl – for in truth she is little more than a girl – will readily agree to that, I am sure."

She noted that he had moved from the conditional to the future tense but she could not trust herself to speak again just yet. It seemed that he had made up his mind.

It was rare for them to disagree. It was true that their temperaments were very different; he was more emotional than she, more excitable except at work when, she was often told, he brought calm and confidence to the most anxious of situations. She was inclined, she felt, to be too serious and although she loved him and the children deeply, she somehow could not show her love as freely as he did. They complemented each other well; she tempered his impetuosity with caution and he brought humour to her gravity. But he had a streak of obstinacy, especially where the welfare of the poor was concerned. As a Justice of the Peace he was known to be outspoken and had made himself unpopular on a number of occasions by being less harsh in his treatment of offenders than many believed was appropriate. There had recently been a case of a female servant stealing some cheese; he had shocked many people by questioning her employer about the amount of food he allowed her, then only sentencing the servant to a week's imprisonment with hard labour. In a similar case, another J.P. had given three months' imprisonment with hard labour to a servant who had stolen two pairs of stockings. Sophia had had to remind him how important it was that he did not upset those in positions of power. He was the most highly esteemed local doctor amongst the respectable classes. It was through the influence of his most eminent patients that he had been made a J.P. and his appointment had then persuaded more wealthy patients that he was the doctor for them. By exploiting their good opinion of him, he had then been able to obtain further funding for the project closest to his heart, the Dispensary on Bideford Quay which provided free treatment for those too poor to pay. Sophia also found that the income from his wealthy patients made her housekeeping accounts far easier, but she did not usually use this argument to influence him, for he was not practical in financial affairs.

She decided to try a different tack.

"Don't forget, William, people generally only take on a Workhouse girl because they can only afford very low wages for a servant. Think, will you not, of all the situations we have known, people who take advantage of the girl's situation and work her almost to death, treating her as they would a slave. I am very much afraid that far from being impressed by our actions, people will suppose that we are doing the same and you know how important it is for you to retain the good opinion of influential people. You would not want any sponsors to withdraw funding from the Dispensary."

But he had become extravagant now in his enthusiasm for his plan, sure that before long all the respectable people in the district would be rescuing girls from the Workhouse. If a training school could be set up in the town, all the girls born in the Workhouse could spend some time there when they were old enough in order to ready them for the outside world. Sophia sighed to herself as she passed a dish of fruit to her husband. She could see the sense in this last plan but she did not consider that it had any bearing on the present dilemma.

She was very proud of her home. In those lonely years as a governess, she had become almost resigned to living in one small room in someone else's house, and she had never expected to be mistress of such a place as this. She took pride in ensuring that everything in the household ran smoothly and that all was calm and pleasant when her husband returned from his rounds. She was most careful in the servants she employed and on the whole had been lucky in finding pleasant and efficient girls from good backgrounds. Only three were employed – a cook, a housemaid and a nursemaid – so just one change could have a considerable impact. The idea of employing an inexperienced, uneducated and probably immoral girl - from the Workhouse! - appalled her. Such a girl would be likely to steal - even the tea and the sugar might have to be locked up. And might she not bring infection to the house? It was always a worry that William might be carrying an infection, although he was most diligent in the use of disinfectant, especially now that there was smallpox in the town. And even supposing the girl was able and willing to learn, how would she, Sophia, possibly find time to train her when her time was already fully occupied? Tentatively she put this point to her husband.

"I'm sure she will learn in no time, my dear, for you are a good teacher and expert at managing your time. And as far as your usual worry with servants is concerned, you need have no anxieties that she will attract followers as you will realise when you see her, for she is a poor, thin creature with sallow skin and sparse sombre hair. Though I am sure her appearance will improve with an adequate diet."

Sophia felt even less encouraged as she imagined the girl, but she knew her husband's mind was made up.

"May we take her on a month's trial? We can then let her go if she is unsuitable."

He agreed readily, for his mood was now genial and expansive. She said a little prayer asking for forbearance until the ordeal was over.

A week later Sophia was preparing for bed. One by one she unclasped the hooks of her second best grey dress and let it fall to the floor. She stepped out of the plain petticoats and dropped them beside the dress. Disrobing did not take long as she agreed with her husband that corsets were deleterious to health. Catching sight of her reflection in the mirror, she regarded the chemise-clad figure with distaste. Her waist had thickened after years of child-bearing and her hair was greying a little; she knew that her youth had gone. Wearily she bent and picked up her clothes and threw them over the back of the old nursing chair. There was dust on the arm. If such oversights were possible when an efficient, well-trained maid was employed, in what state of disorder would the house be when this new housemaid came?

Her husband's plans had progressed, there was to be no gainsaying him now. He had returned to the Workhouse and interviewed Selina Burman a second time and had spoken to Mr and Mrs Eastman who were only too glad to lose one of their inmates. It was arranged that she should return to her parents in Clovelly for two weeks before starting work in Bridgeland Street, timing that would coincide with Mary Tuplin's departure.

Today Sophia had told the cook and the nursemaid of Mary's replacement. They were good, respectable girls who worked hard and Sophia considered them almost to be friends although their manner was never anything less than respectful. Today, however, they had been displeased.

"A *Workhouse* maid!" Jane had exclaimed, aghast.

"She'll know nought but scrubbing and swilling," Eliza had declared, "How can I work with one such as that?"

They had both said that they knew of more suitable girls, as if Sophia were choosing this one for want of any better.

"Thank you," Sophia had said firmly, "but Dr Ackland and I have decided that this girl deserves the chance of a better life."

She could tell by their quickly exchanged glances that they understood the truth of the matter.

"She has a young son," Sophia then told them. "The children will be told that her husband has died." Both had looked shocked.

"Ma'am, I'll not share a room with her," Eliza had said. "I'm sorry, but I will not. If you say that I must, I'll hand in my notice."

Sophia had half-heartedly reprimanded her for speaking so sharply but secretly she sympathised. It would be no use asking Jane to share as she slept in the girls' bedroom.

"There's nothing else for it then, Selina must sleep in the kitchen."

Jane had looked at her almost with compassion. "Ma'am, *you* can't want this girl to come here."

Feeling close to tears and fearing the consequent loss of authority, Sophia had held her head high and turned to go.

"It is what Dr Ackland has decided is best and it is our duty to obey him."

As she walked away, she knew she had revealed her weakness. Since then she had come across them several times talking in whispers together and glancing sympathetically at her before quickly returning to their duties. She hated the servants to think that there was discord between her husband and herself.

She pulled her nightgown over her head and gazed at herself disconsolately in the dressing table mirror while she unwound her hair and brushed it out in long sweeping strokes. He was right, of course he was, that the girl should be given a chance and she would not disagree with him. It was she, Sophia, who was being selfish, putting her own concerns before the suffering of another human being. The words "but she's only a common servant" floated into her mind and she quickly put them aside. She must pray for compassion.

She climbed into the bed and hastily blew out the candle. She had left her husband downstairs reading. She hoped he would not visit her tonight. If it was late when he came up and he saw that her light was out he might pass straight on to his own room. She felt clean and cool between the smooth white sheets and she shivered a little at the thought of the extravagant endearments and the irritation of his long beard, like spiders' legs, on her face.

She should not entertain such feelings. She owed him so much. If he had not married her, where would she be now? In the same situation as her sisters no doubt, who were still working as governesses or struggling to support themselves in a small school. Whereas she was in a fine large house in Bridgeland Street, the best street in the town. She had accepted without hesitation when he had asked her to be his wife and when he gave her the children, her life had been transformed by the love she felt for them. When there were little difficulties between herself and William – of which he never seemed to be aware – she always reminded herself how thankful she should be to him.

She must remember that if the girl was as unsuitable as she feared, they need only keep her a month. She would surely be able to demonstrate to William that the household was suffering. She turned comfortably over on to her side. Before she went to sleep she heard her husband climb the stairs, hesitate at her door and continue along the corridor to his own room.

Sophia Ackland with children, believed to be Annie,
Maud and Charles Kingsley Ackland, c.1866.
(Wellcome Library, London)

Chapter Three

The Workhouse gate clanged shut behind her. Selina heard the Master's footsteps retreating and dared to turn. He passed under the great arch, through a door into the office and was gone. Beyond the arch the dirty grey walls of the main building towered above her and the rows of windows frowned down at her. She stared at them for a long fearful moment then turned her back on them and looked down at Will beside her. She stroked his soft shorn head, took his hand and made her first hesitant steps away from the gates.

Across the road two workmen stared, one muttered a remark and they both laughed. Selina kept her head down and walked down the wide paved road. It was Meddon Street; she remembered the name from years ago when it had been an address where she had so fearfully sought refuge. She looked back, half-expecting to see the Master or Mistress coming after her. She passed a shop, then another, keeping her eyes on the road ahead, not daring to look either side. A man pushed a barrow up the hill but thankfully did not attempt to speak. She came to a forge and felt a rush of heat and saw the sparks flying from the bellows which roared in the dim interior. Looking back along the road she saw that she had walked several times the length of the Workhouse exercise yard. She kept a straight path for the first time in four years, resisting the urge to run, putting one heavy-booted foot in front of the other.

The little footsteps beside her pattered along at double speed and she looked down at Will and squeezed his hand.

"Will. My sweetheart." He walked on stolidly like the little automaton she had once seen at Hartland Fair. "Us'll 'ave 'ee smiling soon, Will." He still wore his Workhouse dress despite Mrs Eastman's annoyance at having to let it go. He had no clothes of his own, having no need for them when he entered the House still in his mother's belly. Selina wore the dress she had arrived in, stored away in the offices all this time. She remembered altering it to fit her expanding waistline, and now it hung off her thin frame in folds. It was worn almost to threads in parts but felt soft after the harsh cloth she had worn for the last four years and she stroked the faded cotton as she walked. The piece of blanket around her shoulders had been her mother's, given to her after that last visit when they had both cried as they hugged each other, quietly, so that Father would not hear them and come in and shout and bang his fists on the table again. She pictured once more the narrow cottage a few steps from the steep main street; she felt the solidity of curved cobbles under bare feet, heard the lapping of waves and crying of gulls from the harbour, and smelled the salt and the herrings. Her parents' cottage would be there at the end of today. Fear surged through her again; she knew that if she could not find the meeting place at the right time - and what was the time? - then both she and Will must sleep on the streets or return to the Workhouse.

The road curved round to the right and two more streets opened up before her. She hesitated, trying to remember what the doctor had said. "Go straight on until you see the river." There was no river to be seen. Two women who had been gossiping in the middle of the road stopped and stared at her, taking in her anxious face and her clothes, which she knew to be even more threadbare than their own, then Will's shorn head and coarse Workhouse garb.

"They'll be after 'ee again if 'ee stand about like that, maid," said one.

Then they spoke quietly but she heard every word as she stood awkwardly, holding tight to Will's hand.

"I don't know 'er, do you?"

"No, her idn't from this part of town, far as I know. It idn't Mary 'Eddon's maid, is it?"

"No! Her's years older than that and I don't know that 'er's in there now. Mind, this one looks like 'er's just as daft, though Mary 'Eddon's maid did know to keep her legs closed, you can say that for her."

When they turned to look her up and down again, Selina stepped quickly towards them.

"Please, be this the road to the river?"

They stared again until one replied,

"The river? 'Tis down the hill there, maid, straight down."

As she thanked them and crossed the road, one called after her,

"Don't 'ee jump in, mind."

The road down which they had directed her was steep and lined with tall narrow houses, almost as steep as that in Clovelly but here there were no cobbles and she trod warily, slipping a little in the mud. Some small children playing on a doorstep stopped to watch them pass and called out a greeting. She looked down at Will but he did not raise his head and she watched him anxiously as they walked. Suddenly he gave a little chuckle, then another, and she stopped and crouched, bewildered, to look into his downcast face. A small smile played around his lips and he gave a sudden little jump on the steep slope.

"Will?"

He pulled her hand from hers and jumped again, three, four times down the hill, the little bubbling laugh escaping from him again.

"'Tis a hill, you've never been down a hill before, Will."

She wondered to think of it. For all his short life his world had been flat, consisting of stone floors, wooden boards, regimented steps and level yards. No grassy slopes to roll down, no hills down which to bowl a hoop or a ball even if he had ever possessed one. How extraordinary to be walking down a steep hill for the first time!

"Just wait 'til 'ee get to Clovelly, Will, 'tis steeper there!"

She took his hand again and he gave a little skip before resuming his subdued, puppet-like walk.

The church clock started to chime, a sound she had sometimes heard from the Workhouse when all was quiet and the wind was in the right direction. It had stopped before she realised she should have tried to count the chimes to see what time it was. The doctor had said eleven o'clock and not to be late. But she turned a corner as the road narrowed between two tall buildings and there, just a few yards away across a paved thoroughfare, was the river.

The outlook before her was one which had caused many to stand and stare, and Selina almost gasped at the open vista, so different was it to the close walls which had limited her view for so long. Her gaze moved over the broad span of the Torridge at high tide, the many graceful stone arches of the ancient long bridge, the smoke from the shipyards on the far side and the silent presence of a jumble of warehouses, then up to the green undulating hills rising beyond and the endless sky above. To her left, the wide Quay beyond the bridge was lined with imposing buildings on the landward side but the tall masts of a clipper and a red-sailed cutter moored alongside the Quay reached even higher than their roofs. Among the ships were the smaller masts and many-stranded rigging of numerous small trawlers and fishing boats and the familiarity of this sight made her reach down to lift Will so that he might see them too.

"Look, Will, herring boats, from home, some of 'em!"

A little weak sunlight lightened the grey November sky and caught the ripples on the surface of the Torridge as it eddied through the narrow arches of the bridge, and reflected on the windows of the hotel beyond. At the far end of the Quay, several people gathered close to the fishing boats and, taking Will's hand, she continued on her way with a little more confidence.

As she got nearer she saw that all the figures on the Quay were male, and she kept close to the buildings on the opposite side, edging past bay-windowed public houses from whose doors drifted scents of beer and tobacco and the sound of loud voices. When finally she was opposite the small group of men she stopped, hiding behind a sleepy-looking horse that stood between the shafts of an old farm cart. Will shrank close to

Bideford Quay c.1880

her and hid his face in her skirt at the sight of the strange creature.

Of the five men, she could see at once from their rough jerseys and sou'westers, that four were fishermen. The fifth, however, standing slightly apart, was taller and wore a top hat and gentleman's long coat. She saw the long whiskers as he turned to glance up and down the Quay and from a familiar energy about him knew him to be Dr Ackland. If she turned around she could, within a short time, be back in the familiar refectory scrubbing the floor; *that* was her home, was it not? Could she walk back along the Quay without being seen? She would have remained half-hidden behind the horse for a considerable time had he not then glimpsed her and calling out a cheery, "Halloo there!" stepped towards her.

"Come! Come and meet the good men who are to take you to your family. 'Tis all agreed and they are ready to set sail. And you, young man", he addressed himself to Will, "are to have an adventure!"

"Why, 'tis one of William Burman's daughters!" one of

the others exclaimed and the four fishermen stared at her, rubbing their noses and stroking their beards to puzzle out which daughter she was and what had kept her away from Clovelly for so long. They looked from her to Will in his Workhouse dress, but the doctor approached and spoke to her quietly.

"Come now, they wait for you. Your passage is paid for and this is to help your parents with your keep until your return." He passed her a small purse. "I shall expect you in two weeks or thereabouts, when the wind is fair. Now, you see this street opposite?" He waved his arm dramatically towards a wide street lined with tall, grand-looking houses that ran up from the Quay. "My house is on the left, just ask any passer-by for Dr Ackland and you shall find it. Now, take courage and be gone!"

She turned hesitantly towards the group of fishermen.

"Come on maid, us'll soon 'ave 'ee home in this wind," and after a brief embarrassment of rough hands and strong arms around her, she was seated in the stern of one of the herring boats with Will in her lap, two of the men boarding the boat with her.

"Now you stay where you be, maid, and us'll work around 'ee."

There were a few minutes of noise and industry as ropes were thrown and the dark brown sails unfurled and flapped noisily. The boat turned around slowly until suddenly the sails filled, the ropes tautened and the boat contracted and banked. The drama was over as quickly as it had started and they were sailing peacefully away from the Quay. The tall, white, many-windowed houses lining the Quay and stacking up the hill behind grew smaller and were replaced along the river's bank by tree-covered slopes interspersed with large houses and green fields. The fishermen were busy coiling ropes and she was able to look at them from the corner of her eye without being observed. The faces were familiar to her; the older she thought to be James Whitefield, the younger perhaps his cousin. But even if she could not recall their names, their very presence was comforting to her. The soft burr of their accents, the way they screwed up their weatherworn faces as they studied the sky, the gentle mockery accepted between lifelong friends and even their practised movements as they measured out a twist of tobacco to chew – all these things spoke to her of home. She sat very still, listening to the occasional crack of heavy sails and the gentle splash as the boat cleaved the water, and smelling the seaweed, the salt and the fish. And she felt herself to be very small, as small as Will, but in her memory she was sitting in *her* mother's lap with her sisters around her and their possessions wrapped in cloths on the floor of the boat. The whole family had locked up their small cottage on Clovelly's steep cobbled High Street and were sailing to Lundy, the island which formed a long low shape on the horizon on clear days. She remembered the rolling water all around the boat and the warmth and comfort of snuggling in close to her mother. She looked down at Will in her arms and recognised the wonderment in his startled eyes. She pulled him in close and held his cold little hands in her own, examining and counting his fingers, gently rubbing his thumb which was calloused from frequent sucking. She saw where the sunlight caught the fairness of his closely shorn hair and smoothed down a few longer wisps behind his shell-like ears, then ran her finger along the nape of his neck where his hair grew the other way. She bent to kiss his cheek.

"Will. Sweetheart. Us be gwain home."

He did not reply, but she felt him relax a little and he leant his head against her breast. She wrapped her blanket closely around the two of them.

"You be gwain to see your Nanna and Grandfer, Will. Grandfer, he'll say 'tis his little princess come home and you'll be his little prince, Will." That was not the way he had spoken to her when she had last seen him, but surely all that would be forgotten now.

Her thoughts were interrupted by a shout, and she looked up to see that they were passing a village with more fishing boats moored at the Quay. A group of fisherman in thick woollen pullovers waved, shouting greetings and a joke made at her expense. The Clovelly men laughed and responded and she turned away, staring across the now very wide river to distant houses on the far bank.

"They don't mean no harm, maid. Don' 'ee pay no attention to 'em. Does your feyther know you'm coming home?"

She shook her head.

"Well, there'll be a fair old party tonight then!"

"I should be bringing two boys home to 'em."

He must have heard the tears in her voice for he didn't question her further, but passed her an old jacket from under a seat.

"Yur, maid, 'twill be getting breezy when us go out over the Bar."

She had heard talk of the Bar in the past. Looking ahead she saw the river widen still further. As she pulled the jacket around her shoulders she saw that the green hills which had run down to the river's edge were now replaced by rolling sand hills, their creamy-whiteness interspersed with tall clumps of pale, wiry grass. As the boat approached an area of white-topped waves, the wind strengthened and the men braced their legs and busied themselves to hold it steady. The boat rolled and swayed alarmingly and Will was suddenly sick down the front of her dress and her arm. When she next looked up after hushing his little cat-like cry and cleaning them both as best as she could with a corner of her blanket, the land was left behind them and they were heading out into the open sea, the boat rolling steadily now and moving fast, leaving behind the thunder of waves on the long pebble-edged beach.

The younger man sat down beside her and took a paper bag from his pocket. She gave him a quick glance. He was a thick-set man with heavy whiskers and gentle, pale blue eyes.

"Would 'ee 'ave a bit of bread, maid? The both of 'ee look like you need a bit of a feed and 'twill settle his stomach." He took Will's hand and placed a piece of bread in it, breaking off a second piece for Selina. Will looked at the bread in surprise, then fearfully up at the man.

"The tender dear! Does 'ee suppose I've witched it? 'Ee's the image of his grandfer, 'tis in the eyes!"

Will started to chew surreptitiously on the bread, as if someone might snatch it from him.

For the next two hours the boat rolled and Selina clung on, breathing deeply when the spasms of nausea threatened to overcome her. The wind was chilling and she kept the fisherman's jacket wrapped close around herself and Will. He gazed out wordlessly at the endless sea, the few scattered trawlers from Appledore and Bideford and the distant, hazy coast. Next to her was an empty space where Thomas should have been and she put her hand on her breast where a wisp of his hair lay next to her heart. The vast, dappled grey sky arched over her and met the great ocean that went on for ever and ever and she almost wished she could stay there, safe in the bucketing little boat with the wind all around as if time itself stood still. Eventually they began to draw nearer to a great wall of cliffs and she looked back and saw that they had almost crossed the wide Bideford Bay. The cliffs towered ever higher in front of them, changing from grey to shades of red-brown and green, softening as their wooded slopes appeared from the haze. There was not a dwelling or a person to be seen, and the only sound the roar of the surf and the mewling cries of gulls.

The mate turned to her.

"There you be, maid, do 'ee see Clovelly now?"

She looked ahead where he pointed and saw a white perpendicular line in the green cliff wall. As the boat approached she saw that the line was made up of small white houses, piled one above another up the steep cliff face as if balanced each side of a long ladder, and interspersed with trees and bushes in greens and autumnal russets and browns.

As they drew still closer she saw the massive dark curve of the harbour wall and the dancing shapes of brown-sailed herring boats. She stared, unfamiliar with the view of the village from the sea, until among the lower, closer houses she saw some she could name; Crazed Kate's, Temple Bar, the Jolly Sailor, and she knew then that the fisherman spoke the truth.

The sails were furled and they glided slowly into the harbour where a row of boats with fluttering windlasses and creaking ropes were drawn up alongside the Quay, close up to the coal cellar under the Red Lion. Beyond the little pebble beach came the gentle splash of water from the waterfall and the musical cries of gulls among the drying nets spread out on the boulders, then a shout from a knot of men who gathered on the wall.

Clovelly Harbour

"Who've 'ee got there, then?"

"'Tis one of William Burman's daughters come home!"

The questioner, a gnarled old fisherman, turned to his

neighbour. He in turn walked a few paces to another who shouted to a woman at the door of a cottage.

"Tell Mrs Esther Burman her daughter's home!"

From there the cry was relayed up the hill in time-honoured fashion until it grew faint among the tangle of whitewashed cottages high above and Selina pictured her mother, busy with the washing or tending the fire, hearing the news and standing stock still in disbelief, then hurrying from her house, down the steep cobbled street towards the harbour.

An hour or two later she sat in her parents' cottage, a second cup of dark tea in her hand, as her mother stood at the table deftly gutting herring for the evening meal.

"Be 'ee making a pie?" Selina asked. "I haven't had so much as a taste of a fish all these years, and I don't suppose Will has ever tasted one." Will was asleep in her lap. He had cried when they arrived in the cottage, overwhelmed by the strange woman who sobbed and tried to take him in her arms, and the swarm of neighbours and cousins who had crowded into the little room. She saw that her mother was close to tears again and she took a deep breath and made herself think of other things, a trick which she had been forced to learn in the Workhouse.

"Ma, what of my sisters? The men told me William's out fishing but I've heard no news of *them*." She tried to put aside the hurt that none of her sisters had ever visited her in the Workhouse and her mother had only done so once.

"Oh my, there's lots to tell!" Her mother, having dropped the rolling pin on the table, stood with her hands on her hips and gazed at Selina with her mouth open and her chins wobbling with excitement.

"Mary Ann's married, and Eliza! And they've both had boys, the two of 'em! Mary Ann married John Hockridge...."

"What, John Hockridge from Burnstone Farm? The oldest of those boys?"

"Yes! And he's rented a farm of his own! Sowden over Hartland way, good-sized farm that he had the chance of, so he came to her and said he wanted a wife, and they've one man outdoors *and* Mary Ann has a girl to help her indoors! Oh, her's done well for herself, Selina. They come here to visit every few weeks, the baby's a plump little tacker, thriving he is! And Eliza, she married last year to a chap from Holsworthy way, William Bowden. They've got a tied cottage over Halwill but it's not too viddy, she told me that when I saw her last, back in the summer it was. And their son, over a year he is now, 'e's called Cephus Parmonious."

"What!"

"I know, poor little toad."

Her mother rolled out the pastry with renewed enthusiasm. Perhaps she would be equally proud of Selina now that she had a good situation, but it was doubtful because the past could never be undone. Her sisters' successes made her even more aware of her own disgrace. Mary Ann, the oldest sister since Elizabeth died some years ago, had always been capable and efficient and had made a good impression in her first place, but it was still surprising that John Hockridge had picked her. Eliza was nearest in age to Selina and they had once been close.

"Any news of Sarah, Ma?"

"No." Her mother's face clouded over. "Not a word."

"And what of Margaret and Ellen?"

"Margaret's working up at Winsworthy. 'Tis her first place and her's been up there two years or more, her's coming on fifteen I think. 'Tis a hard place for she's the only servant kept but they'm pleased with her, I think, so her'll be able to move on. And Ellen you'll see dreckly if her doesn't dawdle home from school."

Her mother put down her rolling pin.

"Selina, I can't tell 'ee what a burden was lifted when I saw them settled. Such worry I've had about you and Sarah! Children *be* a burden, they *be*, when you haven't the means to help them or even to give them food every day when you've so many in the house together. And every one that's born leaves you weaker 'til you've hardly the strength to lift the newest from the cradle. I'm so thankful that some of you at least be settled. And you now, Selina, after all your troubles that's a place to be proud of, with Dr Ackland himself! William too, he's done well for himself, he's fishing with Richard Foley. They'll be setting out before dark and I doubt he'll return 'til morning. They'm expectin' a good catch as the moon's full and the clouds be moving fast."

When she had last seen her mother, her parents had been worried by their only son's determination to go to sea. Her father was not a fisherman, but they had all grown up with the knowledge and fear of the sea. That knowledge was inescapable in a village which clung to storm-scarred cliffs and whose vista beyond the huddle of low cottage roofs was of infinite ocean and sky. The talk was of weather and waves, trawlers and herrings and beneath the good-natured banter the awareness of tragedy was always present. Clovelly had had more than its fair share of heartbreak, even for a village which was so dependent on the treacherous seas. Every fishing village on the north coasts of Devon and Cornwall was resigned to the loss of a seasoned fisherman swept overboard or a young man crushed between boat and harbour wall, but Clovelly had also experienced death on a greater scale. Earlier in the century there had been two occasions on which the fleet had gone out on a calm evening in anticipation of a successful night's fishing when a storm had blown up with such rapidity that the boats were unable to reach the safety of the harbour. Thirty-one men, eleven from Clovelly including her father's older brother, had been lost in the first disaster and twenty-one in the second, their bodies washed up on the beach for their wives and mothers to find. Selina's father had been a young boy at the time and had promised his mother he would never go to sea. Her brother, however, was unscarred by tragedy and had spent much of his childhood at the Look Out watching the boats come in and helping the men down on the Quay whenever he was allowed. When the time came to make a decision, his parents could not argue with his choice as there was in any case no labouring work available. This year, Selina had been told, the herring had returned in greater numbers than they had for several years and the income he brought into the house was welcome, for his father did not always have a full week's work.

She got up and placed her sleeping son on a blanket by the fire, clicked open the latch on the low cottage door and stood outside on the step, taking in the familiar view over grey tiled rooftops and the precipitous hillside topped by tall trees high above her. She wandered down the familiar weed-grown path which wound between close cottage walls and through a passageway built under the little Wesleyan chapel where her family prayed every Sunday. She walked through to the steep main thoroughfare, itself only wide enough to accommodate four people walking abreast, and leant against some iron railings enclosing a tiny garden. The lines of cottages ran down each side of the street, their little gardens and terraces still bright with tall autumn-flowering fuchsias and russet creepers which climbed up the walls and over the roofs. A visitor with his box of paints and cloth-wrapped canvas wished her good night as he climbed back up the hill to the New Inn. The light was beginning to dim and candles glowed in the windows of some of the cottages, illuminating cosy domestic scenes in their thick cob-walled interiors. From the stepped cobbled street there was a narrow vista below of deep blue sea widening upwards to the sky where an almost full moon hung as if suspended on a string. She breathed deeply, taking in the scents of wood-smoke that rose lazily from the cottage chimneys and the salt and fish which drifted up from the harbour, hearing the echoing chants of the fisherman, the mewing of the gulls, raised voices and a crying child from a nearby cottage. All were intensified by the stillness and silence of the immense sea and sky beyond.

It was as if the past few years had never happened, as if she had never been away. Every cobble at her feet was familiar, for how many times had she sat here with her sisters as they walked their peg dolls over the rocky road? Pictures of the interiors of every cottage were imprinted on her mind, the face and character of every inhabitant known, for had she not run freely in and out of every house as a child? The scene was one she had dreamed of many times and she wondered to think that it was now reality and the other just a bad dream. She felt she was growing lighter and taller, as if someone had lifted a yoke or a load of firewood from her back.

She had never felt in control of her destiny. Her sister Mary Ann had been more forthright. Even at twelve years of age she had turned down the first situation she was offered and had helped her mother take in extra washing for a week or two until she found a situation she considered to be superior, knocking on doors and offering her services until she found the right one. Selina would be afraid to do that even now. She knew Mary Ann thought her stupid when she returned home big-bellied from her first situation at Woolsery, but now that it had happened twice, how could she be sure that it would not befall her again? Her work might not give satisfaction at the Doctor's house; would she then be returned to the Workhouse? As the sky darkened, the moon's reflection appeared in the vast dark blue ocean, so still and so quiet. She pushed the fearful memories aside. She was here; she had her son, one son. A figure appeared toiling up the hill towards her and she turned away to return to her parents' house.

That night she lay on the straw mattress she was sharing with Will and her youngest sister Ellen. Her father had returned from ditching in the estate woods to give a very different welcome from that she had received from her mother. His first thought had been of her keep; she wished now that she had realised the anxiety this would cause him, as she knew that it *was* anxiety which made him glare at her and shout so loudly that Will started to cry quietly. It had been the sight of the tears on the small boy's cheeks and his flinching at the sudden movements that had stopped her father, giving her the opportunity to hand him the unopened purse that the doctor had given her. He had quietened then but throughout the evening had thought up one objection after another. She was used to rough work – how should she know what to do in the fine house of a doctor? She was to be on a month's trial – suppose she did not give satisfaction in that time? The winter was coming, the herring would be gone and his own wages would decrease with the bad weather – how would they feed Will if her wages did not arrive home safely? At this point he banged his fist on the table and shouted,

"If I can't put a few shillings aside now, your mother and I will both be in the Workhouse when I'm not fit to work!"

He reminded her of the last time she was taken from the Workhouse for employment and asked how she knew the doctor was to be trusted. At this her mother, unusually, raised her voice in loud objection.

"William! 'Tis Dr Ackland you'm speaking of! There isn't a kinder, better-respected man to be found! You know there's many in this village that speak his name with the sort of reverence that should by rights be kept for chapel. In any case, look at her. What would he want with a maid such as her?"

Her father had admitted that he should not have spoken of the doctor in such a way. Nevertheless there was still disquiet when the candle was carried upstairs.

Selina spent the next day helping her mother with the washing that she took in for the New Inn. Her presence did not make her mother's work any easier however, for every few minutes a visitor called in, having heard of Selina's return. She got used to telling her news and managed to speak of Thomas's death without tears as long as she took a deep breath and changed the subject after one brief informative sentence. Not all were kind to her and some told her earnestly that they hoped she had learned her lesson and would lead a more upright, godly life in future. Several enquired fearfully about life in the Workhouse and one asked whether it was true that human bones were used to make the soup. One woman who had had a bastard child herself was kinder and marvelled at Selina's prospective employment with Dr Ackland.

Throughout the day Will sat looking at the floor, neither replying to the visitors when they spoke to him nor playing, even when his grandmother took a small roughly carved wooden donkey from the mantelshelf for him. By the end of the day her mother asked whether he ever spoke. Did he ever call her name? Selina was confused at first by the question and had to think about it. All the Workhouse children had learnt that it was safer to keep quiet and it had not occurred to her before that she had not heard Will speak.

"But yes, of course he speaks, or he did speak."

She remembered before he was weaned, holding him in her arms in bed when he woke early and whispering quietly to him as she counted and tickled his fingers and toes.

"One, two, two" he used to say. Until his hunger overcame his delight in the game and he'd say "mamamilk" and pull at her clothes. He would point at the other small children and say "baba", laugh at the Workhouse cat and call "puss-puss". And that day when he had been dragged from her arms and he had been so frightened by her anguish, his little fingers had desperately tried to cling on and he had screamed "No! No! Mama! Mama! No!"

"Yes," she said, "He used to call my name."

"Well, you'd better get this washing done and teach 'n to do it again."

So when they had rinsed the last of the sheets, wrung them out together above the stream and thrown them over the bushes above the cottages to dry, Selina made a cup of tea and sat down next to Will while her mother started ironing the sheets and pillowcases washed earlier in the day.

"Mama's going to have a sit down after all her work." She marvelled for a moment that she was able to do so. He stared at her, his blue eyes as deep and dark as the night sky, then looked back at the floor. She thought back to the alternate

Sundays in the Workhouse when she was allowed to spend a short time with the children. Usually she talked to Thomas, asking him if his teacher was fair with him and reminding him to be a good boy. She would hold Will on her lap unless Mrs Eastman was in a particularly bad mood and enforcing the rule of no contact. She did not usually question Will, nor he speak to her. She was not sure now what to say to him. She was afraid he was missing his brother but did not trust herself to speak of him.

She picked up the wooden donkey and walked it along her lap, clicking her tongue in time to its hoof beats. Will looked at it without interest. It occurred to her that he had never seen a donkey and the only horse he had ever seen had been standing still.

"Come on Mama's lap, Will." She sat him facing her astride her knee and jigged him up and down. "Horsey, horsey, don't 'ee stop. Just let your vit go clippetty-clop. Your tail goes swish and the wheels go round. Giddy-up, we're homeward bound!" A little smile played around his lips. "Again, Will, again?" She sang the rhyme again, speeding up towards the end like she used to with her little sisters. He smiled and a glint of light appeared in his eyes. She covered her eyes with both hands. "Where's Mama gone? Boo!" After the third time he laughed but would only look at her fleetingly.

"Mother, can you spare me for a minute? I s'll take Will to see the donkeys."

There was a little late autumn sunshine but the breeze was cold so Selina bent to fasten the buttons on Will's wool jacket, donated by a neighbour whose last child had just outgrown it. His Workhouse dress had also been replaced with some more suitable cast-off clothes and it was pleasing to see him looking more like a normal child. When she took his hand he followed her obediently with his head down and they walked to where old Uncle Daniel waited with his donkeys below the terrace of the New Inn, his long grey beard matching the colour of his charges. He was sitting with folded arms hoping for a late visitor who might want a ride up to see the Dykes or down to the harbour to sketch the trawlers. Selina had rarely seen horses in her childhood for they were not sufficiently sure-footed to negotiate the steep cobbled High Street that provided the only access to the village. Instead it was donkeys that carried the wealthy and the infirm, that transported fish and coal up the hill from the harbour and delivered potatoes, milk and building materials down to individual houses. Any villager who had access to a shed or, better still, a small paddock kept a donkey, as the initial outlay was soon repaid. Each evening children could be seen collecting fodder for the donkeys from the roadside verges in the higher village.

Old Daniel had never been one for conversation so after replying to his "All right maid?" Selina was free to talk to the donkeys and to Will. She sat the child on her hip while she buried her hand in the soft, thick hair on the donkey's forehead and stroked the long, stiff, velvet-covered ears which flicked gently in response to her touch. Will stared and when the donkey lifted its top lip to nuzzle his hand, he pulled it away and hid his face in Selina's shoulder.

"Donkey, Will, stroke the donkey." She patted its neck and held his hand against the thick grey-brown hair.

"Can I give'n a ride, Uncle Daniel?" The old man grunted his assent and Selina lifted Will on to the small felt saddle and pushed his feet into the stirrup leathers. She remembered her sisters crying when first placed on a donkey but Will sat silently, submitting to whatever experience life threw at him. She led the donkey up the High Street, keeping a hand on Will's knee to support him. After a while she looked back at him and saw his mouth twitching as if trying to suppress a smile and he reached out to touch the donkey's soft mane. When they turned back down the hill and the jolting and swaying increased, he started to chuckle and she laughed too as the donkey felt its way over the slippery cobbles back to its companions. She reached up to her son and pulled him off into her arms, moulding his comforting weight to her side and burying her face in his sweet-smelling neck.

"You'll spoil that boy." Selina was holding Will on her lap and helping him to bits of fish from her plate so that he did not cram them all into his mouth at once.

"There idn't time for that, Mother."

It had been two weeks since Selina had arrived in Clovelly and the message had come the previous night that a trawler would be sailing to Bideford in the morning. She had dreaded this moment and had tried to put it to the back of her mind, spending her time helping her mother with the washing and some mornings going down to the harbour to help her brother. Together they shook the nets and counted the herrings into the deep round baskets called mawns, placing them in three at a time until the total reached a meas or six hundred and twelve. It was hard work which left her hands, arms and apron covered in glittering scales but she threw herself into it with enthusiasm, relishing the opportunity to work in the open air with the sounds and smells of the sea around her. The fishermen and their wives and daughters working around her kept up a steady rhythm of gossip and comments on the quantity and quality of the fish, the weather and the state of their respective boats. Selina listened to their soft, familiar accents but kept her head down and her hands busy. She knew that most people thought her both foolish and wicked for bearing children she was unable to support and regarded her with disdain mixed with a superstitious fear, for the fate of the Workhouse was one that they feared above almost all else. This had been confirmed when, desperate to stay near her family, she had gathered her courage and called on two nearby farms where, she had heard, there might be a chance of work. She was politely but firmly turned down at both.

She sat Will astride her knee so that he faced her. He had put on weight in the last two weeks and had some colour in his cheeks; the thin little scrap she had brought home was now beginning to look more like the boy of four that he was. He gazed at her for a moment then smiled beguilingly and she gave him a kiss before he wriggled off her lap and ran towards the door.

"Wait, Will, us'll go for a walk. Mother, I won't be long then I'll help 'ee with the ironing when I'm back."

She took Will's hand and they climbed slowly up the abrupt ascent, winding first this way, now that, towards the road where the carriages and carts stopped. From a break in the hedge there was a wide view over the terraced vegetable gardens on the slopes above the village and down to the narrow pebble beach which stretched round the bay to the narrow white line of houses forming the village of Buck's Mills. Amongst the grey roofs of Clovelly she could see her own house far below and as she looked she saw her mother come out with a bowl of slops.

"Look, Will, there's Nanna, there, look!" She crouched down beside him and pointed until he glimpsed her. Another child might have shouted in the hope of receiving a wave. They watched the little figure moving about her chores until she returned inside the house and the sound of the door closing echoed up the hill to reach them on a faint breeze.

They continued on their way, turning into the Hobby Drive, the carriageway that wound through the woods above Clovelly. Selina walked close to the precipitous edge, gazing down at the village below, while Will dawdled along picking up an acorn here, a curiously shaped twig there. She watched him. He was beginning to do the sorts of things other children did. Now that the time had come for her to go she felt numb with anxiety for him. Her mother would not have time to talk to him and might not notice if he was losing weight or starting a fever. Neither of her parents had been as keen on taking him in as she had expected, for she had not realised how relieved they were at having all but their youngest daughter off their hands at last. Neighbouring children had so far shunned him, finding his shorn-headed appearance strange and his ways peculiar. He would have to go to school and she feared the treatment he might receive from the other children. It was at least a consolation that her sister Ellen would be able to walk with him and look out for him.

From here the view of the village was an intricate grey mass of roofs among the trees, the line of the main street invisible among them. It was so still; so quiet but for the occasional muffled sound of voices from below, a sudden distant laugh and the braying of a donkey drifting up to her, the subdued autumnal song of a robin nearby. She kicked the toes of her boots in the golden leaf litter at her feet, remembering the hard scrubbed floors of the Workhouse, she felt the breeze in her hair and looked out at the azure sea before her and, below her, the village. Her village. The preacher would say it was wrong to have such a thought but it seemed to her that it was a miracle that she was here. And now she had to leave.

She passed over the stream that gushed down the hillside to run beside the village street and followed Hobby Drive as it wound right and then left along the hillside. She stopped again and again to glimpse the village from different angles, to see people busy about their work, tiny figures unaware of the woman and child far above them. On she went until she was able to see a dizzy view of the beach and the harbour wall and across to the measureless ocean. She stood still and hugged herself, not wanting Will to see her tears, dreading telling him of the reason for her sorrow.

She sniffed and wiped her eyes on her sleeve, pushed back her escaping hair. At her feet she saw a horse chestnut shell and she bent to pick it up.

"Look, Will, a conker!"

She held out the hard prickly case and he flinched as he touched it, pulled his fingers back and hid them in his armpit.

"Careful!" She crouched down in front of him. "Mama kiss it better."

She took his fingers in hers and kissed each one in turn, making him laugh, then gave him a hug. She wanted never to forget the feel of his solid little form in her arms.

"Come on, Will, us has to stamp on it, find the conker! Like this!"

She dropped the conker on the stony track and stamped on it.

"Now Will do'n!"

He raised his Workhouse boot, almost over-balancing in the process, and brought it down on the conker until, with her help, the outer casing split open and she showed him the shiny brown fruit nestling in the white interior.

"Ball!" he said, having recently seen one for the first time.

"No, not ball, Will, conker. Look! Here you be. No! Don't eat it! 'Tis to play with, Will."

They walked hand in hand down the narrow path which led from Hobby Drive back to the village, Will stumbling occasionally as he gazed at the shiny conker in his hand. How could she leave him? Poor dear Thomas was dead, though it scarcely seemed possible and she frequently had to remind herself that it was so, and soon she would have to leave Will. Until now she had been too absorbed in him to think about her new post. If she could not give satisfaction and was not able to find other work – and how could she without a character? – she and Will would have to return to the Workhouse.

They reached the first houses and passed through the narrow cobbled side street to the Lookout. A small level platform with an unobstructed view over the entire bay in the centre of the otherwise precipitous village, the Lookout had been used for centuries by fishermen, their families and especially by the elderly to observe the weather and the sea conditions, to watch the fishing fleet and remember the magnitude of past catches and, when a storm blew up, to watch in fear as the boats battled with the violent seas below. Selina hesitated behind the long bench where four aged men with long grey beards were seated. She knew them all, for they had been revered elders even when she was a child. William Lee had told her proudly the other day,

"Eighty-eight I be now, maid, would 'ee b'lieve it?" and Grandfer Whitefield, who was ninety had observed,

"Well, you habn't catched up with me yet, boy!"

William Lee turned and saw her now and shifted a little on the bench to make room for her. They were deep in discussion about a ship wrecked in the bay "five and forty years agone" and paid no attention to her.

Will scrambled up next to her and together they gazed out at the wide, open bay and the protective arm of wooded cliffs. The air was perfectly still in this sheltered spot and not a leaf moved amongst the rhododendrons and buddleias which clung to the rocky slopes around the village. The silence was broken only by the clear voices of fishermen and the squeals of herring gulls rising up from the beach and the emphatic exclamations of the old men beside her. Here in the sheltered rocky crevice everything was clearly-defined – the colours bright, every sound and smell distinct – but when she looked out into the bay which she would have to cross the next day, the pale blue-grey sea and sky blended into one another so she could not tell where they met. The semi-circle of coast which reached as far as Exmoor was just a hazy shape floating in the greyness and although she searched for the estuary which led into Bideford, she could not even identify the headland which preceded it. How was it possible that she should head out into that obscure place, to be with people she did not know and a job which was beyond her imagining? She pulled Will into her lap.

"Somehow I'll come back for 'ee, Will," she whispered in his ear, "I don't know rightly how I be going to do it, but I will."

Chapter Four

On the morning of her departure Selina rose early. All night her mind had been racing over the day's expected events - the preparations, the farewells and the journey across the wide Bideford Bay - and stalling at the unknowable at the day's end. She crept downstairs so as not to disturb the rest of the family and concentrated on familiar tasks.

In the kitchen she relit the fire in the big stone fireplace, set the kettle on to boil then quickly swept the kitchen, emptying the sweepings outside in the hedge and shaking the rag rug from the front door. She stood for a few moments on the cobbled path and watched as the dawn approached. First the high wooded hill emerged from the dark sky then the white cottages which ran down the steep valley beneath appeared from the gloom, each familiar huddled shape holding its own special memory.

It was baking day so she took out the bread tins and greased them ready for her mother to use. She was anxious about the extra burden she was placing on her mother by leaving Will with her and had done all she could before her planned departure. She had cut down and altered the clothes donated by cousins and neighbours, so that her mother would not have to sew for him, even making some in bigger sizes that she could hardly believe that Will would ever grow into. She had taught him to draw little pails of water from the well and stagger back to the cottage with them to help his grandmother and last night they had sat together tearing paper to thread on a string next to the earth closet.

When her chores were done, her father had left for work and her sister for school, she went upstairs to change for the journey. In just a few minutes she would have to leave. She took a deep breath and wrapped her arms around her stomach, trying to quell her increasing nausea. Her clothes were laid out ready on the bed. She had been anxious about what she would need to take to Bideford. Fortunately her sister Mary Ann had visited bringing a plain grey dress and a white cap she said she could spare. The dress had needed taking in and was only a little worn, and Selina was able to make some aprons from a sheet her sister had brought. She had tried on the outfit last night and her mother had run to a neighbour to borrow a small looking glass. The dress fitted well but her hair was all wrong, she pulled at it now in frustration. It had grown only a little since leaving the Workhouse where hair below the shoulders was not permitted. She had parted it in the middle and tied it back but she knew it looked foolish.

She and her mother had decided that she should wear this dress for travelling, in order to make a good impression on her arrival. She also put on a black wool jacket of her mother's for warmth and the boots, now repaired, from the Workhouse. She packed her bundle with the dress in which she had left the Workhouse and another of her mother's cut down to fit, a spare pair of stockings and the extra aprons. Inside the bodice of her dress, next to her heart, she placed a little paper packet folded to contain a small lock of Will's hair cut last night although it was barely long enough to do so, and the wisp of Thomas's.

Her mother insisted she go to the harbour early rather than risk keeping the men waiting and they said their farewells at the cottage. She knew that the warmth of her mother's embrace reflected her pride in Selina's intended destination more than sorrow at her departure. Then she turned to Will and concentrated on the sensation of his fragile little body against hers as she hugged him, the soft hair against her face, the little fingers which curled around her thumb as his eyes, close to her own, gazed seriously back at her. She wanted never to forget.

He did not reply to her farewells but as she closed the door she heard him starting to cry and she sobbed helplessly until she reached the High Street, where the presence of a small group of waiting well-wishers forced her to control herself. In no time she was down at the harbour and was directed into a trawler where she sat, trying to control her tears.

In the Workhouse she had forgotten what Clovelly looked like. Now, waiting in the trawler she gazed at the massive sea wall protecting the busy harbour and the waterside cottages, making herself take in every detail, hoping she would remember this time. To her right the sea and sky formed a uniformity of grey devoid of individual features and she glanced anxiously at the gathering clouds.

She was, surely, presentable enough to knock at the doctor's door? She must find the back door, her sister had reminded her of that, and she must curtsey. What should she say? Who would open the door? As to how she should find the house in the first place she could not bear to think, as she could not remember the name of the street. "Just ask for Dr Ackland," she told herself. Surely there would be someone to ask. It would almost be preferable to be returning to the Workhouse where her life would at least be ordered and familiar, even if hateful, and Will would be at her side for a few hours more.

The nets on the harbour wall were being gathered and folded. The skipper climbed into the trawler which was returning to Bideford to be laid up for the winter, the crew of four returning to Clovelly by road.

"There be rain on the way," he warned. "Us may be in for a wetting."

Selina looked up at the sky and saw the threatening clouds which were beginning to gather beyond the steep green cliffs.

Dr Ackland closed his front door and paused for a moment before stepping down on to the street. He looked up at the sky between the twin spires of the chapel across the road then, swapping his heavy leather bag to his right hand, he strode decisively across the road to observe the sky in the south-west. There was no break in the low grey cloud, nor was there any breeze to blow in a change. That decided it, if he went on horseback he was likely to get very wet, he must take the brougham today. He was glad of an excuse for the extravagance.

He removed his hat with a flourish, "Good *Morning*, Mrs Baxter, and it *is* a good morning, I believe, even if a little grey," then turned right towards North Road, passing purposeful women with baskets on their arms and a delivery cart drawn by a weary grey horse, all making for the Mill Street shops. He had raised his hat a dozen times when he glanced up, as he did every morning, at the tall house which curved round the corner into Chingswell Street, his childhood home which he viewed with a warm nostalgia combined with lasting sadness that his parents were no longer present.

Charles was sweeping out the stable and Toby was tethered in the yard, groomed and ready to be harnessed. The doctor felt in his pocket for the customary carrot as the horse turned and whickered in recognition.

"Charles, would you avail me of your time today? I have calls to make in Instow and Westleigh in addition to a visit to Mrs William Hutchinson and do not relish the prospect of a soaking."

"Yes sir, certainly sir, I can be ready in a few minutes."

"Good man. You get changed and I'll start harnessing him."

Charles could usually oblige him when he needed a driver and if he was busy there were one or two other men who could be relied upon. The doctor spoke quietly to the Shire cross and patted his neck, the sound echoing round the small yard. Two other horses, invisible in their stables, moved restlessly, their hoofs ringing on the cobbled floor.

Ten minutes later Dr Ackland stood behind the brougham as Charles guided it carefully through the narrow entrance into North Road. Toby was a good steady horse and it was rare for the carriage to be scratched. His first call was to a house just above Northam Square. It did not do to call on Mrs William Hutchinson too early; she preferred to have her breakfast and make her toilet so that she could be prettily arranged in the bed before he arrived. So first it was to Castle Street to see a child of whom he had been eloquently informed by the father, knocking on the door last night,

"'Er has the squits awful bad, Doctor."

Having given Charles his instructions and pulled the carriage door closed with the habitual slam, he relaxed into the deep leather seats, absent-mindedly humming the tune that Emily and Lucy had been singing at breakfast, Mr Tennyson's poem that had now been set to music. They gave no trouble, the girls. Clever as well as pretty. He would see that they all had a good education, though he had doubts whether the two older ones, Annie and Maud, were well enough provided for at present. He would have preferred a more solid cultural and intellectual education for them, something less ornamental. Difficult, with it being in the family. He placed his leather gloves on the seat beside him and smoothed his beard thoughtfully. His two eldest daughters were at Compton Gifford just outside Plymouth, at a school run by two of Sophia's sisters. It had only nine pupils and would not be viable if he did not send them his daughters to educate. None of Sophia's five sisters was married and the small annuities left them by their father were insufficient to support them. He frequently helped out with small sums, especially for Frances, the eldest. There it was. By marrying Sophia he took on the sisters as well. He had no regrets. But he would have preferred to have chosen a better school for his two eldest daughters.

They were passing along the causeway which led over the marshlands to Northam with Toby going at a smart trot, his hoofs ringing on the metalled road. A heron out on the marsh staring intently into the watery grasses raised its sword-like bill suspiciously then drew in its neck and hunched its shoulders, ready to fly. As the carriage passed, the Doctor turned to watch and the heron stared back.

The heron. *Ardea Cinerea.* Kingsley would like to draw

Extract from census return, 1871, Mannamead, showing Lucy and Sylvia Lott, and Ann and Sylvia (Maud) Ackland. (The National Archives, RG10/2109/62) that. He showed some talent. His sketches were still childish but were beginning to develop some feeling.

- He must get that talent from his mother for I have none. But he is falling behind in his studies. He must go away, learn Latin and Greek, he is eleven years old and I must see to it soon. Such a sensitive boy though, such a dear, darling boy.

The tune came into his head again and he sang quietly to himself in a rich baritone. It was fortunate that it was his older son who was Mr Charles Kingsley's godson and not the younger, for Hugh was a different kettle of fish, confident and rumbustious. Perhaps it was his godfather's sensitive and attentive influence that had helped form Kingsley's character. - Will I see him again, dear friend that he is? We had such a pleasant time together in August and Kingsley will never forget the trip to Clovelly. Shameful that such a great man is not made more welcome in the town.

The brougham had slowed now as they made their way up the winding tree-lined hill to Northam, the horse only being urged to a trot to pass a donkey cart which seemed barely able to take the gradient, both donkey and driver being equally old and grey and both, indeed, appearing half-asleep.

"Co-o-o-me into the ga-a-a-rden, Maud." He waved his hand in time to the tune. Ah, it was a fine day. A carriage drawn by a smart chestnut approached and he raised his hat with an extravagant gesture to compensate for the obscuring tendency of the carriage windows.

"Good morning, Sir!" The man in the passing carriage would not hear, but no matter. He raised his hat in reply and bowed pleasantly. A good man, Mr Thomas Pynsent, a splendid man, and not afraid to speak his mind. Would there were more like him. It was one of the frustrations of the Doctor's position in society that he could not always speak out openly against injustice. He must hedge the truth with civilities, be courteous to men of influence while raging inwardly at their stupidity and dishonesty. But they recognised his integrity, that was certain, and they liked his use of homeopathy, knowing it to be popular in the very highest levels of English society. And he had found favour with many powerful men, could count such as the Earl of Portsmouth and Colonel Fane of Clovelly among his patients.

- A fortunate man, I am, it is true.

It was through their influence that he had become a Justice of the Peace and from there followed other positions and now this latest, the Medical Officer of Health. He it was who was chosen, although all the doctors in the town had put their names forward. There was no doubting it, he was the most favoured doctor among the good families in the area and since this last appointment two more gentlemen had already approached him. He was confident that, in time, they could be persuaded to support the Dispensary. So, more free treatment for those that most needed it.

In the garden of one of the large houses that could be glimpsed between the trees, a gardener led a small pony pulling a grass-cutter. They turned precisely at the edge of the lawn and cut another neat swathe of grass.

- Well, he knows there to be rain ahead!

At last the Local Board had seen fit to appoint a Medical Officer of Health, a permanent position this time, it was to be hoped. They had finally been forced to take action after the severe outbreak of scarlet fever earlier in the year and now the smallpox. At last he could change things, enforce sanitary improvements, advance the lot of the poorer people through cleaner streets and disease-free water. Only then could they be educated and fix their minds on higher things. No man can do that when he is ill from contaminated water, when his children are dying. It was disgraceful, it was blasphemy, a denial of the intentions of God for his creatures that so many should live in filth and poverty while others reclined in luxury and did nothing to help their poorer brothers.

- But do not speak that word. Utter that word, Socialism, and they will throw up their hands in horror. No Medical Officer of Health then, no Justice of the Peace, no subscriptions to keep the Dispensary open. No. Proceed cautiously. Think before you speak. I am successful at that now.

He chuckled to himself. The impulsive young man that he had once been would not recognise the temperate, careful man he was now. As far as the world was concerned he was a Liberal, but Liberalism did not go far enough. One must intervene, take action, empower the poor so that they might help themselves. Quietly, resolutely, he worked away. There were improvements. Better times were coming.

The brougham bowled down Fore Street and ragged wide-eyed children ran back, fingers in mouths, to watch it pass. Dogs barked and a bare-footed boy chased behind the carriage, shouting,

"Shall us 'old the 'oss, Sir, penny to 'old the 'oss Sir!"

Charles turned into Castle Street and drew up outside a very small terraced house that stood right on the road. Doors up and down the street opened and women and children appeared to see who had arrived, for horses were not frequent in these very narrow side streets. The Doctor opened the carriage door without waiting for Charles and descended the steps. The street, he noted, was tolerably clean, devoid of the vegetable and human waste that was so often thrown from front doors.

"Come in, Doctor, come in." He tipped his hat to the young woman who welcomed him in, blushing and flustered. She could not be more than one or two and twenty. He glanced quickly around the small, low-ceilinged room. It was neat and clean, with a bright fire in the hearth and a rag rug on the newly swept floor. A wooden cradle stood near the fire.

"I've a job to keep her clean, Doctor, the milk goes through her so fast."

A child of about fifteen months lay listlessly in the cradle, her somewhat sunken eyes gazing at him without interest. An ornate bonnet decorated with frills and ribbons combined with the child's dullness to give it a doll-like appearance.

"Lift her out please and place her on your lap."

The young woman hastily placed a cloth on her lap and did as she was asked. He examined the child quickly, talking to it soothingly as he did so. The abdomen was tense and hard, the limbs relaxed, offering no resistance. In response to questioning, the mother stated that the child was fed from the breast except when it was left with a neighbour while the young woman went to do the laundry at Cross House. It was then given a bottle. Upon request she replaced the child in the cradle and ran to fetch the bottle. While she was gone the Doctor stepped through into the scullery. There was no water, all would be fetched from the pump. A small window looked out on to a patch of garden where leeks and cabbages were growing. The privy was at the end, well away from the house.

As he expected, the feeding bottle was the culprit. Inside the rubber teat was black mould. He showed the young mother and the neighbour who had accompanied her back to the house and they marvelled that such specks should be harmful. After an explanation of the uses of disinfectant, directions in the dosing of syrup of ipecac followed by water boiled with sugar and salt, he rinsed his hands with disinfectant at the pump and returned to the brougham, satisfied with the outcome as he knew the grateful mother would tell her friends and neighbours. Education and hygiene; together they saved lives. He waved to the cluster of staring children who had gathered at a safe distance from the brougham.

As they moved off, he slid open the window and instructed Charles, having remembered another call to make in Northam. An old man was dying and there was little more he could do to relieve the pain but his presence was a comfort to the elderly wife. They turned right into North Street and stopped outside a small square house set high above the road. The elderly woman opened the door as he climbed the steps. She seemed to be shrinking away from life along with her husband, and her hand, when he took it in greeting, was cold and limp. She cheered a little, however, as he gave his instructions; a few sips of sweetened weak tea for the patient when the church clock struck the hour, turn him with the help of a neighbour every other hour, the same neighbour to sit with the patient between the hours of midnight and six for it was beneficial for him to have a change of carer. He knew that the old woman would not rest for her own sake but would do anything for her husband. As he bade her farewell there was a greater strength in her hand as she grasped his own in gratitude.

He sighed as he reclined again on the leather seats. The sky had darkened and a little fine rain had begun to fall, forming tiny droplets on the window of the brougham which gradually drew together until large enough to run hesitant races down the glass. Outside, Charles turned up his collar and drew his coat together over his knees. The doctor opened his bag and took out his notebook to make a few pencilled notes.

- *Dies Mercurii 15 Novemb.*

Now on to Wellesbourne. He sat up a little straighter in his seat. What would amuse Mrs Hutchinson today? In truth the remedies were slow to help her melancholia and it was his presence that helped her to rally, but there, he liked General Hutchinson and was always met with courtesy. Charles turned left into Limers Lane then into the drive of Wellesbourne, the gravel rattling noisily under the wheels. The Doctor pulled the bell cord, humming to himself under his breath until the door was opened by an attractive, curtseying maid dressed in lilac and white.

"Good morning, Doctor Ackland. Mrs Hutchinson is ready to see you."

As he strode towards the staircase which wound elegantly up to the first floor, Lieutenant General Hutchinson stepped out from the library, proffering his hand.

"Good morning, Ackland, how good it is to see you again. Will you take coffee with me when you have seen my poor wife? I know it will be of no avail to offer you anything stronger!"

The maid led the way up to Mrs Hutchinson's bedroom and they entered after a knock at the door had elicited a weak reply. The lady, sitting against a mound of lace-trimmed pillows with a grey and white Persian cat curled at her side, greeted him pleasantly, saying how glad she was that he had come.

"And what a pleasure it is to see you, dear lady. I do think you are looking a little better. Do tell me how you are feeling."

It was the usual story. Her nerves were not good and she slept poorly, it tired her to be with the children although to do so did raise her spirits a little, sometimes her shoulders ached dreadfully and that did not help her to rest. He explained again that child-bearing had diminished her vitality and now that she had reached the change of life she had not sufficient energy to meet it. She confided her fears to him in a low whisper and he listened intently, nodding all the while. When she had finished he assured her that with rest, the medicines he would continue to give her, a light nourishing diet – he had some new suggestions for this – and a little gentle exercise when she could manage it, she would, in time, make a complete recovery. They then talked of their respective children and he was able to make her laugh a little at their antics. They discussed the progress of Mrs Hutchinson's son Horatio, who was the same age as Kingsley and at school at Winchester College but was suffering from ill health, and spoke of the opening of the new Music Hall in Bideford which she had fortunately felt well enough to attend.

Almost an hour had passed before he joined the General in the library where they conversed, with great affability, on the subject of golf, and by the time he took his leave it was approaching luncheon.

- But no matter. It was enjoyable for all involved and my fee will equal that of many calls to humbler households.

By now the rain had grown steadier and showed no signs of abating. As they re-crossed the marsh he saw that the heron had been joined by two more, one standing poised in the distance and the other stalking hesitantly through the long grass, all disdainful of each other's company. A close flock of oystercatchers had joined them - high tide then, they had been driven from the riverbank. Yes, high tide, of course it was. Intriguing how the various species of birds differed in their habits, as did humans of course. He chuckled to himself as he imagined his acquaintances in the guise of birds. Yes, he could identify a heron, a chattering starling and a confiding robin. Sophia and the children would enjoy the comparison.

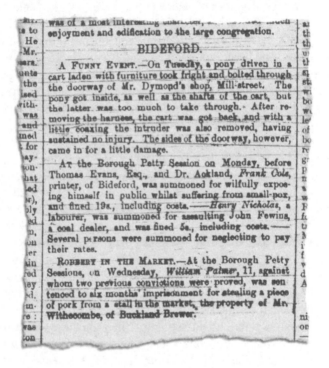

BIDEFORD.

A FUNNY EVENT.—On Tuesday, a pony driven in a cart laden with furniture took fright and bolted through the doorway of Mr. Dymond's shop, Mill-street. The pony got inside, as well as the shafts of the cart, but the latter was too much to take through. After removing the harness, the cart was got back, and with a little coaxing the intruder was also removed, having sustained no injury. The sides of the doorway, however, came in for a little damage.

AT the Borough Petty Session on Monday, before Thomas Evans, Esq., and Dr. Ackland, *Frank Cole*, printer, of Bideford, was summoned for wilfully exposing himself in public whilst suffering from small-pox, and fined 19s., including costs.——*Henry Nicholas*, a labourer, was summoned for assaulting John Fewins, a coal dealer, and was fined 5s., including costs.—— Several persons were summoned for neglecting to pay their rates.

ROBBERY IN THE MARKET.—At the Borough Petty Sessions, on Wednesday, *William Palmer*, 11, against whom two previous convictions were proved, was sentenced to six months' imprisonment for stealing a piece of pork from a stall in the market, the property of Mr. Withecombe, of Buckland Brewer.

From the North Devon Journal 29/2/1872

It was two o'clock and the rain was heavy when the brougham stopped outside 23 Bridgeland Street again; the Doctor took out his watch to check as he settled into his seat. Instow first, the journey there would give him time to digest his meal. He glanced along Queen Street as they passed; there was no water lying there despite the rain. The new sewers were effective and all the houses now drained into it. The re-sewering of the town was almost complete and at last many great and long-standing nuisances had been done away with; at last there would be few streets where every manner of foul effluence oozed from broken drains – he could expect an improvement in health as a result, less typhoid, perhaps no return of the cholera. God willing, the latest outbreak of smallpox would be short-lived. There had already been many fatal cases, mainly in the poorer and more overcrowded parts of the town but there were still incidents of infected persons wandering the streets and putting all at risk. Again it was education that was needed but it was not easy when so many were illiterate. They would learn however when the news of the fines imposed at the Petty Sessions spread through the town, they would know then to keep themselves indoors until fully recovered.

He gazed out over the Quay to the many-arched bridge. It was always a cheering prospect, even in inclement weather, to see the wide expanse of water that divided the town, the brown-sailed fishing boats and the ships that put him in mind of far-flung places and happy journeys that he had made. He turned to watch visitors descending from a carriage and hurrying into the Steam Packet Hotel, the train on which they had arrived chugging out of the station on the far side of the river.

How comfortable it was in the brougham in the rain, almost as pleasant as his own house. His wife and children were warm and secure indoors, all his little ones together in their calm, ordered home. Sophia had mentioned the servant problem at luncheon, Mary was due to leave on Saturday and she was concerned about her replacement. He had almost forgotten about the Clovelly girl - what was her name? He unfastened the straps on his bag, took out his casebook and leafed through the pages. There, Union Workhouse, child of Selina Burman. Three weeks ago, so she should be due to return from Clovelly before long.

Sophia was not enamoured of the plan, he was aware of

that. She had suggested today that the girl might not arrive and that they should perhaps advertise for a replacement. He had assured her that he was certain that would not be necessary. He usually left the servants to her but was sure that his decision in this case was the right one and Sophia had not protested. He smiled as he pictured her, no doubt now sitting with the children helping them with their lessons, his beautiful wife, so serene, - but how he embarrassed her when he found her in the kitchen and took her in his arms when the cook's back was turned! He sighed as he imagined her soft figure in his arms, his wife, who had borne him seven fine, darling children.

- How fortunate I have been. And I have made good choices. In Sophia he had found an ideal partner; beautiful, educated, - in truth, from a family originally a great deal wealthier than his own - but always grateful to him for providing a home and children when she expected none. He would remind her of how precious she was to him as soon as he returned home. Perhaps he would promise to take her to the Dramatic Reading at the new Music Hall; he knew she very much wanted to go.

- Co-o-o-me into the ga-a-a-rden, Maud

I am here at the ga-a-ate alone.

They were well underway and Clovelly was long since lost to view when the first drops came. The wind had risen and the sea was choppy; there were white tops to the waves as far as the eye could see. Selina fought with nausea, breathing deeply and trying to watch the horizon. One of the men showed her the hatch to the little cabin but crouching in the cramped, dark room which smelt of fish made her feel worse and she quickly climbed back on to deck. She was passed an oilskin which she pulled around her shoulders but there was nothing to cover her skirt. As the rain continued she watched as the dark drops on her grey dress multiplied until they joined together and she felt the coldness seeping through to her petticoat, then to her legs, then running down into her boots. She removed her cap and put it inside her bodice to protect it but the rain dripped from her hair and ran down her neck.

The journey was interminable. She clung to the side of the boat with both hands as it leapt and plunged with the strengthening wind. The nausea overtook her and she turned to lean over the side, almost past embarrassment. For a while she felt better but then retched again and again, hardly noticing when the wind blew vomit back on to her dress. Her stomach heaved until it ached and her hands shook with the effort of holding herself upright in the pitching trawler, the shock bringing tears which joined with the rain streaming down her face. An hour passed, and another. Any thoughts of her future were driven away; her physical suffering joined with her anguish at leaving Will and silently she screamed his name again and again as if his presence could cure all her ills.

She was too unwell to look around and saw only the rolling water and the side of the trawler that she clung too; it was some minutes after a particularly rough patch of water that she glimpsed the shore and realised that the boat was now sailing more steadily up the estuary. She managed to turn to a more comfortable position but still gripped her seat with shaking hands as her stomach continued to heave. The unremitting rain was a deluge now that the wind had dropped and as some discomforts decreased so she became more aware of how wet and cold she was. Water ran from her hair and her clothes were completely sodden, for the wind had blown the rain under the oilskin which she had not fastened and her skirts and petticoat lay heavy and cold in her lap with water running from the hems on to the deck. She realised she was shaking from head to foot, whether from shock or cold she could not tell, and she looked down with embarrassment when she realised she was attracting the notice of the men, who were more relaxed now that the Bar was crossed and the journey almost over.

"Well, you'm a bit wetty now, maid. Us'll soon be to

Bideford and 'tis only a step to the Doctor's house, they'll soon put 'ee to rights. Us'll put 'ee down on the Quay afore us goes to tie up."

Within a few minutes she looked up to see the tall buildings and long Quay wall of Bideford. One man jumped ashore with a rope and held the trawler steady while another helped her off.

"There you be maid, straight up that street now!"

She stood and watched as her link with Clovelly and all that was familiar sailed across the Torridge, the fishermen never giving her a backward glance. As she picked up her bundle and turned away from the river she realised that it, too, was running with water.

The Quay was deserted in the pouring rain. She started walking slowly across the road and into the street of tall, imposing houses that had been pointed out to her. The windows lined up along each side of the street to stare at her and she walked with her head down to avoid their gaze. The road resembled a stream-bed but it hardly mattered, she could not get any wetter. Her skirts clung heavily to her legs, making walking difficult and she felt the water in her boots ooze between her toes with every step. She was still shaking and swayed a little as she walked, having become accustomed to the motion of the sea, and this slowed her pace still further, but in any case she was not in a hurry. Knocking on Dr Ackland's door was now an impossibility. She knew she would reach the end of the street before long, and then there was only one place she could go. But she was unsure of the way to the Workhouse and she felt no compulsion to find out.

She heard footsteps behind her and a young girl in a white apron came running past holding a heavy shawl over her head. Some instinct made Selina call out to her,

"Please, which is Dr Ackland's house?"

"Just over there, look, number 23, with the bow windows," and the girl flew into the next house, slamming the door behind her.

Selina stopped and gazed nervously at the grand house that

had been pointed out to her. It was not, in fact, as large as she had imagined, for in her anxiety it had grown from a townhouse to a country mansion. But she saw at once that there was an additional problem. In common with all the other houses on the street it was attached to its neighbours. She could not approach the back door. Even if she had looked as smart as she had hoped she would, she could never have walked up the steps and lifted that big brass knocker, like a lady visitor.

She was standing outside a church and she looked up at it; at least no one would stare at her from its windows. Its design was far more imposing than Clovelly church and had no tower, but instead two spires so tall it made her neck ache to look at them. To the right of the tall arched door was a smaller door, set back from the road and sheltered a little by the stone lintel above and it was here that she sat, her upper body protected from the rain which still beat down upon her skirt. She pulled her mother's wool jacket around her but there was no warmth in the sodden fabric and she continued to shiver uncontrollably. She felt numb, both from the cold and from the hopelessness of her predicament. Her time in Clovelly seemed colourless, as insubstantial as a half-forgotten dream; even her memory of Will did not feel real and she was not sure that she had not imagined him. She looked at the house that should have welcomed her in, with its arched doorway and two large windows that curved out from the wall. In one window stood what appeared to be a small tree in a pot, unlike anything she had seen before. The house appeared utterly foreign, not for the likes of her. She stared down at the rain that was falling past her face and on to her skirt, dripping from her skirt on to the step, running from the step down to join the stream that flowed along the road to the river. She was unaware when an hour had passed, and then another.

Chapter Five

The brougham was returning from Instow at a steady trot, Charles being keen to get home out of the now heavy rain. There had been six calls to make in Westleigh, Instow and at Bradavin Farm; the Doctor had been called to the latter by an anxious labourer who had seen him earlier in the village and had run to alert him. Mr Hookaway had severed an index finger and it had been hanging by skin and tissue only; it was a triumph to save it and he relaxed now in a glow of self-satisfaction.

The River Torridge and Bideford Bridge, 1870's

As they approached Bideford the road became congested with farmers' carts returning home from market and he observed how many of the wives, sitting huddled and wet beside their husbands, appeared downcast in the extreme. He knew their story; up since five o'clock, each would have enjoyed her time in the market with the many social opportunities it offered, but would have then endured a long wait for her husband, ensconced in one of the many public houses around the market square. Now both were irritable, the one from drink and the other from fatigue and cold.

- Ah, the demon drink, what short term pleasures and long term miseries it does unleash.

There was one more call to make before he could return home for dinner, then out again for a Local Board meeting. They turned left and Toby slowed to a walk as they passed under the new railway bridge and up the steep bends of the hill, soon leaving the town behind. A veritable torrent of water poured down the unpaved road carrying leaves, stones and other debris with it, the ditches being unable to cope with the volume of water which ran from the fields on either side. His intended destination was a house on the Alverdiscott road which was being set up as a temporary hospital to receive smallpox patients. Mr Pollard the mineral paint manufacturer had, after much prevarication, offered the house for rent but he was a difficult man and the procedure of renting the house and setting it up as a hospital had been protracted and frustrating both for the Local Board - of whom Mr Pollard was, ironically, a member - and for himself in his new role of Medical Officer of Health. However, progress had now been made and he was to see what preparations were still needed before the first patients could be received.

They turned left at Sentry Corner and the road levelled, Toby now trotting through wide puddles which, in some places, stretched across the road. As they approached the house it became clear that the workmen had gone home. The Doctor fumbled in his pocket for the key and, descending from the brougham, hurried to the door. The house smelled of paint and freshly sawn wood.

- Good, good. The white liming is finished, a good clean job, the floor thoroughly cleaned.

In one downstairs room was stored the furniture and bedding which had been ordered and delivered, another was locked which was somewhat peculiar, just one upstairs room remained to be finished. He checked the windows, three of which were new. All could be opened despite the very damp weather; fresh air was essential. It only remained for him to appoint a nurse and he knew now of a suitable candidate. It had not been easy to find someone willing to take on the post because of the fear of infection, but now there was a widow who had agreed to start work providing she could bring her young son to live with her.

- Good. Now home.

The windows of the brougham had misted, shutting out the torrents of rain and he allowed his eyes to close as he was carried home, picturing a cheerful hearth, a well-laid table and the welcoming faces of his family.

"La feuille donne..." Sophia waited while Kingsley sucked the end of his pen and frowned. Mary had written the words and looked up expectantly. "Hurry up, Kingsley dear. Do your best. La feuille donne la couleur verte."

"That's green, verte is green!" said Emily, who was carefully adding green paint to the leaves she had drawn, approximations of the ivy leaves that stood in a jar in the centre of the table. Sophia liked to adapt the same object to suit the varying ages of her children, in this case French dictation for the oldest, painting for the younger ones. Lucy and Hugh, being younger and more impulsive, had almost finished their paintings. It was frustrating that the children could not all finish their tasks at the same time.

"Des paysages. La feuille donne la couleur verte des paysages. Don't forget to paint the stem, Hugh. Mind the water!"

The children were all lacking in concentration for they had not had their walk this afternoon as the rain had become heavier and heavier. It beat now on the window and hissed occasionally in the fire as it found its way down the chimney. She looked at the clock; it would be as well to finish a little earlier today and play a game. She rose and walked to the window to look out on to the garden. The rain fell in an unremitting torrent, the path had become a veritable river and water spurted from a broken gutter. She must check the ceiling in the maids' bedroom, it dripped sometimes in heavy rain. It would be as well to cut short this dictation.

"Que ce soit des champs ou des bois. Que ce soit des champs ou des bois."

Kingsley sighed. She could see errors in his work even when reading it upside down across the table. At eleven years old he should be learning Latin as well but she did not have sufficient knowledge of the subject to teach it and in any case she doubted whether he would take to it. He was an intelligent child but somehow his interest always seemed to lie elsewhere, anywhere it seemed but where his studies required. His father felt he should go away to school to learn to be more diligent and self-reliant but he was so sensitive, so young still for his years, she could not bear to think of him in what would seem such a harsh, unforgiving environment. Perhaps in another year he would seem more grown-up.

She rang the bell to ask Mary to bring a pot of tea and some milk for the children, then cleared the table and sent Emily to the kitchen with the jar of water and the paintbrushes. It was a nuisance they had missed their walk but the extreme weather made the house seem a haven of warmth and comfort. There would be time for some games and the opportunity for the children to use some energy before teatime. Probably William would return early if there were visits he could put off until tomorrow, especially as he had to go out again to a Local Board meeting later.

"Now, how about a game of Shopkeepers while you drink your milk? Hugh, you come and sit next to me and I'll whisper in your ear if you're uncertain of something. Lucy, what will you be?"

The children all chose their professions and she watched with amusement as they played the familiar game, bouncing in their chairs with excitement when it was their turn to answer.

"I am the draper and I have some silk for sale. Is it animal, vegetable or mineral?" Mary sat up very straight and spoke with the intensity of a natural orator.

When each had had a turn and the younger two had exhausted their repertoire, Kingsley suggested a game of Ball of Wool and ran to fetch a scrap of wool from her workbox. The cloth was removed and she joined in with them all, blowing vigorously on the table to move the wool away from the edge and prevent it reaching the floor, until it fell next to Lucy and it was decided that she should pay the forfeit of imitating a pig. They were all laughing and she must have missed the sound of the front door, for suddenly there was Mary Tuplin white-faced at the door calling "Ma'am, ma'am!"

She was already hurrying to the door when her husband shouted to her, his tone very different from his usual greeting. She saw him standing in the hall supporting a woman who appeared close to collapse, rainwater dripping from her clothes on to the polished floor. Her first thought was that her husband had gone too far this time, bringing one of his poorer patients into their home where the health and security of the children could be put at risk.

"Bring a chair, she cannot stand" he ordered and Mary Tuplin ran to oblige, Sophia being rooted to the spot with the children crowded behind her.

The woman was swaying in his arms as if inebriated, her hair stuck close to her skull like a wet dog, her head bowed and her nose running. If Sophia had seen her on the street she would have given her a wide berth.

William lowered her on to the chair and the woman sat with her head almost on her knees while he continued to support her.

"It's Selina Burman, she has come from Clovelly by sea. I should have thought to send the carrier for her. She was sitting on the church steps – did you not see her from the window?"

Sophia was unable at first to take in what her husband said. The children, who had until now been silenced by the apparition, started to ask questions.

"Who is the lady, Mamma?"

"Why is the lady here, Mamma?"

Sophia took them back into the schoolroom and hurriedly organised another game to keep them busy; they were not to worry, it was just a poor woman whom their father needed to help. How could she tell them the truth? In any case the woman could not stay, it was unthinkable.

She sent Jane to keep an eye on them and returned to the hall. William was still crouching on the floor supporting the woman. Her dress was soiled down the front, she could be carrying infection, they must get her out of the house at once - but he was sending Mary to heat water for a bath.

"Will you help Mary bathe her? She needs to be thoroughly warmed and given some hot soup before being put to bed. Where is she to sleep?"

"To sleep?" How could her husband countenance the idea? "William, surely, you must see, she cannot stay."

"Sophia, we have promised a month's trial! Which room did you intend her to have?"

"William, it is impossible! Think of the children, please. We cannot take someone in from the streets to sully our home."

He looked at her incredulously. "I have promised her a situation! Where is she to sleep?"

Sophia felt her eyes fill with tears.

"The kitchen, for Jane will not share with her and in any case, Mary is here until the end of the week. There is nowhere else suitable." Sophia hoped he would not mention the guestroom, he could not, surely. She thought quickly for she knew the kitchen would be busy.

"I will ask Eliza to change her plans and prepare a cold dinner, I will help her myself. *She* can lie down near the scullery door. We will manage."

Sophia hurried to tell Eliza and calm her indignation as far as she was able, then quickly covered her dress with a large apron and returned to her husband. Between them they helped Selina through the door and down the passageway into the kitchen. While Mary poured jugs of hot water into the hip bath, they sat the woman on a chair where she remained slumped with her head down, grasping a bundle of wet rags in her hands and sobbing, "Sorry, Sir, sorry, Ma'am, I be so sorry." Eliza stared at her incredulously.

When the water was ready her husband left and Sophia saw that she would have to take charge as Mary and Eliza hung back, their expressions reflecting her own state of mind. She instructed Eliza to start the dinner and rolled up her sleeves.

Afterwards she did feel pity, as well as disgust. The girl – such a thin young creature could not be called a woman - was the epitome of misery, so ashamed, so very timid. She had hardly seemed to know how to wash herself and in the end Sophia had taken the flannel and soaped her hair, doused her head with disinfectant and scrubbed her back and her legs, rubbing vigorously to restore the circulation. Her skin was blemished and unhealthy-looking, her nails bitten to the quick. Mary poured warm water from a jug to rinse off the soap but remained grim-faced, offended no doubt that such a creature could even be considered as her replacement. Sophia still had not seen the girl's face properly for she hunched forward in an effort to cover her nakedness and was quite unable to look up.

The bundle the girl had carried was wet right through and proved to hold little but rags. Sophia took out two aprons which might prove sufficiently serviceable for the kitchen and threw the rest in the range where the fire hissed in protest and was almost put out. Then she washed her hands thoroughly and resolved to have a bath herself. When she returned to the kitchen to check that the dinner was progressing satisfactorily and Eliza not too indignant, the girl was lying on a straw mattress that Mary had retrieved from the outhouse and had a blanket pulled up over her face. Sophia saw that she was shuddering a little and approached her.

"Are you still cold?" There was no answer but the shuddering subsided a little. "Can you hear me? Are you still cold?"

"No, ma'am. Thank 'ee, ma'am."

Sophia realised from the barely audible voice that the girl had been crying. It was not credible that she would ever be capable of useful work. The sooner she left the better it would be for all of them, even if the house did have to be run without a housemaid for a time. Would she still be here in the morning however? Sophia resolved to lock up the silver.

It was many hours before Selina dared to raise her head and look around. From under the blanket she had heard clattering dishes, running water and subdued voices, then the floor around her being swept and footsteps approaching and receding. After these sounds had ceased there was the squeak of floorboards above her head, then silence but for the occasional creak as the house settled down for the night. She sat up slowly. There was a candle burning on the corner of the table nearest to her and a chamber pot placed at the end of her mattress. She got up quickly and relieved herself. She found she was wearing a long nightgown which in the candlelight seemed whiter than anything she had ever seen. She scrambled back into bed and looked around, holding the blanket under her chin so that she could quickly lie down again if anyone came in.

The room was large and the ceiling low. The floor was covered with a patterned material which felt waxy when she reached out a finger to touch it. There were two tall dressers displaying coloured plates and dishes; numerous pans hung over a fireplace which contained an iron range, smaller and shinier than the ones in the Workhouse. Could she really he here, inside Dr Ackland's house? She remembered the strength of his arm around her shoulder as he half-carried her in from the street and heard the compassion in his voice. But her shame afterwards – had he been there when she was bathed? No, of course not. But Mrs Ackland was. Selina curled herself up into a tight ball.

The room was so quiet. It was the first time she had ever slept in a room alone. She could sit up and no one would see. She could even get up and look around, but would not, in case someone came. Tomorrow people would come. She would have to speak, she would have to apologise for today and speak up so they could hear her. Would the other servants be kind to her? She would work, if they showed her what to do she would work harder than she had ever done before. If Mrs Ackland saw how hard she worked she would surely let her sleep here again tomorrow.

As she lay wondering at the events of the day, she remembered the paper that had been in her bodice, containing the only memento of her boys. She got out of bed and in desperation searched the kitchen, holding the candle up to high shelves and into dark corners, no longer caring whether anyone might discover her. She found her dress and coat rolled up in a damp pile in a washing basket and shook them out and searched through all the folds and in the sleeves, but in vain. There were some clean clothes on the table which must be intended for her to wear in the morning but there was no sign of her bundle with the two spare dresses and stockings and aprons. Could the precious little reminder of her sons be with them? Finally, she stood in front of the black range in which the fire now died away. She bent down and carefully opened the door. The glowing coals were almost covered with mound of soft grey ash. She stared at it for a very long time.

Chapter Six

It was still dark when Selina stood in the only partially worn violet dress, looking from the closed kitchen door to the cold range. She hoped these clothes *were* intended for her. As soon as she woke she had dressed hurriedly, but she was now at a loss to know what to do and dreaded being considered idle. She knew she could clean out the range but could find no implements to use. There were brooms in a corner cupboard but to sweep the floor before cleaning out and lighting the range would be considered stupid so she stood by the table, hoping it would look as if she had just finished dressing. She had tidied her bed but left it unrolled on the floor, intending to fold it away as soon as someone came, to add to the impression of having just risen. Several times she made forays to the back door in which a large key was waiting to be turned; the range tools might be kept outside but suppose there was a dog? She retied her apron and smoothed the folds, combed through her hair with her fingers again. She jumped a little at a sudden sound but it was only a cockroach scuttling behind a cupboard, but then, yes, there were footsteps, descending some stairs and approaching the door.

As the door opened Selina looked away, pretending to be occupied, but a large black dog rushed at her, barking and wagging its tail and almost knocking her off her feet.

"Jimmy, be quiet! You'll wake the whole house! Come on, outside!" The woman grabbed the dog's collar and pulled him away from Selina, unlocked the back door and let him go outside. Selina turned away to roll up her bed.

"Put the bed out in the outhouse, on the right as you go out the door. Bring in the poker and dustpan and I'll show 'ee how to do the range. Here, take the lantern out first."

She found herself in a small paved area next to two stone outhouses. There were some dimly lit windows beyond a large expanse of darkness. The air was damp and cold. She unbolted the first outhouse, turned back for her bed which she placed on a shelf and found the implements for the stove. When she returned to the kitchen the woman was standing and watching her.

"Well, least I can see your face now, or some of it. Did 'ee get some sleep?"

"Yes, thank 'ee ma'am."

"Don't 'ee 'ma'am' me. I'm Eliza though I could be Miss Stribling to you if I'd a mind. What's your name?"

Selina told her. Eliza Stribling was diminutive but had very large feet in huge, shiny, black buttoned boots below the hem of her skirt.

"Well, Selina, you can watch while I ready the stove then it'll be your job." She attacked the firebox with a poker. "Make sure you get all the ash down then take it out here, see?" She lifted out the ashpan. "Then lay the fire and make sure you have the flue open here and here and the door open here for a draught. Light it after you've cleaned it or a bit before you've finished. There's the blacklead and the cloths. Then scrub the table and the floor. Mrs Ackland wants you in the kitchen, nowhere else this morning. Mary and I will do the downstair rooms. You can make us a cup of tea when the kettle boils."

Eliza went to a cupboard and starting placing dustpans, polish and cloths in a large wooden basket. Selina glanced at her once or twice as she swept out the stove and started scraping off the burnt spillages. She was not much older than Selina herself, small and wiry with brown hair pulled tightly back into a small bun, and with fast, efficient movements; her very large hands matched the size of her feet. Selina rubbed harder at the stove and was glad when she was left alone.

She judged about an hour to have passed before the door opened again. She had heard a clock strike six, so there must be a door open which had shut out the chiming overnight. She had finished polishing the stove, had tentatively turned on the tap above the big stone sink and jumped at the water that gushed out into the bucket unaided, completed the other tasks Eliza had given her and then had looked at the seven pairs of boots lined up by the door. In a cupboard she had found the blacking which she quickly mixed to a thin paste in an old saucer before smearing it on all the boots with the blacking brush, then commenced polishing with the shining brush until her arm ached. The dog whining at the door had worried her for she was afraid he would start barking at any moment but she did not like to let him in. The kettle was boiling and the tea ready in the pot; as soon as she heard the door open she turned and poured the water in, slowly.

"Well, boots done as well! There, Mary, I reckon you'll not have to do those again before you leave."

"Well, I'll not miss them."

The second woman let in the dog, making a fuss of him for being shut out for so long before ordering him to lie down in the corner, which he did, watching them with what was almost a smile and thumping his tail on the floor from time to time. Selina had never seen such a dog before, though it did rather resemble the spaniels that Mr Fane's beaters took shooting at Clovelly.

Selina turned with the two cups of tea and watched them carefully to avoid spillages as she approached the table.

"Have one yourself as well, and we may as well have breakfast for we're ahead of ourselves now with three to do the work."

Selina poured herself a cup of tea while Eliza cut thick slices of bread which she spread with butter. Selina's stomach started to rumble. She sat down at the end of the table and studied her cup.

"So, you're to take my place then."

It was the other woman who spoke to her.

"I, I'm sorry, I didn't mean…."

"Oh, don't be sorry, I'm leaving to be wed. I'm not sorry! But they're good people, the Doctor and Mrs Ackland, the best there are. They can have the pick of servants you know!"

Selina glanced up at her for a second. She was a little older than Eliza and plumper, with fair hair. Her expression was not unkind.

"I shall work hard, I shall do whatever is asked. I knows how to work." She did not add that nothing could be harder than the Workhouse.

"Well, see that you do. But I don't know as that will be enough for Mrs Ackland. I don't know that she'll keep you longer than the month. Anyway she wants to see you later this morning, you're to stay in the kitchen 'til then. You'll find she's fair."

Selina nursed her cup of tea and struggled to hold back the tears at this kindness. They left her alone then for a while, talking of people she did not know. She wondered whether Mrs Ackland would call her Mary. In her post at Woolsery the mistress had always called her servants Mary. At least the food was good here. There was more butter on her two slices of bread than her mother would use in a whole day and she ate them quickly, realising how hungry she had been.

"Do 'ee want more, maid?" Eliza had cut two more slices and was looking at Selina, the bread knife poised. "Lord, I'm offering you bread, not the whole world! You're a strange one and not a bit what I expected!"

They asked her questions then, about the places she had worked before and about Clovelly, of which they had heard stories but had not visited. The Workhouse was not mentioned. She did not know how to describe the households in which she had worked, they were farms and therefore larger and busier than her parents' home but she had no other comparisons to make. She could not answer their questions about the master at the second farm. She rubbed at a knot on the tabletop until the dog, Jimmy, came to investigate and was ordered back to his bed. The conversation soon took a different direction and Selina was able to take occasional fleeting looks at the two women as they laughed over previous positions they had held. Eliza looked less intimidating when she smiled.

As soon as they pushed back their chairs she jumped up

and cleared the plates and cups, then apologised for putting them into the sink instead of the wooden bowl which was kept underneath. She dug her bitten nails into the palms of her hands; she must not make mistakes.

By the time Eliza told her it was almost eleven o'clock, the time she was due to meet Mrs Ackland in a room called the drawing room, it seemed as if days rather than hours had passed, for everything she did had to be done in such a particular manner. She had chopped vegetables for the next day's soup while Eliza prepared breakfast for the family; the carrots had to be chopped like *this* and the onions sliced like *this*, the bones pounded and tied in a bag, the meat chopped as small as could be. But Eliza was clear and direct when she gave instructions and did not grumble, indeed she praised Selina with a curt "that was quick" when all the clearing up after the family's breakfast was completed. The kitchen door opened several times, usually to reveal Mary carrying jugs of water or cleaning equipment but once it was another woman who spoke to Eliza and carried some things out to the washhouse, ignoring Selina. When she had gone Eliza had said that she was Jane, the children's nurse. It had not occurred to Selina that there were children in the house but she did not like to ask questions. When she had returned from the coalhouse with a full bucket of coal she found that Mrs Ackland had just been in to give her orders for the day and her heart pounded because, if she had opened the back door, she would have seen Selina standing still for a moment looking across the long garden to the backs of houses which formed the next street.

And now it was time to meet her. Eliza found Selina a clean apron and clicked her tongue and shook her head. "She won't *bite*, you know!"

Selina followed her out of the kitchen. After a short passageway the wax floor covering changed to burnished wood; she glimpsed a wide staircase with highly polished banisters, then Eliza was knocking on a door and going in. In response to a voice Selina stepped forward on to a blue carpet and curtseyed clumsily.

She knew she must speak. She *had* to apologise.

"Ma'am. I'm sorry. I, - I put 'ee to a load of trouble yesterday, I – the sea was so rough...and..." Her toes were curled so tightly inside her boots that she swayed slightly and she quickly drew herself upright. In doing so she glanced up momentarily and saw a lady sitting very upright on a sofa. She was very stern, with small, fine features.

"Certainly it was not an ideal introduction to a prospective servant. First impressions are important, even of those whose reputations have travelled before them."

Selina stared at the deep blue carpet. She felt her mouth starting to turn down and struggled to control it.

"Dr Ackland wants to give you a month's trial. If, during that time, you give any cause for displeasure you will receive instant dismissal. For the first few days you will work under the direction of Mary, the housemaid who is leaving and I will oversee your work myself."

Selina did not take in all that Mrs Ackland said to her after that. She clasped her hands together and dug her nails into her palms to stop herself from crying. She could feel her nose starting to run but she daren't wipe it on her sleeve. Mrs Ackland told her what a particular household it was, how she liked everything to be ordered, how everything must be in its place for her husband. She told her that the children had no knowledge of immorality and she had every intention that it remained so.

"As far as they are concerned, you are widowed. You will wear this at all times."

Mrs Ackland was holding out something in her long slender fingers. She stumbled forward and was handed a ring, a plain band with sharp edges.

"It is brass so you need not consider it worth selling."

She then read out a list of rules which she said she had written specially. Selina was unable then to hold back the tears for there was not a single rule she would ever dare to break, but she held her breath and managed to remain silent.

"I will place this list in the kitchen drawer and you will read it every day."

"Ma'am, I'm sorry Ma'am…."

"What is it?"

"I cannot read, Ma'am."

There was a long silence.

"Then I shall come to the kitchen every day and read it to you. Now return to your work."

Selina closed the door with shaking hands. By the time she had passed the staircase and found the kitchen door she could hold back the sobs no longer. Eliza looked up from the table where she was rolling pastry and watched as Selina closed the door behind her.

"Here." Eliza took a rag from the table drawer. "Go out to the coal shed with the coal scuttle. Take your time."

Sophia sat back on the sofa. She had made herself clear, that was certain. If there were any transgressions now, it would not be for want of instruction, for she was sure she had omitted nothing. It would not be fair if the girl did not understand the nature of the household in which she now found herself, she had to realise that her previous ways were totally unacceptable here. Sophia looked down the list of rules she had drawn up.

If you encounter one of your betters in the house or on the stairs, you are to make yourself as invisible as possible, turning to the wall and averting your eyes.

Followers are strictly forbidden. If you fraternize with any member of the opposite sex you will be instantly dismissed.

Any breakages or damages in the house will be deducted from your wages. Theft will result in instant dismissal.

And so it went on. Sophia sighed and walked over to the window, leaning on the sill to gaze out on to the street. The truth was the interview had not gone quite as she had expected. She had imagined the girl would be quite recovered from her distress of the previous evening and would walk in without shame and stare brazenly at her, perhaps challenge her authority. She had even half-hoped – and feared, for she hated a scene – that Selina would refuse some of the conditions, then she would have been justified in letting her go immediately and the whole sorry business would have been over. Her husband would accept that he had been over-optimistic in taking her on and they could return to their previous well-ordered stability. She had not expected the cringing, sobbing girl who could not even meet her eye.

An image came to her that she had thought long-forgotten, a small girl sitting with head bowed and lip quivering as she was chastised. The image induced feelings of guilt and shame in her, for she had badly misjudged that situation. It was a long time ago now. When she had first gone out as a governess, lonely, unused to children and deeply disturbed to find herself in a position close to that of a servant, she had charge of three small girls. The oldest, Ellen, was surly in her manner to Sophia, did not apply herself to her books and tore her papers when her errors were pointed out. On the third day Sophia had lost her temper and had shouted at the girl, itemising her failures and her weaknesses. That night the child had had nightmares, calling out in fear so that the nurse had had to attend to her three times. The child's mother spoke to Sophia, shocked that her daughter had been spoken to in such a way; Ellen was a dear child who was heartbroken that her previous beloved governess had gone, once secure in her affections she worked hard and was always sweet-mannered. In time Sophia found this to be true and the memory of the incident still made her feel very uncomfortable.

What had brought back that memory? It was true that it seemed she had misjudged Selina somewhat, but she was no more suited to the household for being ashamed of her conduct; the fact remained that she had acted immorally. And besides she was only trained for rough work; Eliza had already remarked that she did not know the names or purpose of many of the kitchen implements. How would she manage in here? Sophia looked around the room. On the mantelshelf were the glass-domed clock and tall china candlesticks that had been saved from her childhood home; there, on the table, her favourite Staffordshire figure; in the cabinet her mother-in-law's best tea service. All had to be dusted daily and there would surely be breakages. She did not like to upset the already disgruntled Eliza by asking her to exchange any of her duties.

That was another thing, her servants had always been treated well and had responded by being amiable and willing. If there were extra jobs to be done they would set to even if these tasks fell outside their usual remit. Now the balance of the household had been upset and she felt she had to tread carefully if she was not to lose Eliza and Jane. She had always hired bright, intelligent girls with whom one could hold a conversation if one so wished; the younger children could show the servants their books and they would be read and admired. How could such an uneducated girl be suitable?

Sophia straightened the cushions and put the list of rules in her bureau drawer. The thought of having to read them through every day filled her with a deep reluctance.

That evening she checked her hair in the hall mirror and arranged one of the ringlets in front of her shoulder. Her husband appeared behind her with carefully combed beard and twinkling eyes and she smiled at him in the mirror until he started nibbling the back of her neck.

"William, *please!*" She turned and looked at him admiringly in his best dress suit, but he lifted her up and spun her round so she had to look in the mirror again to rearrange her lace shawl.

She had been looking forward to this evening for some time. She and William had been unable to attend the grand opening a few weeks ago of the new Public Rooms that were situated just across the road. On that occasion Mrs Scott-Siddens had given a dramatic recital in the Grand Music Hall. Tonight's presentation was by a less eminent performer but she was still thrilled to be going. She had studied the advertisements in the newspaper and tried to imagine hearing the works of Mr Shakespeare and Mr Tennyson read in the dramatic manner, even finding a few moments to take out her copy of the Works of William Shakespeare and to read through some favourite passages. She and her sisters had often spent winter evenings reading the plays, each taking a part and doing their best to imbue the words with the expression they deserved but, of course, none had ever seen a play acted out on the stage.

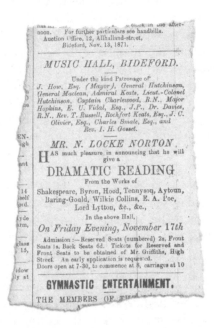

From the Bideford Gazette,
14th November 1871

After a final look in the mirror, they stepped down on to the pavement and crossed the road, arm in arm. Outside the Public Rooms there was a great bustle of people arriving by carriage and on foot and greeting each other before disappearing through the doors. Sir Edward and Lady Green of Pillhead, having just descended from their carriage, waited outside to speak to Captain and Mrs Christie of Tapeley who were being helped from theirs. William bowed his head, then they stood aside so that the new arrivals might enter first.

The foyer was thronged with people and within a few minutes they had clasped a dozen or more hands in greeting before processing up the staircase to the Grand Music Hall and thus to their seats not far from the orchestra. Sophia settled herself and looked around. William had brought her in to see the hall and the ground floor rooms shortly before they opened but that had been during the day. Now the hall was lit by numerous brilliant jets suspended from the ceiling. The light reflected in the stained glass windows and illuminated the elegant decoration of the walls and high ceiling so that it almost put her in mind of a church, though she had to admit it was plainer than would be found in larger towns.

William leaned over and spoke quietly.

"In such a place and amongst such a fashionable company, one might almost imagine oneself to be in London! Does it not seem extraordinary that we are only a few steps away from our home and our children?"

Sophia had never been to London but had once been to a recital at the Royal Public Rooms in Exeter. She had certainly never expected to have such a place on her doorstep.

The Christies and the Greens took their reserved places a few rows in front, bowing and smiling to those already seated. Glancing around, she could see party after party taking their seats until there was a dense mass of faces and hats with nodding feathers.

"Look, I am sure that is a new gown Mrs Hoyle is wearing. She did not tell me of it!"

Dr and Mrs Hoyle acknowledged them as they took their seats and William made a mock salute.

"I'm sure this new hall will be very advantageous for the drapers, dressmakers and milliners in the town, for there will be many wanting new gowns and hats. Look, there is Dr Pridham and his wife also, the place is well-equipped with medical men tonight."

The orchestra began to tune up. There were several familiar faces amongst the musicians but it was hard to know where to look first when everything was so novel. She would have liked very much to turn around and scrutinise the room and all the people sitting behind. How the children would love it here! It might be possible to bring Maud and Annie when they were home.

There! As the orchestra struck up an overture, the curtains slowly opened and an artistic-looking gentleman in a large cravat and velvet-trimmed coat bowed, and, as the music died away, took a dramatic pose, flinging his arms out towards the musicians.

"If music be the food of love, play on;

Give me excess of it, that, surfeiting,

The appetite may sicken, and so die."

Sophia sat enthralled until he reached the end of the speech and the orchestra took up their instruments once more amidst enthusiastic applause.

A chair was then brought on to the stage and the gentlemen sat with a book in his hand which he proclaimed to be The Woman in White by Mr Collins. This was not one of Sophia's favourites but the piece was read with great dramatic effect. It was the third chapter in which the lady of the title is first introduced and there was a perceptible gasp in the room when Walter Hartright felt the ghostly hand on his shoulder. She thought perhaps she might obtain a copy and read it again.

He was a remarkable performer. For two full hours he kept up the pace with brief interludes of music to add to the entertainment and to allow him to change his coat or procure a hat to give the impression of a different character. For his final piece, he announced Portia's famous speech from The Merchant of Venice. He stood for a moment in silence and upon his face an expression of intense sincerity developed.

There was not a whisper or a shuffle from the audience as he launched into his passionate declaration.

"The quality of mercy is not strained.

It droppeth as the gentle rain from heaven

Upon the place beneath. It is twice blest:

It blesseth him that gives and him that takes…"

William reached for her hand and when the actor took his final bow he stood to applaud with everyone else, although she knew that such entertainment did not usually greatly engage him. As they clapped he leaned towards her.

"Such admirable sentiments and so eloquently expressed! Your Mr Shakespeare was a wise man indeed."

Outside, the carriages were lined up almost the length of the street and there was a buzz of conversation as little groups of people met and exchanged impressions of the evening. In their own street to have a gathering which included those of the very highest social standing! They bowed to the Mayor Mr How and the Reverend Gosset then met with Dr and Mrs Hoyle. They all enthused about the entertainment until the two men were sidetracked by the subject of the Dispensary. Caroline Hoyle took her hand.

"So, we must meet soon and you must tell me whether you have resolved your servant problem. I have heard recently of a good housemaid who may soon be available."

In her enjoyment of the evening, Sophia had almost forgotten about Selina. It was to be hoped that Eliza was keeping a close eye on her in the kitchen, as instructed.

"No, it is not resolved yet. The girl I told you about arrived yesterday."

Their eyes met and Sophia lowered her voice so that William would not hear.

"She cannot stay, she is entirely unsuitable. I shall tell you the whole story when we meet! I shall have to find a way to be rid of her."

It rather spoiled her evening, having to end on that note. They made their farewells and as they crossed the road she admired her home. It looked a warm and welcoming house as well as being one of the grandest in the street. It was not for the likes of Selina Burman.

Chapter Seven

Selina crouched in front of the range, adjusted the candle so she could see the area remaining to be done and dipped the cloth in the jar of black lead again. Her arm was aching with polishing but she was nearly finished. She had not slept well, for all the events of yesterday had kept running through her mind and her head spun with the strangeness of it all. She picked up the kindling she had ready and laid it carefully in the firebox then took a spill and lit it from the candle. There was a good draft and the kindling caught. Surely Eliza would come downstairs soon – it must be nearly morning. Would she be cross that the stove was done? She would be expecting to do it herself this morning as Selina was to help Mary with all her work in the house, to learn what to do so she could manage when Mary left on Saturday. Would she be able to manage? She must, for Will. She hugged herself as she crouched by the range and pictured his little face.

- I'll do it for you, Will. I'll learn it all.

Half an hour later she followed Mary and her candle down the corridor. They had been pleased with her and Eliza had thanked her rather brusquely. She had never once been thanked in the Workhouse, but then neither had she ever done any work voluntarily. They had had a cup of tea with sugar and then Mary had made her scrub her hands and change her apron and had checked that her boots were clean. Now Mary's candle flickered, giving brief glimpses of a broad front door with heavy bolts and the polished staircase sweeping up into darkness. Selina straightened her apron and pushed her hair back under her cap. Her boots squeaked a little on the wooden floor. Mary opened the door to the drawing room.

"You're to do everything quietly so as not to wake the family."

Selina nodded mutely in reply to the whisper. The room was cold after the warmth of the kitchen and in darkness but for the dim light shed by the candle; Selina held it up while Mary stood on a chair, which she first covered with a clean cloth. She reached a spill up to a circular glass light hanging from the centre of the ceiling and with a sudden burst which made Selina jump, a light appeared, brighter than any she had seen before, and the room emerged from the shadows. She had never seen such a room before. Wherever she looked there were things of such beauty and rich colour, glass and china which shone like jewels in the dazzling light, fabrics so thick and soft she longed to stroke them, dark polished wood in which she would surely see her face. The carpet, which she had been too distressed to examine yesterday, appeared to have garlands of flowers laid on the soft blue surface. The curtains – *could* they be velvet? – were draped right down to the floor.

"Stop gawping, there's work to do."

Selina quickly followed Mary to the fireplace, carrying her basket of brushes, cloths and polish.

"'Tis a lovely room though. I couldn't stop looking at it when I first started."

The fire surround was of a pearly white stone carved with intricate figures and the mantelshelf was festooned with velvet in the same deep red as the curtains, a fringe ending in little balls along its lower edge. Selina raised her head and jumped when she saw two pale faces looking back her, one stern and pretty, the other surprised and plain. Mary knelt down, sweeping out the ash and talking all the time in a low whisper. Selina tried to take in the instructions, tried to remember which the dust sheet was and that the marble was to be wiped with the damp cloth after the ash was clear, followed by the blackleading. She carried out the ash and fetched the kindling and coal to light the fire while Mary drew the curtains and shook up the cushions. There were upholstered chairs and a long low ottoman - such colours - and how comfortable they must be to sit on! Mary gave her a hard look and she hurried to finish the fire.

Next there was the dusting to do and at first Mary made Selina watch while she dusted the pictures, each of them worth an hour or more of inspection, then removed the china dog, the tall red and blue candlesticks – could they be china too? – and a perfect china Shire horse from the mantelshelf. The glass-domed clock must remain where it stood, for only Mrs Ackland could move that. Mary let her dust the candlesticks before replacing them herself and repeated this performance all around the room accompanied by such rapid instructions that Selina's head began to swim. At each side of the fireplace was a glass cabinet so full of china there was hardly room for another eggcup but these remained shut, the glass being polished to show them to best advantage. She was allowed to flick the feather duster over the tall plant, a tree almost, which stood in a great pot in the window. Stepping forward into the bay window she stared at the church across the dark deserted street until Mary called her away. They sprinkled damp tea leaves on the carpet and Mary watched while Selina knelt and swept them up, the *hard* brush for that or the dust would not come up.

At last they stood and surveyed the room.

"Can you see anything amiss?"

The room was a vision of perfection, of such beauty as she had never imagined. The fire now glowing amongst the white stone cherubs added the final touch.

"Look. That chair's not pushed in and the Bible's not square on the table."

Selina hurried to put this right then Mary pulled a fine chain below the light to dim it.

"Not too much or it will go out."

Next was the dining room. In the farms where she had worked all the eating was done in the kitchen but here was a room set aside for the purpose. The lighting, the fire, the dusting and the sweeping were carried out as before but with a new set of rules to remember, the feather duster to be used *here*, the damp cloth *there*. They were almost finished when a small voice came from the doorway.

"Hugh! What are you doing out of bed! Does Jane know you are here?"

A small boy in a long nightgown stood at the door. At first she thought one of the cherubs had jumped down from the drawing room fireplace for never had she seen a child with such round, rosy cheeks. He stared at her.

"What are you doing here?"

"This is Selina, Hugh. She's going to do my work for me. You remember I told you how I'm to be married but will come back often to see you?"

"I've lost my rabbit."

He still stared at Selina. Coming to herself she hurried to the chair where she had seen a soft, worn, toy rabbit and took it to him, crouching down in front of him and stroking his hair. He shook her hand away and marched out and up the stairs.

"How old is he?"

He was four, the same as Will, but taller, stockier. She watched him climb the wide stairs one at a time until he disappeared around the first turn.

Two hours later Selina saw Hugh again, though she dared take only occasional fleeting looks. The family were seated around the dining table talking and eating, and she stood by the sideboard in an agony of embarrassment waiting for Mary to return from the kitchen. She had spent the last ten minutes or so in the kitchen toasting bread on a fork in front of the open range, her face burning and her hand sore from the heat. She had tried changing hands but had dropped a slice of bread in the fire; fortunately Eliza was arranging boiled eggs on a dish and did not see. When enough toast was done she had carefully slotted it into a silver rack and was told to follow Mary to the dining room, then Mary had whispered to her to wait while she fetched more cocoa. So here she was, standing alone with the family sitting there before her. She looked up without raising her head and saw Hugh sitting opposite her, playing with his toast, not taking part in the conversation which buzzed around the table. She jumped when, suddenly, the Doctor addressed her.

"Ah, Selina Burman! You are somewhat drier than when I last encountered you! Are you comfortable now? Do you have everything you need?"

She murmured a reply. She kept her eyes on her boots but was still aware that all the children had turned to look at her. At first when the Doctor spoke again she assumed his remarks were again addressed to her, but he was talking to the children, asking what they intended to do that day. A clamour of voices answered him and she stole a glance at them, three girls and two boys, the loveliest children she had ever seen. Eliza had told her there were also two older girls away at school. At last Mary returned with the cocoa. After pouring it for Mrs Ackland and the two smallest girls she handed the jug to Selina with a meaningful look. With a shaking hand she approached an older girl, then a boy, pouring the cocoa carefully into the mugs. When she reached Hugh, to her surprise, he looked up and smiled at her.

When the breakfast things were cleared away it was time to clean the bedrooms and she was to do them with Mrs Ackland herself. She stood at the foot of the stairs trying to look attentive but invisible at the same time, listening to the children's voices from the dining room and waiting for the door to open. She twisted the ring on her finger for it cut into her a little. Should she dust the banisters while she was waiting? It was to be her first time upstairs; Mary had taken up the cans of hot water earlier while she helped Eliza in the kitchen. Had she not been told to turn to the wall whenever any of the family was near? Mary did not do so, she just stood aside and if it were one of the children that was passing she sometimes spoke and once ruffled the older boy's hair. When they were alone, Selina had gathered her courage and asked Mary what she should do.

"Rules? She read you rules?"

She had not needed rules, she said, she knew how to behave, she had had a good character from her previous post. She looked at Selina frankly for the first time.

"It's different for you of course. Mrs Ackland has to be careful. You're working hard, Selina, and you seem a good quiet maid. How you came to have that misfortune I don't know but you know that by having it, you couldn't ever have expected to work in such a position as this. 'Tis only down to the Doctor that you're here; Mrs Ackland will let you go after a month if she can. If she's made rules 'tis best you keep to them."

The task seemed harder than ever now. She only had one more day to learn the work from Mary and the rules could not be learnt from her for she did not know them. She would have to listen very carefully when Mrs Ackland read them again.

And now here she came, sweeping out from the dining room in her beautiful dress. Selina turned half towards the wall but it felt wrong, as if she was avoiding the prospect of work.

"Bring your things and follow me."

She was half way up to the first landing by the time Selina picked up her basket of cleaning materials and followed her. With Mrs Ackland's back to her she was able to quickly look around as she climbed the stairs. On the first landing where the stairs turned to the left were two very tall arched windows looking out over the garden with alcoves to each side of them, one of which contained a statue – naked! – of a tall lady and the other a thin vase with dried grasses and seed heads. They reached the first floor and carried on up, past another landing with matching windows and alcoves containing tall empty vases and on to the second floor. Mrs Ackland turned right into a very large bedroom with steeply sloping ceilings and stood in the middle of the room while Selina hurried after her with the basket.

"This is the girls' bedroom and Jane sleeps here also. At present just the three youngest sleep here as Annie and Maud are away at school. *Their* beds do not require any attention at present as they have dust sheets over them as you can see. We are not lighting fires here at present but when it is colder one of the first jobs will be to clean the grate and re-lay the fire. Before that the chamber pots are to be emptied and thoroughly scrubbed. You have learnt how to do that already I believe. For now, place them by the door."

Selina had dealt with the chamber pots yesterday, tipping them into a water closet at the back of the house. She had not seen such a closet before and had to be shown how it tipped up to empty into the underground drain.

Mrs Ackland then inspected Selina's nails for dirt and showed her how to turn and shake the two mattresses on each bed. It was a job for two and she was told that either Mrs Ackland herself or Jane, the children's nurse, would help her. They worked together shaking out and tucking in the sheets and blankets and plumping up the pillows. Selina soon remembered the familiar rhythm and began to relax a little. They were to be vigilant for bugs at all times and report any sightings immediately. The jugs and bowls were to be washed thoroughly in the hot water brought up in the can and dried with this cloth. Then the bed frames wiped down with the damp cloth, the wardrobes and chests polished like this.

They moved on to the servants' bedroom where Eliza and Mary slept, a tiny room with ceilings so low and sloping it was impossible to stand upright. Mrs Ackland watched from the door while Selina cleaned the room. Then they repeated the routine in the other large bedroom where the boys slept and from there they moved downstairs to Mrs Ackland's beautiful big room, the Doctor's dressing room which also contained a bed and the guest room which only needed dusting. Mrs Ackland reiterated her instructions each time adding short explanations as to why a damp cloth or polish was necessary. Selina had not considered before the reason for such routines and suddenly the tasks seemed simpler, she was sure she would remember now what to do. As Mrs Ackland turned to go downstairs, leaving her to deal with the chamber pots, she took a deep breath and spoke out before she lost her nerve.

"Ma'am."

Mrs Ackland turned.

"Yes, what is it?"

Selina looked down at the floor.

"Thank 'ee, ma'am. For showing me what to do."

Sophia sat at her bureau in the drawing room with her account book. Before she went out shopping she must look up Mr Holman's bill, for it was now due. There was the list to write too, she had memorised the items that Eliza needed. She sat back in her chair. She normally enjoyed her mornings. While Jane dressed the children and took them out for a walk she was able to organise the household, plan the meals and do any necessary shopping before the children's first lessons. Today the house did not feel as if it were her own. It felt invaded. Tainted. She always found it difficult when there was a new servant, but this was different. Selina was not the right person for them, not right at all. Why could he not see it? At breakfast she had felt that there was a stranger amongst them, a stranger listening in to their private conversations. The girl had stood there pretending to be so demure but obviously avidly interested in everything they had to say. Goodness only knows to whom their business would be communicated. And she had such a sly look about her, hunching her shoulders and looking away as soon as someone approached – even one of the children!

She picked up her pen again and dipped it in the inkwell.

6lbs onions

3lbs carrots

2 cabbages

3lbs braising beef

Sometimes she sent Mary out to order the shopping. Would she ever be able to trust Selina out in the town? She might meet up with – oh, she shuddered to think who she might meet with, what infection she might return with. Yet she knew these arguments would not influence her husband for he would simply tell her she was being fanciful, would laugh and stroke her hair. The only reason he would accept for dismissing the girl would be flagrant bad behaviour or an unwillingness to do the work. On the latter point, Sophia had to admit, she could not be faulted. She had been told how Selina had unexpectedly completed tasks in the kitchen before the other servants had even descended the stairs and in the bedrooms she had been eager and had thrown herself into the work. But was this not related to her slyness, her determination to insinuate herself into the household? And much of the work was beyond her capabilities. Mary had reported that she had not had the first idea of her duties in the downstairs rooms, Eliza that she did not know how to handle glasses. It was also clear this morning that her personal hygiene left much to be desired; that, too, would have to be addressed. The thought filled her with distaste.

She tried to put the matter aside. She consulted her recipe book, added a few more items to her shopping list and rose to get her coat. Selina was on her knees polishing the hall floor. She looked down and away in that irritatingly furtive way. Sophia watched her for a few moments.

"Please be careful not to leave any flecks of polish lest it gets walked into the carpets."

She closed the front door behind her and took a deep breath. It was a relief to leave it all behind. The day was bright and she could just hear the musical chanting of the girls in the Misses Beer's school across the road; somewhere a horse whinnied and the distant church clock struck the hour. Mill Street was congested with carts, carriages and packhorses trying to pass in both directions and as she made her way through the chaos she was, as usual, replying to greetings every few steps.

"Good morning, Mrs Pridham."

"Yes, lovely day, isn't it, Mr Davis."

She saw Mrs Elizabeth Rooker and Marianne, wife and youngest daughter of Mr James Rooker. He was the senior partner in the legal firm Rooker and Bazeley and they lived just a few doors down the street. Would they have heard about the servant from the Workhouse? Sophia took their hands in greeting. Mr and Mrs Rooker had been at the Music Hall the previous evening with two of their daughters but there had not been an opportunity to speak; now they were as enthusiastic in their praise of the readings as Sophia herself and she relived the pleasures of the evening as they discussed the merits of each before going their separate ways.

The words from The Merchant of Venice came to her again. She must find more time for reading; such pleasures left a glow for the rest of the day. How could one worry about such trivial issues as servants when Mr Shakespeare's words were still resounding in one's mind?

Her first call was to Mrs Emma Cooler's greengrocer. She squeezed past the carriage of the Reverend Harding of Littleham which the new groom had drawn up right at the door and waited her turn in the queue. She made her order and crossed into the High Street to look at a new display of fine woollen cloth in the window of Mr Boyle's shop. A man carrying a box of oranges on his head wandered along the pavement, stopping every now and then to advertise his wares:

"Oranges! Best oranges fifty a shilling!"

She stopped and he lifted down the box so she could examine them, but some were wrinkled and dry and she noticed that the man's hands was dirty; she smiled politely and declined his offer. Further up the High Street three carts waited patiently while a very large farm cart carrying a full load of hay swayed out of Grenville Street and turned down the hill and the first cart was forced to back amongst much shouting of directions and advice. When she was a girl in Honiton huge loads of hay used to pass along the street and the boys riding aloft were able to look right into the first floor windows of her home, to the consternation of herself and her sisters. Now, to Mr Holman for the beef and to pay the bill, then Mr Coles for the bread, three loaves which she said she would carry with her now as they were needed for luncheon. One of the Doctor's patients stopped her to request that he attend as soon as possible. She frequently had to memorise messages as she went about the town. Now, that was another thing. How was Selina to manage answering the door? She would have to be taught the correct responses, how to speak up clearly and politely – and how was she to take messages? The servants had a book in which to write messages for the Doctor and were meticulous in their efforts to convey the correct details even if their spelling was sometimes somewhat amusing. But now she had a servant who could neither read nor write.

She turned into Bridgeland Street. She felt an unusual reluctance to return to the house. She would take in the bread and walk on to meet Jane and the children returning from their walk. She felt she needed more fresh air and the tide would be high. She needed a view of the river to cheer her.

Chapter Eight

Dr Ackland closed the door of the small cottage on Chapel Street and hesitated for a moment. The lane in which he stood ran between Allhalland Street and Bridge Street and was exceedingly narrow; if he reached out he could almost touch the house opposite. The houses had not yet been connected to the sewers and there were still some inhabitants who emptied their refuse and their filth into the gutter which ran down the centre. At the top of the lane lay the old burial ground, no longer used but who knows what contamination might still be lurking there? All in all, Chapel Street provided the worst possible conditions for disease prevention. And now, a case of smallpox.

He replaced the bottle of disinfectant in his bag, strode down into Allhalland Street then paused again, raising his hat and murmuring a 'Good morning' to several well-wishers. He took out his watch and glanced down at it. He should have brought his horse; he would be late for the Dispensary. But he must go, there was no time to waste. A messenger would not suffice on this occasion.

He turned and walked quickly along the street of tall eighteenth century houses, jumping on to the pavement to avoid a butcher's cart pushed by a boy who shouted out an apology as he raced around the corner from the High Street. He had not gone to Chapel Street to visit a patient but to inspect the houses. There was much urgent work to do as Medical Officer of Health – more than enough at the best of times and now with this epidemic… He had visited each house, had seen that the floors were of earth and that the walls ran with water and then – that man, lying on a bed of rags with extensive papules already on his face and neck. Two weeks, then, since infection. The longer he stayed in that milieu the more cases there would be; two others in the household had admitted that they had not been vaccinated.

Variola. He cursed under his breath and automatically requested pardon of himself. It was spreading faster than he had expected, no doubt the unseasonably warm weather was playing a part. If it continued to spread at this rate the Smallpox Hospital would soon be overcrowded – but thank the Lord there were at least some beds.

He passed the bow windows of Grimes jeweller's and opened the door to Mr William Vinson's draper's shop causing the bell to ring loudly. The sound was quickly absorbed by the rolls of cloth that lined the hushed interior. A young man behind a display of black and gold sewing machines looked up and bowed his head in greeting.

"Your father, if you please."

Dr Ackland removed his hat and contained his impatience while the boy disappeared upstairs.

Vinson is a good man, one to be relied upon. A sensible man. Unlike so many on the Local Board. He came. They shook hands. It was as he thought, the Board of Guardians had still made no decision about provision for pauper patients and until they did so only those who could find the five shillings a week for their accommodation could be admitted to the Smallpox Hospital. Out of the question for many, especially as food and medical attention were additional costs.

"That settles it, if you will speak on behalf of the Committee and accept this man I will pay for him myself. If he remains where he is we shall not see the last of this disease before the spring."

They shook hands again.

"One other matter, Doctor."

Mr Vinson stepped aside into a back room and gestured to the Doctor that he should stand close so that the communication should not be overheard.

"Have you heard of the allegations being whispered abroad about our Mr Pollard? A servant girl once in his employ, who is now with child, has put it about that he repeatedly assaulted her. I mentioned this matter to him, as tactfully as I could, for fear that the lie, if lie it be, should reflect badly on the entire Board but his reaction was most disturbing, – he cursed me, the board and the hospital and he threatened to beat me, I had to run from him – and all this on the street for all to see! I do not know what his next actions will be but I fear he will put obstacles in our way as far as the running of the hospital is concerned."

More difficulties. Dr Ackland cautioned him to keep the matter strictly to himself for the time being and they made their farewells.

Dr Ackland walked quickly down High Street and crossed the Quay, dodging between a hansom cab and two farm carts and tipping his hat in apology. The walk across the bridge would allow him time to gather his thoughts. It was a fine morning and unusually warm for December; getting into his stride he breathed deeply, glad to be away from the close stench of Chapel Street and enjoying the hint of salt carried by the incoming tide. He thought of the wide open expanse of the golf links where the river met the sea and regretted that it would be some time before he had sufficient leisure to play again. There was still a slight haze over the river, softening the outline of the shipbuilding sheds and warehouses from which an insistent clamour arose. Glancing over the parapet as he walked, he saw two young boys guiding their rowing boat towards one of the channels where the water rushed and eddied under the arches of the bridge. A terrier stood in the bows yapping at the fast-flowing brown and silver ripples.

- So. Was *that* what had upset our Mr Pollard? He was always a difficult man. Unpredictable. His temper easily roused. He had been obstructive about letting his cottage for the hospital. He had been a member of the Local Board for some years but remained an outsider, and was not to be trusted. At times he was affable, perhaps trying a little too hard to be accepted, at others one barely felt safe to turn one's back on him. Unfortunate that the cottage had to be rented from him but there was none other available which was suitable for the Smallpox Hospital. First he would let it, then he would not. When a higher rent was offered, then, of course, he agreed. But now... this was a different matter. This was a serious matter.

He had heard the man had been obstreperous again and now it seemed that his awkwardness may have been due to this insinuation, but was there truth in it? If it *was* true, well. Well, well. It was likely it would not be his first offence. This could have a bearing on the young servant, Selina Burman. He would have to look into it.

Reaching East-the-Water he turned into Torrington Street, glancing up to the site where the new railway station was being built. So many new developments, such modernisation! There was no doubt, the town was thriving. Before long, please God, every house would have mains water. At last there was an isolation hospital. In time there would be a general hospital; he had been determined Bideford would have one ever since his training at University College Hospital. A man shuffled forwards from the doorway of the Swan Inn.

"Any messages to take, Sir? I'm an honest man, Sir."

"Thank you, not today."

Past the tiny cottages where he could touch the first floor window sills if he reached up, past the brewery and the Blacksmiths Arms and into Torrington Lane. Now, it was number 37, was it not?

Mr Philip Paddon had been appointed as messenger to the Smallpox Hospital, an essential role as it was so far from town and the nurse was unable to leave her patients in order to come in for requisitions. Food, blankets and other things needed to be fetched, and patients too, as those who had to go to the hospital and indeed some who had to leave needed to be carried. Until now he had used a farm wagon hired from Mr Pollard, now the offer seemed likely to be withdrawn. He found the messenger, Mr Paddon, at home.

The man told him that on the previous day he had gone for the wagon and had been spoken to most rudely. Mr Pollard had cursed the hospital and said he rued the day that he agreed to let it.

"He said, Sir, if you'll pardon me saying it, that the Committee are liars and you are a fool, Sir. If you'll pardon me, Sir. And when I asked him the reason for his saying so, he cursed me too, Sir, and sent me away."

It was as Mr Vinson had told him, but of course whether the reason for the upset was correct, that remained to be seen. He instructed the man to hire a cart from a different source and to line it well with straw in order to carry the patient from Chapel Street to the hospital immediately. The man put on his coat and set off at once.

Dr Ackland took out his watch; already it was eleven o'clock and his patients would be waiting for him at the Dispensary. He would walk steadily but not too fast. It would not do to arrive over-heated.

Later that evening he sat at his desk in the study, his casebook illuminated by the single oil lamp that had belonged to his father. Just outside the immediate pool of light stood his inkwell and the silver-framed photograph of his family, above on a shelf a grimacing human skull gazed emptily at an elegant statue of Asklepius, the Greek god of medicine and healing; and beyond, in the shadows, were his leather armchair and the book-lined walls. The dog, Jimmy, snored softly in front of the dying fire.

He put aside the brochure he had been perusing, dipped his pen in the well and wrote in his casebook.

Dies Veneris 8th December 1871.

Mr Prance's sister. Birth of 7th boy in succession.

Extraordinary. But the woman had not seemed to expect otherwise and had remarked that it was just one more mouth to feed.

Mr Elliott, attend.

Mrs Bradburn, dropsy, attend.

Vaccination. Westleigh, 5 patients. Instow, 3 patients.

The demand for smallpox vaccination was increasing all the time. Why could people not take it at the proper time? It would be too late for some. Two more beds had been added at the hospital and all eight were now full. Ah. The hospital.

He sat back in his chair and sighed. So, Mr Pollard thought him a fool. Now why was that? He did not for a moment think that it was as a result of a foolish action. He was not often thoughtless and, if he was, Mr Pollard certainly did not know about it. No, the man resented him for some reason. Was it possible that he had heard that Selina Burman was a part of the household and feared what might be revealed? Certainly it *was* possible, for many had shown interest and surprise at their taking on a Workhouse girl, though few knew her name. If there were truth in this charge against Pollard...*Could* he also be Selina's seducer? She had told him that the man in question was a farmer living to the east of Bideford but was too fearful to say more. Well, Pollard was a farmer and owner of the paint mines at East-the-Water. And if it were he, what to do about it?

As if on cue, there was a soft knock at the door and in came the girl in question with his cocoa.

"So, Selina!"

She started, then recovered herself and gave a little bob. She was looking a little better now, more colour in her cheeks, a little plumper perhaps. What colour were her eyes? He never saw them for her gaze was always on the floor.

"Sir?"

No use to ask her about Pollard.

"Are you settled now? Learning about our ways and our preferences?"

She bobbed again.

"Ah, I almost forgot, I have news of your son!"

"Sir?"

She looked right at him for a moment. Her eyes were blue.

"Yes, I visited Clovelly yesterday and had cause to visit several households so I enquired after him."

"Oh Sir! 'Ave 'ee see'd 'n Sir?"

Her voice shook a little. He had not thought that she would be so affected. But of course, of course she was. It was only natural.

"No, I did not see him but I heard that he is lively enough."

He did not tell her that the child had been chased from a cottage with a stolen crust in his hand. It was not uncommon for a child that had been half-starved in a workhouse to steal food at opportune moments. She stood looking down at his cocoa on the tray, forgetting to place it on the desk.

"He's vitty then, Sir? No sickness, Sir?"

"He is well indeed and attending school. The herrings are plentiful this year so he will not want for fish. You do not doubt your parents' ability to look after him, I am sure."

"No Sir. Only they'm old, Sir, and they'm wore out with rearing children."

It was the most he had heard her say since she had been in the house. He leaned back in his chair and observed her.

"How long have you been here now, Selina, three weeks? And we are, what, about three weeks from Christmas?"

She was looking a little confused.

"Perhaps some time in January when the household is settled again and I have cause to visit Clovelly I'll take you along with me, shall I? Then you can visit your son while I carry out my business. It will be in the brougham this time, mind, not a storm-tossed trawler!"

She curtseyed and thanked him and curtseyed again and for a moment he thought that she was about to cry. As she turned to leave he had to remind her that he would rather like his cocoa.

He sighed and picked up the brochure that he had put aside earlier. It was no good to look at it any longer, he wanted to talk to Sophia, and they could decide between them what to do.

d
e
y
y
n
er
ay
d-
ate
der
g to
oard

measur.
washed in at Bucks, near Bideford ; and another boat,
15 feet by 6 feet, was washed ashore at Peppercombe.
She is painted white, with a brown streak at the top,
and the name, as at present deciphered, is Hioane, of
Whitehaven, One of the oars is marked S. D.

THE HERRING SEASON.—The present
season is likely to prove unusually profitable to the
Clovelly fishermen, who have had some enormous
takings during the last few days. On Friday the fish
were so plentiful that all the boats available would
not meet the demand, and many of the nets were left
behind. Mr. Berriman informs us that his takings on
that day were extraordinary.

launch
the-W
was a
to trac
on Th
she w
The
Jury
his op
mitted
Rev.
ary n
found

From the Bideford Gazette,
21st November 1871

Sophia put away her account book, removed her shoes so that she could curl up comfortably on the chesterfield and took up her sewing basket. The hem of Lucy's dress was coming down, there were buttons to sew on Hugh's shirt and a repair to Kingsley's jacket, but they were simple tasks and by the end of the evening they would be finished. Usually Jane did the repairs to the children's clothes but she had had several disturbed nights due to Hugh not sleeping well, so Sophia had allowed her to go to bed early tonight. Before updating the accounts she had written out her menus for Christmas. Annie and Maud would be home at the end of next week and when the family was complete again the festive season would begin – too early of course but there would be no containing the noise and excitement. She smiled at the thought. She leaned over and added 'paste' to her shopping list, plenty would be needed for making cards and decorations.

She heard her husband humming as he came into the hall and opened the door to the drawing room. He was waving a leaflet at her.

"What shall we do about this then, dearest?"

It was the brochure for Winchester College that General Hutchinson had obtained for them. She knew that William would rather like Kingsley to go there but she had made the calculations and it really was not possible. She hoped he would not insist on it. If Kingsley were to go then it would be only fair to send Hugh also and with five girls to cater for as well... She showed him the figures; they did look quite frightening when multiplied to cover the requisite number of years.

"I know his godfather might help but we could scarcely ask for such a favour. And apart from the cost, William, I really am not sure that such a large place would be suitable for Kingsley. I do not think he would get the individual care there that he so needs, do you? He is such a special child, so very sensitive that I think he could be desperately unhappy at Winchester."

"Certainly he would be either miserable or so very changed by it that we would hardly know him. When I talked to young Horatio Hutchinson, he seemed to have learnt an entirely new language and I could make neither head nor tail of what he told me, so full of strange new words was it."

William did not mind that it could not be Winchester. If only the school planned for Westward Ho! were to open soon, he would not have to go away.

"So, is it to be Mannamead?"

Sophia's sisters had run the girls' section of Mannamead School near Plymouth before setting up their own school just a short distance away. Mannamead, a small school with just ten or a dozen boarding pupils but many more local boys, was still run by the Reverend Peter Holmes and his wife, a charming couple who seemed to take a real interest in their individual pupils and ran the school on homely rather than regimented lines. The Reverend Holmes was also a prominent Latin scholar and there could not be a better man to introduce Kingsley to the classics. He would also have the comfort of being near his sisters and his aunts, and would be in a place that was familiar to the entire family. Sophia dreaded him leaving home – it was different for Annie and Maud who had been able to go together – but she could not think of a better place for him to go. There was no school in Bideford where he would get such a good grounding in the classics and it was so very important for him to get on.

Her husband stretched out his feet towards the fire and clasped his hands behind his head.

"Well, if he is to go, it should be at once. It is scarcely worth him starting at Easter for he would be barely settled before the long holiday started."

"We could wait until next autumn. We could arrange for him to have a start at Latin with Mr Wood -"

"No, Sophia. He will be nearly thirteen then. Too much time has been lost already. If he is to get on and win a place at university he must make a start now before it is too late. He does not have a good attitude to study. He does not see the necessity of applying himself when the task is hard or does not interest him a great deal. He will never progress until he sees the necessity of hard work. I am sure that is something Reverend Holmes will instil in him without unkindness. He needs the inspiration of a dedicated teacher and I hope he will find that at Mannamead. But he must start immediately. He desperately needs the company of other boys of his age too. He spends far too much time in the company of his sisters."

Sophia knew that it would be useless to disagree. Besides, she knew that her husband was right. But it seemed so hard. Kingsley was so young for his years, so loving of his parents and his home. Perhaps it would have been different if he had had a brother closer to him in age. She was well aware that William would have liked her to produce more sons. She nodded while William, full of enthusiasm now, proposed that they both went on the train to Plymouth next week to visit Mr and Mrs Holmes and make the arrangements. They could bring Annie and Maud back with them at the same time so they need not travel alone.

How would she have everything ready in time for next term? Kingsley would have to be gently introduced to the plan. There would be clothes to have made, books and pens to buy, a new trunk - her husband was delighted at the thought of his son having a trunk:-

"I did not have one until I went to University College! We shall see, he may still be able to take the same path if he settles down to study."

Her husband's face always showed every emotion he felt, he could not dissemble. She leaned over and kissed his cheek.

"He's a very special boy, William. He will do well, I'm sure of it."

They clung to each other for a moment. She felt her emotions welling up again but she must not let William see, he had enough concerns of his own without her adding to them. There were plans to be made, letters to write, she would keep busy. She would write to Mr and Mrs Holmes in the morning and ask them whether they would be happy to take Kingsley. She glanced up as the drawing room door closed. She had barely noticed Selina making up the fire; the girl was learning to work unobtrusively. That was something else that must be addressed, the month would soon be up and it must be decided whether or not Selina would be kept on. So much to be settled before Christmas. She picked up her mending again, glancing at her unopened book on the table. There would not be much time for reading.

Selina cut herself a slice of fruit cake and sat with her cup of tea at the end of the long kitchen table, trying to take in the news she had been given. Earlier she had lit three candles which were ranged along the centre of the table in the dark kitchen and she watched as their flames rose and fell, reflected in the copper pans hanging above the fireplace and the gleaming plates on the dresser. Eliza and Jane had gone to bed early and she had washed the cups and tidied the kitchen as she had been told. She moved slowly for she was tired and her arms and back ached after sixteen hours of toil but she had worked well, hadn't she? The coal settled and cracked in the stove and when the silence returned it was so complete it seemed to wrap its arms around her. Eliza was in the habit of talking all the time she worked, commenting on what she was doing and demanding how the devil she would get the next meal ready on time, although she always did. The only time Selina could sit quietly was for a few minutes before she went to sleep in her bed on the floor. Now she could make a second cup of tea without fearing a reprimand. She had never been scolded here but she still felt guilty even when Eliza passed her a slice of cake. She licked the last crumbs from her fingers. She still could not quite believe she was in a place where you could eat cake almost whenever you wished.

Will was thriving and she could go to Clovelly to see him, could hold him and kiss him and talk to him. The Doctor was so kind! The house felt different when he was there, she was always aware of where he was and what he was doing. That had also been true of her last master – she would not even let herself think his name – but that had been because she was always so very afraid.

She had almost run back to the kitchen when he had told her the news. She had told Eliza but she had not been interested. She had once asked Selina about her life, but then had not seemed to listen although she had said she was sorry that Thomas had died. After that Selina knew that it was best not to talk about Will. Jane was even more standoffish than Eliza. She was always busy with the children and was closer to Mrs Ackland, speaking to her almost as if she was an equal rather than an employer.

Dr Ackland had said he would take her to Clovelly after Christmas. Did that mean it was agreed that she could stay? Mrs Ackland had not read her the rules again so she could not be sure she was keeping to them, nor had she told her whether her work was satisfactory, and the month was now almost up. If she had to leave they would both have to return to the

Workhouse, she and Will, because there would be no money to keep him in Clovelly. Surely the Doctor would not let that happen? Every day she hoped that Mrs Ackland would notice that she was trying to do her work even better than the day before, polishing the banisters until they gleamed, cleaning the boots so well they looked like new, always making her footfalls as silent as they could be and never leaving the gas too high in the two front rooms. Sometimes Mrs Ackland stood and watched for a few moments as Selina worked. Usually she looked stern but once she had nodded a little as if pleased with what she saw. When would she make her decision?

Chapter Nine

Dr Ackland unwrapped a glass tumbler from a white cloth and placed it on the farmhouse table along with a small lidded ceramic jar. His patient sat with the injured hand outstretched on the arm of the wooden settle. His face was turned obdurately away with his gaze to the window with its long-familiar view of orchard and fertile pastures. The Doctor glanced up at the man's wife who was stirring a large pot hanging over the fire in the huge open fireplace and checking the loaves rising in their tins on the hearth.

"You did well to call me, another day and gangrene would have set in. 'Twould have been better still for me to see it a few days ago."

"I told 'n and told 'n to call 'ee, Doctor. If I hadn't seen your wife in town, 'e'd still be saying no."

"There's no call for us to be running to you for every little scratch, Doctor."

The man's other hand clenched in his lap. The pain and anxiety in his expression indicated that he knew full well that it was more than a scratch. His bill hook had slipped when laying a hedge, cutting deep into the base of his thumb and exposing the bone. He had done his best to ignore it until the pain prevented him sleeping. It was now excessively inflamed and deep purple in colour. Dr Ackland sighed. It was always the same, he rarely saw a patient in the early stages of illness. Even many of those who could pay, like Mr Richard Taylor here, would only do so if it could no longer be avoided, but then the farmers were always the worst for spending money unless it were for improving their land.

He looked over his glasses at Mr Taylor.

"An ounce of prevention is worth a pound of cure, Mr Taylor, a principle I'm sure you apply when it comes to your cows, do you not?"

He spread the clean rags out on the table and lifted the man's hand on to them. He removed the lid from the jar and tipped four large black leeches into the tumbler where they writhed and thrashed against the slippery sides. They were first-rate specimens, vigorous and healthy. Carefully he inverted the tumbler over the wound and watched as they first contracted into firm round spheres, then gradually extended, crawling over the surface of the wound until one by one their narrow black heads fixed into the flesh and proceeded to gorge themselves.

"Good. Excellent!"

Mr Taylor continued to stare out determinedly of the window. It was time to distract him, the leeches needed time to do their work and it would be well for him to relax a little.

"How's the boy then? Helping on the farm yet? What is he now, six or seven years?"

There had been five daughters before the long-desired boy arrived to assure the future of the farm.

"'E's getting pretty handy. Gets the cows in already and I'll give 'n his own calves to rear next year. Get 'n used to the work now and 'e'll go on all right."

Mrs Dina Taylor brought some tea in one of her best china cups and placed it on the table. Less squeamish than her husband, she looked at the hand and the contents of the glass which the Doctor held steady.

"There, they'm doing their job. Will 'ee have a cutround, Doctor? I have some fresh from the oven."

He was always assured of good food when he visited a farm but on this occasion he declined. The waistband of his trousers had been feeling a little tight lately, a result no doubt of his being so very busy and unable to take his accustomed exercise on the golf links. Wherever he went he could be assured of a cup of tea and when on calls out of town he often left with half a dozen eggs, a cabbage or a bag of apples. Most of the poorer homes were aware that he would reduce his fee according to their ability to pay and were happy to show their gratitude, although there were always some who exaggerated their poverty. Inevitably it would be the whining voice and ingratiating manner that gave them away. There would be no such problems today; he had noted the newly thatched roof, whitewashed walls and firmly hinged gates as he rode down the lane to Cadd's Down Farm, the result of the confidence engendered by an inheritable lease.

He peered through the glass. One of the leeches, now almost double its original size, had released its hold and rolled on to its side, drunk with blood. Good, the others would soon follow suit. Mr Taylor had relaxed a little and was complaining about the poor prices being reached at market. He addressed the wife.

"Is that linen sufficiently hot? It will soon be needed and will encourage more bleeding. And a bowl of cold water. You will need to place the linen in it promptly if you do not want it stained. And a cold salt solution, if you please."

After a few more minutes the three remaining leeches rolled away from the wound and he tipped them from the glass into the salt solution and applied the hot linen cloth to the hand. The cloth soon turned red whereupon he dropped it into the bowl and replaced it with another. The bleeding was now abating and the wound looking much healthier. He sprinkled on a little camphorated spirit of wine and carefully bandaged the hand; there, Mr Taylor was now brave enough to watch. Now for the leeches. They had disgorged much of the blood into the now red salt water and he took them up one by one, holding each firmly by the tail and drawing his finger and thumb firmly up the body almost to the head, causing the creature to expel the remaining blood. Now back to their original size, he dropped the leeches into the jar and screwed on the lid. Mr Taylor was gazing at the window again.

"Now, if I may just wash my hands I'll be on my way. Take plenty of rest and keep the hand elevated as much as possible. I'll look in to see you again in two or three days."

He accepted the bag of warm cutrounds that was pressed into his hand and stepped out into the yard of Cadd's Down Farm where his horse was tethered alongside a net of hay. The wind had risen and the air was cold after the warmth of the kitchen; glancing up at a cold and distant sun, he buttoned his coat up to the neck and pulled on his leather riding gloves. Toby blew warm breath on to his face as he unhitched the reins and he patted the horse's dark bay neck. Riding up the steep narrow lane to the main road he considered the remaining calls he had to make. He should call on Mrs Buck at Moreton House before she went away again, see Mr Bazeley to ensure that his leg was making good progress, then there was Mr Hayward's son at the White Hart – and should he go to the hospital? Damn the hospital!

It was not the hospital that was the problem, it was that man Pollard. Apparently at last night's Local Board meeting he had made serious allegations about the running of the hospital, claiming inefficiency and mismanagement and even making personal attacks against Mr Vinson and himself – Mr Vinson had knocked on his door this morning in quite an agitated state to tell him about it. Curse the man! The claims would now be published in the newspapers and there would be some – those who did not know Pollard - who would believe them. How dare he say such things! Did he attempt to discredit Vinson and himself in order to throw doubt on any allegations they might bring against him? Certainly his actions suggested a man on the defence for there was but little truth in his claims. Yet it was true that the hospital was little more than a dormitory for smallpox victims and certainly did not bear comparison with the great city hospitals, though it was unlikely Mr Pollard knew much about those. Bideford had a very long way to go as far as hospital provision was concerned. Then there was this business over Dr Hoyle's servant who had died at the hospital and who, of course, should not have been sent there without permission. It would not have happened if Richard Hoyle had been in better health himself and now there was that dreadful poem in the paper. But there, Mr Pollard had said what he had said and now there would have to be an extra meeting to look into the claims. Yet another evening away from his family.

... it will be seen how frivolous was the ground of the impeachment.

THE BIDEFORD SMALL POX HOSPITAL

To the Editor of the Bideford Gazette.

SIR,—Just one question if you please. Is it not a little singular that the unfounded charges respecting the arrangements at the Small Pox Hospital should have been brought by the owner of the premises, who until very recently refused to allow the board to become tenants of the house? I think I understand the secret of this outburst of passion; but whether I do or not, I think it disgraceful that a committee who have done their best in a case of emergency should at a meeting of their body and by one of their fellow members be denounced as liars, and that unwarrantable accusations should be brought against them. I see in your paper of Tuesday that before these charges were made a member of the board had to defend himself from equally false charges respecting his servant, and to contradict the lie direct. All this must be exceedingly unpleasant, and I thank God that I am not a member of a board at whose meetings personal recriminations are so frequent, and where the lord of disobedience appears to reign supreme—a state of things which, in my opinion, is far more disgraceful than any Small Pox Hospital mismanagement can be. I have it on authority which I cannot doubt that the charges were a tissue of misrepresentation; in other words, that the devil of want and mismanagement has not been let loose at the Small Pox Hospital. By giving these few lines a corner in your excellent *Gazette* you will confer a favour on a constant reader, who desires to be known only as

ONE WHO KNOWS THE ARRANGEMENTS.

Bideford, Dec. 16th.

A SERVANT'S FUNERAL

FROM THE BIDEFORD SMALL POX HOSPITAL.

There's a bristled old hack, harnessed fast to a cart,
From Local Board hospital has just made a start
O'er a road that is rugged, and the cart has no springs,
Whilst the driver's a boy who whistles and sings.
    Rattle her bones o'er the stones,
    She's only a servant whom nobody owns.

Scarcely gone—the poor mortal's screwed into a box,
From dying, 'tis said, of fever—small pox;
Then with 'dobbin' and cart they convey'd her remains,
And a boy who can whistle has taken the reins.
    Rattle her bones over the stones,
    She's only a servant whom nobody owns.

The pall—was it velvet? No, 'twas 'twas tarpaulin
Good God! o'er the coals some deserve a good hauling
Not a bearer we see, undertaker there's none—
Enough to draw pity from adamant stone.
    Rattle her bones over the stones,
    She's only a servant whom nobody owns.

Oh, where are the mourners? Only one there we see—
A Sister of Mercy, who oft bends the knee
At the bed of the dying, ere from earth they depart,
And she's done the same thing for the one on the cart.
    Rattle her bones over the stones,
    She's only a servant whom nobody owns.

Let ye who have blundered atone in some way,
As the drama will live for many a day.
Enough! From her dark grave, if we are not mistaken,
A cry has come, "My God, why was I thus forsaken."
    Rattle her bones over the stones,
    She's only a servant whom nobody owns.
                VINDEX

SEAMEN'S ORPHAN HOME, BRIXHAM.

From the Bideford Gazette,
19th December 1871

He reached the road that ran from Hartland to Bideford and reined in his horse. A man was walking towards Bideford, his steady measured stride suggesting one who spent much of his time on the move. The brim of his faded top hat hung over his eyes, having become partially detached from the crown, and he wore two coats, one that barely reached his knees and another that had no sleeves. He carried a bundle wrapped in a blanket and, curiously, he had a small brown and white terrier at his heels.

"Good morning, Sir! And where are you heading this fine day?"

The man removed his hat. His eyes were dull and red-rimmed, his skin dry and flaking. Psoriasis diffusa from the appearance.

"Bideford, Sir, to the Workhouse, then after to look for work, Sir. Do 'ee have a consideration for me, Sir?"

"You are going to the vagrants' ward no doubt, but what of your dog? I have not yet heard that the Guardians will give relief to a dog."

The dog sat down in a neat, considered manner and looked up at the doctor with interest. Poor relief or not, he was in better condition than his master.

"Oh, he'll wait for me, Sir. I'll do my day's work and have my night's rest, Sir, and he'll be waiting for me when I comes out, Sir. He's a good friend to me, Sir."

Well, there was a story! He reached into his saddle bag and took out two of Mrs Taylor's cutrounds.

"Here. These will, I'm certain, be far better than anything you will have in the Workhouse. Be sure to share them with your friend!"

The man sat down in the hedge while the dog looked on, bright-eyed and attentive. There now. And now from one who had no home or worldly possessions to one who owned the biggest estate in the area, for next he must visit Mrs Buck. How strange that both should have a small dog as their best friend.

He turned left on to the turnpike road then right on to the

private drive through the woods that led to Moreton House. The trees were bare now but the old carriage drive winding between the towering trunks formed a very pleasant vista nonetheless. The tune of a well-loved hymn came into his head. Toby's hooves rang on the stones that lay beneath the crisp fallen leaves and the Doctor leaned forward a little, encouraging him into a trot. It was a pleasant day, a fine wood, why should he care about the likes of Pollard?

   - All things bright and beauteous,
All creatures great and small,
All things wise and wondrous...

Selina tugged at her apron to straighten it, pushed her hair back behind her ears and opened the front door, being careful not to let the dog push past her. The steps looked perfectly clean but Mrs Ackland said they had to be done every day. She put down her bucket and spread out the folded rag to kneel on, then dipped the brush in the bucket of water and rubbed the bar of hard soap over the bristles. She began to scrub vigorously over the surface of the top step, back and forth across the rise and gradually down to the lower step. The steps should really be cleaned before breakfast as there were not too many people about, but Mrs Ackland had said she wanted them to be done after breakfast this morning. She did not dare to look around yet. It was the first time she had been allowed outside. Did Mrs Ackland finally trust her?

A chuggy-pig appeared from a crack at the base of the step as the water flooded in. She watched as it bumbled away along the pavement, keeping close to the house wall and pausing every now and then to poke its head into likely cracks in search of a new, drier home. A woodlouse, Mrs Ackland would call it. She had complained that she had seen a woodlouse in the dining room and Selina had not understood what she meant.

People were passing every minute or so. She could glance

quickly up and down the street as she worked, as long as she was careful to keep her head well down if someone approached. All the boots that passed were shiny and new, not worn at the heels at all, and the footsteps were brisk and purposeful. A very pretty pair of small dark green boots passed by, shown to advantage by their owner lifting her skirts away from the wet pavement around Selina's steps. Looking up just a little she could see a dark blue wool skirt and green velvet cloak. As more people passed she caught snatches of conversation. A lady said 'he will still press his claims upon me', then two gentlemen spoke of 'a disgraceful performance' and 'such unsubstantiated claims about the hospital should not be aired in a public arena'. It was very hard at times to understand what gentlefolk said.

It was a very *smart* street the Doctor lived in. Bridgeland Street. It was broad and there were no shops, just big houses where rich people lived, the tall church with the two spires and the Music Hall. They were all joined one to the other with no alleys or drangs between. Even the church was attached to houses either side. She had seen from the windows of the house that although hawkers' carts or farmers' wagons carrying sheep or hay passed by sometimes, many of the vehicles were well turned-out carriages with beautiful horses. They stopped at houses in the street and sometimes even Mrs Ackland looked out to see what was happening. Once when there was a big occasion at the Music Hall across the road she had been allowed to look out of the window, along with Jane and all the children, to see the ladies and gentlemen arriving in their carriages wearing all their finest clothes.

She glanced over now at the Music Hall. A boy standing outside carefully attached a poster to the billboard then brushed it all over with paste from his bucket. Even from here she could see a picture and some writing. The Doctor and Mrs Ackland often talked at breakfast about the coming events and it seemed that the Music Hall was something new even to them. The boy stood back to look at the poster then, turning her way, called out 'Good Morning!' She quickly looked down and scrubbed harder than ever at the bottom step. When she was sure he had gone back inside, she stood up and swished the bucket of water down over the steps to rinse them and used the broom to sweep the water across the pavement and into the gutter, retreating to the doorway when she saw two more gentlemen coming up the road.

Now she was to take in the brushes, bucket and broom, that was in case someone tripped over them. It felt very strange to be opening the front door as if she owned it and she was glad there was no one in the hall. The cheerful voices of the children rang out from the drawing room where they were doing their lessons today; they were more often in the schoolroom at the back. Did Will sound so happy when he was at school? She had not liked school on the occasions she had attended. She preferred looking after her younger brothers and sisters at home which was what her mother had usually wanted her to do anyway.

Next came the brass; the doorknocker, handle and letterbox and then the brass plaque which Mrs Ackland had told her had the Doctor's name on it, as if she didn't know already. She carefully opened the front door again. She was not yet allowed to open the door to callers although some mornings the knocker went every few minutes, usually with messages for the Doctor. She carefully rubbed some polish on to the brass plate. She could recognise the A for Ackland and there were some more letters underneath. The polish seeped into the letters and she had to push her nail through the cloth to wipe it out. It would be easier if her nails were not so short. Eliza was forever shouting at her for biting them.

A shiny black carriage drawn by two grey horses at a fast trot came down the street and stopped outside a nearby house. The driver jumped down and opened the door and a man in a top hat stepped out and went straight into the house. She paused for a moment in her polishing. Suppose that man, the one she so feared, was to come along the street? Farmers' carts sometimes came this way. A shiver ran down her back. But he would not be expecting to see her here, all dressed-up outside a doctor's house. And surely he would have no call to come to this street. She would try not to think of him anymore. An old lady dressed all in black wearing a hat made of feathers passed by, then another younger lady with a small long-haired dog on a lead. Selina kept polishing and only glanced up after the people had passed but it was good to have something different to look at.

There, all the brass was shining now and not a smudge of polish anywhere. Next she had to do the windows. She fetched another bucket of water and again there was no one in the hall. Mrs Ackland must be staying in the drawing room with the children. They were big bay windows with small panes and she could only reach the bottom half but Mrs Ackland had said that was all right. The view into the room was obscured by the lace curtains and her own face was reflected back at her. She stopped polishing for a moment and gazed at herself, then turned to see her profile and lifted her chin like Mrs Ackland and Jane did. She had become more used to seeing herself, as there were mirrors in almost every room. Her hair was beginning to grow a bit; turning to try and see the back she could see that she might be able to put it up before too long. If only it would curl like Jane's.

The pavement was narrow here and she had to squeeze against the wall when someone passed to allow them plenty of room. Perhaps it would be all right doing the steps every morning, at least it was a change of scene.

Every Sunday, when she had the afternoon off, she stayed in the kitchen. Mrs Ackland had said early on that she would prefer her not to go out for the time being. In any case she had nowhere to go. Eliza and Jane always went out so she had the kitchen to herself, but the time went very slowly. For the first hour or two she was happy just to sit by the range, to doze a little and listen to the kettle murmuring. She would make herself a cup of tea and perhaps have something to eat, just because she could. But the kitchen was very big and empty. Just imagine if Ann Champion could come through that door! Could Ann really still be in the Workhouse? Could they really all be sitting in that room, Ann Champion, Harriet Braddon, Fanny Mock and the rest of them with that sour-faced woman who came in to read them bible stories on a Sunday? Just fancy if she could invite Ann round for tea and they could sit and plan for the future! Ann would bring her William and they would have apple pie and cake to eat, and of course Will would be here and Thomas too and Ann's baby son George who had died when he was just a year old. One Sunday, when she had been thinking of this, Mrs Ackland had come in and seen her cuddling a baby doll that one of the girls had left behind.

There, that was all the drawing room panes done and there was still enough water left for the dining room.

Mrs Ackland always left her a picture book to look at on Sunday afternoons. It was a book for children really and had brightly-coloured pictures from the bible on every page. Jesus had a kind face and dark eyes like Dr Ackland. In one picture he held out his hand to help a little girl from a bed while other people wearing long robes stood around wringing their hands; in another there was a big crowd of people all looking at him and he held some bread in one hand and a fish in the other. She knew that story from Sunday School. The picture she liked best was Jesus in a boat on a very rough sea holding up his arms to calm the waves; the men looking on reminded her of the Clovelly fishermen. She knew that Mrs Ackland intended the pictures to encourage her to say her prayers as the whole household did every morning, but Jesus had done nothing to help her when she really needed him so why should he now? But last Sunday when she looked up from the book to see the warm kitchen with all the shiny pots and pans and the pantry full of food she did say a prayer to Jesus asking him not to send her back to the Workhouse.

There now, the windows were finished. She paused in the doorway and looked up at the sky between the spires of the church. Almost imperceptibly, the ashen clouds drifted a little to form a peephole through which she could see a distant sliver of blue.

JOHN CORNISH SANDERS
Quay, Bideford, Nov. 27th.

SERVANT-GALISM IN BIDEFORD.

To the Editor of the Bideford Gazette.

SIR,—I live in the quiet neighbourhood of Bideford, I have only a small family, I am indulgent towards my servants, who are unrestricted and have all they require from a well-stocked pantry, and yet within the last six months I have had no less than five changes in my domestic assistants. The last housemaid I engaged, a most dressy and unloveable creature, who has just left me for dishonesty, brought with her among other things five costly silk dresses, three chignons, one long hair plait, bonnets and shawls which would have graced the windows of the finest millinery and drapery establishments in London, and a larger stock of jewellery than either I or any of my friends could ever think of possessing. She also had in her room several sensational novels and books of a questionable character, which formed her chief amusement. The girl who left before her was precisely of the same disposition. After living with me three weeks, she told me that unless I allowed her out every Sunday after dinner and two evenings a week she must leave, and she left. Another went because I endeavoured to dissuade her from quarrelling with her two fellow servants and objected to her encouraging the visits of a man of low character, with whom on more than one occasion of my absence from home she had danced in the drawing-room. These are only a few of my domestic experiences, but I fear they are only the beginning of greater troubles to come. We hear much at the present time of the necessity for the higher education of women. Would it not be well to have some systematic training for domestic servants, that they may learn to know and keep their position? When we compare domestic servants of the present day with those of the last decade the contrast is amazing. I fear there is no remedy for the evil of which I complain, nor do I think I am the only one of your readers whose experience of domestic servants is unpleasant.

I am, Sir, yours truly,
A RESIDENT IN THE NEIGHBOURHOOD
Nov. 25th. OF BIDEFORD.

From the Bideford Gazette,
28th November 1871

Sophia stepped forward a little when Selina had moved over to the dining room window. The girl had conducted herself fairly well, no gawping at the gentlefolk passing by, no calling out to that boy at the Music Hall. Sophia had feared that she would try to attract the attention of the male sex after being cloistered indoors for so long and it would, of course, only be the very worst sort who would be interested in her. However there was nothing immodest in her demeanour at all. How had such a timid girl managed to get herself into a predicament on two separate occasions? Sophia shivered a little. She really did not want to speculate on that matter. She must try to forget Selina's past and decide what to do now.

"Mamma, *when* will it be my turn to be the bear?"

Hugh tugged at her skirt and she turned and swept him up into her arms and kissed him.

"You're a little bear now! Look, I can see the fur all over your face and your paws!"

"Then I'll growl at you, grrrrr!"

She put him down on a chair where the rest of the children sat around the table. They were reading through a play that Mary and Emily had written together and were intending to perform for the whole family at Christmas, complete with costumes, though heaven only knew when there would be time to make them. Mary had given herself the lead role as the princess and was issuing instructions to the rest of the cast.

"Come on, Hughie, I've told you I'll wag my little finger when it's time for you to growl, you just have to watch me."

Sophia suggested that he might need a more obvious prompt and persuaded Mary to increase the number of his entrances so that he did not get too bored.

"Mamma, I have just had *such* a good idea! Hugh can chase the goblin off the stage and then I can write the stage direction, *Exit, pursued by a bear* just like Mr Shakespeare did."

"Wonderful, darling! And you could write it on a board for the audience to read so that they do not miss the joke."

Now that they had told Kingsley that he was to go away to school and he had accepted it happily, she could relax and enjoy the Christmas preparations. She never expected him to take the news so well. She and William had sat down with him that morning and gently explained the plans. She had expected tears but instead he had wanted to pack his trunk at once and ran upstairs to plan what he should take with him as though he were going immediately instead of two weeks after Christmas. She and William had just looked at each other and laughed. He might of course, feel differently when they visited the school later this week, but it was a good start.

He was intent now on copying out his lines from the play. He dipped his pen in the inkwell, keeping his place in the script with a pointed finger, completed the sentence in his careful, flowing style and blotted the paper. He would make a scholar yet for he was quite capable of applying himself when he was interested in the task. She rose and stroked his glossy dark hair. He pretended not to notice but his mouth twitched a little as he tried not to smile.

She walked to the bay window again, standing back a little so she would not be seen. Selina was still polishing the dining room window, her tongue protruding a little in concentration. Really, she did look a drudge with her bodice all askew and her cap crooked on her straggly hair. She was one of those who always looked untidy even when her clothes *were* provided for her. At least she was not quite so scrawny now. She was inexperienced but a hard worker and she did not appear as brazen and vulgar as had been expected. She knew her place. The truth was she could have been very much worse. Finding a good servant was a problem these days, it was a major topic of conversation. Even girls with good references turned out to be rude and presumptuous and soon left for another post if things were not exactly to their liking; there had been a letter in the paper just recently on the subject. Perhaps she could do worse than keep Selina on, even if it did mean taking the time to teach her to read and write. It would be such a relief to get the matter settled before

Christmas.

Should she discuss it with William? He would agree for certain, in fact she knew he would oppose any other action as Selina was giving satisfaction. It was not worth bothering him with domestic matters when he was so very busy, all this worry with the hospital in addition to everything else.

Selina was wringing out the cloth and coming to the front door with her bucket. Sophia crossed the drawing room and opened the door into the hall.

"Selina? Put your bucket away and then just step into the dining room, would you?"

Chapter Ten

Dr Ackland turned from the cold, windy street into the council chambers, taking the door being held open for him by a smiling Mr Heard.

"Thank you, Sir. A most unwelcoming night for leaving the warmth of the hearth and the family, is it not?"

"It certainly is, Dr Ackland, and I suspect we're all of us reluctant to be here, given the nature of the business."

He followed Mr Heard down the panelled passageway to the cloakroom from which came a hum of voices. Mr Vinson, Mr Burrow and Mr Joce turned as one and he noted the tension in each face dissipating as they recognised the two new entrants. They all made their greetings with rather forced joviality as he and Mr Heard removed their hats and overcoats, and tried to warm their feet by stamping them on the cold stone floor. Mr Vinson voiced the thoughts of each of them.

"Perhaps the gentleman will not turn out on such a night as this. I think if that were to happen, it would be a welcome Christmas present for us all, don't 'ee think?"

"I shall pull no punches whether he's here or no. I'll not have the Committee publicly criticised in such a way."

"Don't 'ee speak of punches however, Mr Heard, you'm a bit too near to the mark there!"

The Doctor smiled along with the general laughter at this remark but in truth he felt little mirth. If he could turn and walk back through the brightly-lit streets to his family he would do so right now, but he had to be here to repudiate the accusations against him and try to undo the damage that had already been done.

How people loved a scandal! Never content with good news, they sought out any story that might cast doubt on the reputations of others. Ah, and here came one who lived off that desire for tittle-tattle, for the reporter from the North Devon Journal-Herald now entered the room, closely followed by his counterpart from the Bideford Gazette. Both were greeted with some reserve.

Damn that man Pollard! The Doctor was not used to public criticism. The truth was it was not his duty to run the hospital. He had given advice on the improvements that were necessary to convert the cottage but it was the committee's remit to see that it was running smoothly; nevertheless his reputation might already be tarnished. Although the allegations would not be believed by many, were they to be believed by just a few, considerable damage could be done.

There was this latest matter concerning Mrs Elwes's estate at Walland Carey. He would not want that to be jeopardised. He had attended her for many years until her death last month, had always been careful to call promptly when she sent for him, had spent time sitting with her and gaining her confidence until she knew she could depend on him to be honest and truthful. Then he had told her of the very poorest people of Buck's Mills, those whose cottages she preferred not to visit when there was illness about, told her how they suffered when the herrings did not arrive or when wet weather laid the labourers off for weeks at a time. He described the households to which he was called only when it was too late for him to treat the effects of months of undernourishment and the disease which had already spread throughout the family, households where children cried from hunger and old women tried to nurse their sick husbands while barely strong enough to stay on their feet themselves. Like many wealthy people, she had been ignorant of the true extent of poverty on her doorstep but was willing to help alleviate it when better informed. So for many years she had paid for him to attend those most in need. The results were evident both in the fall in the death rate and in the more frequent smiles on the faces that greeted him. He had spoken of the need for the work to continue and consequently Mrs Elwes had left one thousand pounds in her will, the interest on which was to be spent on medical attention for the very poor of Buck's Mills. He had had no doubt that the firm of London solicitors dealing with her estate would appoint him to continue the work – until this latest matter. Suppose they were to read these latest reports in the papers? They would not know that the truth had been distorted.

More members of the Board arrived and the group started to move into the chamber, talking jovially of the weather and the forthcoming Christmas celebrations, anything but the matter foremost in all their minds. He remained apart from the main group and took a seat in the body of the hall; he was not a member of the Board and was there only to listen and observe. It was a role he preferred; committees were confounded things.

As Mr How started to read the minutes of the last meeting, the door opened and in came Mr Pollard. A barely audible sigh travelled around the room and eyes met in silent communication. Mr Pollard glared at Mr How and gave a somewhat sardonic apology as he took his seat. As the tedious preliminaries of the meeting progressed, Dr Ackland observed the new arrival. The man was obviously ill at ease – as well he might be – and shifted restlessly in his seat while staring challengingly at the members of the Board sitting opposite him. Those sitting beside him leant away a little and moved their chairs an inch or two when they could, while maintaining expressions of professional interest in the proceedings.

Dr Ackland had had no personal or professional dealings with him despite having known him for many years. Who was his doctor? It might be interesting to find out and gain more insight into the man's character. Certainly he seemed to put personal gain before public service, that had been clear from the wrangling over the rent for the hospital, but in truth the same could be said at times of every member present that night. They were all keen to avoid paying what they considered to be excessive tax, even if it benefited those less well-off. It was not his selfishness that set Pollard apart from the others. Dr Ackland let his gaze move around the room, from the fire burning in the hearth to the panelled walls and the inscribed board listing the previous mayors of Bideford, but always returning to Pollard. He was already worked up, moving restlessly in his chair, his hands constantly fidgeting and his jaw set. He might almost be grinding his teeth. Was he capable of real wickedness as had been suggested? The Doctor had not met the woman who had made the allegations against him, but there was seldom smoke without fire. Should he act, that was the question? Should he question the woman and make further investigations concerning Selina Burman? Selina was doing so well now, was settled and thriving, was there any merit in opening old wounds in order to bring her seducer to justice?

Ah, now the action was beginning. Mr Heard was being invited to read the committee's report, written in response to the allegations made about the hospital. The Doctor listened carefully as his own recommendations for alterations and improvements to the hospital were listed. All, Mr Heard stated, had been carried out. It was true. Then the matter of the windows was brought up. Mr Pollard, Mr Heard read, had refused to allow windows until it had been pointed out that they would increase the value of his property. At this he was stung to reply, he glared at Mr Heard and called him a liar; it was clear that he was close to losing control. Next, Mr Heard referred to the occasion when Pollard told Mr Paddon that both Mr Heard and Dr Ackland were fools. The Doctor looked down at his feet, meeting the man's eyes now would further infuriate him, Mr Heard, however, continued reading and stared threateningly at Mr Pollard whenever he looked up from his paper. There would be trouble, he could see it coming. The Committee had not restricted themselves to repudiating Pollard's claims but had turned the tables on him. It was not wise, it was not wise at all. Pollard reminded him of a fox at bay. His hands were clenched on the arms of the chair and his eyes were wild; at the next allegation, this time a reference to the large profit he was making from letting the cottage, he leapt to his feet and all was confusion. Those nearest to him hurriedly moved away as he raised his chair above his head and flung it violently towards the fire, then sprang after it and, grabbing the poker, ran at Mr Heard shouting oaths and curses all the while. In the general melee that followed he was restrained, some members fortunately being more inclined to move towards him than away and, after a struggle during which more fearful oaths were uttered, the poker was restored to the fireplace and Mr Pollard, shamed into something approaching acquiescence, to a different chair, his own now being in need of repair. He was almost crouching in his chair now, his long, narrow face besieged by anger and self-doubt in equal measure.

The claims and counterclaims continued. There was some truth in what he had said. The hospital *was* merely a facility for those who wished to be removed from their houses in order to protect others from the smallpox. In practice this generally meant servants whose employers would meet the bill in order to have them out of the house. It *was* an inadequate hospital compared to the big city hospitals but for Bideford it was, at least, a start. Would Pollard be prepared to pay higher rates to help fund a better one?

Ah well. Dr Ackland relaxed a little as the meeting drew to a noisy and chaotic end. At least his name had been cleared. The allegations would, no doubt, be included in the newspapers but it would be clear, after these scenes, that they were made by a man who had now been completely discredited. The reputation of the hospital would be damaged, however.

Pollard was the first to leave and their eyes met briefly. He glared as if challenging him to utter the as yet unspoken charge, before striding out. The Doctor rose and joined the group who, after a moment's silence as Pollard left, were now reliving the events of the evening.

"I thought I would meet my Maker when he picked up that poker!"

"When he threw the chair it caught me just here on the ear!

An inch nearer and I'd have been calling for the Doctor here! Have a look, Doctor, I'm not severely injured, am I?"

He carried out a mock examination amidst general laughter and pronounced Mr Joce whole.

Mr Vinson was rather more thoughtful than the rest.

"By the next meeting he'll be calm and almost sensible again, that's his way. One would almost think it were drink enraging him but he'll not touch a drop."

He moved closer and spoke quietly.

"And what of this other matter, do we address it?"

"Perhaps I'll speak to the woman who has made the allegations. Will you let me have her name?"

Mr Vinson wrote the name and address in his notebook and tore out the page.

"My main concern now is how the reporting of tonight's meeting will affect the hospital. I fear that confidence in it will be lost"

They found their overcoats and gloves and settled their top hats comfortably. Stepping out on to Bridge Street away from the fusty, fire-lit room, the air was sharp and raw. The reflections of the gaslights on the bridge glittered on the silent river and Allhalland Street was empty but for a scavenging dog, the shoppers that had crowded the festively-lit streets having returned to their warm hearths. They walked along slowly together, leaving the concerns of the evening behind in the Council Chamber. Mr Vinson, also, would have all his family with him for Christmas day; it would be a day of rest. At the corner of High Street they shook hands warmly and Dr Ackland continued along Mill Street where a few shops remained open. He raised his hat to an elderly man sitting in a donkey cart outside Mr Hopson's shop.

"Season's Greetings to you!"

"And to you Doctor, a very happy Christmas to you!"

And it would be; it would.

THE BIDEFORD WEEKLY GAZETTE---DE

BIDEFORD LOCAL BOARD.
THE SMALL POX HOSPITAL—EXCITING SCENE.

The Bideford Local Board held an ordinary general meeting on Thursday, when in the course of a discussion upon the alleged mismanagement of the Small Pox Hospital an extraordinary scene was witnessed in the Council Chamber. The Mayor (Mr. How) occupied the chair, and there were also present: Messrs. Joce, Pollard, Heard, Vinson, Burrow, Tremner, Down, Martyn White, W. White, and Pain.

Mr. Heard, on behalf of the Hospital Committee, brought up a report relative to the arrangements at the house at Moor Park in reply to the charges made by Mr. Pollard at a previous meeting. It appeared from this document that after the board became tenants of the house Dr. Ackland inspected the premises and gave certain directions as to what should be done, all of which had been complied with. The whole of the inside had been white-limed, the floors had been well-cleansed, sufficient light and ventilation had been provided, and the house put in an efficient state for the reception of patients. Mr. Heard gave a list of the furniture, bedding, etc., purchased by and lent to the committee, and alluded to the difficulty experienced in engaging a nurse. They had engaged the services of a competent person at a salary of 12s 6d per week, this person being allowed, at her own request, to have her son with her. A man named Paddon had also been engaged as messenger, and it was his duty to attend the hospital every day and render whatever assistance might be required. A charwoman had been engaged as an assistant, and she had also watched the patients at night. When this man Paddon went, as requested, to ask Mr. Pollard to remove certain dung from the exterior of the house he replied, "Mr. Heard is a fool and Dr. Ackland is a fool." [Mr. Pollard: That is an infernal lie.] In fact, the whole of the Medical Officer's recommendations had been carried out. With regard to the charges brought against them by Mr. Pollard, which were wholly untrue, he would say what he had to say without any feeling of animosity. He regretted that such an untruthful report had gone forth because it branded the town with what it did not deserve—a disgrace worse than the Hampstead Heath Hospital. [Mr. Pollard: Every word he says is untrue.] Moreover, Mr. Pollard had kept from the committee a room which should have been occupied as a bedroom by the nurse. This room had been stored with potatoes and locked, in consequence of which the nurse had not had the accommodation she required and her son had taken the disease. [Mr. Pollard: It is a ———— lie.] It should be borne in mind, too, that the accusations made against the nurse when she was first appointed came from Mr. Pollard, who described her as a " drunken and worthless woman." [Mr. Pollard: I say it is an abominable lie ; I never said so.]

An exciting scene—a scene of indescribable confusion—took place before Mr. Heard concluded his defence. Irritated by accusations of selfish motives, Mr. Pollard became very violent, and, after throwing his chair on the fire-grate, seized the poker, which he aimed at Mr. Heard amid cries of "Order." Epithets which no provocation could justify were also indulged in ; the report was denounced as a tissue of lies ; and Mr. Pollard said he despised the board as well as the committee, for there was not a truthful man or a gentleman amongst them.

The Mayor feared that the reports that had been published in the papers would have the effect of preventing servants and other persons from going to the hospital. He was very sorry that such serious charges had been brought forward. It was painful to him to listen to the accusations made at a previous meeting, when it was said that all the committee had asserted was false, because such accusations were untrue.

Mr. Vinson believed Mr. Pollard to be a well-meaning man ; but he could not help saying, for unfortunately it was the case, that he had been led away by this matter by statements and representations made to him by others, and before making inquiries as to their truthfulness had made charges which could not be substantiated. He was much obliged to the committee for the satisfactory way in which they had discharged their duties.

Ultimately, on the motion of the Mayor, seconded by Mr. Down, it was resolved that the confidence and thanks of the board be accorded to the committee, and that they be requested to continue their services. All the members voted for the motion with the exception of Mr. Pollard.

THE PUBLIC STREETS.

The dirty state of the public streets was complained of by several members of the board. Mr. Burrow alluded to the inconvenience which they occasioned to the inhabitants, and Mr. Joce considered that they were a disgrace to the town. Mr. Heard also thought they ought to be kept in a cleaner state, and moved that the Surveyor be requested to employ able-bodied men to cleanse the principal thoroughfares, which was seconded by Mr. Joce and carried.

THE WEIGHBRIDGE HOUSE.

The following tenders were received for the repair and alterations of the weighbridge house in accordance with the plans and specifications prepared by the committee : Mr. John Sing, Littleham, £165 15s 8d ; Mr. James. Howard, Bideford, £165 ; Mr. J. H. Glover, Bideford, £93 10s ; Mr. James Bale, Bideford, £52 10s. On the motion of Mr. Heard, seconded , by Mr. Joce, it was resolved that Mr. Bale's tender be accepted provided he can furnish sufficient sureties for the performance of the work in accordance with the specifications and to the satisfaction of a clerk of the works to be hereafter appointed. Mr. Pollard, who did not consider it necessary to ask for sureties, refused to vote for the motion.

THE WATER AND DRAINAGE WORKS.

A letter was read from the Surveyor, requesting that Mr. Crokam's time of maintenance be not allowed to commence until his return to Bideford ; and a letter was read from Mr. Crokam, requesting that the amount due to him on account of his contract and for extras be paid, less his maintenance money, and that the £500 deposit note held as security for the due performance of the work be handed back to him. The consideration of the former part of this letter was deferred, but the deposit note was ordered to be handed over. The Surveyor having certified that Mr. Hookway was entitled to the sum of £500 on behalf of his contract for the drainage works and for extras, the same was ordered to be paid.

SMALL POX IN THE BIDEFORD STREETS.

To the Editor of the Bideford Gazette.

SIR,—While turning the corner of Mill-street this afternoon I came in close contact with a young man who, judging from his appearance, had not completely recovered from a severe attack of Small Pox. His face presented a most repulsive appearance, and the scales left by the disease were falling from him. Only a few days ago I saw a girl not more than twelve years of age in a similar state playing with other children in the New-road. Ought this to be allowed ? The sight of the young man I fell in with this afternoon was enough to predispose any one to an attack of the malady ; it gave me such a sensation that I have been suffering from feverish excitement ever since. It is a pity, I think, that local authorities have not the power to prevent persons just recovering from Small Pox from moving about the streets, for while the epidemic is spreading to such a fearful extent the appearance of semi-convalescents in the streets and amongst people moving about and meeting together cannot but have a very serious effect in circulating the disease. The

Selina stood aside while Mrs Ackland and Miss Annie stepped out on to the street, then closed the front door and followed them as they walked arm in arm up Bridgeland Street. The evening was cold and windy and as she gazed up at the dazzling gas lights she fastened her jacket and put the big wicker basket on her arm. It was the first time she had been out after dark. This morning she had accompanied Mrs Ackland to the pannier market so that she might carry home the joint of beef for the Christmas dinner, as Mrs Ackland did not trust the delivery boys to be on time. Selina's arms had ached with the weight of the huge piece of meat and when they arrived home she found that blood had leaked through the brown paper wrapping on to her dress, but it had been worth it to see the huge market thronged with shoppers and the stalls piled high with poultry.

It had been an extraordinary week. First Mrs Ackland telling her she was to stay, then Miss Annie and Miss Maud arriving back from school and the whole house in an uproar – excited children rushing from room to room, Jimmy barking, Eliza stamping her big feet around the kitchen in a frenzy of anxiety and excitement at all the preparations for Christmas, the rooms to be prepared for Dr Ackland's sister and her family arriving by train from Exeter tomorrow - and now this, being allowed to leave the house twice in one day!

She followed Mrs Ackland and Miss Annie around the corner into Mill Street. The pavements were thronged with people and the shops were lit as bright as daylight. She stopped and stared, causing an old gentleman to bump into her.

Miss Annie turned to her.

"Look, Selina, isn't it pretty? I do so love this time of year. Mamma, we must bring the little ones out one evening to see this."

As they made their way along the busy street Selina peered through the crowds to see the shops on either side. In the illuminated windows was a profusion of goods of every description; in this one were pyramids of oranges, lemons and apples, and cauliflowers arranged in a ring with one in the centre like a gigantic flower; in that one dozens of loaves and cakes in every shape and size. Another had dozens – hundreds, surely – of pairs of shoes and boots all carefully arranged in pairs. Some windows had brightly-coloured pictures of happy, smiling children and decorated trees, others had shiny coloured letters strung across their length. Miss Annie turned to her again to point to one of these.

"Selina, that says 'Here's a Merry Christmas', just like the letters we put up in the dining room."

Miss Annie had spoken to her several times since her arrival, almost as an equal, she did not seem disturbed to learn that Selina could not read and had urged her mother to teach her soon. Selina could not think how to reply to her remarks so she curtseyed and said 'Yes, Miss' every time she was addressed and watched her admiringly, marvelling that a girl so much younger than herself – she could not be more than fourteen – could be so confident and composed.

"Mamma, may we have a tree this year instead of the Christmas bush? Gertrude and Catherine both told me they are to have trees in their homes and it sounds such fun to hang them with candles and baubles."

"I have already arranged it with Mr Cann – look, he has some outside his shop now. But it is to be a surprise for the little ones so you must not say a word."

The fir trees were arranged outside a window filled with flowers, holly and scarlet berries. Selina had never seen a decorated tree before but there used to be a Christmas bush in the entrance of the Workhouse each Christmas. It was made of two hoops, one inside the other and each year she had helped to decorate it so that it formed a globe of holly, ivy and mistletoe. That and the special Christmas dinner had helped make the day bearable, but she had always cried to think of her family celebrating in their simple way in Clovelly.

As they made their way along the street their progress was impeded by the many people who stopped to exchange greetings with Mrs Ackland and to comment on Miss Annie's height.

"My, her's a proper young lady now!"

"Are you ready yet? There's only a few days left now!"

"'Ave 'ee seen the queue at Miss Powe's? I'm sure I'll never find a goose to buy!"

The pavements were so crowded that they were forced to step out into the road and squeeze between a carriage and a donkey cart, and outside Miss Mary Powe's poulterer's a queue of people wound out into the street and a boy helped customers choose from the dozens of turkeys, geese, chickens and ducks that were hanging from hooks all around the shop front. They paused and Mrs Ackland consulted her list.

"We must come out again tomorrow for more provisions. Tonight I want to buy a few little gifts. I would like to get each of the children a present this year, though not for you tonight, Annie dear, for it must be a surprise. Let us go to Mrs Murphy's shop."

They looked in the window of number two Mill Street. The small panes were illuminated by several dazzling lights and within, on shelves lined with red and gold paper, were an assortment of toys such as Selina had never even imagined: china dolls nestling in boxes of tissue paper; an engine with red wheels; a little china tea set decorated with pink rosebuds; a miniature shop with toy fruit and vegetables all made of wood and even a Noah's ark with a procession of brightly coloured animals. They went inside and Selina gazed around while Mrs Ackland asked to see the engine and some skipping ropes. There was a sailing boat with a big white sail and a rocking horse with a real mane and tail. There were many smaller toys too, soldiers, farm animals and a little tin drum. At home in her box, locked in a kitchen drawer, she had three silver crowns, her first month's wages. Fifteen whole shillings. She had taken the coins to bed with her so that she could feel their weight in her hand and run her thumb along their ridged edges. In her last position she had been paid only a shilling a week and had not been allowed any tea or sugar.

Her wages were, of course, to be sent with the postman to her parents to support Will; that very evening Mrs Ackland was to write out their address for her to copy. But surely she could buy a little toy to send him for Christmas so that her parents could tell him she was still thinking of him? She picked up a little toy train. The wheels did not go around as they did on the bigger ones but it was still quite perfect. But, of course, he had never seen a train. A boat would be best, he knew about boats, he could sail it on the stream that ran down the side of the street to the harbour.

Mrs Ackland's paper-wrapped packages were being put in the basket on her arm and she quickly held it out to help. It was no good; she had not got the crowns with her and she dare not ask Mrs Ackland to lend her the money.

Next they crossed High Street to look in Mr George Boyle's window where Mrs Ackland and Miss Annie admired the ribbons arranged as a rainbow. From the public house next door came the sound of a badly-played piano, noisy singing and shouts of laughter. Selina could just see through the window to the bright, glittering interior lit by hanging gaslights reflected in a large wall mirror. There were women inside as well as men. Might this be the sort of place to which Harriet Braddon came when she discharged herself from the Workhouse? She tried to see if there was anyone she could recognise but Mrs Ackland gave her a sharp look and she quickly turned away. They went into Mr Boyle's shop and chairs were drawn up for Mrs Ackland and Miss Annie while a young man brought trays of silk handkerchiefs for them to examine. The walls were lined from floor to ceiling with scores of shallow drawers with brass handles, each marked with a little label to identify its contents. On the other side of the shop, rolls of cotton, velvet, silk and brocade in every imaginable colour and design were arranged on deep shelves. Perhaps one day she might be able to spare just a little from her wages to buy a ribbon or two or a piece of cotton for a new dress.

Their next call was at Mr Squire's silversmith and

jeweller's shop at number 12 High Street. There were already several ladies peering in at the windows and the display was quite dazzling, each window carrying a different show, this one of pocket watches and clocks, that one gleaming cutlery and tankards, on the right, necklaces, earrings and bangles and all backed by mirrors which doubled the quantity and brilliance of the exhibits. Miss Annie stared at the earrings, her breath misting up the glass.

"Mamma, look at those perfectly dear drop earrings with the little pearls! Would Maud not love those! Selina, look, which do you like best?"

No one Selina knew had ever possessed earrings. There were some with dark red stones in the shape of little flowers, others with jewels the colour of the sea surrounded with silver, still more like tiny trees with emerald leaves and little pearl earrings that shone like the sun reflected in dewdrops.

"- I, I like all of them."

Miss Annie laughed.

"It is so difficult to choose, is it not? Mamma, it would be wonderful if Maud and I had some very nearly the same but I really do not want to know which ones, I love surprises so much!"

Mrs Ackland went into the shop and they watched while two assistants hurried to greet her and draw up a velvet-cushioned chair.

"Now, I really must not look for I do not want to know whether or not Mamma will choose some for me. Let us turn away, Selina. Oh, it will be such fun at Christmas! We shall open presents and play games and Mamma always lets the servants watch *and* buys you each a present, a new apron or something similar. Have you bought any Christmas gifts yet? Mamma tells me you have a little boy about the same age as Hugh. It must be so hard to be parted from him, I just cannot imagine being away from my family at Christmas. What present have you bought for him?"

"I -, nothing, no presents, I've never bought a present, Miss."

"Oh! But your parents will buy him one, I am sure, he must miss you so much."

"We never had presents at Christmas, Miss, save for an orange if we could get it."

Selina looked down and grasped her hands together to stop herself biting her nails. She felt herself under close scrutiny.

"I would like to get Will a present, Miss, but I must send my wages home to pay for his keep."

"Oh, but surely you could send some little thing! A lollipop perhaps, it could be posted with your wages. Here comes Mamma. Mamma, Selina has no present to send to her son! She could get one on the way home, could she not? A lollipop or a bag of sweets so that he might be reminded of her?"

"Selina's wages have to be sent home, Annie. Her parents will have many expenses. Come, I wish to buy some cinnamon from Mr Cadd and we must hurry for it will not be long before your father's meeting is finished."

How her skirts swished when she turned away like that! Selina followed as they crossed the busy High Street to a chemist's shop, its window containing brightly-lit jars of green and red glass.

"But Mamma, Selina must be able to send him a little present and a Christmas message, she must! Think how hard it would be if we were parted from Hugh at Christmas, we would hardly bear it."

"It is not the same at all, Annie. Now come, we still have much to do."

"Why is it not the same? He is her son, a little boy of just four years! You would like so much to send him a present, would you not, Selina?"

Selina looked down into the basket, gripping the handle tightly. She could not answer Miss Annie.

"Very well. We will buy a lollipop on the way home. I will pay for it myself for it is not worthwhile breaking into the crowns. But, Annie, I would like to speak to you when we get home. I am afraid you have been forgetting your manners while you have been away. I hope you do not speak to your aunts in such a way."

As her mother turned to open the door to the chemist's shop Annie smiled conspiratorially at Selina, obviously delighted that she had achieved her aim. Later, as they strolled back through the emptying streets where some shops were already closing their doors, Miss Annie linked arms with her mother again and they laughed together as they planned a Christmas morning surprise for Dr Ackland, so their disagreement could not, after all, be serious. Selina's basket now held, in addition to all the other packages, a twist of paper containing a bright red lollipop. Soon she would be able to visit her son and meanwhile there would be all the extraordinary happenings which seemed to make up Christmas in this astonishing household. Surely she was one of the luckiest people in the town?

Letter, Dr W.H. Ackland to Charles Kingsley Ackland.
(From the papers of the Ackland and Littlewood
families. Reproduced by permission of the Wellcome Library, London)

"Bideford Thursday
6.30 pm
My dear Kingy,
You were a very brave good boy and kept up wonderfully
well. Of course you could not prevent a tear or two at
parting when you saw that both Annie and Maud were red
about the eyes - Do your best, it will be for a very little
time dull - play & work & kind friends so near and around
you will cheer you and make you contented. I went away
from home alone, at 8 years of age & among strangers &
and even had at one time to stay in the school during the
holidays & so was away a whole year. God bless you my
brave boy.
Dear Mamma sends lots of love - give mine and Mummy's
to Annie and Maud. Jimmy is lying on the big arm chair &
would send you a wag of his tail if I could make him know
what I am doing.
Ever your affectionate father,
W.H. Ackland"

Chapter Eleven

Sophia put down her pen and read through her letter. What else could she say to make him feel a little happier? It was such a struggle when she was close to tears herself. She picked up his note and read it again, although she now knew it by heart.

- Please, please Mamma and Papa, may I not come home again? I miss you all so very much so shorely it would be better to go to school when I am older. I would work very hard at home and would never be lazy again, I promise you. I tried to be brave last night like you told me but when the light went out it was too hard.

She took a deep breath and picked up her pen again. She must make him know how much she loved him, above all else he must be assured of that. But somehow she must keep her distress from him. How was she to do it?

There had been such excitement when his letter had arrived this morning, properly addressed in his careful hand. Her husband had claimed it from the other children and had opened it carefully to a chorus of,

"What does Kingsley say, Papa, what does he say?"

She had seen his face alter as he read the letter quickly, then passed it to her.

"He says he is with some splendid boys and is having a wonderful time and misses us only a little! Now then, let us look at the globe to see where Kingsley is, for he is really quite close, then who will come up on my shoulders and gallop around the dining room before I go to work?"

When they had had a moment alone she had pleaded with him, but he had been adamant.

"He *must* stay a term at least, he *has* to have time to settle and find his feet. What is his future to be if he is not properly educated? The poor, dear, *dear* boy - I would take the train to visit him, now, this very minute, if I thought it would help him but I fear it would only further unsettle him, if that is possible."

He was right, of course, it was so very important for Kingsley to do well in his studies if he was to follow in his father's footsteps. Oh, but he was still so young for his years, so very sensitive. It had been different when Annie and Maud first went away, she had wept then but they had been excited at going off on such a big adventure together and had quickly made friends. Besides, their aunts' presence had made things comfortable for them. Mr and Mrs Holmes were kind but it was not the same.

Yesterday morning when the first sad little letter had arrived, she and William had hoped that it was just nerves at settling in and had assured each other that he would soon recover. William had sat straight down to write to him and throughout the day they had reminded each other of what he might be doing at that moment, now eating with the other boys, now having his bedtime wash – would the water be hot? But then this morning just when they had been sure that he must be a little happier this next letter had arrived.

They had had such a very happy Christmas, the family complete again with Annie and Maud home. The house felt almost empty now by comparison. Kingsley had been very cheerful and had frequently talked about going to school and the things he might do there, and when it was time to pack his trunk he had been so excited she had felt a little hurt that he did not seem to have any qualms about leaving home. He had been a little tearful of course when they had said their farewells at the station, as were Annie and Maud, it was only natural – how forlorn *she* had felt when the whistle had blown and the train had chugged up the track taking her boy away! William had helped her into the brougham and had held her as she sobbed in his arms. Her sister Lucy had written by return of post that all three children were in good spirits when they arrived in Plymouth and that Kingsley had gone bravely to school after a night with his aunts. But then his first letter and arrived, and now this.

What was he doing now? Would he feel better now his lessons had started and he was kept busy? Or would he find the teaching too hard and feel even more miserable? For eleven years she had known what he was doing almost every minute of the day and now it was almost intolerable that he was apart from her and she could not hold him in her arms and comfort him. How must it feel to sit in a strange classroom with boys he did not know?

When Jimmy padded over to her and put his head on her knee, she knelt and put her arms around him and buried her face in his long, soft coat while he stood very still and wagged his tail gently in silent sympathy. Eventually she dried her eyes and, finding herself kneeling on the floor, folded her hands on the seat of the chair and said a little prayer for Kingsley and for herself, that they might both become reconciled to his being away. She would advise him, too, to pray for forbearance. The thought of him kneeling at a strange bed, perhaps in tears, made her own flow again.

The children were with Jane, copying the map of Devon that hung on the wall so that they might mark the place where Kingsley was. She had arranged to give Selina another writing lesson before lunch. She was tempted to call it off but she had no good reason to do so. The girl was learning slowly but she was making some progress. She could write her name now and was so pleased with herself you would think she had achieved something remarkable.

She took her letter out to the hall table for the postman to collect and called to Selina who was carrying buckets of coal up to the top floor. She was proving a good worker and was always deferential in her manner; it had been a wise decision to keep her on. Good, this time she had remembered to wash her hands and change her apron. With a good diet she had put on some weight and her hair and skin had improved, she was looking sufficiently respectable to answer the door now, so must be trained to write messages.

"Remember to say the sound of each letter as you copy it.

That's it. No, that one is M, M for mother."

It was really no different from teaching children – the tongue poking out in concentration, the scratching of the pen, the staring into space when the memory failed, but she did look rather ridiculous. She felt a sudden pang that it was this creature rather than Kingsley sitting opposite her. She rose and walked to the window. A dejected-looking horse between the shafts of a cart loaded with potatoes stood outside Mrs Ley's Establishment for Young Ladies.

"Now try to write these words. Consult the alphabet you have written to remind you. Cat. C-a-t."

A man in dirty, dishevelled clothing climbed into the cart and the horse moved off, barely lifting its head as if in a deep melancholia. Did Kingsley sit by a window? Did it have a pleasant view to cheer him or would he be reprimanded if he looked out?

"Dog. D-o-g."

She wandered back to the table. Selina was running her finger along the alphabet and looking worried. These lessons would have to become more frequent if she was to write down the messages that came for William.

"No, that's P. There, that's G. Good, your copying is improving."

"Please, Ma'am, may I try to write William?"

Whatever was the girl thinking of? Sophia was confused for a moment. Could Selina know that that was the doctor's name and, if so, how could she dare to speak it?

"My son Will, ma'am, I would like to write his name and to write him a letter, if you would please help me, ma'am. I'm afraid he'll not mind me else, ma'am. My sister might be able to read it to him, ma'am."

Sophia had not heard her say so much before. Red-faced, she looked into her lap and twisted the brass ring that she wore on her finger. Of course she had not meant William, what a silly mistake. Sophia could have made herself look quite foolish if she had reprimanded the girl for using her husband's first name.

"Don't forget, Selina, the purpose of teaching you to write is to increase your usefulness to the household. Any personal concerns are secondary to that. Now write Sit, please, S-i-t. No, it is an I, there, the vowels are always the hardest. Now I shall cover the alphabet. Now write Sad. S-a-d. Well done, yes, it begins with the same letter as sit. You are making progress, you see. Now copy this sentence that I shall write for you and see if you can read it back to me afterwards. Remember to rest your wrist on the table to steady your hand."

Sophia sat back in the chair. A letter did not seem enough for Kingsley. How dreadful if he were to feel abandoned! He must know that his parents were keeping him in school *because* they loved him, anything else was unthinkable. What could she send? They had ensured that his trunk had been full but she had thought afterwards that she could have included one of the fruit cakes that he liked so much. Yes, that would do well, she would make one this very afternoon. He would know that she was thinking of him and he could perhaps share it out amongst the other boys. A fruit cake was sure to win friends.

"Good, that is quite accurate, quickly use the blotting paper. Now see if you can read it."

The girl made a good attempt and was able to read some of the shorter words without help.

"Well done. 'They do not love that do not show their love.' Those are the words of Mr William Shakespeare from a play called The Two Gentlemen of Verona."

She dismissed Selina and returned to the window. Would Kingsley have finished his morning's lessons now? How hard it was to be a mother! You gave birth in agony, you fretted over every rash and pale look and if they lived – thank God that they had – you suffered the anguish of separation when they started to grow up.

- Well, I still have four at home. Let's see how they are getting on and whether these maps are finished. The distance to Mannamead will not seem so great on a map.

Letter, Sophia Ackland to Charles Kingsley Ackland.
(From the papers of the Ackland and Littlewood
families. Reproduced by permission of the Wellcome Library, London)

"Saturday
My own dear boy,
I trust I shall have a letter from you tomorrow, telling me
you are getting more reconciled to being away. I know
my own dear good brave boy, you will try to make
yourself happy - of course it must be hard at first for you,
but you see the sooner you go, the sooner you will be able
to leave. You know my own dear son how important it is
that you should get on, all your future welfare depends on
how you do get on and every month lost now will keep
you so much further behind. Pray to God to make you
happy and cheerful. Mind the texts in your little book - it
will make <u>me</u> so happy if I get a happy letter from <u>you</u>. I
will think of you so much tomorrow, what a great comfort
it is that you are so near dear Annie & Maud & Auntie &
how kind dear Mr & Mrs Holmes are. - Are you to have a
"top" hat? as Papa thought you ought. I can't fancy you
in one, write and tell me what you have. I have been
thinking that very likely you have gone into town this
afternoon to buy one. How important you will look in it.
God bless you my own dear loving boy.
Papa sends his best love so do all the little ones and
myself. I send you thousands of love.
Your own dear Mother."

Dr Ackland locked the door to the Dispensary and strolled over to the boy who was holding his horse. A tall, thin boy, always scruffily dressed but with a certain intelligence in his eyes, he was always lingering on the Quay ready to wait with a horse, push a barrow, carry a sack on his thin shoulders or do anything honest - and in all probability, dishonest as well – to earn a few pennies to help support his widowed mother and younger brothers and sisters.

"No sick people today, Sir? I'll stable 'n if you want, Sir, I can walk 'n up the street, Sir."

"Thank you, my boy, but I have further calls to make. No patients in the Dispensary but plenty elsewhere."

He took the reins and handed the boy a coin.

"There comes Mr Taylor. If you run you'll be the first to meet him."

The boy darted off along the Quay, his bare feet skilfully avoiding the roughest stones, and reached the farmer as he dismounted from his horse.

Dr Ackland smiled. The boy would be about the same age as Kingsley. Poor, dear Kingsley! He mounted his horse and trotted towards High Street, raising his hat to passers-by and casting an appreciative glance at the tall-masted clipper moored alongside the Quay. The Dispensary was not open today but he had called in to replace some papers he had needed for Thursday's very satisfactory annual general meeting. The Dispensary was going from strength to strength. There were more subscribers than last year, more patients had been treated and he had persuaded the two doctors new to the town to offer their services as Dr Hoyle was now so unwell. He had given examples at the meeting of some who had benefited: the shoemaker who was able to resume work after attention to his injured hand, saving him and his family the shame of applying for poor relief; the housemaid whose cough was cured before her employers became affected; the young smallpox victim who had made a full recovery after attention was given to his diet and nursing care. He had praised the subscribers for their generosity in helping those less fortunate than themselves and had known that the self-satisfied smiles would lead to many conversations at well-laden dinner tables and further potential subscribers being urged to add their support. Was it possible that eventually there would be none in the town who had to suffer and perhaps die without a doctor to attend them? He had plans. The next stage would be to provide beds at the Dispensary, there was space for eight or nine. And then one day a hospital, a real hospital where care for all who needed it would be provided.

Well. There were more pressing concerns for now. There was no need to be too hasty in attending a birth as Nature so often had her own way of solving problems but he had been long enough. Having allowed Toby to walk up High Street and Grenville Street he now pressed him to a trot, passing the marketplace and continuing to Honestone Street, calling out a cheery,

"Mind your toes now!" and

"Look out for the little ones!"

as children scattered beneath his horse's hoofs. The scrap of paper in his pocket directed him to Hyfield Place, Mr Carpenter the cabinet maker. He chuckled to himself.

- Our Mr Carpenter must be going up in the world.

Finding number nine, he tethered Toby securely to a nearby gate. Almost before he had time to remove his hand from the door knocker a rather pale-faced man opened the door and ushered him past two anxious-looking women to an upstairs room. A young woman lay in bed, her knees drawn up towards her chest. As he entered she drew a deep breath and uttered a long, low groan which ended in a shriek. He held her hand and quietly reassured her until the spasm passed, then reached under the covers. Ah. In his hand he held a tiny foot. A breech birth. He saw now that there was an older woman in the corner of the room. She told him that the labour had been going on for seven hours and that it was a first child. The bowl of water by the bed was freshly boiled and he rapidly removed his frock coat, rolled up his sleeves and washed his hands. The room was tolerably clean. Now. He explained to the woman who was now lying exhausted on the pillows that he would place the child in a better position.

"Have no fear. You will soon have your child in your arms."

Please God. He waited until the next spasm passed then gently pushed the little foot back inside. Good, the child was not large. Should he turn it? He could – but no, the knees were flexed now, a complete breech. Leave it like that. The umbilical cord had not dropped, all would be well. But it was a first child, no track record. Please God all would be well.

"All right. Well done. Not long now."

He sat back quietly for the next ten minutes or so, speaking soothingly when the spasms came, writing in his notebook to pass the time when the woman lay back and closed her eyes. When her groans intensified he moved forward quickly. She panted, then screamed. There, the buttocks were delivered. He held the child's hips lightly, eased the legs out.

"Gently now…"

He waited, then worked with the contractions, giving himself curt, silent instructions. Now stop. Wait. There, the arms.

"Hold back now if you can."

She screamed again. Dear God, he must do his best. He eased out the shoulders. Gently, gently. Now for the head. He reached inside, placed a finger inside the child's mouth to pull the jaw down, then two fingers to flex the head towards the chest. Slowly now. Here came another spasm. There. It was a boy.

"It's a boy. You have a fine boy!"

The child moved, cried, the blue eyes opened. A fine head of hair. A lovely boy. He cut the cord and handed the child to its mother. All was well, he had managed it, thank God he had managed it. She thanked him, crying, held the child and touched its cheek, stroked the tiny arms.

"Lewis. His name is Lewis, Doctor."

He rode up the road. He would allow himself ten minutes to compose himself. A birth always moved him, always gave him a glimpse of the divine. Birth and death; it was an honour to witness them and it was doubly affecting when the two were closely linked as they inevitably were in a risky birth. And always he was reminded of the seven precious births of his own children. Lewis Carpenter, the first child of a new little family. Pray God they would be happy and healthy.

Now this trouble with Kingsley. He turned into Abbotsham Road, leaving the town behind and continuing past the new villas until the road narrowed and there were fields on either side. To think of his own dear boy so unhappy – did he not know himself how it felt to be away from loved ones and a familiar home? His memories of those dreadful first months at boarding school had never left him, and now the emotions he felt at the thought of Kingsley experiencing such a thing threatened to overcome him. But what was the remedy? Where would he be now if he had never gone away, had never learnt to be independent and face up to adversity? But it was a bitter lesson for his dear boy!

He reined in his horse and looked over the fields and across the valley. A buzzard glided from the bare branches of an old oak, mewing a complaint at the unwarranted disturbance. There was a beauty in the lifeless trees and the dormant fields, though it required man's intellect to see the promise of spring in the sleeping landscape. And Kingsley, what did he look on now?

At least they could write frequently – he would write every day! When *he* was at school the cost of a letter was prohibitive and he only received one every two weeks or so. Ah, *there* was progress, now for just a penny the letter would be with Kingsley the very next day, sometimes the same day if it was sent early.

The buzzard circled overhead then settled warily in an elm

at a safe distance. Then there was Dr Hoyle, poor, dear Richard Hoyle. For weeks he had dismissed Dr Ackland's questions when he was again unable to attend the Dispensary but last week he had finally addressed the subject.

"Just cast an eye over me, would you, my friend? You know how I value your opinion."

He had been shocked at what he found. Richard had winced when the area below his right ribs was palpated. The liver was hard and greatly enlarged.

"Have you vomited?"

"Yes, many times over the last few weeks."

"And you are lethargic?"

"I am. And I am losing weight."

Their eyes met. He knew that the knowledge he could see in Richard's eyes was mirrored in his own. They could not hide it from each other. The outcome was clear, for the disease was already advanced.

Cirrhosis. Alcohol, so often the cause, was not implicated in this case. He had known other doctors, abstainers, who had succumbed to the disease. Why? Could it be through contamination of the blood? Some infection contracted during surgery? They were all more careful now, but in the old days - the blood, the unwashed hands. It was possible that Richard had carried this infection for many years, he too might harbour it. Richard was forty years old. He had a wife and four dependent daughters.

Now, this would not do. There was business to attend to; he would visit his friend later. Now he must visit Mrs Daniel and then, well, then he must visit Pollard's servant. He had put off that business for too long. He took Mrs Daniel's letter from his pocket to remind himself of his purpose. Mrs Daniel, like so many of his older patients, was unable to write, so it had been written by a friend.

He turned and urged Toby into a swift trot back up Abbotsham Road, passed through Old Town and was again in the country. On reaching Adjavin, he found Agnes Daniel seated as usual on the old oak settle by the fire in the farmhouse kitchen, issuing shrill reminders to her daughter-in-law who was preparing luncheon. She pulled up her thick black skirts to show him her swollen knees; at the age of eighty four she was quite beyond any sense of shame at showing her pantaloons.

"The knees is awful bad, Doctor, and the pain in my hips is wuss still. Do 'ee want to see?"

He assured her that would not be necessary and produced the tincture of guaicum.

"Is that the same stuff you gave me last time? 'Twas marvellous how it took the pain away!"

Back on the road he considered his next call. The truth was he would like to have gone straight home, not because he was reluctant to talk to Pollard's former servant but because, if the rumours proved to be correct, he would have to take further action. How to approach that would indeed be difficult. Amongst a small sector of the population it was considered almost acceptable to abuse a young vulnerable servant, commit the most heinous crime against her and then abandon her and the resultant unfortunate child, condemning the two of them to a life of immorality or of separation and near-starvation in the Workhouse. Toby shied a little as the Doctor slapped the saddle in anger and frustration.

- I *will* not have it!

Such criminals must be brought to justice and if necessary he would do it, however difficult it might prove, he would do it.

He stopped in Old Town, tethered Toby and stood for a moment with his hand on the horse's neck. When he knocked on the door to which Mr Vinson had directed him, it was opened by a young pregnant woman wearing neither apron nor cap, her dark hair in disarray. She looked at him with some suspicion.

"Good morning. Is Mr Short at home?"

"There idn't no Mr Short here. I don't know of one hereabouts."

"Is that so? Then I must have been given the wrong

address. I'm so sorry to have troubled you."

He turned as if to go, then hesitated.

"I seem to recognise you. Did you not work for Mr Pollard at one time? I'm sorry, I must introduce myself. Dr Ackland."

He held out his gloved hand but she did not take it.

"That bugger! He should be locked away, he should, he's a madman! I wouldn't work there again if you gave me five guineas!"

"He is an awkward customer, it's true. I would be interested to hear of your dealings with him. Would you mind if I step inside for a moment? I'm sure you don't want your neighbours overhearing your unfortunate experiences."

She glared at him.

"They know right enough what I think of Mr Pollard. But you can come in if you want. I know you, you healed my ma."

He followed her into a small, sparsely-furnished room. The fire was out and the earth floor damp. He could hear people talking in a back room. Although there were two chairs the young woman, quite devoid of social graces, did not suggest that he should sit, but stood staring out of the window.

"Pardon me troubling you, but I have heard that Mr Pollard treats his servants very badly. I am always keen to iron out any injustice."

He gazed at her and she met his eyes momentarily. She had a large face and wide mouth and could have been attractive were it not for the acquired harshness of her expression.

"Badly? He's a pig! I tell 'ee, he's mazed! He should be locked away! His wife'd be better in the Workhouse than with him! But what are 'ee going to do about it? Can 'ee get him locked up? Can doctors do that?"

"I am a magistrate as well as a doctor. There are things I can do when the occasion warrants it."

He reached for her hand and this time she let him hold it although she turned her face away from him.

"Do you wish to tell me how he treated you?"

She withdrew her hand and sat heavily on the hard chair.

"He was as changeable as the weather, one minute smiling and all going well then of a sudden he'd be shouting and lashing out. He'd hit any of us who was near and many a time I thought he'd kill me! I tell 'ee, I wouldn't go back there for *no* money!"

"And your expected child?"

"Well, 'e threw me out of course. *She'd* have waited 'til I had a house to go to but not him! I was out in the dark and the rain and had to walk to town like that. No shawl on my back! And afraid all the time he was coming after me. 'Twas lucky I had had my sister to go to else I'd have been in the Workhouse that night!"

"You have had a very hard time. You must be glad you are more settled now. Has he made amends to you?"

"Amends? I haven't seen him since and hope I never do. I got a new life now, this chiel coming" – she placed her hand on her belly – "and I'm to be wed next week!"

She grinned up at him. So, now the truth was coming out. There was light and optimism in her eyes when she smiled.

"Wed! So you will have some security for your child."

He patted her shoulder and smiled down at her. "I heard some stories about Mr Pollard. Some said he was the father of the child. I am glad, then, that it is not the case."

"No!"

She looked rather shamefaced.

"I shouldn't have said that, not really. He was bad, but he never did that. I wouldn't have let him! But my man, the one I'm to marry, he'd gone away. I thought I'd end up in the 'House or on the streets, I really did. So I thought, well, Mr Pollard can pay. He's done enough harm. So I said it was him. But my man's back now. I don't want no more to do with Mr Pollard now."

Dr Ackland rode home in pensive mood. So. Pollard's

unpredictability was not confined to his public life. That was not surprising. But there was no further evidence that he was Selina's seducer. Toby swayed from side to side as he braced his legs on the steep descent of Coldharbour. Over the rooftops the view, which at high tide displayed the River Torridge to its best advantage, now presented a sombre expanse of mud extending to the distant huddled cottages of Instow. The Doctor braced his own legs in the stirrups and leaned back in the saddle to make the steep hill easier for Toby. Now he had two problems: whether he should again broach the matter with Selina and encourage her to divulge the name of her seducer, or whether he should take action over Pollard. At what stage did a man's irrational and aggressive behaviour become a medical or judicial matter? It was particularly difficult when he was a public figure.

- Oh, leave it. Leave it for now.

A man climbing the steep hill looked up in surprise and the Doctor chuckled quietly. He would himself get a reputation for irrational behaviour if he did not take care. There were better things to think of than Pollard. The family in Hyfield Place with their precious new child, Pollard's servant starting a new chapter of her life and soon to be a mother herself, and his own home and family, a little smaller now that his older son was away.

- I will write again to Kingsley. Reassure him of our love.

The thought of his family, secure in the warmth of their home, sustained him as he stabled, unsaddled and fed his horse, leaving the animal comfortable for the night.

Chapter Twelve

Selina cast her eye over the kitchen again to make sure that everything was in order. She had put away all the clean dishes after lunch, swept up more of the black beetles with which they had been plagued for the last few days and, yes, Eliza had put out the tea things before she left the house. Five cups, the Doctor was going away on a train and staying the night. She looked into the scrap of mirror that Eliza had given her and straightened her bonnet ribbons under her chin. Then, after checking the kitchen one last time, she tiptoed through the hall, knocked on the drawing room door and entered.

The four children were seated around the fire with their parents, Mary reading to her two younger sisters and Hugh curled up on his father's knee looking at a picture book. Mrs Ackland sat somewhat apart with a small leather-bound book on her lap. Eventually she looked up and Selina curtseyed.

"Please, Ma'am, may I go out now? I've done all my work."

"Let me look at you."

Selina flinched as she was scrutinized from the top of her simple straw bonnet to the toe of her worn black boots.

"Very well. You are going straight to your cousin's, are you not?"

Selina curtseyed again.

"Yes Ma'am."

"Well, do not overstay your welcome and see that you return by seven o'clock. I hope you have an enjoyable time."

"Yes Ma'am. Thank you Ma'am."

She stepped out on to the street with relief. It was mild for the beginning of February and across the road a little weak sunlight glimmered on the small turrets that surrounded the two tall church spires. It was the third Sunday that Selina had been allowed out. The two previous weeks she had had nowhere to go so had walked tentatively around the lower part of the town, carefully avoiding the streets that led up to the Workhouse. She longed to see Ann Champion, to tell her about all that had happened to her and to hear news of Fanny Mock, Harriet Braddon and the rest of them but the very thought of seeing the Workhouse again made her feel shaky. At first she had kept to the shopping streets she knew but had then ventured along the Quay, looking at the fishing boats from a safe distance in the hope that she would see someone from Clovelly who might have news of Will, but there were no familiar faces among the groups of men standing about and she had hurried away when one called out to her. There were some young women walking arm in arm along the Quay and she guessed them to be servants like herself on their afternoon off, although there were also some who looked less than respectable. She considered crossing the bridge but it stretched at such length across the expanse of water that she hesitated, like a rabbit unwilling to venture too far from its burrow. Instead she walked a little way out past the deserted wharves until the town and its inhabitants were left behind and the empty road wound between shrub-covered crags and the gleaming river. She had sat on a large stone on the bank staring at the tranquil expanse of water and its green backdrop of undulating fields and woods, the silence broken only by the shrill calls of a flock of small birds which rose and fell above the river bank like so many dandelion clocks.

But now she had somewhere else to go. She walked towards North Road where Dr Ackland stabled his beautiful bay horse, Toby, then turned cautiously into Coldharbour. The narrow street climbed steeply and she hoped that her cousin's house was not close to the Workhouse. How lucky she was to have bumped into Mary Venning! She had been out on an errand to buy some washing soda last Thursday when someone had called her name. She had not recognised her cousin at first for it had been many years since they had met and they had never been close friends. Mary had lived at the Lodge out near Eastacott, a mile from Clovelly village.

She was plumper now and well-dressed, though Selina did not think her particularly pretty. There had not been time for an exchange of news on Thursday although it seemed that Mary had already heard where Selina was working. Selina had promised to come to tea if she was permitted. Now, as she made her way up the hill, she wondered with some trepidation whether Mary would have remembered the arrangement and whether she knew about the Workhouse and the two fatherless children. Mary had been away from Clovelly for several years and when she did see her family, she probably had better things than Selina to talk about.

She carefully studied the numbers on the front doors of the little cottages as she climbed the steep hill, searching for the one she had memorised.

- There. Twenty-one, a two and a one.

Mary answered the door and Selina followed her into a tidy front room. A baby of a year or thereabouts stood on uncertain legs, holding on to the seat of a chair. As he looked up at Selina he lost his balance and sat down with a bump. Mary picked him up and kissed him.

"This is Thomas."

Selina caressed his soft downy head, taking in every detail of his clear blue eyes and smooth skin.

"Thomas. You'm a lovely boy. My first son was called Thomas."

"Oh, I'm sorry, Selina. I heard about your two babies. The younger one's in Clovelly, isn't he?"

"Yes, 'tis three months since I saw him. Have 'ee heard any news of him?"

Mary had not but it was easy to talk about their respective children, how old they had been when they first stood, how well they slept, the anxieties caused by their illnesses. Mary spoke with confidence of the way she cared for her son and her plans for his future; she had an air of certainty that made Selina feel still a child by comparison.

Selina sat with the seductive weight and warmth of Thomas on her lap until he cried and Mary unbuttoned her dress to feed him. Selina looked around the room. It seemed very small after the rooms to which she had become accustomed but she could imagine herself living as Mary did in this little house.

"Do 'ee have the whole house, Mary? You be married now, be 'ee?"

Mary told her she had married Thomas Parkhouse, a mason, nearly four years ago.

"You wouldn't know him but he worked in Clovelly alongside my father for a while. He's out working now but you may meet him later. He don't like to work of a Sunday but us needs the extra money as the rents are high in Bideford if you want a good cottage. My brother lives with us as well, us helps each other out and us've got all our furniture now. We need the money especially 'cos it's important that us eats well, he so's he can work hard and me so's I can feed Thomas here properly."

Selina gazed at her.

"I learned that when I was working in London. I was nursery maid to a big household in Hyde Park Gardens, Mr Holland's house, twelve servants were kept. You won't know it of course but it is a very fine address, the rooms are so large you could fit this whole cottage into just one of them and there is a balcony looking out over the garden and Hyde Park. Mrs Scriven from Clovelly was the nurse, she got me the job and us had seven children to look after. I learnt a lot there. Are you going to stay in the position you've got?"

"Yes, I passed my month's trial."

"But will you stay? What about your son?"

As Selina hesitated, Mary handed Thomas back to her and got up to make the tea, so she was saved the difficulty of formulating a reply. She could not imagine having the luxury of planning her future and then making it come true. It had not occurred to her to expect any more changes, despite missing Will so much. However when, after a tea of a potato pie and cutrounds with jam, Mary showed her around the little cottage, all she could think of was how much she wanted to have such a house to live in with Will. There was a kitchen with a small stove, a scullery and a privy next to it, a small garden which Mary said was important because Thomas needed plenty of air, and two bedrooms upstairs which meant that if Mary's brother left, Thomas would have his own room when he was weaned. Selina stood at one of the upstairs windows looking out at the view over roofs and chimneys to the fields beyond, fascinated that she could see the twin spires of the church but, try as she might, unable to see which roof belonged to Dr and Mrs Ackland's house.

As they leaned out of the window pointing out landmarks to each other, the front door banged and Mary hurried down to see her husband. Selina followed tentatively. Thomas, wearing dusty work clothes, was a thick-set chap with a full set of whiskers to compensate for prematurely thinning hair. He greeted her loudly and threw himself into a chair. After standing about rather awkwardly for a few minutes while Mary clattered about preparing his tea she thanked them both and prepared to leave.

Mary accompanied her to the door.

"Come and visit again Selina. Us could go for a walk together if the weather's fine. I like to take Thomas out when I can."

She held out the baby to be kissed and as Selina walked down the hill she tried to relive the baby's artless chuckle and sweet scent so that she could remember them when she had a moment to herself. There was now another aspect to her life and as she worked her way through the long days, she would be able to think of Mary and her baby in the wonderful little house. Mary had not said whether she should visit again the next Sunday but another visit so soon would, in any case, seem just too many riches.

Letter, Eveline, Countess of Portsmouth to
Dr W.H. Ackland
(From the papers of the Ackland and Littlewood
families. Reproduced by permission of the Wellcome Library, London)

The whistle sounded. What *was* that note? B? B flat? His daughter Mary would know at once. Dr Ackland leaned forward to watch as the steam-wreathed platform with its usual gathering of admiring small boys slipped away and the slow wheeze of the engine gradually increased to a rhythmic exhalation. They chugged under the bridge and the river again came into view, serene in the late afternoon sunshine. He sat back, glad to have the compartment to himself. Even after all this time, it was enjoyable to take a train. Would it had been available years ago when he travelled more frequently! As an undergraduate at the University College Hospital he had experienced many journeys of twenty four hours and more, travelling between Bideford and London in the cramped discomfort of a small horse-drawn coach. The luxury and speed of modern train travel was, by contrast, always a pleasure. He remembered the excitement when he and Sophia had travelled on the very first train to run on the new line from Barnstaple to Bideford. It was shortly before they married, 1855 and the start of the new modern era and, as the immense power of the engine drew them forwards, they had hardly known whether the cheering and flag-waving was for their own future or that of the train.

He gazed across the River Torridge. The town was now left behind and on the far bank smoke rose from the lime kilns, and men worked in the shipyards. *They* would soon be finishing their day's work, whereas he had already attended eight patients today and would now be seeing two more *and* would be away from home for the night. The train gathered speed and, relaxing into the rocking motion, he debated taking out his book, the Quarterly Journal of the Geological Society, but no, for now the present was preferable. On Captain Christie's fields a fine flock of pedigree sheep grazed, their lambs gathering to race and leap like so many children, as his children had leapt around him as he left. And Kingsley. What would Kingsley be doing this fine Monday afternoon? No doubt there would be a walk, there would be some quiet time for studying. Please God he would be tranquil, his letters suggested he was now more settled. Dear Kingsley.

The tower of Westleigh Church was visible on the skyline and now they were slowing – there was the whistle again! – and swaying past the marsh and towards Instow, with its twin village of Appledore across the river.

Splendid, he still had the compartment to himself. If he could not spend time with his family, he did not want to share it with anyone else. He brushed a speck of dust from his best frock coat. It *was* his best but it was, nevertheless, showing signs of wear. He pulled at a loose thread on the cuff.

- Confounded thing!

He certainly did not want to go to the expense of a new coat. This was perfectly adequate for best and his older one did well for everyday. But one did have to be careful on occasions such as this, one had to appear well-dressed.

– Curse it!

178

He rubbed at a mark on his trousers. Where had *that* come from? Sophia had fussed over him when he left but perhaps he should have taken more notice.

The first time he had made this journey he had taken very great care to make a good impression. What excitement there had been when he had first received a letter asking him to attend the Earl and Countess of Portsmouth at Eggesford, travelling by train and staying overnight! He had been recommended by Lieutenant Colonel and Mrs Hamlyn-Fane at Clovelly Court whom he had been attending for some while. It was, of course, the making of him. When the news spread that he was attending both the Fanes and the Portsmouths and that he was willing to use the esteemed homeopathic remedies, he was the doctor that all the worthy men in the area wanted for their families, and before long he had also been recommended as a Justice of the Peace. But it was not all plain sailing. He gazed out across the broad stretch of the Taw. He was now sent for quite frequently to attend the family or one of the higher servants but, once the novelty of visiting Eggesford had worn off, it had not been a duty he enjoyed. But there it was.

The whistle sounded again – *was* it a B flat? – and they rattled over the bridge and eased into Fremington, the engine hissing gently. He looked out over the marshes, desolate even in the late afternoon sunshine. A solitary figure in a battered hat slid over the mud in search of bait, a wooden bucket swinging from his hand.

The fact was that Isaac Newton Wallop, the Earl of Portsmouth, thought more of his horses than he did of those who worked for him, perhaps more even than his family. Horses, hunting, racing and gambling were what motivated the man.

- But there, I'm only the doctor. I can attempt to heal the body but can do little for the mind.

Of course that was not strictly true, he could frequently did soothe disturbed minds and set wayward temperaments on the right track, but not those as resolute and powerful as the Earl's.

The rhythmic chugg-chugg-chugg of the train slowed as it wheezed and swayed into Barnstaple station. This time there was more shouting and slamming of doors but again he was left in peace. The train then steamed through the meadows of the wide Taw valley, crossing and recrossing the meandering river.

He was, however, hoping he might have the opportunity to converse with the Earl today. His plan for some years had been for a general hospital in Bideford in addition to the isolation hospital that had at last come into being. He was no closer to securing a new building, but it should soon be possible to provide some beds in the Dispensary. More funding was needed before the Local Board would agree but, if the Earl of Portsmouth could be prevailed upon to provide some sponsorship, doubtless others would want to follow suit. Assuming he was invited to dine with the family, it should be possible to bring up the subject. He took the Countess's letter from his pocket and reread it.

They passed the little stations of Umberleigh and the Portsmouth Arms, through a deep cutting then out into the open again where a man with a gun, and a dog at his heels, strolled through the water meadow. A toll house and the rich lands of the Portsmouth estate came into view. The Doctor gathered his belongings and opened the door as the train creaked to a halt at Eggesford Station.

He was the only passenger to disembark and he watched as the men stoked the engine and the immense strength gathered itself and slowly drew the carriages from the platform, gathering speed as they disappeared around the corner.

Now. He turned from the platform and went past the station to the road. It was empty but for a donkey cart laden with sacks disappearing around the bend and two men on foot who took the turning towards Eggesford House. There was no sign of the promised brougham. He gazed out over the valley to the isolated church on the hill, below which sheep grazed on the lush parkland grass. The sun was now low in the sky and the magnificent trees adorning the parkland cast long shadows. A perfect pastoral scene, but he had no intention of walking the mile-long drive to the house. After a few minutes there was still no carriage descending the hill so he knocked on the door of the station master's house.

"I was expecting to be met. Have you any knowledge of a carriage?"

"No, Sir. There were no other guests on the train, Sir. Lord Portsmouth just returned from hunting and 'e's got a crowd of guests with 'im, Sir, so it may be as all the grooms are busy with the 'orses, Sir."

"I *was* expected. Are there any carriages available here?"

"Well, there's a cart in the sawyer's yard there, Sir. I could ask for that to be got up for you, Sir."

"Thank you. I shall wait for ten minutes first in case the brougham is on its way."

The man asked him in and he drank a welcome cup of tea, listening all the while for the sound of an approaching carriage, eager to learn that the apparent slight was merely tardiness. When his tea was finished he asked the man to have the cart prepared.

As the cart drove back down the sweeping carriage drive, he stood back and looked up at the three storey castellated façade of Eggesford House and the multitude of twenty foot high chimneys towering above it. The vast scale of the place never ceased to impress him. He rang the bell by the immense carved oak door and waited for several minutes before a liveried footman appeared.

"Dr Ackland. The Countess is expecting me."

He was led through the entrance hall with its sweeping staircase and into the long gallery. He had once, while waiting to see a patient, paced out the length of this hall so he could impress Sophia with news of its sixty-five foot oak-floored extent, the many doors, seemingly constructed for giants, which opened off it and the ancestral faces which gazed gloomily down from ornate frames on its walls. Today he was shown perfunctorily into the library.

ECCESFORD HOUSE, DEVONSHIRE.

THE SEAT OF THE HONOR.BLE NEWTON WALLOP FELLOWES M.P. TO WHOM THIS PLATE IS MOST RESPECTFULLY INSCRIBED
BY THE PROPRIETORS.

London E. Jennings W. Chaplin 1832

"You will tell the Countess that I am here?"

"Yes, Sir. The family are dining with guests at present, Sir."

The library was cold and somewhat musty. No fire had been lit in the stone fireplace and a single lamp burned on a large table in the centre. He had heard that two servants were employed exclusively to tend to all the lamps in the house, if true it would appear they had overlooked this room. From the adjoining dining room came the murmur of many voices and occasional loud laughter. He walked up and down a few times and gazed from the windows at the rapidly darkening view down across the park, then took the lamp and held it up to the bookshelves that lined the walls. Little of interest, at least on the lower shelves that were illuminated by the lamp. Dull historical tomes that had, from the look of them, not been opened for a century or more. He returned the lamp to the table and took his own book on fossils from his bag.

An hour passed. He was beginning to feel cold despite

having kept on his coat and was decidedly hungry. The laughter from next door had increased and he had heard doors opening and closing. Suddenly the library door opened and a woman of thirty years or so in an elaborate evening gown scurried in and immediately turned her back on him, waiting by the half-open door in a state of obvious excitement. A moment or two passed, then a man slid through the door and put his arm around her waist, pressing her close, and simultaneously perceived the Doctor sitting at the table. It was Lord Portsmouth.

"What the devil are you doing here?"

"I might ask the same of you, my Lord. Were you seeking a book? Perhaps you would allow me to recommend one, Sir?"

In one smooth movement the Earl guided the woman out of the room and moved a few steps nearer the Doctor.

"Well, Dr Ackland! I was not aware that you were calling. Did my wife ask you to attend?"

His manner was obsequious and there was something insincere about the fleshy mouth and slightly hooded eyes.

"She did indeed, my Lord, but I have not had the pleasure of seeing her yet or receiving my instructions. I had just for a moment assumed that the lady who just entered was her Ladyship."

The Earl turned away and wandered towards the darkened window.

"My wife has finished dining now and I'm sure she will see you. We gentlemen are retiring to the smoking room."

He turned but did not meet the Doctor's gaze.

"I can, of course, depend on your discretion. I wish you good night."

Dr Ackland inclined his head but did not reply.

He caught the 11.11 train the next morning having, this time, been driven to the station in the brougham. The visit had been successful after its inauspicious start. The Countess had eventually come to him in the library, full of apologies when she realised how long he had been waiting in the unheated room. It was, in fact, his experience that the servants were frequently offhand but he had kept this thought, and the earlier occurrence, to himself. He had been ushered into the Countess's own cosy sitting room and had been supplied with a commendable dinner, after which he had attended the lady's maid. He had then drunk coffee with the Countess and her mother, Lady Carnarvon, and they had conversed on a range of topics until he had been able to bring the conversation around to the subject of Lady Carnarvon's health. She had accepted his advice and a tonic and had agreed to see a Harley Street doctor that he recommended, so the Countess was very thankful. He had spent a comfortable night in one of the smaller guest bedrooms and had eaten a hearty breakfast. A further consultation with the maid this morning, and his business was done. He would be well-rewarded, but the visit gave him little satisfaction. He had not, of course, been able to bring up the subject of the Bideford hospital.

The train stopped at South Molton Road and he watched as a woman carrying two live chickens in a basket struggled into a compartment and pulled her small child in after her. The line repeatedly crossed the Taw and he gazed out at the river and at the hills that rose from the broad valley floor. A large dog fox trotting through the riverside meadow stopped and stared at the train then ran swiftly to a sheltering wood.

- Watch out, Reynard, the Earl of Portsmouth and his huntsmen are about. He is more than a match for you in cunning.

He had chosen to breakfast in his bedroom that morning, not wishing to socialise with the Earl and his guests, but he had seen them mounting the beautifully turned-out horses below in the stable yard and had recognised the lady he had seen in the library.

Well, some who were called gentlemen were not worthy of the title, yet he had known some poverty-stricken men who were gentlemen indeed. He was not one of those that felt that England would become a benighted nation now that the working man had won the right to vote. He did not even believe that suffrage would lead to radical change, although he sometimes wished that it would. There were incidents of self-indulgence and immorality in every class but it was particularly unfortunate when it was seen in those who should have been setting an example to those beneath them.

Lord Portsmouth was one case in point, and a certain member of the Local Board another.

- Mr Pollard. What to do about *him*?

That was another problem he had still to solve. And he was no further ahead with the funding for the hospital.

Chapter Thirteen

Selina clung to the seat as the carriage jolted on the rough road. Toby was trotting so fast that the hedges seemed to stream past the windows and the bends in the road ahead, though partly obscured by Charles on his high seat, arrived almost as soon as she caught sight of them. Through a gate she glimpsed a flock of sheep with their lambs and then a man clearing a ditch waved to her. She shuffled back on the slippery seat and a little closer to the side of the carriage which was lined with soft buttoned leather, for she was afraid that at the next bump she would bounce right up against Dr Ackland. He did not appear concerned at their speed, indeed he was humming to himself as he looked out of the window and every now and then he broke into song.

"The ash grove, the ash grove alone is my home!"

She had to be careful not to laugh.

It was last night that he had given her the news. She had been removing the tray from the drawing room and Mrs Ackland had been yawning and saying she must go to bed when Dr Ackland suddenly spoke.

"Ah, Selina!"

"Yes, Sir?"

"I have calls to make in Clovelly tomorrow. You may come with me if you wish in order to visit that young son of yours. We shall leave after breakfast."

She had nearly dropped the tray, but Mrs Ackland had not been pleased.

"Tomorrow? Who is to do all the work? And Mrs Bazeley and her daughters are coming to tea – there is *extra* work to do!"

She could hear raised voices after she closed the door, but she had known that the Doctor would not go back on his word.

She had got up extra early this morning to make sure she would have time to change into her new dress and do her hair after breakfast. Her hair was just long enough to put up properly now, although it was still inclined to escape and fall down. The dress was an old one of Mrs Ackland's that she had given her to wear on Sundays. It was a dark blue and very plain but now that she had taken it in, it fitted very closely and well and Eliza had said that the colour suited her complexion. She had a small piece of ribbon in a lighter blue at the neck that she had bought out of her last wages, she also had a present for Will and the rest of the money was tied in a handkerchief to give her parents.

She would see Will today! She would like to have jumped out of the carriage and run all the way to Clovelly because it was so hard to sit still when she knew she would soon be able to hold him and to hear his voice. A sudden thought struck her and she must have gasped because the doctor turned to her enquiringly.

"'e'll be in school! Will'll be in school 'til the end of the day!"

"Oh, don't let that worry you! You can just go to the school and take him out, I'm sure the teacher'll not object."

Of course. He made everything so easy. A good thing he did because she would not be here otherwise. Mrs Ackland was not the only one who had been displeased at her going. When Eliza had heard the news she had marched off to see Mrs Ackland and when she came back had shouted at Selina.

"*I* never get a day off! And why not? Because *I* haven't got a bastard child! *I* know to keep my legs closed 'til I'm wed!"

She had still been irritable in the morning.

It was hard to see anything much from the carriage because the hedges were so high and their seats low down but suddenly the Doctor pointed to the window.

"There! There's the sea! Do you not wish you were on the open sea with the wind in your face instead of in this musty carriage?"

187

"No Sir, I don't. 'Tis too rough and makes me sick."

He laughed. She always felt like joining in when he laughed.

"I confess I am not a great sailor myself although I often have to sail to Lundy when the lighthouse keepers or others in that windy place are sick. But my dear friend Mr Charles Kingsley, after whom Kingsley is named, always prefers to go to Clovelly by sea."

Even from this distance the sea looked vast, grey and forbidding. She could hardly believe she had travelled all the way to Clovelly on it. Such a long time ago it seemed, yet she could still remember the soft, warm weight as Will slept in her arms, his head resting on her breast.

"He returned to Clovelly regularly to gain inspiration for his books. No doubt you met him when you were younger – he was very well known and liked in the village."

"Yes Sir, I did."

She remembered Mr Charles Kingsley coming to the cottage and talking with her father on several occasions; he seemed to be friends with everyone in the village. He always caused a flurry because he was a gentleman and the best cups had to be taken out and the pile of ironing hurriedly hidden behind a chair. She seemed to remember that when she was very young he once took her on to his knee and she had been rather afraid, he seemed to frown and smile at the same time and she hadn't been sure whether or not he was cross. She did not like to tell the Doctor this; it embarrassed her now to think of sitting on a man's knee.

"Now we are coming to the Hoop's Inn so we know our journey is half completed."

Toby was walking down a hill now and ahead of them in a little valley was a thatched inn, as long as a whole terrace of cottages. She could remember passing it when she was walking to the Workhouse, for there was little to notice on the long road from Clovelly. She had stopped to ask for a glass of water, and a kind woman in the kitchen had given her a piece of bread and cheese.

"I walked past it when I was expecting Thomas."

"Ah. Poor Thomas."

He turned to observe her.

"That was not such a happy journey as this, I fancy?"

"No Sir. It were a long way and I was afraid. But worse still was the journey back to the Workhouse when I was expecting Will. I knew what lay ahead then."

"Ah yes. And you had been very badly treated, had you not?"

"Yes Sir."

"It was a farm to the east of the town, I believe."

"Yes Sir."

"There are several I know out that way. Southcott and Tennacott and Stone. Was it one of those where you worked?"

"Sir. I'm sorry, Sir, but I don't want to remember it."

"Very well."

He patted her hand.

"It is often difficult to relive painful memories. Some think that doing so can lead to great instability of mind but I prescribe to the view that these things are better mulled over and understood. That way one can progress in life. Now here we are at Buck's Cross. On our return journey we must descend into Buck's Mills for I have two pauper patients to attend there. In Clovelly I have to see Miss Christine Fane and then make several calls for the Clovelly Mariners' Society."

She knew Dr Ackland would like her to tell her that man's name but she could not. Dr Ackland did not look cross. He had taken some papers from his bag and was trying to write something with a pencil, although she could see that his writing was shaky because of the movement of the carriage.

At last they reached the turning down to Clovelly and began the long descent through the upper village and she cried out and pointed, for there in front of them was the sudden immense view of the sea that reached out to meet the sky, a vast, silent presence that made her catch her breath.

"Yes, there it is. You are home again."

She stared at the sea as Toby, walking again now, drew them ever closer. The small group of women outside the cottages, the carriage from the Rectory passing by, the turning to the church, all these were seen as if in a dream and it was only the ocean, the hugeness of it, that held her attention. At last they reached the top of the High Street and the Doctor was telling her he would come to her parents' cottage in the afternoon and she was walking down the steep cobbled street in the fine misty rain and it was just the same as it had always been, the close cottage windows looking in at her, the first flowers already in bloom in the little gardens and the sounds echoing from the sides of the deep cleft that held the village - the braying of the donkeys, the raised voices calling from garden to garden and the barking of the dogs. And now here was Mrs Harris outside her cottage staring and then calling out -

"'Tis Esther Burman's daughter!"

And others came out to look until she reached her parents' cottage and her mother was already running out to greet her.

Almost at once she set off again to the newly-built school to which her mother directed her, hurrying back up the cobbled street and into Wrinkleberry Lane with her heart pounding, running with her skirts held up away from the long wet grass that grew in the centre of the lane, arriving out of breath at the school door and only hesitating for a moment before going in.

The room was quiet. A smell of warm bodies, chalk dust and the smoking stove. Every face looked up and stared at her. She could not see him. Sitting in the front row, her sister Ellen gasped, her hand over her mouth, smiling.

"Yes, what can I do for you?"

He sounded confrontational rather than helpful. It was old Mr Dannell and he did not recognise her.

"I be looking for William Burman."

"William Burman is in the next room."

She pushed past the forms, squeezing Ellen's hand as she passed, to reach the door when she heard Mr Dannell's voice again.

"You will knock on that one, Miss, please."

She knocked and entered. They started singing as she went in, almost as if they had planned it, one shrill female voice carefully enunciating the words and twelve childish voices straggling along behind.

"Now the dreary night is done,
Comes again the glorious sun,
Crimson clouds, and silver white,
Wait upon his breaking light."

She scanned the little upturned faces gazing at her and there he was. A bit plumper and more grown-up, opening his mouth in time to the music. Their eyes met and he gazed at her, puzzled.

She turned to the teacher who had put her finger on her lips to hush the children.

"Please Miss, I've come for William Burman. I'm his mother."

And there they were, hand in hand outside in the drizzly rain. She knelt down to him, careless of her skirt, hugged him to her breast then held him at arm's length and looked at him.

"Will, Mama's back, Mama's back to see you. You remember me?"

He nodded solemnly, his head down, gazing up at her through his lashes. His mouth was a tight little bud. She straightened his cap and buttoned his jacket, which almost outgrown, and re-tied his dragging bootlaces.

"What a big boy you be now, going to school! Are you a good boy and learn your lessons? Mama's learning to write too, Will! Us'll write letters to each other when us gets good at writing!"

He pulled away and ran down the lane, looking back to see if she was coming. She followed him, almost tripping as she watched him pause with rapt concentration and jump over a puddle with feet together, pull a stick from the high hedgerow and slash at the roadside weeds. He was a fine, strong-looking boy now with good sturdy legs. Her son! All those months when she had been Selina, the housemaid, the one from the Workhouse, seemed to vanish. She was Selina Burman, from Clovelly, mother of William Burman and there he was running down the lane, just as if she fetched him from school every day.

When they reached the cottage, Will opened the door and ran in.

"Nanna, Mama's here!"

Then he sat on a chair and stared at her as she came in. Her mother had made tea and they sat and had a cup together – Will too; she had never seen him drink tea before. When he had finished he ran to the door but Selina called him back, so he sat on the chair again, kicking the rungs.

"Here, Will, I've a present for 'ee. I bought it special from my wages 'cos Mama's working now, you see."

She unwrapped the little wooden boat she had chosen at Mrs Murphy's toy shop when she was out on an errand, agonising over the limited choice she had for her tuppence. It was small and roughly carved but had a little figure sitting in it, a mast with a white cloth sail and a string to pull it along. He took it and examined it carefully. He liked it, she was sure. He pulled it along the floor and over the edge of the rug as if it were riding the waves, murmuring to himself all the while. There was fluff on the floor by the fireplace and she resolved to have a sweep up when she had finished her tea. The whole room looked as if could do with a good clean.

Will was lying on his stomach now, sailing his boat past the chair leg.

"He's looking well, Ma. He's strong, in't he? There haven't been any illnesses or fevers?"

"No, no, nothing like that. He's not easy tho', Selina. He's been in a bit of trouble in the village."

"Trouble, what sort of trouble?"

"Well, he goes running in people's houses without asking."

"Us all did that. Us knew everyone."

Her mother was looking down, folding and re-folding the

hem of her apron.

"Yes, but he runs in and takes things, food mostly. Folks have complained to me several times. He's not easy and I'm getting too old to have a little one like him around."

She dropped her apron and looked at Selina.

"I do it for you Selina, but 'tis hard sometimes."

Her mother was making something out of nothing, she was sure. She would see things differently if Selina were married or if Will was one of her sister's sons. She could see he was a good boy, good and quiet, not unruly. They had all got into scrapes when they were little and had been yelled at a few times by one neighbour or another.

"Well, if he's taking food he must be hungry, he wouldn't do it else. You can't be giving him enough to eat."

"Of course he gets enough to eat! Any case, he don't always eat what he takes. Folks wouldn't mind if, well, I dunno, if he was just normally cheeky I suppose. They say 'tis the way he just runs in and runs out without looking at folks. And last week he let all Mr Headen's chicks out of the coop, just opened the door and ran off and some of them were lost."

Her mother wasn't making any sense. It was because she was ashamed of Will, that was what it was. Selina bent down and lifted Will and his boat on to her lap. They were silent for a while.

"I'm sending you enough money, amn't I? I send you all of it, only keep a penny or two for myself."

"The money's useful Selina, I won't pretend it isn't. And of course I see that he gets enough to eat, you know I wouldn't see him go without, not while us has the money coming in."

Her mother turned her cup round and round in her hands. It was a new one with a blue pattern on a white background. There were some matching plates on the dresser; they would have come from the pedlar. Selina pulled Will closer and he rested his head against her neck. It was true that her mother would not let him go hungry, but the money she sent was more than enough for his food.

"Anyway you'm looking bowerly, Selina. I don't know when I've seen 'ee looking so well. The extra weight suits 'ee."

"I *feel* well, Ma. 'Tis the food I reckon."

"They feeds you well then?"

"I've never had food like it! Us has meat everyday and cake, near enough as much as us wants."

"Well, you've got colour in your cheeks, you really have, and that despite having an indoor life."

"My monthlies have started again, first time since Will was born. In the Workhouse lots of women said their monthlies had stopped."

"There! And the work's not too hard at the Doctor's?"

"Oh, 'tis hard 'cos everything has to be just so, not a speck of dust anywhere – and the water! I be for ever carrying bath jugs of water upstairs 'cos they're for ever washing, all of 'em. All the water has to be carried up to the top floor for the five children, fresh for each of 'em then the dirty water down again. Water and coal. The coal that's used - a fire in every room! You wouldn't believe how much! I'm fit to drop by the end of the day. But I've learnt heaps, it's not like any house I'd been in before."

"And they'm good to you?"

"Oh, they're fair. And Dr Ackland, he's so kind, Ma, and so good and loving to his children. I'd do anything for *him*!"

She helped her mother peel the potatoes for dinner but kept stopping to watch Will who was still playing with his boat. Her father came in having been laid off for the afternoon, there being a shortage of work at that time of year. His face lit up when he saw her and she broke off from the dinner preparations to explain to him how she came to be there.

"Oh, you'm not staying then?"

He seemed quite disappointed that she was only visiting for the day.

"Look at 'ee now! You'm looking a proper lady!"

He said he had been telling everyone about the good

situation she had in Bideford and the money she was able to send home.

"Come on out now, come and see Gran and Grandfer Tucker, let 'em see how vitty you'm looking!

They left Mrs Burman to her preparations for a while and called on the neighbours where her appearance was admired and she was questioned about the grand house that she lived in and the number of other servants that were kept. But as they left, Granny Tucker patted Selina's arm and said confidingly,

"'Tis important to have a good situation, chiel, seeing as 'tis likely you'll always have to earn your living. There bain't many men as'll take a wife who's been rumpsin' about."

Selina turned away in shame, although the remark was meant kindly. There were plenty of girls who got pregnant out of wedlock but she knew that to have done so twice with no chance of marrying the father and, particularly, to have spent so long in the dreaded Workhouse was a stigma that would never be forgotten.

After dinner she told Will she would take him down to the harbour. He looked up at her quizzically.

"See boats, Mama?"

She was reminded of Hugh having conversed knowledgably about the schooners and cutters on Bideford Quay and felt a pang of anxiety. But then at five Hugh was a year older than Will; Will would catch up, she was sure of it. After all, he was going to school now.

"Yes, see the boats, my flower, and us can sail yours in the stream."

Will had insisted on holding his boat in one hand during dinner, but still managed to eat a good meal. Although she would not have told her mother so, Selina enjoyed watching him eat rather more than she enjoyed the somewhat over-salted fish and potato stew herself.

They stepped out of the cottage together and walked hand in hand through the narrow cobbled passageways to the High Street.

"In Bideford, Will, there are grand buildings and shops with windows as wide as that cottage, so's you can see all the things you can buy!"

He pulled his hand away and crouched down by the stream that ran down the side of the street. Despite its fast current, it was a muddy brown and carried debris of doubtful origin. Had it always been that dirty? She and her brother and sisters had always played in it as children, but she felt uncomfortable seeing Will putting his hands in it. She knew the difference now between clean dirt, like coal dust, and dirty dirt, like rotting things. You could get ill from dirty water.

"Come on Will, us'll sail your boat in the sea."

There, he was not a bad boy, he did not protest when she pulled him away and began the steep descent. The fine rain had cleared, and a little weak February sunshine filtered through the slowly drifting clouds, illuminating the blue-grey roofs and whitewashed walls of the cottages below. Beyond the steeply tiered roofs lay the shimmering silver-grey sea, the ever-present backdrop to her childhood, and now to Will's.

"Shall us throw pebbles into the water when us gets there, Will?"

Four visitors had just arrived outside the New Inn; the two ladies in fine travelling costumes of purple and dark green with matching hats and the gentleman in frock coats and top hats. Their numerous pieces of luggage were being unloaded from the donkeys, having been carried down the hill from the afternoon coach, while they exclaimed at the prettiness of the cottages and the steepness of the path they had descended, declaring it to be more staircase than street. They wished Selina a good afternoon and smiled at Will. It was strange that whereas in Bideford she was just an unimportant maid, here she was considered to be part of the attraction.

Her descent to the harbour was slow, as she was greeted first by Mrs Parsons who sat knitting in her doorway, then by old Mr Stevens. Both asked about her new employment and others came from neighbouring cottages to listen; twice she was told she should keep a close eye on Will. Next she saw

Grace Whitefield. They had played together as children, but Grace eyed her rather warily. She was courting William Howard, she said, and they hoped to marry one day. She looked away as she said it, as if marriage was beyond Selina's understanding. She did not look at Will or say anything about the last eight years of Selina's life. All the while Selina could feel Will's little hand in hers as he stood by her, good and quiet, but it seemed that no one would forget the circumstances of his birth, however he behaved.

The bench at the Lookout was empty and she sat for a while, glad to be alone with Will before the final descent to the Quay Pool. She tried to ask him about the other children at his school and whether he had any friends but, although he was able to list the children's names, he could not tell her about any games they played together. But still, he was strong and healthy, that was the most important thing. She stroked his hair, it reached his collar now and was almost blond, just like she remembered it when he was a baby. But his neck was dirty, despite it being only three days since his weekly bath. She wondered whether he was left to wash himself.

"See boats now, Mamma."

"Yes, us'll go and see the boats now, my flower."

She glimpsed a clock as they passed the open door of a cottage above Temple Bar and thought of the glass-fronted clock that ticked away the minutes and the hours in the dining room in Bridgeland Street. She had learnt to tell the time and often glanced at it to know whether she was getting behind with her work. The clock hands were moving and time was passing even though she was here with Will; it would not be very long before Dr Ackland came to take her away.

When they reached the harbour she went hesitantly to the blue-jerseyed fishermen who sat outside the Red Lion and passed the time of day with them, knowing that they would otherwise stare at her all the time she was on the beach. They returned her greeting laconically and glanced at her briefly, their eyes deeply crow-footed from long hours spent gazing at the sea. She led Will down the slipway on to the pebbles. She was adroit at stepping quickly from one to another, but Will's little feet slid down between the rounded stones, so she carried him to the sea, even though she knew the fishermen would be making remarks about her babying him.

The afternoon was short, but provided memories for her to dwell on for many weeks. The calm immensity of the ocean and the gentle, repetitive swish-swash of the waves at its edge; the incessant splashing of the waterfall at the base of the cliff and Will's delighted laughter as they ran through it together; his concentration as he gazed at his boat bobbing on the edge of the water, dwarfed by the moored fishing vessels and ancient harbour wall beyond; then the moment when, tired from throwing pebbles, he climbed into her lap and rested his head against her, holding tight to her thumb as if he too were savouring the moment, aware that she would soon have to leave.

Dr Ackland strode down the street, swinging his bag and scattering the hens that pecked between the cobbles. As always, he was brought to a standstill by the vista that opened suddenly in front of him and he paused by the railings that guarded the sheer cliff. It was a view of which he would never tire. The precipitous grey-roofed cottages and vivid green woodland, the grey pebble beach that curved alongside the steep, verdant cliffs as far as the distant village of Buck's Mills and, beyond it all, the vast and silent ocean. What had changed since he leant here on the railings ten, twenty or even thirty years ago? It was as if time had stood still, for the deep fissure that held the village shut out the noisy modern world; here neither the power of steam nor even that of the wheel could hold sway. The birdsong, the calling voices and the cries of gulls that rose and echoed from its sides – were they not the same songs, the same voices that he had heard so many times before? How strange to think how *his* life had changed since he first came here as a boy! How was it possible that he now had seven fine children of his own? But of course in reality the cycle of life continued here too. There were births, there were deaths, there was pain.

He consulted his pocket watch - a few more minutes would do no harm - and turned to lean back on the railings and view the scene from a different angle. Above the patchwork of little gardens with their beds of leeks and tall brassicas, their lines of motionless washing, their pigsties and henhouses, the wooded hill rose up to a silver grey sky. The cottage from which he had just departed had a row of fine cabbages and a tumbledown linhay crammed with flotsam and jetsam for firewood. The old fisherman had told him of the sudden and violent pains across his chest that came on without warning, but seemed more frequent after climbing a stretch of the street, "going upalong" as he said. What a place to live for one suffering from *angina pectoris* - for that was, no doubt, the cause of the pain. He had recommended rubbing warm applications onto the chest, had prescribed an anodyne and reassured the anxious wife, but he knew that the disease would soon take its course and the end was likely to be sudden. There were no children. The tiny income from mending nets would end, the unfortunate widow would be prevented by her rheumatism from keeping up the garden and the Society would not be able to support her, so it was probable that she would end her days in the Union Workhouse. A harsh environment for whoever had the misfortune to go there, but for one who had spent her entire life in surroundings such as these... He sighed. There were times when the little he could do fell so far short of what he would wish.

Well, Selina at least would have had a happy day. He stroked the small grey cat that was winding itself around his legs, picked up his bag and set off down the hill to her parents' house, calling out a greeting to two small children who ran to the safety of their front door, before turning to gaze at him, wide-eyed.

He took out his notebook but Charles, who had hoped to be home before dark, was driving at such a pace it was impossible to write. He had been somewhat terse when Dr Ackland and Selina had returned to the brougham and, after they were both seated, had made a point of lighting the lamps to emphasise their lateness, quite unnecessarily as there was still some time to go before sunset. He checked his notes. The calls in Buck's Mills would probably not be lengthy, although one was to a house he had never before visited and advice about hygiene would no doubt be necessary, perhaps details of the landlord obtained if the house was very broken down.

Selina was subdued. He glanced at her. She was looking down and fidgeting with the edge of her jacket; he did not speak to her again, having already realised that she was close to tears. Well, it was natural enough, she had, after all, just bade farewell to her son. He knew only too well how painful that was.

When he had knocked on the door he had heard scurrying within and the mother's voice declare,

"Oh, my dear life!"

He had chuckled to himself. Most cottagers found it necessary to hurriedly tidy up when he called but he soon saw when he entered that Selina had been the main instigator of the hasty organisation. Many girls returned from service with the view that their mother's housekeeping was inadequate, having been exposed to higher standards of cleanliness and new ideas about decoration. There was uneasiness in this household however, a tension between mother and daughter. Now why was that? Mr Burman was a solid sort and had reacted to the perceived need for deference by roaring out his answers to enquiries about estate work, in the mixture of embarrassment and defiance often seen in the labouring classes.

While drinking his tea and discussing the season's herring catch – the son's occupation was apparent from the navy blue garments drying over chairs and the fishing lines, blocks, pulleys and sail thimbles littered over the dresser – he observed the child sitting on the rug in front of the fire. His manner was somewhat peculiar. He neither listened to nor craved attention from the adults around him, but neither was he truly absorbed in his play, which consisted of repeatedly pushing a toy boat along the floor. Selina fussed over him, but he shook off her attentions as he would those of a fly. He did not appear to be an imbecile. He had seen a child this week, a girl of two years or so whose vacant eyes and delayed development spoke clearly of that condition and he had had to indicate gently to the parents that their first child was not normal. Young Will's eyes possessed intelligence, but there was a strange lack of emotion. Perhaps it was the child's ways that were causing its mother extra grief now.

"Young William looks a strong healthy boy."

She turned to him gratefully. "Oh, do 'ee think so, Sir? *I* do, and Mother says 'e's not had a day of illness. Do 'ee think 'e'll thrive, Sir?"

"I do indeed. He's a fine boy. And good at his lessons, is he? And not too much trouble to your mother?"

She stared down at her jacket again.

"'Tis not easy for Mother. Her's wore out with rearing children. But her should take more care of him!"

She looked up at him, her distress overcoming her shyness.

"Folks are all talking about 'im! Saying 'e's a bad boy - 'e's not! I know 'e's not!"

"Ah. And why do they say that of him?"

"They say he steals! And Grandfer Lee, us met 'im when us came up off the beach, 'e said Will'd end up in prison if I don't take'n in hand. But what can I do? I can't 'ave 'im with me when I be working!"

"No indeed, you cannot. And do you believe what they say?"

"No, I don't. 'E's a good boy. 'Tis only that, - 'e's got no father. And 'e was born in the Workhouse. So they've made up their minds 'e's no good."

"Yes, I'm afraid that may be so."

No use to voice his fears that there was something amiss with the boy. He reassured her that her son was in the best possible place that the situation allowed, and had his family and the community to keep him on the right path. In truth he wondered whether there was something in the boy's parentage that predisposed him to unsocial behaviour. Was he indeed Pollard's son?

Chapter Fourteen

Sophia hesitated outside the tall, forbidding door. She was aware that her hands, grasping three bunches of wild daffodils bought in the Pannier Market earlier that day, were shaking a little. If she turned away now, surely she would be seen from one of the many windows. Might someone not call after her? Without allowing herself to think further about what could lie ahead, she raised the door knocker and banged firmly on the door.

It was the disagreement with her husband two days previously that had brought her to the Workhouse. He had been adamant that Selina was to go with him – as if the girl's desires were of greater importance than his wife's! They had not often come so close to an argument and this time she had attempted to stand her ground. She was sure he had never spoken to her in such contemptuous tones before. His words still stung her. He had asked how she could consider tea-drinking and idle chatter more important than Selina's need to visit her son. Had she any idea of what Selina had suffered? Did she feel no sympathy? He seemed to have forgotten that Selina had brought about her own downfall. And he had overlooked what she herself had experienced as a young woman - did not she, of all people, understand adversity? Well, now she would prove it. He would not be able to accuse her of ignorance again.

He would not approve of her visiting the Workhouse, she knew that. He preferred her to support his work by maintaining a comfortable, happy home to which he could retire at the end of the day; he did not wish his wife to be involved with his patients, even though he agreed that the ladies who visited the poor could sometimes help a little to alleviate suffering. Well, she was here, whether he liked it or not.

She could hear someone approaching now. Suddenly the metal grille in the heavy door slid open and a face looked out at her suspiciously.

"Yes?"

"I have come to pay a visit."

It was, of course, absurd but she had worried that the purpose of her call might be misconstrued. She had changed from her dark brown day dress into the rather smarter grey and had put on her dusky pink bonnet that she generally kept for Sundays. The idea of being mistaken for a gentlewoman fallen on hard times was too embarrassing to contemplate. As the man stared out at her challengingly, she raised her chin a little and spoke out again with forced confidence.

"I have come to pay a visit to the ward for infirm women. I have brought some flowers as a gift."

"Nobody's made arrangements for a visit this afternoon. Us isn't expecting no one."

"No, I have not made arrangements but I would like to visit nevertheless. I am Dr Ackland's wife."

The man's face changed at this. He stared at her a moment longer, then unbolted the door. She had been advised that it would be best to visit the ward for elderly and infirm women, at least on the first occasion. It was said that some of the language and behaviour in the able-bodied women's ward could be quite shocking and that the children's ward was too distressing. The men's ward was, of course, quite out of the question. She followed the man across an empty yard to the main building where they passed through a series of doors, the sound of each as it was unlocked and relocked echoing around the bare walls and stone floors of the corridors. A strong smell of carbolic overlay something sourer, a most disgusting odour, as if stale clothes and the contents of drains were being boiled together with cabbage; she felt her stomach tighten and she lifted her skirts an inch or two above the floor.

They passed a deep, dark stairwell where a coarse-featured woman of indeterminate age looked down on them expressionlessly as she swept the stone stairs, then a clanging bell reverberated through the building, making Sophia flinch, and was followed by the sound of chairs scraping on stone floors and then loud footsteps. Suddenly the next door opened and a young woman stood back as a column of children passed through. Sophia opened her mouth to greet them but they approached and passed with heads bowed like little automatons devoid of vivacity, first the biggest boys of ten or twelve years then descending in size to the smallest of two or three years, followed by the girls ranged in the same way. All had their hair cropped viciously and unevenly close to their heads, all wore a uniform of coarse striped cloth. Most seemed oblivious of her presence; the few who looked up at her incuriously had sore, red eyes and one or two had thickly running noses. Then they were gone, the unsmiling young woman following, her keys in her hand.

As her guide opened the final door, he stood back to let her pass.

"'Ow long would 'ee like, Ma'am, one hour?"

Too flustered to disagree she stopped just inside the room and heard the door being locked behind her. The bitterly cold room was bare but for two long forms along its walls and a rough wooden table in the middle. Around the table sat four elderly women on hard chairs, apparently engaged in sewing. Another eight or nine bent shapes sat on the backless forms, all dressed in shapeless, blue-striped gowns, white aprons, grey shawls and small white caps. One twisted around to gaze sightlessly at the ceiling, moaning,

"Help me! Help me! Help me!"

Sophia felt her heart pounding. Those who were sewing and one or two on the forms peered up at her and in every lined face was despair and degradation. This was not what she had imagined. Where were the grateful smiles and the welcoming fire? If she had not heard the doors being locked she would, at that moment, have turned and ran from the building. As the futile cry for help continued, she forced herself to step forward.

"Good afternoon. I have come to visit and to read to you, if you would like that. And, look, I have brought some daffodils!"

As she held up the flowers with their stems wrapped in bright green moss, their vibrant yellow trumpets shone out into the dreary room. For a moment she thought them to be the most beautiful things she had ever seen. A faint - aaahhh! - of appreciation came from one or two toothless mouths. One woman eased herself from her chair, shuffled over and took the daffodils.

"Thank 'ee, Ma'am."

She gave an awkward little bob, her knees being too stiff to curtsey, and hobbled off to a cupboard, returning with a jar. Several women continued to gaze vaguely in Sophia's direction but none spoke except the one who was still pleading for help. She made herself walk across the room and draw up a chair at the table. She felt uncomfortable to be sitting among them but it seemed preferable to sitting on the end of the form. As she did so, she realised that the sour smell was that of urine. She pulled her skirts close, quickly opened her Bible at Psalm 23 and took a deep breath.

"The Lord is my shepherd; I shall not want. He maketh me to lie down in green pastures: he leadeth me beside the still waters. He restoreth my soul: he leadeth me in the paths of righteousness for his name's sake. Yea, though I walk through the valley of the shadow of death, I will fear no evil: for thou art with me: thy rod and thy staff they comfort me."

The old woman sitting across the table, who had been trying short-sightedly to thread her needle, put her sewing in her lap and started to cry silently. Sophia carried on to the end then turned quickly to Psalm 121, then 123. She had the attention of all around the table now and several on the forms were leaning forward to hear. She read through several more psalms, gradually slowing down her delivery and gathering her courage until finally she closed her Bible and looked up. A murmur of appreciation went around the table. She began to realise that the ones sitting with her were those who were more competent, probably the only ones who were capable of attempting to sew the rough cloth they held. As she spoke to them of God's mercy she observed the sad remnants of humanity on the forms. Several looked far too ill and old to be sitting on hard backless benches. One had an expression of exaggerated contentment on her face which was more unsettling than the expressions of despondency. One woman, a lot younger than the rest, was clearly an idiot. She rocked rhythmically back and forth on the bench, intently watching her hands which writhed and intertwined close to her face. There were bald patches amongst her closely cropped hair.

Sophia saw that those around the table were watching her intently, but one or two were clearly too deaf to take in unfamiliar words. Surely they were visited regularly by the minister? She stopped, then raised her voice, addressing the one who had fetched the water for the flowers. Was she comfortable in this place? Was she well cared for? Gradually, in response to further questioning, the old woman told falteringly how most people were kind and the food was sufficient, but she missed the broken-down cottage with the ancient rose tree by the door where she had lived until her friend died. She missed her chair by the fire. She would like her old plate with the faded willow pattern, as here all the plates and mugs were of tin and she was unable to make a cup of tea when she wanted. She missed hearing the sparrows chirping at her window when she woke and she did *so* miss the old oak tree. She had hoped to die in sight of that tree. Sophia sat very still; she felt quite unable to reply. As the old woman spoke she stared at the wall with weak, watery eyes as if she saw there all the mourned accoutrements of her former life. Also, she said, she missed the solitude, for she had never married and even as a servant had been accustomed to her own room.

"I 'as to share a bed with 'er", she said, indicating the woman across the table, who had stopped crying but still gazed into her lap.

"'Er misses 'er 'usband, 'e's in the men's ward."

The other now looked up and started to plead with Sophia in a high wavering voice. Please, would she help? Would she speak to the Guardians about the funerals for herself and her husband? They'd always dreaded having a pauper's burial and years ago had paid a little into a Burial Club so they could have bells and decent coffins. She was afraid the Guardians did not know about the money they had saved and, the sparse tears started to run down her lined cheeks again, she could only see her husband once a week for a few minutes and in any case he had lost his mind. Her children were dead or moved away. Please, would Sophia speak to the Guardians for her?

Sophia promised she would. She was afraid she, too, would start to cry. She fingered the coarse calico that the woman was sewing.

"What is it that you are sewing?"

"'Tis shrouds. Us is all sewing shrouds."

Sophia withdrew her hand quickly. The plea for help from the old woman on the bench grew more insistent. Sophia felt she should sit nearer to read from the Bible in case deafness had prevented her from hearing, but she felt her nerves were not up to it.

"'Er does that all day and all night. 'Tis all us hears - Help, help, all the time."

How was it possible to bear the knowledge that one would end one's days in such a place? She tried to calculate how long she had been here now. It seemed far longer than an hour. She pulled one of the jars of daffodils closer and, turning it this way and that, started to talk about the hedgebanks out in the country which were now starred with wild daffodils and primroses, and the buds on the trees that would soon burst forth, and her children who loved to run in the woods and gather the flowers, but the despair that surrounded her was beginning to drag her down. This was not her life, she told herself silently. She was not one of them. She would not sleep here tonight. She would not share a bed and inhale that fearful smell. She was apart from this. She was

Mrs William Ackland. She was Sophia.

Later she lay in her own bed, gazing unseeingly towards the curtained window. She had tried to have tea with the children but could not respond to their chatter. After a while she had complained of a headache and had come upstairs, and Selina had brought her cocoa and a flannel to soothe her brow. Her husband had returned and, after running up the stairs, had gently examined her and pronounced her overtired, a diagnosis to which she had contributed by closing her eyes against his loving concern. She did not tell him where she had been. He had been wrong when he had said she had no understanding of adversity. If she turned away from suffering, it was because it distressed her so very much. Now she stared at the window and she let the years fall away, the memories that she had tried to bury playing out as if on a stage before her.

She was 25 years old, in her father's house in Honiton. She and her five sisters sat in the drawing room, Lucy holding her neglected embroidery in her lap, Eliza sitting listlessly at the piano that had remained unplayed for days and Frances pacing restlessly at the window. None of them spoke. At last they heard the front door open and waited, hardly daring to breathe, until their brother Herman entered the room. His demeanour told them at once the news they waited to hear. The crisis had come. The Honiton Bank, the historic bank of Flood and Lott, had failed.

After the death of their father twelve years previously Herman had tried his best to take his place in the bank. Their uncle Harry Lott and his partner Mr Flood had been supportive but it had soon become clear that the strain of supporting his six sisters was too much for Herman. He had begun to come home late, with red-rimmed eyes and an aroma on his breath that Sophia could not identify until she heard one of the servants say that it was drink. The expected partnership in the bank had not materialised. The sisters had had every expectation that they would make seamless transitions from the comfortable household in which they had been brought up to running comfortable households of their own. Even when Herman had married, suddenly, and against the wishes of his wife's family, they had thought only that their dowries would be reduced, but it was not long before he cut their allowances. Frances and Lucy had started to sell small pieces of their lacework, and professed themselves to be amused at earning a few pennies through their handiwork. But this – it was as if they stood on the edge of a precipice. The Bank had been the fortress that protected them and they knew that their lives would never be the same again.

The drawing room that had been the secure base from which they ventured forth became their prison. She and her sisters hardly dared to leave the house when the knowledge of the bankruptcy spread, for the feeling in the town was so strongly against them. Even those who had been lifelong friends of her father averted their faces and on one occasion Frances had returned in distress when a man, no gentleman to be sure, spat on the floor at her feet.

Sophia closed her eyes for a moment and pulled the coverlet higher. She remembered the strain of being confined to the house, all the sisters together in one room and quarrelling over trifles, with Herman visiting infrequently and providing no satisfactory answers to their frantic queries. The servants came, first one, then the other and curtseyed and said they were sorry to leave, but had found new situations. When she woke in the night shaking and drenched in perspiration she would hear one or other of her sisters crying out.

It was Frances who finally took charge and declared that they must find themselves situations. They had all stared at her, uncomprehending at first.

"We have no choice. We must go out as governesses or starve."

"Governesses? We cannot! To live in a stranger's house, to be little better than servants! Frances please, anything but that!"

What Frances said next had shocked them all to the core and none of them ever protested again.

When news spread of their predicament, the aversion with which they had been met was replaced by pity. It was almost harder to bear. They were thrown on to the mercy of the few friends who stood by them and eventually, after many applications and set-backs, positions were found. Up to this day Sophia sometimes woke, sobbing and frightened, at night and she acknowledged now that it was the memories of that time that caused her distress. The final shock had been the forced separation of the sisters. Emily travelled all the way to Lancashire to be governess to a clergyman's children; Eliza went to a farming household in Bridgwater; Frances, Lucy and Sylvia took in pupils in Compton Gifford. Sophia was sent on a long, lonely journey to St Dominick in Cornwall where she was to be governess to the children in a Rector's family. To save money she had to travel third class and was terrified by her uncouth companions, a woman who drank liquor and used foul language and a man who attempted to insinuate himself into her confidence until she broke her silence and pleaded with him to leave her alone.

What sad, solitary years followed! Reverend and Mrs Bazeley were kind enough and sometimes invited her to join them in the drawing room in the evening but she knew it was only out of pity, although they tried hard to include her in the conversation. She preferred to sit alone in the bare schoolroom or in her tiny bedroom, writing her letters or just staring out of the window at the empty garden. It was over a year before she felt resigned to her position, living in one small room at the top of someone else's home, neither part of the family nor a servant. Although glad to be in an area where none knew of the shame brought on her family, she felt lonely and isolated living in a small village. It was a little easier when, after some years, she was moved, like so much baggage, with the family to Bideford.

Extract from census return, 1851, St Dominick, showing Sophia Dillon Lott.
(The National Archives, HO 107/1901/28)

The fear, however, did not leave her. She knew her situation to be precarious and there was nothing she could do to improve it. Her wages were low and she had to spend sufficient on her dresses to present a respectable appearance. She also had to buy paper and stamps for her letters and occasionally books to keep up her knowledge. She could save nothing. She was lucky that she had enough to eat; poor dear Emily was always hungry. She knew that when the children grew up and she was no longer needed it would be hard to find another situation. All the sisters had told untruths about their ages to get situations, as all families wanted a young governess; everyone knew that any governess would be worn-out by the onerous duties and quite incapable of work by the time she was forty. When that time came – it was not something Sophia had cared to think about. None of them could rely on Herman. She heard little from him and only infrequently from his wife Elizabeth, letters which hinted that Herman was still drinking despite his accountancy work and new appointments.

It was a lonely life. Her only social contact with her equals was through writing to her sisters, several times a week to each of them. Through them she heard of the fate of other governesses. One, it was said, being without family and unable to find a new situation, led a desperate and immoral life. One was overtaken by madness and ended her days in the County Asylum. One was forced into the Workhouse. Another preferred starvation. A certain death was preferable to degradation and a slow decline in the Workhouse. There were days when she felt the Asylum would be the way for her.

Then she had met William and the fear was taken away. From the very first time that he visited the Rectory to examine little Ernest and gazed at her rather than at the child, she knew she was safe. He became her fortress, her link with society; he gave her security and love and her beloved children. As Dr Ackland's wife she became respectable again and had to conduct herself in a confident manner, as one deserving of respect. She had put the past behind her. She must not let him down. She never acknowledged her previous precarious existence and stepped forward into the world with the confident certainty of the successful doctor's wife, beyond reproach, beyond doubt.

> A. Holdswo... o.... ...
> October 13, at Sydney, New South Wales, the wife of Edwd. Chapman, Esq., of a daughter.
> **MARRIAGES.**
> January 15, at Northleach, by the Rev. H. Miniken, M.A., the vicar, and brother of the bride, assisted by the Rev. C. H. Wainwright, B.A., brother of the bridegroom, George William Reed Wainwright, Esq., of 15, Pembridge-crescent, Westbourne-grove, and Staple-inn, to Alice, widow of Edward O. Payne, Esq., of Dorchester.
> January 12, at Charles Church, Plymouth, by the Rev. F. L. Bazeley, rector of Bideford, William Henry Ackland, Esq., surgeon, Bideford, to Sophia Dillon Lott, of Wentworth Villa, Mannamead, Plymouth, daughter of the late Edward Lott, Esq., banker, of Honiton.
> January 10, at Camelford, by the Rev. W. R. Brown, Mr. Saunders, of Chulmleigh, to Ann, third daughter of Mr. John May, Luffenton, St. Teath.
> ....ary 8, at Welland, near Malvern Wells, Major John J. ...l Horse Artillery, son of the late Robt. ... 'b. Northumberlar'

From the Exeter Flying Post 24th January 1856

For her sisters, the fear was still there. She saw it in their eyes. It was there when they talked of the future, or of a friend who had been asked to leave because she was too old, another who was worn out and could no longer work. After Herman died such a dreadful, shameful death just a year after her own marriage – the relief flooded through her anew that no one in Bideford had ever got to hear of it - her sisters had only their tiny annuities and William's goodwill to fall back on. Lucy and Sylvia struggled on with their small school in Mannamead; Emily was passionate in her care of the boys at the Bloomsbury choir school and was so brave and independent; solitary Eliza nearly always refused help despite looking so pale and thin that Sophia sometimes feared she would be extinguished altogether; and Frances – poor, dear Frances. She was no longer strong enough to work and eked out her small annuity by visiting charitable friends, a week here, a week there. She passed the time by reading and lived in an imaginary world.

Sophia turned on to her back and sighed. She heard footsteps on the stairs and Lucy's dear little voice pleading,

"But I *want* to see Mama! I want to give her my drawing!"

Jane's low tones proscribed and coaxed, and the footsteps continued up to the next landing.

Sophia knew she was impatient sometimes with her sisters. She had not wanted to think too much about their lives. Ever since her marriage she had taken on the role of the oldest sister, especially so since Frances had failed. She was the one who advised, encouraged and set high standards. She was the one to look up to, the one who had returned to her rightful place in society. But she knew that, although her sisters confided their fears to each other, they would not do so to her. She was brisk. She did not deal in sympathy.

The visit to the Workhouse had awakened the old fears. She had buried them so deeply she had forgotten they were ever there. *She* was once as vulnerable as those poor old women; *she* could have fallen as low as them. Another voice told her it was nonsense, she was above that, but she knew it was not true.

To end one's days in that dreadful place! No comfort, no warm hearth or familiar possessions, no caring faces or old companions! To sit, day after day, on that hard bench with the wailing and the sobbing echoing from those merciless walls! Surely those poor aching bones should have some respite for their last few months or years? Surely they should be made comfortable in bed? Why had she not been more aware of this before – were not her very sisters afraid of such an end?

And the children. Those poor, neglected, unhappy children. She shook her head against the soft feather pillow, shaking away the thought that *those* children were different, less deserving, less sensitive than her own. They were not. Her children could be in that cold, unwelcoming place if some misfortune befell William. Had not the unthinkable happened to her family all those years ago? She knew that William had made provision, had bought property when he could in order to protect his family, but had not her father done the same? She imagined seeing Emily, Lucy and her beloved Hugh in rough Workhouse dresses, their red infected eyes gazing reproachfully at her, and she reached a shaking hand to her constricting throat as her heart pounded. Surely she was going mad! Where were this morning's certainties, the confident woman who had strolled around the market smiling, inclining her head politely, buying daffodils as if they alone could assuage suffering?

And Selina. Had she felt such despair and desolation? She had never before considered Selina! Those rules, those dreadful rules, the bed on the kitchen floor – the girl was just out from the Workhouse, separated from her child, the other dead - and she had shown her no mercy! Where had been the reassuring smiles, the comfort and the Christian welcome? And the child, the child that she, Sophia, had tried to prevent her visiting! Could Selina's feelings at being parted from her son be similar to her own?

There was a knock at the door. Selina entered and curtseyed, carrying a tray. Her cap was, as usual, a little askew above the too-short hair that was escaping from it. She looked curiously at Sophia before gazing demurely at the floor again.

"Eliza's sent some tea, Ma'am. Us hopes you'm feeling better, Ma'am."

What deprivations had the girl suffered? No doubt tears had been shed, here, in this house. Did the fearful memories and the longing disturb her sleep, in the kitchen, where all should be warmth and cheerful industry?

"Ma'am?"

The blue eyes were gazing at her anxiously.

"Your son, Selina, is he well?"

The girl looked startled.

"Yes, Ma'am, thank you."

"You must miss him very much. Is he well cared for, Selina?"

"He is, Ma'am. Thank you. Leastways, my ma does her best."

"You must visit him again one day. And, Selina, remember you have a secure situation here. Are you happy here now?"

"Yes, Ma'am."

There was a long pause. How solitary it must be, living in this house with her son far away. And not even a small room to call her own.

"Would you like the tea now, Ma'am?"

When she had gone, Sophia lay back on the soft pillows and found that she was crying. The sobs came from deep within her and she cried until she gasped for breath, burying her face in the pillow lest the children or servants should hear her and hardly knowing what sorrow was flooding from her.

Eventually her breaths steadied. She lay still. The creamy drapes around the bed, the majolica vase on the mantelshelf seemed brighter, clearer than before. What a day, what a very strange day it had been! She sat up against the pillows. She felt drained, but calmer now. The tea was only lukewarm, but welcome. She would sleep. William had said she was overtired, and she was. She would sleep and tomorrow she would write to her sisters, she would even write to poor Frances. Perhaps next week she would go to the Workhouse again, after she had spoken to William. She would persuade him that she was stronger now. Might she one day visit other wards? Visit the able-bodied women's ward where Selina had been? The prospect filled her with foreboding; it was too much to consider today. But she wanted to be really useful. She would try to make a difference. How easy it would be to slip back into her old, comfortable ignorance! She finished her tea, and closed her eyes. And Selina? What was to be done there? A new mattress, that was the least she could do, a new softer mattress and a pillow. And she would smile, let the girl see her work was appreciated. Assure her that her situation was secure, that was the main thing. But now she would sleep.

...........eteen days.

..ne Hannadine, of Teignmouth, John Hore, master, that sailed from 'hence on the 8th of September, had arrived out a few days before the above vessel sailed.

HONITON.

At the meeting of the Town Council of Honiton, on the 9th inst, J. H. Townsend Esq., was unanimously elected Mayor, for the year ensuing.

HONITON BANK.—On Wednesday, last week, this town was thrown into a great state of excitement, by the issue of the following circular from Messrs. Flood and Lott, announcing their being obliged to close their bank:—

" It is with great pain we announce that under the unprecedented state of the Money Market, we are compelled to suspend our payments. We shall be prepared in a short time to satisfy our creditors that our resources are ample to discharge all the demands upon us, and leave for ourselves a considerable surplus. Our embarrassments have been caused by the extreme pressure of the times, and our anxiety to continue that extensive accommodation to our friends, which it has always been our wish and our custom to afford. We propose to submit a statement of our affairs to our creditors on Tuesday, the 16th day of November instant, at 11 o'clock, at the Public Room, at the Dolphin Inn, which we feel confident will satisfy them of their certain ultimate safety, and in the mean time we have to entreat their forbearance.

"FLOOD AND LOTT.

" Honiton Bank, 3rd November, 1847."

On the afternoon of the same day, a meeting of the creditors was announced to take place at the Dolphin Inn, on the following morning, and which was numerously and respectably attended. Mr. Player, on behalf of the firm, handed to the creditors a statement of the assets and liabilities of the bank which was read as follows:—

Liabilities	
Ledger Balances, about	£20,000
Deposit Notes, about	55,000
Notes in Circulation, about	16,000
	£91,000

Assets	
Securities and Balances, about	£100,000
Mr. Flood's Net Private Property	57,000
Mr. Lott's ditto ditto	28,000
	£185,000

The above statement was deemed satisfactory by the creditors, and a resolution to that effect was carried unanimously. After the appointment of a committee, &c., to assist Messrs. Flood and Lott in the winding up their affairs, the meeting was adjourned to Tuesday the 16th inst., when a more detailed statement will be laid before the creditors. Such an untoward circumstance as the closing of the Honiton Old Bank, must necessarily, for a time, impede the progress of trade in this town and neighbourhood; indeed, to such an extent as will be severely felt by every one, and unfortunately, perhaps, to some few it will involve ruin. But we must not dwell on the dark side too long, affairs are in some quarters already bearing a brighter prospect, for "when things are at the worst they must mend;" and we trust and believe the shock by some experienced is from fancied rather than real danger. That every demand on Messrs. Flood and Lott will be fully and honourably met, no one individual questions, they are *able* and *will* pay to the utmost farthing. On Monday a notice was industriously circulated throughout the town and neighbouring villages, the following of which is a copy:—

" Honiton Bank.—Notice.—The tradespeople and shopkeepers of Honiton continue to take the Notes of this Bank for goods, and in payment of debts, and without requiring any abatement, allowance, or discount to be made on such Notes, and the goods rendered at the usual prices. All persons indebted to the Bank will be entitled and allowed to set off any Honiton Bank Notes against their respective debts.

" Dated Honiton, 8th Nov., 1847."

Confidence is being more and more felt in every quarter, but in none is it more so than it is deserved. Messrs. Flood and Lott will, from their statement, pay twenty shillings in the pound,—well would it be could every man do the same.

NORTH DEVON.

BARNSTAPLE DISPENSARY.—On Sunday se'nnight, a ...the .... of St. Peter an....

city, on ... ... "On the nutritive value of different oil-.... , and substitutes for oil-cakes."

A COLLISION.—On Saturday, a carriage and two sprightly grey horses, belonging to Capt. Levett, of Culver, came into violent collision with a phaeton, belonging to the Rev. Mr. Northcote, which was standing outside Mr. Tucker's shop, grocer, High street. The phaeton was considerably damaged, but no harm was done to the pony which was in it.

MELANCHOLY DEATH IN THE DEVON COUNTY GAOL.—An inquest was held on Monday afternoon in the hospital of the Devon County Gaol, before R. R. Crosse, Esq., on the body of Mr. Herman James Lott, of Honiton. It appeared from the evidence of Mr. E. H. Rose, governor of the gaol, that on Tuesday, the 6th inst., the deceased was committed to the debtors' ward, under a warrant from the County Court at Honiton. He was then in a very excited state, and was evidently labouring under the effects of drink. He went to bed almost immediately, and continued much in the same state, scarcely touching a bit of food, until he died. Mr. Webb, the surgeon, was called in, and he received every attention from him, as well as from the officers in attendance, and from the other debtors. The warder of the debtors' prison, Thomas Pennington, stated that when deceased arrived there he was in a very excited state, and appeared to him to be tipsy. He was supplied by his wife with a cup of coffee, as he appeared very thirsty, and went to bed. The next morning he was much in the same state, and drank cold water, which he asked for, and a teacup full of gruel. He asked for the surgeon, and Mr. Webb was sent for at nine o'clock on the Wednesday night. Deceased was attended to by Samuel Johns, who has charge of the sick in the debtors' ward, and on Friday night, shortly after nine o'clock, he died; and on Friday night, Mr. Webb, surgeon, stated that when he first saw the deceased, on Wednesday, he was apparently recovering from drunkenness. Anticipating *delirium tremens*, he requested him to remain in bed, and prescribed for him accordingly. On Thursday he saw him again, and he was then suffering from *delirium tremens*, but he was sensible. He ordered him medicine, and saw him on Friday, when he appeared much in the same state. At nine o'clock at night he was sent for, and immediately went to the gaol, but found that he had just expired. His opinion was that death was caused from excitement, terminating in convulsions. In answer to a juror, Mr. Webb said the fact of his being brought to the gaol might have increased the excitement under which he was labouring. Mr. Rogers, the brother-in-law of the deceased, stated that previous to his committal he had suffered from convulsions; that on the Saturday before his removal he had sold an estate, called Branscombe, as agent for another party, by which a considerable profit had been realised, and he was of opinion that this had greatly excited him, which, with the fact of his having had convulsions previously, would go far to account for the cause of death. The coroner said that if deceased had died out of the gaol there would have been no necessity for holding the inquest. He bore testimony to the attention which was paid to the prisoners by the authorities of the gaol, and the satisfactory nature of the evidence which was always given in cases of this sort. The Jury returned a verdict that "death was caused by convulsions."

EXETER COUNTY COURT.—TUESDAY.

From The Exeter Flying Post January 15th 1857

219

Chapter Fifteen

Selina dipped her brush in the hot water again and scrubbed at the scullery floor, sending eddies of suds towards the skirting in the corner. From the kitchen came the sounds of Eliza clattering dishes and singing loudly, almost drowning out the rhythmic scratching of Selina's brush on the stone floor.

"For men must work and women must weep
And there's little to earn and many to keep."

The song changed to a la-la-la every now and then when she couldn't remember the words. Selina noticed there were splashes of grease on the plank doors of the cupboard, she would scrub them down tomorrow before doing the floor. Today, being Friday, the dining room was to have a thorough clean and she must start it as soon as she had finished the floors in the scullery, pantry, passage and privy, otherwise she would scarcely finish it before luncheon.

She finished the floor with a cloth, moved on to the privy and then fetched a clean bucket of water to start on the passage. The passage ended in a glazed door leading out to the garden; she stood for a moment watching the daffodils waving wildly in the strong breeze and the small clouds that sped across the bright blue sky. Where was Will now? In the school playground perhaps, for the time was about right. Was he running around with the other children or did he stop to watch the clouds too? On his way home did he pick daffodils from the hedge to give to his grandmother?

Ever since she had returned from Clovelly she had thought about him almost all the time but already she was finding it difficult to picture his face. And as for Thomas - she could hardly remember the look of him at all. Her strongest memory of him was of holding him in the days after his birth, and the sweet milky scent of his breath as she gazed down at him drowsing in her arms. If only she could have had likenesses made of both her sons! There were photographs of all the Doctor's children displayed in the drawing room. She had seen Mrs Ackland gazing at Kingsley's likeness several times since he had gone away to school.

She wiped away the steam that her breath had made on the window then got down on her knees and started on the floor. Every time she thought of Will the same question came into her head.

- What can I *do*?

And there was never an answer. She couldn't think of a single way she could earn enough money to keep them both and have him living with her. Instead she would start to dream. In one dream she and Will lived in a little house like Mary's. During the day Will went to school and she cleaned the house until it was spotless and then she could sit back and admire the bright rug in front of the stove and the flowered curtains at the window. Then she would go shopping to buy what she needed for supper and would make a meat pie like Eliza had shown her or some bacon and potatoes, and it would be ready by the time Will came home from school so they could sit together to eat it.

In the second dream Will was living here in the Doctor's house, almost like the other children except he went to school and ate with her in the kitchen and at night he had a little bed in her room, for in her dream she had been given Eliza's room.

Hearing footsteps, she turned and saw Hugh hopping along the passage towards the privy.

"Mind now, Hugh, the floor be wet in there. Don't 'ee slip now. And don't 'ee make a mess."

She would probably have to wash the floor again, he was a messy little toad. He reappeared, still pulling up his breeches and she sat back on her heels to look at him. He put his arms around her neck.

"I'm going for my walk now. Are you coming with us?"

One day last week when Mrs Ackland was unwell, she had

accompanied Jane and the children on their walk, holding Jimmy's lead and keeping an extra eye on the younger ones, as the more Hugh and Lucy jumped around, the more excited Jimmy became and they were too much for Jane on her own.

"I can't, my lover, I've a heap of work to do. There, now there's someone at the door!"

Hugh ran back upstairs to find Jane and she quickly dried her hands, changed her work apron for her white one and ran to the hall.

"Good morning, Sir."

She was careful to pronounce the 'or' in 'morning' correctly as she had been taught, then listened very carefully to the message before curtseying and saying,

"Thank you, Sir, I will ask the Doctor to call."

She repeated the message to herself as she hurried in to Mrs Ackland who was writing letters in the drawing room.

"Mr Headon's wife, Ma'am, stomach very bad, 63 Meddon Street."

"Thank you, Selina."

Mrs Ackland wrote the message carefully on a scrap of paper and Selina copied it into the book on the hall table, sounding out the letters carefully as she had been taught. Mrs Ackland thought she would soon be ready to write the messages on her own but she was very afraid of getting them wrong and sometimes, when the caller talked a lot, it was difficult to know what the most important part of the message was.

For the last few days the sound of the door knocker had caused her extra trepidation. On Tuesday there had been a delivery of chops for dinner but instead of the usual boy, the butcher's son stood smiling on the doorstep. Recently she had been embarrassed to go into the shop to place the orders because he always noticed as soon as she joined the queue and he would smile and say to no one in particular,

"Now my morning's brightened up!" or

"Here comes my favourite customer!"

She would keep her eyes down and try not to giggle,

which was hard because he was so very attentive when he served her, telling her he would deliver the sweetest lamb chops or the leanest beef he had in the shop.

Then, there he was on the doorstep. He had handed her the parcel but after that had given her a folded sheet of paper, saying in a low voice,

"This is for you."

Then he was gone. Confused, she had carried the meat towards the kitchen but had paused in the passage, looked around to make sure no one was coming, and unfolded the slip of paper. There were words on it but no numbers, so it could not be a bill. She slipped it inside her dress. All day she was afraid that Mrs Ackland would demand to know the whereabouts of the note from the butcher.

When everyone had gone to bed, she sat down by the candle and took out the paper. There were two lines of writing. The first word began with a Y, then an O, then a U. The sounds did not seem to make sense. The next word was hard too. The next was V, E, ve-ry, very, then the last P – R, pr-e-tt-y. A shock went through her, making her hands and feet tingle and her heart pound. She looked back at the first two words and it made sense. You-are-very-pretty. But was it sense? Was it really meant for her? She looked at the next line. This was easier. M-a-y, May I, s p-ea-k, May I speak, to, that word again, -you, May I speak to you, o-n-e day, one day. She clutched the paper to her chest and drew her feet up on to the chair. She tried to see his face and could not, but could hear his voice,

"Now my morning's brightened up! This is for you!"

It echoed through her dreams all night.

She had not had occasion to go to the butcher's shop since then and he had not called again, although one day the young boy came with a delivery. She thought of him whenever she was not puzzling over a way to be with Will. He was tall with a broad, confident face. He liked her! How was it possible? She imagined him standing very close to her, talking in a low voice as she gave him the order for the meat and the thought of it made her legs feel shaky and gave her an itch down there. She had not felt like that about a boy since she was at Stroxworthy and she used to wait in the barn for Joseph Andrew to come and meet her.

She had hidden the slip of paper in the bottom of her tin in the kitchen cupboard, wrapped in an old apron that also contained her mirror, an egg cup with just a very small chip in it and an odd teaspoon, not a silver one. She did not really know why she had taken them, except that she had hoped she would one day be able to use them in a home of her own. She was sure they would not be missed. The note, too, gave her hope. Something might happen.

She finished scrubbing the passage and emptied her bucket in the scullery. Eliza was still singing and changed the words to,

"Can you scrub, scrub the carrots and peel, peel potatoes?"

"I've got the dining room to do! I'll have to be quick."

As she scrubbed and peeled, Eliza told her of her planned visit to her sister, Jane, who was the servant to a watchmaker in Barnstaple.

"What be 'ee gwain to do then, Sunday?"

"I shall visit my cousin up Coldharbour. There's something I want to ask her."

She knew better than to discuss Will with Eliza, but perhaps she could talk to Mary Parkhouse. She knew a lot of people around the town so perhaps she would know how Selina could find a house. But she wouldn't tell her what people were saying about Will in Clovelly because she was afraid Mary might think it was true. As for the butcher's son – but no, she would not mention him either. She dare not trust anyone with the knowledge of the note she had received.

"Can you sew?"

Mary was staring at her dubiously. Her small round eyes reminded Selina of currants in a lardy cake.

"I should think your hands'd be too rough for fine work."

Selina was sitting in Mary Parkhouse's little front room with Thomas asleep on her knee. She had explained to Mary that she wanted to leave her situation in Bridgeland Street and find work and a house of her own so that Will could live with her. She knew the idea sounded absurd as she told it, and Mary's reaction confirmed her feeling.

"You'd be mazed to leave that situation you've got – what would 'ee do instead?"

Selina had explained that she hoped Mary might have some ideas, might know of someone who was managing to bring up a child on her own. She did, but certainly none who did so through choice. Most found a husband as quickly as they could if they found themselves in a predicament. Trying to feed oneself and a child, as well as paying the rent, was very difficult; the most Selina could expect was lodging in one room. A house of her own was quite out of the question. Selina asked how much rent Mary had to pay.

"Four shillings a week. 'Tis a lot but of course our food bill is much more 'n that. I spend four shillings and sixpence just on bread each week. 'Tis hard sometimes, but we manage. Thomas is a skilled worker so he earns a guinea a week."

It was more than Selina earned in a month. Of course she had no rent to pay or food to buy – but no one would pay for a servant to live out.

"Us couldn't manage here if my brother wasn't lodging with us and us is better off than most. But if you could sew p'raps you could do gloving at home. Of course if it was me, I'd never have left my child in the first place."

She offered to take Selina to see a woman who lived up the hill at New Row and who was a gloveress with two children. Mary's tone of voice suggested that this was not something to be admired. However, Selina felt encouraged. If it was possible to support two children surely she could manage with Will, although she was doubtful whether her sewing was good enough.

Mary put on her bonnet and wrapped a blanket around Thomas. She was so brisk and efficient it was clear that *she* would never have to support herself and two children through gloving. Out on the street some boys kicked a pig's bladder to and fro across the steep hill. Mary shouted at them to watch out for her child.

The cottage at New Row was along a narrow path where a couple of small children played in a puddle. Mary held up her skirts and knocked at number four. There was one small, bare room, clean enough but cluttered with boxes and with the air of a workroom rather than a room for a family. Two women sat sewing at a table and the one who had opened the door for them returned to her chair and picked up her work.

"I'll carry on while us talks, I'm that behind."

All three wore white aprons and there was a worn white sheet spread over the table. Standing there in her best dress and with Mary in her fancy bonnet, Selina felt like one of the lady visitors who used to call occasionally at her parents' cottage in Clovelly and, in her discomfort, realised that she had already missed some of the answers to Mary's questions. The younger woman, Jane Richards, was explaining that there were six of them in the house, herself, her two children, her mother and two boarders, James and Mary Lugg from Frithelstock. The three women all worked in gloving. She looked at Selina.

"Is your sister good with a needle?"

Selina had almost forgotten that Mary had advised they should say they were looking for work for Selina's sister; it would not do for the news to spread that Selina was thinking of leaving her post.

Jane Richards showed her the work she was doing. The glove, which she held in a white cloth, was a very fine cream-coloured silk and she was sewing a decorative seam along the back with the finest needle Selina had ever seen. She said that if she worked from eight until eight she could make two pairs a day, perhaps three if they were leather. Working seven days a week, she could earn five shillings.

Five shillings! The shock must have shown in Selina's face because the woman retorted,

"Well, what did 'ee expect!"

Five shillings was only a little more than she earned now and she did not have to pay for rent or food for herself. How would she be able to afford even one room for herself and Will on five shillings?

Suddenly the two children who had been playing outside burst in through the door. The younger woman yelled at them.

"Get out the back, now! Look at the state of you! They know not to come near when us is working; us can't risk having dirty fingerprints on the gloves."

Selina had imagined being curled up in front of the fire with Will while she sewed in the evenings. She was doubtful, too, whether she would ever master the work. Perhaps she was more suited to being a washerwoman – although she knew what hard work that was and for very little money. Mary was now distancing herself by talking about a pair of leather gloves she owned; it was time to go.

"'Tis no good, you see," she said, as they walked back down the hill.

"Men's wages are higher. Women were never meant to keep their children theirselves. If you could find a husband, Selina, and if he'd take on Will as well as you, *then* you'd be able to leave your work, maybe just do a bit of washing or scrubbing if he didn't earn as much as my Thomas do. 'Til then you'm better off where you be."

Her beady eyes stared, emphasising her meaning. Selina said goodbye when they reached Mary's door. Thomas's cousins were coming for tea so, as she had not been asked to stay, she carried on down the hill. It was a grey day and there was a bitingly cold breeze. Usually she looked forward to walking through the town and looking in the shop windows, planning what she might buy with the few pennies that she kept aside from her wages. Today the prospect bored her, but it seemed a waste of her afternoon off to return to Bridgeland Street and sit in the kitchen. She walked slowly along Mill

Street. There were few people about, just the idiot man who stood on the corner twitching and waving his arms, a smartly-dressed lady with a small dog on a lead and a couple of maidservants walking arm in arm. Her afternoon off would be more fun if she had a friend to walk with. Mary was too caught up with her husband and child. But she knew she would be shunned if she let it be known that she had been in the Workhouse, and it seemed difficult to make friends without telling the truth about her life.

She turned into Lower Gunstone and then into a street she had not been along before. It was narrow with many small, low cottages in a bad state of repair pressed one against another. There was rubbish strewn around and slops had been thrown out into the street despite the fact that the drain in the centre of the road had been filled in. Men lounged in the doorways, drinking from jugs and shouting to each other across the street, and a dozen or more half-dressed children fought and chased each other from house to house. Her pace slowed for a moment, but already several men had turned to look at her and she had the sense that if she turned now, she would be pursued like a cat fleeing from dogs. She kept her eyes on the ground and walked faster, flinching as her best dress swayed above the dirt but afraid to lift it and risk showing her ankles.

"Sarah, come and take a look at this! Here's a pretty one!"

A woman ran forward and she glimpsed long greasy hair and a low-cut bodice.

"'ere, give us a penny missus. Give us a penny or your ribbon!"

A man said something she did not catch and coarse laughter rang out. She walked faster, aware that the children were now chasing after her and that one clutched at her dress and the others laughed and jeered. She gathered her skirts in front of her and walked faster still although the street was slippery with mud and mess.

"Selina? Selina, 'tis you, i'n't it?"

She hurried on; it could not be meant for her.

"Selina Burman!"

Someone stepped out from a doorway, grabbed Selina's arm and was staring at her face. It was Harriet Braddon!

"Well, it *is* you! Look at 'ee, you'm quite a lady! Fancy, seeing you again!"

Harriet looked dirtier than she had in the Workhouse and wore a frayed bonnet that barely concealed her too-short hair. Behind her, men and women looked on with interest from the cottage doorways.

"You'm still at the Doctor's then, from the look of 'ee! Well, you'm the last person I expected to see! Come in with me and 'ave a cup of tea and meet my man!"

Selina found herself being led to the door of the nearest dilapidated cottage. Inside a man sat at a bare table, a cup and a bottle in his hands. He stared at her and grunted a reply when Harriet told him who she was, "an old friend of mine" she said, without mentioning the Workhouse. He continued to stare while Harriet crouched to pour a cup of tea from the pot on the hearth.

"Tell me all about the Doctor's house then, Selina. You'm well fed from the look of 'ee! You'm allowed out on a Sunday then, be 'ee?"

How could she tell Harriet how much her life had changed? She answered her questions briefly. She was discomforted by the difference that had always been there between them and that now seemed to have magnified; she felt herself to be proper and self-important in Harriet's company. Yet Harriet had achieved something despite her slovenly ways, for she was managing to live independently. The man having slouched away to the door, she asked Harriet where Emily was and how she supported them both. Emily was with a friend, she was told, and Harriet paid a few shillings a week for her keep until she had got herself set up. The man she was with did casual work and did not earn a lot, so Harriet supplemented their income in the way she was accustomed to, but he was expecting more work soon and then she would stay at home. She would settle down with her man, she said. She had had enough of the old life. It was harder now, men wanted younger women, but Selina could earn a *lot* of money now she was looking so pretty. She put her hands on Selina's shoulders and stared into her face. But then, said Harriet, why leave your situation if you're well treated and live in a grand house with good food, it was worth being parted from your child for that.

"Well, maid, you'm no more talkative than you ever were, that's for sure."

As soon as she'd finished her tea, Selina got up to go and submitted to Harriet's enthusiastic embrace, agreeing that she would call again. She hurried along the street, looking straight ahead until she found herself in the High Street. She turned up the hill and paused, pretending to look in the window of the chemist's shop. No one followed her from the narrow turning below. The broad High Street with its tall buildings and decorated shop windows was safe and familiar. She turned her back on the narrow side street and continued up the hill.

She remembered her first weeks in the Workhouse where there were so many strange faces, such a press of women with callous, rough ways. There were many who would have stolen from one other had there been anything to steal, and who lied and cheated against each other, and others who were mad and had terrifying, unpredictable outbursts. It seemed that parts of Bideford were as rough as the Workhouse. There was no reason to be afraid of Harriet Braddon of course, in fact it had been good to see a familiar face. But she was afraid of what Harriet offered.

She turned into Grenville Street and stopped to look in the window of Heywood's, the drapers. Suppose she was to bring Will to Bideford and find a room to live in. Would it be in a street like the one in which Harriet lived? She wanted to take him away from people who thought ill of him but he would be no better off if they lived somewhere like that. And if she could not be a glove maker might she even end up like Harriet? Perhaps it would be worth it, in order to have Will living with her. Harriet had said she could earn a lot of money. She wanted so much to be with Will but she could not imagine herself in such a life. Perhaps Mary was right, she was better off where she was.

She walked past the empty pannier market. Was she, then, to spend the rest of her days as a housemaid? Was she only to see her son two or three times a year? Outside the New Inn a family waited for the coach, the mother in a green cloak and matching bonnet talking animatedly to her husband, the children, a boy and a girl, laughing and trying to push each other off the large wooden trunk. She walked on, hesitated outside the Portobello Inn, then turned into Silver Street. She knew where it led. Had she not avoided this way ever since her new life had begun?

The bitter wind stung her face and made her eyes run as she turned the corner into Meddon Street and walked slowly up the hill, keeping close to the cottage walls. There it was, further on across the road. She stopped. The stone walls, the railings, that fearsome arched entrance, ready to swallow up any that came near. She pressed her back against the cottage wall and stared at the Workhouse. She would go no nearer. It had consumed eight years of her life, eight years, from the age of sixteen to twenty four. Whatever happened she would never, never go back in there. She would rather die than that. Was Ann Champion still inside those gloomy walls? How she would love to see Ann again, to tell her of all that had happened, to gossip about Harriet Braddon. And Fanny? Poor Fanny Mock was in there still, she was sure of that. Any one of them in there would give anything to be in her situation, living in a warm and beautiful house with plentiful good food, wearing smart clothes that fitted and having the freedom to wander the town on Sunday afternoons. She took one long last look then turned and retraced her steps.

So this, then, was her life. But something might happen. She might get married. Men did marry women who already had children, of course they did. And wasn't she pretty enough now for someone to want to marry her? At the top of Bridge Street she paused and stared down at the grey band of water that meandered through acres of mud. In Clovelly the tide rising and falling made little difference to the huge expanse of ocean but here the river almost disappeared when the tide was low. She folded her jacket more tightly across her breast and tucked her hands under her armpits. It would be wonderful to be a lady and wear a pair of those fine leather gloves. She might as well return to the kitchen. It was, at least, warm there.

She descended the steps that formed the top of the street, then made her way down the precipitous hill. It pleased her that Bideford was set on such a steep hill for it reminded her of Clovelly. If only there were more familiar faces, people with whom she could pass the time of day, perhaps even, eventually, walk with and share confidences. Perhaps after a while she would find a friend. Two men were pushing up the street towards her, long energetic legs striding quickly despite the steep hill. She looked up and she caught her breath. One was the butcher's son! There were no side streets down which to escape and it would be foolish to turn around; she walked on, her eyes down. Should she look up at him? What should she do if he spoke? He would speak, wouldn't he? The two drew near and she kept her eyes down until she could do so no longer. He was staring at her but – not in the way she expected. He stepped aside to pass her and almost knocked into her and his voice was harsh.

"It's that whore from the Workhouse."

She carried on walking. She went home. She sat in the empty kitchen and later she knew she must have sat there for a long time, seeing nothing. At first the words that rang in her ears had no meaning. Then she thought perhaps there had been another woman there, on the other side of the road, and the words had been meant for her. But she knew it was not so. Someone had told him of her past. She should have known it would happen. It would always happen.

She went to bed although it was barely dark. She lay on the new soft mattress that Mrs Ackland had given her and she stared out at the shadowy kitchen until the shadows thickened and the true darkness came and, finally, the longed-for oblivion.

Chapter Sixteen

Dr Ackland sat back and looked over the top of his glasses to observe the woman sitting opposite him. She gazed past him, seemingly perturbed by whatever it was she saw on the unadorned wall of Mr Eastman's office. She was heavy-featured with a determined jaw, downturned mouth and dark brows. A large wen was prominent on her right cheek. Her dark hair, shorn close under the Workhouse cap, was greying; her large eyes were brown and devoid of light. Were the features asymmetrical in any degree? The ears malformed or projecting? The nose perhaps was a little crooked, but that might be as a result of injury. He glanced down at Mr Eastman's notes again. Fanny Mock, aged 42.

He had been reading Mr Maudsley's latest book, *Body and Mind*. It would be satisfying if he could bring any of the theories introduced therein to bear on this patient. Dr Pridham had not yet read it and there was some pleasure to be found in introducing him to new ideas for he was, at times, inclined to be condescending in his assumption that his wide reading had earned him superior knowledge. The book put forward the theory that insanity had physical roots, that the signs of mental degeneration could be recognised in physical defects. Fanny Mock's features were strong; there was nothing in them that suggested that an inherited physical inferiority was the cause of her insanity. If the truth was to be told, the tone of the book made him a little uneasy at times. Of course, a healthy mind depended on a healthy brain in a healthy body. But to place emphasis on inherited inferiorities - where would such a view of humanity end? Had not the work of Mr Darwin demonstrated that we are all from the same root, that we were not created as master and slave but are all equal? Would not the belief that some individuals were evolutionary failures lead some to think that they should be removed from the tree of life like so many dead branches? It was true that, unlike smallpox which attacked rich and poor indiscriminately, insanity favoured the poor, but why? Not, surely, because they were inferior but because the circumstances of their poverty maddened them.

So, what was it then that maddened poor Fanny Mock? Dr Pridham, tiring of the Workhouse Master's complaints, had asked him to give his opinion. The notes spoke of delusions, increasing recalcitrance and lengthy episodes of weeping punished by a reduced diet or a few hours in solitary confinement. She had been in the Workhouse for some years and was a native of Bideford, but before her incarceration had been a servant in London. Curious. He knew her father, Mr John Mock; he had been a blacksmith in Allhalland Street and had once spoken of disowning a daughter who had caused embarrassment to the family. He looked over his glasses again. She was not unaware of him for she shot him occasional nervous glances, otherwise staring at the wall while her hands grasped and pulled at each other in her lap. When first brought in she had not replied to his greeting and it had only been after Mr Eastman had spoken threateningly to her that she had muttered a 'Good morning, Sir'.

He smiled at her, knowing the smile would be in his voice even if she did not look at him.

"Fanny, I see you used to work in London. I was there myself at one time, many years ago now."

Her eyes remained on the wall but the hands became still.

"A thrilling city in many ways, but inhospitable. There is little loving kindness to be found there. Coming from Bideford, as I do too, you must have found it an immense and chaotic city. Where was your place of work?"

Her eyes flicked to his face, and away again. She was listening intently, he was sure.

"There are very many great houses there of course, many opportunities for work."

"'Twasn't a house, Sir, 'twas an hotel."

Ah, he had hooked her. She sat very still now, as if

transported back to the past.

"Many, many stairs up to the top. But 'twas dark in the basement."

"What was the name of the hotel, Fanny?"

"The Great Northern Hotel, Sir, Kings Cross."

"Ah yes, I know it! Who does not, indeed? The railway hotel! A very elegant, imposing building. Were you happy there, Fanny?"

"Us had candles – thousands of them! And soap, up to the ceiling. Mrs Myers used to count 'em."

A shadow passed over her face. What memories were hidden behind those troubled, dark eyes? She looked at him suddenly.

"Do 'ee know him, Sir? My husband? He'll take me out of here when they tell him I'm here. He'll take me away, take me home. Do 'ee know him, Sir? Will 'ee tell him? I don't like this place! I want to leave this place!"

There, the mania was come again. She started to cry, gazing at him as if he held the key to her freedom. Alas, he did not. Poor Fanny was not married, but perhaps a germ of truth lay in her misconceptions. Was there a man who had once cared for her? Or one, more likely, who had taken advantage of her? Perhaps there had been a child, as was so often the case. Or this male figure might be merely a desperate imagining, an embodiment of longed-for security. Poor Fanny. He reached out and took her hand.

"Fanny, tell me, what is your work here? Are you in the washhouse? Or in the kitchen?"

She looked down at their joined hands.

"I scrub the floors, Sir."

"Then I think you need a change. You can sew, no doubt. Would you like to sew, Fanny? There will be more company, perhaps someone who will befriend you. I will enquire."

He questioned her further and, although she was able to answer his enquiries with some semblance of intelligence, her mind soon wandered when he was silently writing his notes. Monomania, undoubtedly. He ordered purgatives to be followed by a strengthening diet, and opiates when the occasion warranted it. It was so little. What else could he do? Years ago, she would have been better off in the Exeter Asylum, there would have been pleasant rooms, flowers and pictures to calm the restless mind, a better diet and useful toil. Asylums were now so overcrowded that conditions were little better than in the Workhouse. Send her to Exeter and he would merely be exchanging one prison for another, and an unfamiliar and disturbing one at that. So many minds gone astray, female minds particularly. Why? Was it perhaps the increasing pace of modern life, the bustle and the stress? The certain tendency of bad and insufficient food in the parents to produce insanity or imbecility in the offspring? Or was their madness simply the desperate communication of the powerless?

He patted her hand and rang the bell for Mr Eastman. He would talk to Dr Pridham of Mr Maudsley's book but he did not think that its theories applied to Fanny. With kind treatment, fresh air, exercise and good food no doubt her mania would decrease, perhaps even disappear. But where could she go for such treatment? He was helpless in the matter.

He walked out on to Meddon Street. It was a fine March evening and not yet quite dark. Above the line of roofs to the west the sky glowed and the thin wisps of cloud were suffused with pink from the setting sun. Would Fanny ever stand outside these gates to see such a sight? It was doubtful. He turned away down the hill. In the valley behind the terrace of houses a song thrush flung forth his soul in a complex melody that encompassed both grief and hope. He stopped for a moment to listen.

"There is comfort in the natural world, is there not?"

He addressed a hunched old man leading a small donkey.

"Does your heart good to hear it, Doctor, 'tis true."

But it did not seem right that he was seeking comfort when Fanny Mock and so many like her were incarcerated; when his dear friend Richard Hoyle was gravely ill with his grief-stricken family around him. He could do little to help Fanny, and nothing for Richard, but there were others who would be easier to reach. Had he not saved Selina, given her a comfortable home, security, employment, a good diet, not to mention a better future for her young son? There would be others in the Workhouse who would make reliable servants and surely there would be families who would follow his example. He must do more! It was too late for poor Fanny Mock, but he would see to it that others were helped. He resolved to speak to Sophia that very evening.

He turned into Silver Street, nodding and murmuring a "Good Evening" to a woman hurrying out on an errand, her shawl wrapped close against the cool evening air. The freedom to come and go as one pleased! Selina could enjoy that now, to a degree. And today he had made a discovery. While he had waited in the office for Mr Eastman to fetch Fanny Mock, he had perused the record books that were ranged on the shelves behind the desk. It had not taken long to find the name of Selina Burman. And there it was! She had indeed gone out from the Workhouse to be a servant, leaving her son Thomas behind, and she had indeed returned because she was with child. But her employer was not Mr Pollard. His conjectures had been wrong. Her assailant - if her story was true, and he was inclined to think that it was – was not one he would have thought capable of such heinous behaviour. And he had misjudged Pollard, in this particular matter at least. The knowledge disturbed him. He would see Pollard at the Local Board meeting tonight; there would perhaps be the opportunity to assuage his conscience.

He had been on foot all day, going from the Dispensary to the top of town and back, across the bridge twice and along the Abbotsham Road. He had lunched with Mr Vinson and they had discussed this evening's meeting. The number of smallpox cases was, thank the Lord, falling steadily and only a handful of patients were now being cared for. It was now time to consider the future of the hospital. Neither he nor Mr Vinson had relished the thought of discussing it with Mr Pollard. Well, this new information would make the task easier.

Outside the pannier market the lamplighter reached up his long pole and the bright light flooded out, intensifying the darkness in the corners beyond its reach.

"The evenings are drawing out now! Spring will soon be on the way."

"'Twill indeed, Doctor. Goodnight, Doctor."

His own home would be bright and warm. Jimmy would be wagging his tail by the welcoming fire. Sophia, dearest helpmate and companion, would be ready to greet him. She was better now, quite recovered from her escapade. To go to the Workhouse without informing him! It seemed that his rebuke had stung her more than he had intended. Perhaps he had spoken a little too sharply. She was too readily influenced by her society friends at times; it was not right that her wish to impress them should prevent Selina from seeing her son. But to visit the Workhouse! She was too sensitive for that. She seemed a little rebellious now, for she had stated her intention to go again. It really was not necessary; he asked only for moral support. But she seemed possessed of a new resolve. It made him slightly uneasy.

Late shoppers dawdling in Mill Street, gathering in little knots to gossip, turned to greet him. On a whim he turned into the sweet shop and bought lollipops for the children; only four, for were not three of his darlings now away at school? He then asked for another three to be wrapped; they could be posted so that Annie, Maud and Kingsley would know he was thinking of them. No doubt Sophia would be sending parcels to them soon.

As he opened his front door Mary and Emily ran from the drawing room and no sooner had they thrown themselves into his arms than Hugh came sliding precariously down the banisters, closely followed by a shrieking Lucy, bumping down the stairs on her bottom with her skirts bunched in her lap and her drawers displayed for the world to see. He jumped forward and caught them both so that all four children were gathered in a wriggling, giggling mass in his arms.

"Just in time before Mamma saw you! Come, I'll run up the stairs with you and we'll all slide down together!"

And he strode up the stairs with the shrieking children.

"There! Now look, Mamma has come to spoil our fun, but it is as well for I should spoil my coat."

He handed out the lollipops and came down to greet Sophia, pretending to examine her for signs of tiredness or nerves.

"No, the eyes are bright and clear, the lips do not quiver nor the mouth turn down; I pronounce you quite recovered!"

She smiled at him and returned his kiss. He sensed a new confidence. Well, so be it. Her happiness was his main concern.

COPY OF MEDICAL CERTIFICATE.—*Sched.* (F), No. 3.

(a) *Set forth the qualification enabling the person certifying to practise as a Physician, Surgeon, or Apothecary, ex. gro.— Fellow of the Royal College of Physicians in London, Member of the Royal College of Surgeons, England; Licentiate of the Apothecaries' Company, or as the case may be.*

I, the undersigned,

being a (*a*) *Doctor of Medicine of the University of St. Andrews and a Fellow of the Royal College of Surgeons of England by examination*

(b) *Physician, Surgeon, or Apothecary, as the case may be.*

and being in actual practice as a (*b*) *Physician & Surgeon*

hereby certify that I, on the *Ninth* day of *November* 1883

(c) *Here insert the street and number of the house (if any), or other like particulars.*

at (*c*) *the Union House, Meddon St in the Borough of Bideford in the County of Devon*

personally examined

(d) *Insert residence and profession or occupation (if any) of the patient.*

Fanny Mock

of (*d*) *Bideford an inmate of the Union Workhouse, Bideford* and that

(e) *Lunatic, or an Idiot, or a person of unsound mind.*

the said *Fanny Mock*

is a (*e*) *Lunatic* and a proper person to be taken charge of and detained under care and treatment, and that I have formed this opinion upon the following grounds, viz:

(f) *Here state the facts.*

1. Facts indicating Insanity observed by myself (*f*) *She is wild & incoherent in her talk - Has no just ideas on recent events - Becomes wildly excited at times both by day & night - Has the delusion that she is married to a Clergyman but is unjustly prevented from living with him - Says she has been shot through the brains by a bullet connected with an electrical wire.*

(g) *Here state the information, and from whom.*

2. Other facts (if any) indicating Insanity communicated to me by others (*g*) *Her talk is very unreasonable and at times indecent - She is very violent in her conduct and will throw anything she has in her hand at a person giving the slightest offence - Cannot be left alone with safety. Has attempted to climb the walls of the yard of the Union House. Her conduct has been gradually getting worse - This information has been given me by Caroline Steute resident Nurse at the Union House*

Signed, *John Thompson M.D, LRCS Eng.*

Place of Abode *Lynton House, Bideford*

Dated, this *Ninth* day of *November* One Thousand Eight Hundred and Eighty *three*

Fanny Mock, medical certificate.
(*Devon Record Office Ref 4034A/UH/2/18*)
Fanny was sent to Fisherton House Lunatic Asylum, Salisbury, in 1883 and transferred to Devon County Asylum in 1891. She died there in 1908, aged 72.

Later he sat in his study and pushed aside his casebook. Today's notes were written up and tomorrow's visits were planned, it only remained to put up the medicaments that would be needed. Then time to sit with Sophia – he had scarcely seen her today. After a hasty dinner he had gone straight out again to the Local Board meeting. Mr Pollard had, of course, been present and he had decided to try a different tack with the man. He had to admit he felt more favourably disposed towards him since his discovery in the Workhouse that afternoon.

He had approached Pollard before the meeting and had shaken his hand, thanking him for allowing his premises to be used and emphasising how valuable had been the facility of treating paupers there. He enumerated the cases that had been particularly difficult and explained how different the outcome might have been had the hospital not been made available – why, if the patients had not been isolated, Bideford might even now be in the grip of a most serious epidemic! There had, of course, been some difficulties, some disagreements, but fortunately Mr Pollard had recognised his public duty and had not withdrawn his offer. By the time he had finished, Pollard had been glowing with pride. The meeting had passed off well, agreement being reached that for the time being the facility of the hospital would be retained and all present joining in thanking Mr Pollard, albeit some rather half-heartedly.

So, perhaps that was the way to handle him. It was possible that his outbursts of violence were in response to a perceived inferiority, in which case ostracising him was not helpful. Was it not true that inside the most disturbed or angry individual lay a more sensitive soul in need of some love and recognition? Admittedly it was hard at times to believe it of such an unattractive character as Mr Pollard. There was no doubt he had had his setbacks in life, including a bankruptcy back in the late 'forties, but that certainly did not excuse his behaviour. In any case, since then his paint mines had gone from strength to strength.

He yawned and stretched. No doubt they would see more of Mr Pollard's unpredictable side in the future. At least gross immorality was not, it would appear, part of his nature. Instead, Selina's seducer was one he would never have suspected. Ah well, human nature is complex. It is never dull. He would keep an eye on this particular individual, make sure no more hapless maids from the Workhouse were sent to work for him. And Selina? All was well there. Why disrupt her tranquillity?

DEATH OF A MAGISTRATE.—We regret to have to announce the death of Dr. Hoyle, who has been for many years a magistrate of this borough. The deceased gentleman died at his residence Bridgeland-street, early on Wednesday morning, after a long and painful illness, in the prime of life. He has left a widow and several children behind to deplore their loss.

From the North Devon Journal, 25th April 1872

243

Chapter Seventeen

Selina hesitantly unlocked the door of 23 Bridgeland Street, walked in and closed it behind her. She leant back against the door and listened as the unaccustomed stillness of the house settled around her. She heard a horse and cart outside on the sun-drenched street, then a questioning voice followed by a laughing reply. In here it was cool and quiet. Motes of dust danced in the sunlight streaming through the stained glass above the door. She carefully placed the key on the hall table.

She was to have two weeks here alone. She had not understood at first when Mrs Ackland had told her the family were to have a midsummer holiday; where could they go that could be better than this house? She glanced into the downstairs rooms to make sure they were really empty then walked through to the kitchen and stared at the mess, the result of the morning's hectic preparations. It would have to wait; she was hungry after all the activity. She cut a slice of cold meat and potato pie and placed it on a plate. Such a rush it had been! The train had been leaving at 10.40 and at one time it had really seemed as though at least part of the family would miss it. It had taken four trips in the brougham to transport the seven children, Dr and Mrs Ackland, Eliza, Jane, and all the luggage to the station and after the third consignment had left, Mrs Ackland had decided that there was insufficient space for those remaining and had handed Jimmy's lead and a picnic basket to Selina, telling her to make her way to the station as fast as she possibly could. The picnic basket had been heavy and awkward and Jimmy, already excited by the unaccustomed activity, had pulled on the lead, making her afraid she would be dragged under the wheels of a carriage on the bridge.

She had never seen a train at such close range before. Its

huge size and deafening roar as it pulled out of the station had so overwhelmed her that she had not realised that the children were waving goodbye to her until it was too late and they were gone.

Mrs Ackland had told her this morning, along with all the other instructions of which she had been reminding her for weeks, that as the weather was so pleasant she could sit in the garden with her cup of tea occasionally if she wished.

"After all, there will be no one there for you to disturb."

Well, she would take her pie out there. Mrs Ackland had not said *lunch* but then, who was to know?

She had never sat on the garden seat before. She was used to coming out to shake out the dusters or beat the rugs and always took a moment to look around, but this was different. This was the best view of the garden. She took a mouthful of pie. The sun was warm on her face. The rose bed was a picture, in full bloom now. The roses were Mrs Ackland's particular favourites. There was honeysuckle climbing over the trellis and attracting a multitude of bees. She watched as they fumbled their way into the creamy throats of the flowers, the deep murmur of the bees and the accompanying sweet scent of the honeysuckle reminding her of childhood days in Clovelly. A large bumblebee landed on the grass and crawled clumsily towards her foot, a blackbird was singing at the end of the garden and a woodpigeon crooned in the big tree. Beyond the garden wall came the sound of hammering from the blacksmith's shop behind the Swan Inn and beyond that were the backs of the Mill Street houses and shops with their windows staring down at her. It would not do to sit out here too long, for suppose someone told Mrs Ackland?

She would not, in any case, have much time for sitting. While the family were away, she was to clean the entire house. When she first heard of the plan, she had pleaded that the responsibility was too great, but Mrs Ackland had told her that she was perfectly capable. She just hoped she could get through the two weeks without breaking anything or losing the front door key. It was late really for the spring clean but

Mrs Ackland had said it was much easier to do when the house was empty. They were gone to Lyme Regis where they had rented a house. Eliza would cook as usual and Jane would see to the children and a daily woman would come in to clean. Eliza had been very excited about it; she said she would have time to walk by the sea and look at the shops in Lyme and was sure that Selina must be disappointed not to be going. Well, *she* was to have a holiday too. When the family returned she was to stay to help them settle back in and then have a whole week in Clovelly with Will. A week! It was hard to believe. She got up and picked a bright pink rose, buried her nose in its heady scent and tucked it in her buttonhole.

She wandered into the dining room and then into the drawing room, gazing at the familiar spaces made strange by their emptiness. The glass-fronted corner cabinet was bare as Mrs Ackland had washed and packed away the most delicate china before she left and the silver had been locked up, but it was the silence that struck her most forcefully. She stared at the likenesses of the children in the drawing room, then lifted the lid of the piano and experimentally pressed a few keys. The sound was harsh and tuneless in the silent room. How clever the girls were to play as well as they did! She sat on the edge of the sofa and surveyed the room. Dare she sit in here this evening? Perhaps she could try to read one of Mrs Ackland's books; there was one on the table. She picked it up and tried to read the writing on the spine. Lorna Doone. There were a great many pages and no pictures; it made her head ache to think of reading so many words. Mrs Ackland had left a bookmark part way through, so probably she had intended to take the book with her. Well, she surely wouldn't miss such a dull-looking thing and in any case had put several other books in her trunk.

She walked slowly from room to room, peeping into Dr Ackland's ordered study with its firmly locked desk and the dreadful skull and into the children's rooms where Jane had carefully folded the clothes, then into Mrs Ackland's bedroom. She thought she would see how much work there was to do in there, but then was drawn irresistibly to the wardrobe. The lighter summer dresses had been packed for the holiday but the pale grey wool and the black silk were neatly folded on the shelf, along with a dark green wool that she realised, as she examined it, could be let out for pregnancy. Tentatively she took the pale grey and stood before the mirror, holding it against her. The colour seemed to suit her. She would have liked to try it on but as she pressed the waist against her own, her mistress's perfume wafted from it. She hastily pushed the dress back into the wardrobe and went out on to the landing, listening until she was sure she was still alone.

Going back into the room she removed a dark pink bonnet from its box. There was a long hair caught on the fabric, a little fairer than her own. Her hair was long enough to put up properly now and she resolved to try some different styles while she could make use of Mrs Ackland's mirror. The bonnet looked well on her. She turned her head this way and that. Had she been pretty when she was younger? She had never thought so, although Joseph Andrew had told her she was. Would anyone ever say so again, before she grew old?

The next morning she had just finished her breakfast, having slept a little later than usual, when Charles arrived to help her move the furniture. He was to come every morning that she needed him; he had fewer horses to care for now that Toby was out to grass for two weeks so was able to help out. She felt a little shy of him as they had never spoken without anyone else being present but he had an easy, careless manner and did not seem greatly interested in her. She took him up to the girls' bedroom on the second floor and together they moved the beds and the chests of drawers, putting as much as possible out on the landing and the rest away from the walls.

She wished afterwards that she had asked him to carry

down the heavy rugs because by the time she had done that and beaten them in the garden until her arms ached, she already felt tired and the rest of the room was not even started. It was not until she returned upstairs that she remembered that the feather mattresses and pillows should also have been carried down for beating; she felt sure that this was quite beyond her and that both she and the mattress would fall down the stairs if she tried. There was nothing else for it; they would have to wait until the next day. By mid-afternoon she had swept the walls down with a soft brush, washed down the paintwork, scrubbed all the joints on the beds, and swept and scrubbed the floor. She hung the summer curtains and left the window open to air and dry the room.

After a supper of cold lamb, potatoes and beans, she walked again through the empty downstairs rooms. She felt restless despite her fatigue and eventually put on her bonnet, picked up the key and went out. She knew that it was likely that her comings and goings would be reported to Mrs Ackland by any neighbours who happened to see her, but what was the harm in it as long as she was doing no wrong? She had, after all, finished her work for the day.

The street was quiet in the evening sunlight and empty but for two gentlemen sauntering towards the Quay. People who lived in Bridgeland Street never sat out on their doorsteps or gossiped idly on the pavement and their doors were kept firmly closed. She crossed the road and looked at the billboards outside the Music Hall. There was a picture of a lady singing, wearing an evening gown and with a serious expression. Other boards had a lot of words on them and some numbers, probably dates telling when things would happen. As she gazed at them a man in livery fastened back the doors and wished her a good evening. She walked on. She would be able to watch the comings and goings later from the drawing room window.

Down on the Quay men were securing boats that had come in on the high tide, moving with the slow efficiency borne of long practice. The cart owners whose horses waited patiently for their loads stood about in small groups, watching the boats and talking. A young couple seated on a bench were, Selina noticed, surreptitiously holding hands. She wandered down to the Quay edge where two small boys were fishing with pieces of string, their legs in outgrown trousers dangling over the edge. She addressed the nearest.

"'Ave 'ee caught anything yet then?"

"No, but us will soon when the tide turns."

He turned back, uninterested in her. He was a little older than Will and the back of his neck under his cap was very dirty. She would have liked to have taken him home and given him a good scrub. Was Will playing down at the harbour this evening? The older boys would be jumping from the harbour wall into the sea, their voices echoing back to the village on the hillside. When she closed her eyes she could picture Clovelly, the glowing colours of the flowers that clambered up the whitewashed cottage walls and the windows reflecting back the last rays of the sun as it descended towards the edge of the vast blue sea.

As she passed the boats, one man called out to her,

"Us'll be going up the inn dreckly. Why don't 'ee come with us, maid, 'ave a drink?"

She walked on quickly. She must be careful. Mrs Ackland had told her again and again what would happen if she had any followers. In any case she would never dare to go to the inn.

She turned into the High Street. But why? Why not go to the inn? How was anything ever to happen if she never spoke to anyone? But if she did she would be dismissed. And anyway, what man would be interested while she wore this ring on her finger? It was a lie, that ring, and it forced her to tell lies.

She had made friends with Martha Jeffery, the young servant who worked next door for Miss Hatherley. Martha was friendly despite knowing that Selina had come from the Workhouse and being told that she was not to be trusted. They had walked together several times on Sunday afternoons and

Selina had been entranced by Martha's carefree ways. She complained that Miss Hatherley's house, where she was the only servant, was as dull as ditchwater and envied Selina for working in a lively household full of children. Martha spent all her money on bonnet ribbons and lace collars despite the fact that Miss Hatherley – the old witch – forbade her to wear most of them. Once, they had walked with two other friends of Martha's and the three of them had giggled and made eyes at all the young men who passed. They did not ask Selina why she remained aloof because they had already commented on the ring she wore. She would not have wanted to join in even if she had been allowed to tell them the truth. Sometimes she felt she had lived so many lives that it hardly seemed possible that she was still only 24 years of age.

Well, it could not be helped. She walked along Mill Street and gave a bow and a polite "Good evening" to Mrs Hoyle, Mrs Ackland's widowed friend. It could not be helped. She had never been to an inn and was not going to one now. She would go home and sit in the drawing room with the curtains closed so that no one could see she was in there. She had seen a copy of the Englishwoman's Domestic Magazine on the table. She knew it had pictures to look at as well as writing for she had seen them over Mrs Ackland's shoulder. She might even make herself a cup of cocoa.

The next morning Charles came again. They carried the mattresses from the girls' and the boys' rooms down the stairs. It was very awkward on the corners and she was glad that she had removed the statues and vases from the landings as they would surely have been knocked down, the mattresses being so big and cumbersome. Charles marched down with the mattress held high; he looked so comical that she could not help laughing and nearly lost her footing on the second turn and had to plead with him to slow down.

He was driving for Dr Pridham that day but stayed to beat some of the mattresses for her, hitting them far harder than she could have done herself and producing clouds of dust that were carried away on the warm breeze. He promised to come back in the evening to help her carry them back up. When he had gone, she sat on the seat for a few minutes before starting her work. His back had looked so strong when he had beaten the mattress. What would it be like to have a husband who looked at her lovingly like the couples she saw out walking together? But Charles was not interested in her; he barely looked at her at all. Probably she would never marry. Who would ever want to marry her? She wasn't even sure that she minded, or wouldn't if it wasn't for wanting to be with Will. She had a better situation here than she could ever have hoped for and Mrs Ackland was pleased with her work. And she trusted her too, even trusted to leave her here on her own.

The day seemed harder than the last. Beating the mattresses and rugs was exhausting as it was necessary to hit them very hard to raise any dust. When she started work upstairs, she had to come all the way down three times to answer the door, twice for patients who did not seem to believe the notice that Dr Ackland had put up, directing them to Dr Pridham or Dr Burns Gibson, and once to the French polisher, Mr Barry, confirming arrangements Mrs Ackland had made for him to come and renovate two side tables. In the evening she sat in the shadowy, flower-scented garden and relaxed, releasing the tension from her aching muscles. She could feel the warmth still rising from the old stone wall behind her. Using her fingers, she counted the days and the rooms still to be cleaned. Mrs Ackland had been right; there were more days than rooms. Tomorrow she would just do Eliza's little room and the top staircase; that would be easy. The intoxicating scent of the honeysuckle mingled with the rich, languorous song of the blackbird in the lilac tree. She stretched her arms behind her head and closed her eyes. She would go early to bed tonight.

The next day she finished her work by mid-afternoon. She tidied the kitchen and washed up her lunch dishes. Mr Barry, the French polisher, was out in the yard working on the table and she wasn't sure that she wanted to sit in the garden with him there. He was not very talkative. When he had arrived after lunch she had started to tell him about all the work she was doing and he had put on a polite expression but had soon interrupted her and said that he must start work. She looked out through the open door to the yard where he stood with his back to her, rubbing slowly at the table, back and forth, back and forth. His shirt sleeves were rolled up in the hot afternoon sun and the dust from the table was settling on the hairs on his arms and on the long apron that protected his clothes. Perhaps she should offer him a cup of tea; it looked like thirsty work.

He turned – yes, thank you, he would like tea. So polite, and so distant. He came in and sat in the kitchen to have his tea and she sat down too for she had nothing else to do. The table did not look very shiny yet, she ventured. No, for he had not yet started the polishing, he replied. He was sanding it first, he explained, removing all the old polish and making it very smooth. She felt rather foolish. He gazed at his cup and there was silence again. After a minute or two she got up and busied herself around the kitchen; if he didn't want to talk, that was his business. After being alone for several days she would have been glad to hear a voice other than her own. She had even started giving herself orders to break the silence.

Mrs Ackland's bedroom was the most difficult room so far. All the clothes had to be removed from the wardrobe and chests of drawers and aired in the garden while the inside of the furniture was scrubbed out. Mrs Ackland had asked her to be particularly vigilant in her search for vermin. Charles came to help her with the mattress and rugs again but she could not beat them until all the clothes were safely put away, for fear of getting dust on them. Mr Barry had finished sanding the first table and was polishing. She watched him as she paused to get her breath back from another trip downstairs with her arms full of shawls and chemises. With his head bowed he rubbed back and forth along the length of the table in slow, rhythmic strokes, quite oblivious of her.

He went home for his lunch but she offered him a cup of tea again in the afternoon and this time they sat in the garden to drink it. She felt rather uncomfortable sitting next to him on the seat but he was respectful and did not stare or try to sit too close. He was more talkative this time. He told her he did not find the work dreary.

"You have to get the rhythm just right and make each stroke important, each one smooth and even, so there are no smears. Just keep going, nice and steady, and don't think about the time. 'Tis like feeding the wood, see, you keep feeding it and feeding it and in the end you've got a table that is as good as new, a beautiful table that you can see your face in, it's so shiny. And 'twill last, the polish will last years if it's cared for properly."

His eyes shone as he talked about it. It was surprising that a man could like work that was very much like cleaning.

"So," he said, "have 'ee worked for the Doctor for a long time?"

He looked right at her this time, as if he was really interested. He was quite old, about the same age as Dr Ackland probably, but his face had more lines.

"Only since a little while before Christmas."

"And where were 'ee before that?"

Afterwards she could not imagine why she had told him, except perhaps that she was tired of telling lies.

"I was in the Workhouse."

"Oh, you poor maid!"

He was really concerned.

"However did 'ee come to be in there?"

So she told him. She told him the whole story, or most of it. She was embarrassed when she had to say why she had had to go in and could not look at him; she was in the family way the first time, she said, and the father of her child would not marry her because she was beneath him. The second time, she said, she was taken advantage of, and she felt herself blush scarlet, but he nodded sympathetically and she went on to tell him how the children were forcibly taken from her when they were old enough, how Thomas had died without ever having left the Workhouse and that William was now with her parents in Clovelly and how much she missed him. She had been in the House for eight years she said, from when she was sixteen until she was twenty-four.

When she had finished they sat in silence for a while, then he said quietly,

"I'd never have thought you'd been through all that, you know. What with you being so young. You just never know about folks, do 'ee, until you ask. I don't believe in judging folks, not 'til you know what they've been through."

And he went back to his work.

She went back upstairs and as she worked their conversation kept running through her mind. Why had she told him? He might tell other people, Mrs Ackland might find out that she had not kept her past a secret. But she also felt she wanted to talk to him some more, because he had listened to her and had not thought badly of her. As she came down the stairs with the bucket of dirty water after finishing the floor, he was standing at the door with his box of tools and cloths. He looked up at her.

"Ah, you'm there. I'm off now then."

She came down into the hall.

"I wanted to say -"

"What did 'ee want to say?"

He was smiling at her.

"I've never told no one my story before. No one who didn't already know. Mrs Ackland makes me keep it secret, she makes me wear this ring and I'm to say my husband's dead..."

"Don't 'ee worry about it, maid."

She looked up. He had a gentle smile.

"I'll see 'ee tomorrow then."

And he was gone.

Chapter Eighteen

Sophia paused to regain her breath and turned to look back down the grassy hill, tilting her parasol against the fierce heat of the sun. Already the thatched and slated roofs of Lyme Regis far below had disappeared from view and the only visible part of the town was the protective arm of the Cobb enfolding a portion of the chalky blue sea. She could see the trucks carrying limestone out along the Cobb to the waiting sailing ships, and hear their rattle above the breathy whisper of the sea, and the raucous cries of the seagulls that had accompanied every waking hour since their arrival. She wiped the perspiration from her forehead with her handkerchief and turned to watch her family. William had Lucy on his shoulders, Hugh strode along bravely holding his father's hand and the remaining five all crowded around him, engaged in animated conversation as they walked. Even Annie, who at almost sixteen was beginning to hold herself apart from the rest of the children, was skipping along beside her father in a touching recollection of her younger self. He let go of Lucy for a moment to wave his hand vigorously, no doubt to clarify an explanation of some aspect of natural history and Jimmy, trotting along beside them, wagged his tail as if in agreement.

Their days had been filled with butterflies, wild flowers, birds, insects and fossils. They had picked them, captured them, identified and classified them, drawn them and dried them. The bag William carried on his back was filled with books, notebooks, boxes and geological hammers; the children carried butterfly nets. Lucy and Emily nursed their dolls who also, they said, liked to see the pretty flowers and butterflies. William was enjoying every moment. It was true she had been a little concerned about him when they first arrived. He had had so much business to put in order before their departure that he had scarcely slept for two nights and had been so tired when they arrived that at first he had not wanted to leave the house they had rented on the Esplanade, preferring to spend the time sitting quietly in the little sitting room reading and writing letters while she walked along the seafront with Jane and the children. Now that he was sufficiently rested however, his energy and enthusiasm seemed to be infinite. He had even been out fossil hunting before breakfast, when he could explore the slippery rocks on the shoreline alone.

Jimmy ran down the path towards her and thrust his nose into her hand before dashing back to the rest of the family. The steep path ran through a meadow starred with eyebright, kidney vetch and meadow saxifrage; she paused again for a moment to watch the Small Blue butterflies that danced in the sunshine above them. The sun really was extremely hot. It was a constant battle trying to persuade Hugh to keep his hat on but it was quite essential. The plan for today was to head for the Undercliff again, where the strange landscape had been formed, William said, by landslides caused by the unusual geology of the place. There were small meadows interspersed by steep crevasses and peculiar towers of chalk and flint, sudden hillocks and little valleys, all clothed in lush vegetation the like of which she had never seen before. They were to have a picnic lunch which Eliza and Jane would bring to them when it was prepared, an adventure which the servants found almost as exciting as did the children. In truth, she was a little anxious that one of them would turn an ankle or that they would become lost because the place, for all its beauty, was wild and remote. She had given detailed instructions as to what they should do in case of such an eventuality, but William had teased her for her nervousness and in the end both she and the servants had joined in with his laughter.

Look at him now! With Lucy still on his shoulders he crouched, roared and leapt forward, the children shrieking with fear and delight.

"Mother, look! Papa is a plesiosaur! Come quickly and

see!"

"And a very poor one I am too for I am sure the plesiosaur never roared, but its neck was so long it could reach a very great distance – like this!"

The children shrieked again and Hugh, Emily and Mary pulled their father to the ground, jumping on his back and pulling his beard until he pleaded for a rest. Sophia calmed them and they all sat to regain their breath. William put his arm around her and she leant against him. There was no one to see, so where was the harm in it?

The previous night, when she had lain in his arms again after straightening the bed linen, he had turned to caress her face.

"May we have been lucky, do you think, my darling? May we have made another dear child, another little son perhaps?"

Please God, no, she had thought. Not another. She could not go through all that again. She had snuggled closer to him.

"I'm rather afraid it is too late, dear. I am, after all, 47 years old now. I think my child-bearing days may be over."

"Well, one can never be certain, we may be blessed. I rather think the health-giving air of Lyme might help. I have known many cases where an adored child has arrived after a gap of some years, when the mother has given up all hope of more."

It was true, once born it probably would be adored, children carry with them the imperative to be loved. But one cannot truly love a child that lives as yet only in its father's imagination. Please God, might this one remain there.

She reached, now, for his hand and he caressed hers fervently, moved, she knew, by her unusual demonstrativeness. If only she could feel like this more often! If only all their days were as pleasure-filled, as tranquil as these. He was usually so very busy with his patients, his committees and his record-keeping, she so distracted with household affairs.

Kingsley came and sat beside her and leant his head against hers. He was deep in thought, staring down at the butterfly jar he held in his hand. What a serious young man he had become since he had been at school! But there was a new confidence about him. He seemed to take the genuine interest in his studies that had previously been absent, and he showed every sign of having a keen and enquiring mind. This week he had been reading his godfather's book *Glaucus: or the Wonders of the Shore* with great enthusiasm. She and William often exchanged contented glances when their son spoke.

"Father, where does the Adonis Blue lay its eggs?"

"That I do not know, Kingsley. Perhaps if we were to watch a specimen very carefully, we might discover the answer."

"But it will be on a plant that the caterpillar can eat, will it not? How does it *know* when it has found the right plant?"

"Ah, that is the key question, my boy. It is that knowledge that has enabled it to survive so that we may see it now in your jar rather than as a fossil embedded in the rock."

Sophia watched the brilliant blue butterfly flutter helplessly against the side of the jar. When it became still for a few moments before recommencing its futile attempts at escape, it quivered a little, almost as if it was panting. She was reminded suddenly of the young woman she had seen on her last visit to the Workhouse, whose eyes rarely left the high window even when she was spoken to. Sophia shivered despite the heat of the sun.

"Kingsley dear, you already have an Adonis Blue for your collection, do you not? Perhaps it would be better to release this one."

Lucy crawled over to watch the butterfly. Her white dress was already grass-stained.

"Yes, let it go, Kingsley. It must be missing its children."

"You silly goose! It doesn't care for its children; they are quite independent of it."

"Well, let it go anyway. It may want to lay some eggs. I hate to see the butterflies trapped like that, then pinned down in a case."

William pulled his youngest daughter to him.

"Don't you fret, my sweet; the pretty butterflies do not feel things the way we do. But I think you could release this one, Kingsley, as its variation is not very marked. Have you made a sketch of it?"

Sophia watched as her son removed the lid of the jar and encouraged the butterfly out with a blade of grass. It rested for a moment on the glass lip, closing its wings to hide its beauty, then suddenly took flight and was gone, invisible against the boundless blue sky.

They walked on, descending to the Undercliff by a narrow path that twisted between field maple and ash trees, past a picturesque farm and out into a small meadow. They had rarely seen other visitors on their walks, once or twice lone gentlemen intent on fossil-hunting, once a bare-headed young woman walking alone. Certainly no other family groups like their own, most visitors seemed to confine themselves to the town and the seashore. She had suggested alternating walks with days on the beach, and it was pleasing that the plan seemed successful. She had not had to consider such matters before as their previous vacations had consisted of just a few days in an hotel in Ilfracombe, taken partly so that William might gain inspiration for the development of Westward Ho! The days on the Undercliff were quite strenuous for her and the younger children; she was unaccustomed to taking so much exercise, and it was pleasant the next day to sit on a hired chair on the beach, reading and watching the children playing in the sand. Jane, with Annie and Maud's help, kept a close eye on the younger children as they paddled, but none of the party had bathed yet with the exception of William, of course, who usually bathed on a remote part of the shore early in the morning. The ladies' bathing machines were on a nearby beach especially designated for the purpose. She and Jane had shot covert glances in the direction of the ladies emerging in their revealing costumes and floating off into the sea and had agreed that they would not be participating. Quite apart from the considerations of decency, Sophia felt that she would be at a social disadvantage should she decide to join in as it was apparent from the way the ladies called to one another when in the water that they were well acquainted.

When looking in the shop windows on Broad Street or taking the air on the Promenade in the evenings after dinner, she and William mingled with the people who came from the grand houses on the hillsides around the town. They seemed very superior and barely replied to polite greetings. She suspected that in this fashionable society, one was beyond consideration if one's husband was not an Army or Naval officer. William seemed immune to such concerns and she tried to take strength from him as they strolled together, he musing on the finds he had made that day and she observing the fashions of the perambulating ladies. She had not yet seen such narrow skirts in Bideford. Her own home-sewn outfits seemed clumsy and old-fashioned by comparison but nobody seemed to look at her.

Here on the Undercliff there were no such anxieties. What a picture her daughters made as they skipped through the meadow starred with the bright yellow horse-shoe vetch and pink and mauve clovers, the azure sea in the background!

"Mamma, look! What is this pretty pink flower?"

She stooped to examine the spike of delicate pink flowers and Mary and Maud exclaimed as they found others nearby.

"It is an orchid, of course, and I believe it is a fragrant orchid."

William found the illustration in his book which confirmed the identification and they carefully picked several spikes for the flower press. There were wild irises, too, near a little stream and rock roses on the stony slopes above. She felt the memories of these days would remain with her for ever. To have all her children together in such a beautiful place and all so happy and healthy! She felt truly blessed.

They reached the appointed place at lunchtime, a level clearing amongst shady trees, and waited with some trepidation for Jane and Eliza. Eventually they heard voices and soon recognised Eliza's unmistakeable grumbling tones. Even the younger children were laughing by the time the two servants came into view, struggling along with the picnic baskets and Eliza declaring it was a wonder she had not broken an ankle.

"I've a mind to stay at home and clean the house another time and Selina can come away instead! I'm not paid to risk my life in a vuzzy ol' place like this!"

They all ate together, the children telling the two newcomers of their adventures. How lucky she was, too, to have good and trustworthy servants! Even Selina had turned out so much better than she had thought would be the case, leaving her alone in the house six months ago would have been unthinkable. It was true that it would have been preferable to leave Eliza at home as well if a cook could have been found in Lyme, but Selina had proved to be a hard worker and had never given any concern as regards her honesty or morality since she had been with them. It was indeed remarkable how her character had improved.

There was more than enough lunch for all of them and by the time the remains had been packed away she began to feel a little sleepy. The heat was intense, the air still but for the faint whine of insects and, in the distance, the echoing drum of a woodpecker. She leant against a tree and Annie came to join her, resting her head in her mother's lap. William reclined on his elbows, gazing out at the sea, his broad-brimmed hat and his jacket cast aside.

"Jane, would you keep an eye on the younger ones?"

She was sure she would sleep. She stroked her daughter's hair. Such a poised young lady she was becoming. All the children growing up, even Hugh becoming a little more manageable. Seven children. It was enough.

Chapter Nineteen

Selina was woken early by birdsong and the sun streaming in through the kitchen window and when she opened the back door it already felt warm outside. She stretched and yawned. What did she care if she was standing in the open doorway in her shift? There was no one to see, unless any nosey people were watching from the back windows of Mill Street. If they had nothing more to do, they were lucky, *she* had work to do. And Mr Barry was coming back.

It was to be the guestroom today. The mattress and rugs had been carried out and she was lifting down the pictures and the mirror for cleaning when the knocker sounded at the front door. She glanced at herself in the mirror she was holding. She was surprised at what she saw. She was used to a tired, rather anxious face looking back at her, but she was looking – now, how did she look? Happy, she supposed that must be it. She pushed her hair into place under her cap and hurried down to the door.

"Good morning!"

His eyes were very blue against his weathered face. She followed him into the yard and watched as he set up his materials. They talked a little of the hot weather and he told her how he had watered his garden before coming out. He told her he grew beans, peas, lettuce and potatoes, they were growing well and he would have a good crop. She pictured neat rows of vegetables in a small walled garden behind his house on the Strand but he said there was no garden there; he had been able to rent a small piece of ground at the top of the town. He started polishing and she returned upstairs to her work. Each time she came to the kitchen she glanced out of the back door. It was comforting, knowing that he was out there working. She was tired of being alone.

He had brought his lunch with him and they sat together in

the garden. She glanced over surreptitiously; he was eating a large slice of potato pasty. She felt as if someone had punched her in the belly and she spoke without thinking.

"Did your wife make that for 'ee, then?"

He stared at her and laughed, but in such a way that she had to laugh too, and the pain disappeared.

"Wife? Whatever made 'ee think I was married?"

"I don't know, just that most men are by the time they get to your age, I suppose."

He told her that he had not had the opportunity to marry, having been a soldier most of his life. She was surprised; she had assumed he had always been a French polisher. He nearly married in Barnstaple when he was young, he said, but the girl married someone else. He had not wanted to stay around then so he went away and enlisted, not much caring what would befall him. He had served for twenty-two years and had a pension of one shilling and eight pence a day to prove it. He had asked for his discharge so he could come home and look after his sister who had been widowed with two young children to care for.

"Oh! You live with your sister, then."

"No, not now. Her died earlier this year. I have to care for the boys on my own now, though Mrs Beer just along from me does some cooking from time to time, and the washing. 'Tis hard 'cos they miss their Ma, the youngest especially, he's twelve years old now. But they'm good boys on the whole."

He had finished his pasty and leaned back on the seat with his hands behind his head, closing his eyes in the warmth of the sun. His forearms and face were brown from the sun and there were fine white lines around his eyes, as though he smiled a lot. Suddenly his eyes opened and met hers. She looked down quickly.

"Would 'ee like a cup of tea?"

"Thank 'ee, I would."

She sensed he was watching her as she walked down the path and she tried to move slowly and calmly.

As they drank their tea he told her of the households in which he had worked and how it was the general rule that the grander the house, the less well he was looked after. But he had a good business. It had been a struggle when he first returned home, his sister had gone out cleaning and sometimes cared for other people's children to bring in some money while he built up his trade. Now he had plenty of work and he only went back to places that treated him well.

"I'd be happy to come back here to work!"

She laughed and looked away, feeling herself blush.

At the end of the day he called upstairs to say he was leaving. She came down to the first landing.

"I go for a walk on a Sunday, generally. Would 'ee like to come with me tomorrow?"

She was taken aback but said that she would, she was well on with her work and would be able to have the afternoon free.

"I'll call for 'ee at three o'clock then."

A sudden thought struck her – would Mrs Ackland object? He wasn't a follower of course, he was too old, he just wanted some company. But suppose the neighbours saw it differently?

"I, - the mistress might not like it, perhaps I shouldn't...."

"That's all right, us'll meet on the Quay then, by the Pill Bridge."

And he was gone.

How stupid of her! What would he think of her now? He would think she believed them to be walking out together when it was nothing like that at all! She wouldn't go, she would stay at home.

But when the next afternoon arrived she changed her mind. He had been kind to her and she did not want to hurt his feelings by leaving him to wait for her. She could tell him what she had thought and he would understand that she had to be careful in her position and they would laugh at the foolishness of employers. She changed into her blue dress although it was rather hot for the time of year, took the key and let herself out.

She had checked the time on the grandfather clock before she left but he was already waiting on the little bridge that crossed the Pill stream. He was wearing a dark coat and it was strange to see him without his usual long apron. As she approached, two boys came over from the Quay wall.

"I've brought my nephews, I hope 'ee don't mind. They generally come along with me on a Sunday."

They walked out along the riverbank. There were several couples walking together including one lady and gentleman, the lady carrying a parasol to protect her face from the hot sun. Selina looked away, hoping she was not a friend of Mrs Ackland's, but she felt less embarrassed now she was not alone with Mr Barry. The boys loped along in front, pushing and teasing each other and turning to glance shyly at her every now and then. Their hair and complexions were darker than their uncle's but the younger one had his smile. He told her about the older boy's apprenticeship in ship-building and how the younger one, John, showed some aptitude for French polishing so that he hoped he might be able to train him up. The boy turned and grinned.

"No, I'll go soldiering like you did, uncle!"

"You will not! I'll not have you signing your life away for the sake of a shilling and a red coat!"

He seemed annoyed, and she asked him whether it was not a great thing to serve one's country. No, it was not, he told her, the private soldier was treated as the lowest of the low, being given a poor diet and cramped and dirty accommodation. In India, where he had spent six years, very many had died from disease and from exhaustion. Either they were forced to march up to twenty miles a day in the unbearably hot climate, sometimes ankle deep in sand, or they were confined to overcrowded barracks, infected with scorpions and snakes, for months at a time. Even worse than the barracks were the tents where there were no fans to stir the stifling air. The water they were given to drink was sometimes visibly swarming with life and the bread black and rotten. He had seen his comrades injured and dying and had had to bury them with his own hands. He dropped his voice a little.

"The blood runs cold in my veins when I remember the sights I've seen. So we've both known hardship, you see."

Many men, he said, stayed drunk for much of the time in an effort to forget their troubles. For others, this was not enough and they turned their guns on themselves. He had just kept his head down and got on with it, telling himself it was a job and had to be done.

"'Tis only since I've been back in Old England that I've realised how bad it was, I think. I'll not have those lads signing up."

She was surprised he spoke of his nephews with such emotion.

"You love those boys, don't 'ee?"

He was a little embarrassed. "Yes, I do. They'm good boys."

They walked on, past the shipyard and the little beach at Cleave Houses. The river glistened in the warm afternoon sun and swallows wheeled and shrieked above its glassy surface. She remembered the spot with its scattering of large houses on the wooded hillside running down to the river, though it had looked very different when she had passed by in the fishing boat. She could hardly believe that she was here now, strolling along by the river in a pretty dress, with her head held high. She told Mr Barry about her journey from Clovelly when the sea had been grey and angry, and how ill she had felt, and how she had been so wet she had been to afraid to knock at the Doctor's door. He did not like to travel by sea either and told her of the journeys he had made to the southern seas, when they were weeks together without seeing dry land and many had been seriously ill.

He told her then about the wonders of India, for he admitted that it had not been bad all the time. He spoke of the noise, the constant jabbering of the natives, the women chattering and shrieking at each other, the roaring of the camels and buffaloes and the trumpeting of the elephants in the camp. The sometimes beautiful countryside through which they marched, fields of standing corn under the deep blue sky, the impenetrable jungle and the woods dotted with temples. He had seen a maharajah and his chiefs seated in howdahs on elephants decorated with gold and silver trappings, a firework display, a huge tiger kept as a pet in the palace gardens. Best of all, he said, were the elephants, the massive but gentle animals that seemed to walk like dancers yet could carry huge guns on their backs or could kill a man if they took a dislike to him. Selina had never seen an elephant and could not begin to imagine such a huge creature. Mr Barry did not seem to look down on her for her ignorance although he was knowledgeable about so many things.

They did not walk a long way but she felt elated that she had been somewhere different from the streets with which she was so familiar. They returned by a different route, up a hill where gentlemen's houses stood in large gardens and then down again and across a marsh to re-enter the town through North Road. When they reached the corner the boys said goodbye and Mr Barry hesitated a moment, then said he would see her tomorrow. He seemed a little embarrassed, and she was too. She went back to the house thinking of the strange shores, the burning sun and the dark-skinned people of which he had told her, but she wished she had thanked him for letting her come on the walk. It was strange, thinking of him with his nephews in his house down the road, while she sat here alone.

She was glad to be working on the ground floor. She moved between the dining room and the kitchen, carrying china to wash and mirrors to shine, and as she passed the open back door she could see Mr Barry out in the sunshine, the side of his face and his right arm with the sleeve rolled up, rubbing and rubbing at the table. As he bent over his work she could see his scalp, looking bare and vulnerable through his thinning hair, like the heads of her boys when they were babies. He looked relaxed but completely focussed on his work, unaware of her comings and goings. After she had worked in the kitchen for an hour or so, she went outside. He stopped work straightaway and stretched his arms above his head, looking at her and smiling. She could smell a warm, spicy scent from his skin, the effect of the sun and the polish he was using. She leant against the open door and they talked, though of what she could not afterwards remember. He had a very direct way of looking at her and she was beginning to be able to meet his eyes; they were very blue against his brown face and she liked the way they crinkled at the edges when he smiled and the way he listened so carefully when she had something to say.

When the postman called with the letters she was surprised to see her name on one. She took it through to the yard to show him.

"Well, you'd better open it, maid!"

She had never received a letter before. She took it through to the drawing room and carefully used the letter knife that always sat on Mrs Ackland's bureau, not liking to break the seal. The writing inside was hard to read and she took it back to Mr Barry.

"I *can* read now but this is hard to make out."

They sat on the garden seat together and she peered at the words as he read them, anxious as to what they would say. It was from Mrs Ackland.

"Dear Selina, I hope this finds you well and that the spring clean is progressing satisfactorily. I think you should be well advanced by now. Please will you ensure that you only use the soft brush on the furnishings in the drawing room? The curtains should only be aired for a short while as the sun is very strong. Please take care not to misplace the front door key."

"- My goodness, you'd think her'd forget about such things when her's on her holidays!" put in Mr Barry, but

Selina was intent on hearing the message. He continued to read.

"We are enjoying our stay very much indeed and the children look very healthy from all the fresh air and have good appetites. If Mr Barry, the French polisher," - "hello!" - "is still at work, please would you ask him if he would be so kind as to also polish the small bookcase in Dr Ackland's study, but only if he can complete it this week as I do not wish to have workmen in the house when we return. As previously indicated, we will return to Bideford on Monday. You may, perhaps have a chance to enjoy the garden on Sunday, if the weather holds. With best wishes, Mrs William Ackland."

"Well, that's a turn up!"

She hardly knew why he was laughing; it was such a surprise to receive a letter that she was finding it hard to take in the message.

"I'd have been finishing today but that will keep me going for a couple more days! I can put off my next job for a while."

She didn't understand him at first.

"You'd like that, wouldn't 'ee? We're company for each other, aren't we!"

She nodded, and covered her confusion by asking him to read her the letter again. It made her head swim, having him speak out like that. He moved a little closer so that she could see the letter better and his bare arm brushed against her hand momentarily. She did not move away.

By Wednesday afternoon they were both reaching the end of their work. She still had the kitchen to do but she reckoned she could do that in a day and a half. They had sat together each day to eat their lunch and for the last two days she had prepared bread, cheese and pickles for them both, arranging it carefully on the plate to make it look attractive. Her work seemed to have passed in a dream but it seemed less important now and the times she and Mr Barry spent together were what she looked forward to. She did worry sometimes that she had not done her work thoroughly enough and so had worked until very late every evening after he had gone, concentrating on the dirtiest jobs for which she had to put on her oldest apron and tie up her hair.

Each lunchtime they sat for much longer than was usual. Their conversations repeated in her head in the evenings when she was at work on her knees, wondering whether she had been too honest, remembering things that he had said and the way he had looked. She had told him more about the Workhouse, how her father had turned her away and the long walk to Bideford on her own, how frightened she had been by the rough ways of the other women when she first arrived, the cruelty of the Master, the hunger, the hopelessness of it all. He had been leaning back on the seat with his arm along the back, gazing at her sympathetically. His arm had been close to the back of her neck and once, as she moved, she brushed against it. She had longed for him to move his arm down and around her. He had told her that in India there were no Workhouses, that over there, women in her situation might give birth in a ditch and both they and their babies starve to death. She had been shocked; she hadn't thought of the Workhouse as a benefit before. One's heart could burst with pity sometimes, he said.

He asked her all about Will and he talked more about his nephews. He worried that he did not provide them with a comfortable home. It lacked a woman's touch and sympathy, he said, but there, he was too old to marry now. He had smiled at her;

"You should have seen me in my red coat when I was young, Selina, I was quite a sight then! Quite the dandy!"

He finished the bookcase by the end of the afternoon and they stood together, admiring it. The sun sinking below the roofs of the houses was still hot and the paving stones and walls of the house burned with the warmth absorbed during the day. He had brought out the beauty of the mahogany and the wood glowed, a rich, dark russet against the greys and whites of the house and the paving. She ran her hand over its smooth surface; it was a shame, really, to hide its beauty under rows of old books. He reached out to her hand and lightly held the tips of her first two fingers.

"Well, that's my work done. We could walk again on Sunday though, couldn't us? And come back to my house for some tea after?"

She dressed in her dark blue dress again and tied on her bonnet with the new blue ribbon that she had bought in Mr Boyle's shop. She went upstairs to look in Mrs Ackland's big mirror. The ribbon was rather narrow but the wide ribbons were too expensive. Still, it was an improvement. She walked slowly down the stairs, flicking a speck of dust from the windowsill, and wandered through into the kitchen. She thought she had made a good job of it. She had scrubbed and scrubbed the stone floor until it was almost white and the copper pans shone from their rack. The whole house was immaculate; Mrs Ackland would surely be pleased. The thought of their return the next day filled her with dread as she had become so accustomed to having the house to herself and arranging her work as she wanted. Perhaps it would have been different if Mr Barry had not been there, perhaps she would have been lonely by now.

When she saw Mr Barry walking towards her, smiling and purposeful, she found she was smiling too, she could not seem to stop herself. He was on his own this time. He said the boys had gone to visit their cousins but would be back in time for tea. Mrs Beer, his neighbour, would be there too, he had thought it best. She realised that he was thinking of her, afraid of what others might say if she was seen entering his house. She did not know how to reply, so she said nothing and tried not to think about what Mrs Ackland would say if she knew.

They walked up through the town and out on the

Abbotsham Road, a way that was new to her. The day was even hotter than before and he soon took off his coat, throwing it over his arm and rolling up his shirt sleeves. Selina could feel the perspiration running down her back; she would have worn her lighter cotton dress if it had not been faded and worn almost threadbare at the cuffs. They passed the last of the houses and walked out along a broad country lane. In the hedges the vivid greens and yellows of late spring had given way to tawny flowering grasses and the muted pinks of foxgloves and dog roses that looked tired and dusty in the heat. Selina picked a foxglove flower and slipped the velvety pouch on to the tip of her finger as she used to do as a child. Mr Barry smiled at her and reached up to pick a creamy-white wild rose.

"Here, this'll suit 'ee better."

He moved close to her and she could smell his perspiration and felt the hairs on his arm brush the side of her face as he pushed the stem of the rose under the ribbon on her bonnet. Embarrassed, she stepped away but, as they walked on, she moved a little closer so that their arms touched occasionally, as if accidently. He had an easy, swinging walk and she had to run a little now and then to keep up.

"You walk fast! It's hot to be going so fast!"

He apologised. He had been used to walking long distances in very hot weather in India, he said. She saw again how a shadow passed over his face when he remembered his soldiering days.

"But us is in no rush now. Here, us'll stop for a rest."

He turned into a gateway and helped her around some nettles. They leant their arms on the top rung of the wooden gate, their shoulders almost touching. She was aware of his chest rising and falling a little with each breath and she was reminded suddenly of Will, of holding him close and feeling his heart beat against hers. A field sloped away from them, down into a wooded valley and up again to a ridge above. A chestnut horse grazing in the field raised its head to stare, then walked steadily towards them, swishing its tail to rid itself of the flies that buzzed around it. It lifted its long, gentle head over the gate to rest between them, snuffling and blowing at their clothes as they stroked the quivering, velvety nose and lips.

"There, my beauty, you'm a beauty, you are."

She liked the calm, confident way Mr Barry handled the horse and the gentle way he had of talking to it. He picked a handful of grass and the horse ate it greedily and then shook its head noisily, making her jump. He laughed and put his arm around her for a moment to reassure her, and she saw a shadow pass over his face again.

They strolled on and began to talk easily, of the job he was now doing in Northam which required him to walk four miles each day, of the scrubbing and scouring she had done in the kitchen – she showed him her hands which were even more red and calloused than usual - then she found herself telling him about the plans she had had of finding different work in order to have Will living with her. He listened quietly while she told him of the desire to be with Will and the futile visit to the glove makers. She left out her meeting with Harriet and *her* ideas for earning money. He seemed subdued and she had to ask him what he thought.

"You'm in a good situation. You shouldn't leave, not in my opinion."

"But what can I do? I want so much to be with Will."

"You'm young. Something'll turn up."

She didn't see how anything could turn up when she spent all her time cleaning the Doctor's house.

"I need to know Will's properly cared for and not getting into trouble."

They continued along the road with its view over pastures and woodland. Cattle wandered along well-trodden paths in search of grazing, for much of the grass was burnt brown from the weeks of hot sun. Mr Barry was quiet for a while, staring down at the rough road as they walked. She tried to match the rhythm of her footsteps to his. He was frowning; she had not seen him look so serious before. She would have liked to reach out and touch his hand.

"I'm lucky to be at the Doctor's, I know that, but Will is all I've got and I want to be with him."

She continued to look at him but he kept his eyes on the ground and did not return her glance even when he eventually replied.

"You'm young. I know you've seen misfortune but you've still years ahead of you. Something'll turn up. You'll meet someone and marry one day most likely. You can have your son with you then."

He sounded almost angry. She was taken aback. It wasn't what she wanted him to say; she wanted him to help her, to make suggestions. Then they would have a reason to meet again and she would be able to tell him how the plans were progressing. He might know someone who could help, or find some rooms where she could live.

"It's too late for me. I gave all my best years to the army. All I can do is keep working and care for my nephews, see that they stay on the right track."

He told her that someone he knew in the army had taken his discharge and had married a woman many years younger. There had been no children and they had not made each other happy and after a few years she had run off with a man her own age. His friend had been completely broken by it; he had fallen ill and died a few months later.

"He loved her but he was too old for her, see. It wasn't right."

They walked on in silence. Selina was unsure why he had told the story. What had it got to do with him? Did he think of marrying? He could marry if he wished, what was there to stop him? The thought infuriated her. Lots of women would like to marry him, he could take his pick. He was very fortunate, he had a house and plenty of work. He was his own master and was respected. Of course he could marry. Whereas no one would ever want to marry *her*. Most people despised her when they heard about her past life. The whore from the Workhouse, that's what she was. A pain came into her throat and she felt her eyes fill with tears.

They reached Abbotsham village, a small group of thatched cottages alongside an ancient church. He asked her if she was tired yet and said that they could perhaps, one day, walk as far as the cliffs that were another mile or so further on. She would then, he said, be able to see right round the bay with Clovelly in the distance.

"'Tis a long way in an afternoon but us might manage it."

"Mrs Ackland'll never let me come out with 'ee."

She blurted it out without thinking, and having said it, felt a chasm open up before her.

They walked slowly down the lane where children running with their hoops stopped to stare, past some more cottages and an inn, and took a right turn that would take them back to Bideford.

"Perhaps I should never have asked 'ee out. I could get 'ee into trouble."

He spoke very quietly. She felt herself to be an encumbrance. He would be glad to be rid of her.

They talked very little on the way back. She tried to enjoy the time that was left but the joy had gone out of the day. The heat was oppressive and clouds had begun to build up over the sea, obscuring the sun for the first time in two weeks.

Back in Bideford they walked along Mignonette Walk to reach the Strand and she waited to see which house was his. They continued walking, however, and when they had passed the row of tall houses, she hesitated.

"I thought you lived here in the Strand!"

He laughed.

"What, in those big houses! I'd have to be a fine gentleman to live in one of those! No, I'm further on, other end of the Rope Walk, though some still call it the Strand."

He pointed out Willett Street where Mrs Beer lived. Selina began to feel apprehensive about meeting her and seeing the boys again, in their own house this time. They continued along a narrow lane beside a very long, low building where Mr Barry said ropes were made, until they came to a row of

275

small cottages on the left. She followed him through a low door. When she felt sufficiently confident to look about her, she saw that the cottage was larger than it appeared, with a second room on the other side of the passage through which they had entered and a scullery behind. A narrow staircase led up from the room in which they sat. The rooms were dreary, however, and dark from the proximity of the work sheds across the narrow lane. She guessed that Mr Barry did not think to make them more comfortable.

Mary Beer cast her some curious glances, but was pleasant enough and very talkative on whatever subject came into her mind. She made them tea and brought cold meat, bread and a pot of jam to the bare table, refusing the invitation to join them and saying she would make some pies for the following day, but she continued to call out comments and bits of news, sometimes appearing in the doorway to wave floury hands in illustration of the point she was making. Mr Barry sat opposite Selina with the boys to either side. It was the first time she had faced him for any length of time. Every time she looked up from her plate, their eyes met. The conversation about John finishing school continued, yet Mr Barry's eyes were sad and spoke only to her in an exchange quite separate from the other. She was aware that the boys were watching her and she tried to take part, but she wanted only to be with him. Why had they allowed the day to be spoiled?

Finally Mary Beer said she had finished the pies and must return to her own family. Selina realised that she would have to leave also. It all happened so quickly, suddenly she was in the road and he was in the doorway with the boys behind him, watching. There were a few stilted words about how they had enjoyed the walk, there was his dear melancholy face, and then she was walking away. She saw nothing and scarcely knew how she got home until there she was, sitting motionless on the chair in the hall. Tomorrow the Acklands would return. There would be work, and confinement to the kitchen. Mr Barry would not visit. Her future stretched before her, cold and barren.

Chapter Twenty

"So, do tell me about your reading."

Sophia had been sitting sewing with her sister Frances since they had finished lunch. When Frances had arrived yesterday she had brought news of their other sisters, particularly Emily whom she had recently visited in London, but that topic was now exhausted and at times it was hard to keep the conversation going. William had had to go out to a patient in Instow and Annie was curled up in the armchair with a book, so she was no help. While they had sat sewing in silence, Sophia had glanced up at her sister now and then. Frances was looking even paler than usual and she had surely lost weight again. Her greying hair was scraped back in the harsh, old-fashioned way that she had not altered at all over the years and which only served to emphasise her thin, pinched face. Her black dress was quite faded and worn in places. Sophia sighed. Perhaps she would be able to find her something to wear, but it would not be easy to persuade her to take it. Frances relied so much on the generosity of others that she had, over the years, developed a studied lack of interest that, while it may have been contrived originally to conceal her humiliation, now seemed quite genuine. Nothing animated her, except perhaps her books and her Bible.

"Have you read the latest instalment of Middlemarch yet? I have *so* enjoyed it."

"No, I have not. Emily had not yet acquired it and I have not had the opportunity to buy a copy. Perhaps I might find it at the bookseller's here in Bideford. It would be interesting to know what is to happen to Mr Casaubon."

Sophia knew that Frances could not afford to buy the book, but the pretence had to be maintained. She assured her that there was no need to buy it unless she had a particular desire to own it; she was very welcome to borrow Sophia's copy. They went on to discuss other books. Frances had read Mr Hardy's Desperate Remedies while staying with a friend and had found it rather shocking. Sophia was amused that despite this there was for the first time a sparkle in her eye as she described the details of the plot and the goings on among the rather low characters. Annie looked up from her book to listen.

"Might I read that one, Mama? I have nearly finished Mr Trollope's Dr Thorne."

"Perhaps not, Annie dear."

"Do you allow her to read Dr Thorne? I am surprised."

"Of course I do. Mr Trollope is always quick to show the results of immoral actions. You like Mary Thorne very much, do you not, Annie?"

Again they sewed. The clock ticked. The children's voices could just be heard from the schoolroom; Jane was keeping them occupied for an hour as Frances found their chatter and constant leaping around so very tiring. It was true that Hugh in particular seemed to have an excess of energy that was unusual even for him. It was almost impossible to keep him from launching himself from the arms of the chairs. He was practising being a pterodactyl, he said.

The door knocker sounded from the hall and Annie leapt up.

"That will be Ellen, Mamma. I will take her in the dining room."

The clock ticked again. Frances bent over her sewing, an embroidery in browns and beiges depicting sparrows.

"I have not told you of my latest plan."

Probably Frances would show little interest but there it was; they must converse about something.

"You have seen, I think, how well the maid, Selina, has turned out."

Frances said that she seemed tolerably well trained.

"I was most reluctant to take her on, but I must admit William was right; she is a good quiet girl and I feel I can trust her entirely. She worked very hard completely unsupervised while we were on holiday, I had no grounds for complaint at all. I would now like to help other young women in the way that we have helped Selina."

Sophia explained that she had been paying visits to the Workhouse in order to support the work her husband did amongst the poorer people. She did not touch on the emotions the first visits had aroused in her, for the subject was far too sensitive to discuss with Frances; as it was, her sister was giving increased attention to her needlework. Generally, Sophia said, she had visited the elderly women but she had also, on two or three occasions and with a companion, entered the ward for able-bodied women. There were some who had reached the depths of depravity and were, perhaps, beyond redemption but there were other younger girls who she was sure could be helped. She had made enquiries among her acquaintances to ascertain whether any would be willing to take on a girl to train. William supported her and believed he could arrange for regular training courses on aspects of domestic service. She wished, she said, to give unfortunate young women a second chance, and perhaps even find supportive accommodation for their young children. The Workhouse is such a harsh environment for innocent young children!

Frances nodded, without looking up from her sewing.

"I see. I would have thought you had quite enough to do with a house to run and the children to see to."

"I am busy, of course. But I feel it is my Christian duty to help those who have strayed. With just a little effort it is possible to achieve so much! Selina had led a base and immoral life – I can speak of this now Annie has left the room and, in any case, you are familiar with her story. She and her sons were forced to endure shocking deprivation in the Workhouse. No more than she deserved, you might say, but from what William tells me she was led astray and suffered terribly. Now that I have witnessed the conditions in the Workhouse I do not believe they are conducive to reformation, indeed I believe some are drawn into a life of immorality through the company they are forced to keep. Now Selina has been given the chance of a better life, she has become a useful servant and her character is quite reformed."

"It would have been far less trouble for you to take on an experienced servant."

The drawing door opened and Selina appeared with a tray of tea.

"Ah, Selina, what a welcome sight! I think that is just what we require."

"I've brought milk for the children as well, Ma'am. Would 'ee like me to call them in?"

"Yes, if you would, please. Do you feel sufficiently rested now, Frances?"

"I'll have my tea, then I may lie down in my room for a while."

"Very well, as you please."

Sophia became aware that Selina, having placed the tray on the table, was hovering indecisively.

"What is it, Selina?"

"If that be all, Ma'am, may I go out now?"

Of course, it was Sunday. The afternoon had passed so slowly, she had almost forgotten. It seemed more than a few hours since the whole family had gone to church, with the exception of William who, again, had been too busy.

"Of course you may. Shall you visit your cousin?"

"Yes, Ma'am."

She curtsied and left the room. It *was* satisfying to see such a well-behaved and contented servant and to know that one had been an effective moral guide and teacher. To think that she had might have been still in the Workhouse with her unfortunate child! It was regrettable that Frances did not feel strong enough to involve herself in charitable work.

Selina walked quickly along Mill Street and turned into Coldharbour. She didn't particularly want to see Mary Parkhouse, but there was no one else to whom she could talk.

She reached number 21 and knocked at the door. The house was silent, the steeply-sloping street empty but for a small dog sniffing in the gutter. A fine drizzle was falling, so Mary and Thomas would surely not be out in the little back garden. She knocked again. She was not expected; it was over a month since she had seen Mary. She turned away. Where should she go now? If only Will was with her now! She turned, half expecting to see her son idling along behind her, wanting to reach out and feel his little hand in hers. She continued up the hill, passing the top of High Street and turning into Abbotsham Road. This was the way she had come with Mr Barry. He might be out for a walk today. The thought made her catch her breath. He would know what she should do about Will. But he would not want to see her again. It was two weeks since they had parted and she could still picture the contours of his face as he smiled at her, hear his voice and smell his warm, masculine smell as clearly as if he had been by her side all the time. But she would probably never see him again.

Throughout her week in Clovelly she had thought about him. He would have liked Will, she was sure of it. She could have shown him around the village, the places she used to play as a child, the view from the Lookout, the waterfall on the beach. They could have walked along Hobby Drive, arm in arm under the trees if there was no one around, with Will running and playing alongside. She imagined the things he would have said and her replies and the way he would have looked at her. But she must not think of him. It was wrong, she would think of something else.

She had watched Will carefully all week. It was the longest time she had spent with him since the two weeks in November. He was younger than Hugh, of course, so it was only natural that he should not understand as much and say fewer words, but he *was* nearly five and Hugh had been five when she first went to the Doctor's house. It wasn't just that he was slow to talk. When they were down at the harbour there were other children about, vying with each other to throw pebbles the furthest and chasing each other around the boats on the beach until the old men shouted. None of them asked Will to join in and she realised he was not even watching them. He made a tall pile of pebbles over and over again and when she spoke to him he did not often answer her. When she tried to tell him he was a naughty boy to take things, as her mother said he did, he just stroked the pebble in his hand, over and over again.

She wondered whether Will had always been like this. Was he stupid? Was he different from poor Thomas? It was almost difficult to remember Thomas now. But she could still picture his anxious little face looking around the Workhouse refectory, taking everything in. Will did not take things in like that. She sighed and paused outside one of the new villas, a large black and white house standing confidently in its own grounds, but a man came round from the back and glared at her, and she hurried on. She had never imagined her life would be like this. She had thought she would marry, perhaps stay in Clovelly, have many children as her mother had. She never expected that she would have to spend all those years in the Workhouse, that Thomas would die, that she would be parted from Will. It was all her fault. If she was more like her cousin Mary those things would not have happened to her. Tears of self-pity filled her eyes. Mr Barry would understand, if only she could see him and talk to him.

She walked quickly, past the houses and out of the town. Will loved her though, she was sure of that. He sat on her lap and rested his head on her breast and she wrapped her arms around him, right around so that he was part of her again. At night they lay together and she gazed at his little face in the candlelight, the half-moons of his closed eyes edged with dark lashes, his little rosebud mouth twitching a little as if searching for a word. She remembered how it had felt when Will was in her belly and she clasped her arms around her waist as she walked. She had thought of asking the Doctor if there was something wrong with her son, but he was always busy and the words in her head sounded foolish. Besides, Will was not ill. Who else was there to ask? If Mary Parkhouse had been at home she would have looked at Selina with those hard little eyes, then she would have told her all the new words her Thomas could say, although he was not yet two.

There was the gateway where she had stood with Mr Barry. She leaned on the closed gate. The chestnut horse was there again, half way down the field. It raised its head and stared at her and then went on eating the grass. There had been several big thunderstorms with very heavy rain since she was last here and the grass was growing again. She wondered what time it was. Might Mr Barry be going out for a walk, or returning? She stepped out on to the lane again and looked both ways. It was empty. In any case she must not see him. Mrs Ackland did not seem to have been told of their walks together but she could not take the risk again.

She walked slowly in the direction of Abbotsham, the fine rain gathering on her shawl and her hair. She stopped and gazed back along the road. There would be no harm in just meeting by accident and passing the time of day. Mrs Ackland could not object to that. Perhaps she might see him in the town, along the Quay or returning by another route. She turned and walked back.

She walked down Pitt Lane alongside fields that ran down into the valley, then past Dr Pridham's big house and gardens and into North Road. Suppose she should see Dr Ackland, returning with his horse? But as she passed the stable she saw that it was empty. She kept her head down as she walked quickly past the top of Bridgeland Street, not daring to walk past the house. On Mill Street a few couples strolled together, stopping to look in the windows of the closed shops, and her heart leapt as she saw a man walking towards her. He was of Mr Barry's height and wore a dark coat, but she saw at once that it was not him. As they passed each other she saw from the corner of her eye that he was ugly and that he stared rudely at her.

BIDEFORD BRIDGE AT LOW TIDE.

She crossed over the Quay. The tide was low, a narrow ribbon of water oozing sluggishly over the broad expense of mud. Mooring ropes snaked out to boats leaning drunkenly on the wet sludge with their masts askew while others huddled under the Quay wall. He might have walked out this way. Was it only three weeks since they had walked out along the riverbank together in the hot afternoon sun? She paused on the Pill Bridge where they had met and looked down at the broad stream that trickled almost imperceptibly between the bare muddy banks to meet the river. Across the Quay was the narrow entrance to Rope Walk. She was afraid to look at it directly in case she was seen. She could imagine Mrs Ackland's voice.

"You were seen staring at the entrance to Rope Walk, where Mr Barry lives."

She walked back the way she had come so that she could look without drawing attention to herself. There was Rope Walk and there was the bottom of Bridgeland Street. His house was out of sight, around the corner of the narrow lane that wound between high buildings. In Bridgeland Street she could just see the bay windows of Dr Ackland's house, then they were obscured by a carriage that stopped nearby. On the Quay the inns and public houses were closed, their windows shuttered against the damp Sunday air, and a woman in a low-cut yellow dress strolled, stopped and looked boldly at a man across the street. Selina turned back. She would walk for a while along the riverbank, and then back in case he was returning from a different direction.

"Come then, Hugh, you can draw some more dinosaurs in your book while we sing."

Sophia rose and walked to the piano. Frances had not gone to her room and neither had she wanted to take a gentle walk along the Quay, saying the dampness in the air would not be good for her chest. The children needed some exercise, but perhaps there would be an opportunity later. Sunday afternoons could be very trying when Jane had the afternoon off and William had been called out.

"Mary, you have practised your piece very well, have you not? I think you know it well enough to accompany us."

She found the music and set it up for her daughter and the children, with the exception of Hugh who could think of nothing but plesiosaurs and pterodactyls, gathered around the piano. Frances said she hoped it would not be too loud.

Mary played the introduction very prettily and Sophia relaxed a little. The sound of the piano and then the voices of the children as they joined hers filled her with pleasure and, as she sang, she smiled at Lucy and Emily watching her carefully so that they might remember the words.

"Whoso beset him round with dismal stories,
Do but themselves confound; his strength the more is.
No lion can him fright, he'll with a giant fight,
But he will have a right to be a pilgrim."

She drew Kingsley and Lucy's attention to the words on the sheet as they came to the last verse that they had not yet learned, then they all laughed as they reached the end and Mary finished with a resounding chord.

"Very well done! Though we do lack the deeper tones when Papa is not here. Frances, why do you not join us, you have such a lovely contralto?"

She saw that the sentiment of the hymn had moved Frances and she held out her hand as her sister rose reluctantly, saying that she was sure she should spoil the song.

"On the contrary, it shall be perfect."

She took her sister's arm and drew her into the circle.

Selina paused again on the Pill bridge. She had walked some distance along the riverbank. There had been several families and couples out walking and once a man on his own, but it was not him. She stood as if looking along the Quay but from the corner of her eye watched the entrance to Rope Walk. He might have returned through the Strand. Why had she not thought of going that way? But she must not walk along Rope Walk. It was wrong, she should not think of him. So should she return to the kitchen and look at the dull books with pious pictures that Mrs Ackland left for her? Sit alone with her sewing? Without another thought, she crossed the Quay. Within a few seconds she had turned the corner and was alone in Rope Walk. His cottage was ahead. She walked slowly, feeling her heart beating hard. She walked past the cottage, glancing at the dark windows, trying to look as though she had other concerns on her mind. She continued past it, past the long, low rope workshops until the road began to widen. Ahead a lady and gentleman walked together and she stopped, not knowing which way to go, but they turned into Chingswell Street and disappeared from sight. She waited, standing so that she could see both ways and be ready to walk if anyone came into view. No one did. She turned and retraced her steps, glancing at the cottage windows, fearing to see a face looking out at her.

The desire to see him overpowered her. His face, his smell, his touch. She felt she would die if he did not appear. She reached his door and still no one came. The bend in the road leading to the quay was close, and if someone were to come around the corner she would be seen immediately. She knocked at the door. If anyone were in they would surely hear the beating of her heart. The cottage was silent. She almost ran back to the quay but knocked again. There was a movement, footsteps. The door opened.

So strong was her desire to be away from the street that she almost fell towards him, only half aware of his expression of surprise, his exclaimed – Selina! Then his arms were around her and he was standing so close that their bodies touched and she felt that she was home. She drew back suddenly.

"Your nephews!"

"'Tis all right, maid, they'm out."

He put his hands on her arms and stood back and stared at her until she had to look away.

"'Tis so good to see you! Selina! I've missed you!"

Then his arms were around her again and she put hers around him, feeling his back beneath her hands and his chest against hers. When he spoke his voice was close to her ear.

"I wanted to call for you! But I daren't, knowing you'd lose your job. And then I knew you'd be in Clovelly. When did 'ee get back? I'd have been out searching for 'ee if I'd known!"

She told him how she had been back for two days and then it all came out in a rush, how she was worried about Will because he stole things and did not say very much or play with the other children, how she had wanted so much to talk to him and had been out on the streets looking for him and had been so afraid she would be seen, and he held her again and stroked her hair.

"Hush, maid, 'twill be all right, us'll sort it out together. Will'll be all right when he's with you, us'll make plans."

They drew back again and looked at each other and she saw that his arms and shoulders were exposed; he was wearing just his trousers and a vest and his feet were bare. She looked away in embarrassment.

"I was in bed, to tell the truth, maid. I haven't been too well the last few days. 'Tis a fever I got in India which comes back now and then but I'm on the mend now."

He drew her to him again.

"I've wanted so much to hold 'ee like this!"

Their lips met and for a moment she felt herself to be awkward and uncomfortable but then he drew her closer, stroking her back and her hair and she relaxed and felt herself respond, opening to him, feeling her body coming alive. His heart was now pounding as strongly as hers, she felt it through her dress.

He took a deep breath and looked at her; gave her two, three, more gentle kisses.

"I'm sorry, maid, I shouldn't do this."

She could not answer. She looked at him, his dear face, his eyes full of emotion.

"Selina."

He stroked her face with his hand.

"Is this what 'ee want, maid?"

Still she could not answer. There were no words she wanted to say. She leaned towards him again and their mouths met and this time he was fiercer. Again he pulled away.

"Selina?"

"Yes. 'Tis what I want."

He took her hand and led her towards the narrow staircase.

Chapter Twenty One

Dr Ackland stepped out of the little draper's shop on the High Street and stood on the pavement, deep in thought, until forced to move out of the way of a woman carrying a child. His patient, Mr Christopher Pedler, had pneumonia. His wife was also unwell and the single servant unsuited to nursing. A young woman lodger was occupied with running the shop. Was not this a prime example of the necessity for a hospital? Not that examples were hard to find, he saw such cases every day. In a suitable environment and with careful nursing, Mr Pedler had every chance of making a good recovery but, in this household, where his instructions were not likely to be closely followed, the outcome was less certain.

He *would* have a hospital! The smallpox hospital, or isolation hospital as it should rightly be called now that the epidemic had passed, was all very fine but was not suited for a general hospital. Plans were in hand for eight beds in the Dispensary and most of the funds were now forthcoming. There were two rooms that would be suitable with just a little refurbishment. It would have to suffice until a purpose-built hospital could be afforded, but what a long time even such a modest project took to reach fruition! But it *would* open. He had promised Richard Hoyle before he died that it would open.

He turned down the hill. He missed his friend very much. There was not another doctor in the town who could take his place and to whom he could converse the way he had with Richard. Dr Pridham was feeling his age and had lost some of his customary shrewdness. And the others - they had not a shred of wisdom between them. Dr Cohen and Dr Thompson had already been jostling for position, trying to take over Richard's patients, but he did not want them involved with the Dispensary, however unpopular that made him. And now, here was Dr Cohen himself. He touched his hat as the man on the grey cob rode past him down the hill, but the greeting was barely acknowledged. He had not been forgiven yet for the diagnosis of a tumour which Dr Cohen had failed to find.

He consulted his watch and turned into Mill Street. He would be just in time for lunch. He had fitted in the visit to Mr Pedler after a morning spent in court. There had been only three cases, a woman of forty found clinging to a lamppost in a state of inebriation; a boy of twelve who had stolen money from a missionary box; and the mother of an illegitimate child applying for maintenance from the supposed father. After lunch he had nine calls to make in Northam, Appledore and Abbotsham. It would be wise to take the brougham if he wanted to avoid indigestion.

Selina leaned the broom against the wall in Mrs Ackland's bedroom and glanced out of the door. The children's voices floated down the stairs from the rooms above. She stepped back inside the room and quickly pushed her hand down inside the waistband of her skirt, inside her underclothes and between her legs. Her flesh felt damp and warm. There was none of the sticky moisture of blood that she longed to feel. She pulled out her hand and looked at her fingers. Nothing. She held her breath and leaned back against the wall. Soon it would start; it had to start. Twenty times a day, whenever she was alone she performed the same action, imagining she felt a twinge of pain or a hint of wetness, praying that this time she would be right.

Several weeks had passed since it had happened. She had hardly left the house during that time, scurrying out with her head down when she was sent out on an errand, staying in the kitchen on a Sunday afternoon, pleading tiredness or a mound of sewing when Mrs Ackland expressed her surprise. She dare not go out for fear of seeing Mr Barry. The butcher's words came into her head again. The whore from the Workhouse, that was what she was. She had forced herself on him. She had said it was what she wanted.

She quickly swept through Mrs Ackland's room, squeezed the water from the cloth into the bucket and started to wipe down the furniture. He had been so gentle, so loving. She felt a rush of love for him again. If only she had not been so shameless, perhaps they would still have been able to meet sometimes, to talk and to be friends. He would want nothing to do with her now. He knew what she was. Had she not already had two fatherless children? If he ever married, it would not be to the likes of her.

He had gone to sleep, afterwards. She had lain with his arm around her and had seen that a little of the fever remained with him; he was flushed and his breath came unevenly. A few drops of perspiration stood out on his forehead. She had gazed at him, loving the contours of his face, his softly parted lips and the lines around his mouth, his greying hair. But then the dream had started to recede and she realised what she had done. She dreaded him waking and seeing the look of contempt that would surely appear on his face, the words he was certain to utter. When he turned in his sleep, murmuring a little and pulling his arm from under her, she lay very still for a few moments and, when she was sure he would not wake, slid silently from the bed. She had crept on to the landing and had pulled on the rest of her clothes, then had listened for a moment at the door, not daring to look at him for one last time. She had tiptoed down the stairs, quickly checked her fastenings again and let herself out of the front door. All the way home her heart had pounded and she had to force herself to walk and to look unconcerned although everything was changed, the street was different, the houses transformed, the sky above her seemed quite unlike the sky that had shielded all her earlier years.

How was it that Mrs Ackland had not seen the difference in her? She had been there in the hall when Selina had let herself in and had greeted her pleasantly and Selina had tried to appear normal until she reached the kitchen.

He had come to the house, once. She had been dusting in the drawing room when the knock had come on the door and Mrs Ackland had answered it. Her heart pounded again as she thought of what might have happened had she answered it herself. She had heard his voice at once. She had moved closer to the wall to ensure she was not seen and had stood, her duster in her hand, listening.

"Good morning, Ma'am. Mr Barry, the French polisher, you may remember."

It had made her catch her breath, hearing his voice again.

"I just wanted to make sure you were satisfied with the work I did, Ma'am."

"Yes. Yes, I was most pleased but is there a problem? I have paid the bill, I am sure."

"Oh yes, Ma'am, thank you. I just wanted to make sure you were satisfied."

"I was indeed, as I have said."

"And will you be requiring any more work, Ma'am?"

"No, no more at present but I will contact you in the future if I do."

And she had closed the door. Another day Selina had been cleaning the windows in the drawing room and had seen him walking up the street. She had had to hurriedly stand back from the window and he had passed three times, giving quick glances towards the house all the time. Did he hope he would see her so he could tell her what he thought of her? Did he want her to come to the house again so he could use her again in the only way she deserved? But she still longed for him, although she knew he must despise her.

She picked up the bucket in one hand and the pail of slops in the other and walked heavily down the stairs. She could feel an ache low in her belly but she knew it was not the pain for which she longed; it was the ache of fear.

Dr Ackland turned from the chapter he was reading to the photographs in the centre of the book. It was really quite remarkable for the text to be illuminated by such dramatic likenesses. But then one expected nothing less than remarkable from Mr Darwin, truly a master intellect. He studied the spine, *The Expression of the Emotions in Man and Animals*, then turned back to the illustrations. The book combined unfamiliar concepts with those that he met every day in a wonderful melange that served to elucidate both. Look at this example of a melancholy face! The oblique eyebrows, the depressed corners of the mouth were, Mr Darwin suggested, the vestiges of the screaming fits observed in infants; the face resembled somewhat that of Fanny Mock, the woman in the Workhouse. The photographs of apes were astonishing, their expressions of pleasure and sulkiness greatly exaggerated forms of those one observed in mankind. How alike they were! He had shown Sophia but she had been unimpressed. She preferred her religion to Mr Darwin's theories. He looked up at her and smiled, aware of all the muscles around his mouth brought into play as he did so, just as Mr Darwin described. She, however, was engrossed in her own book.

The illustrated human expressions of horror and agony were fearful, the raised brow, the wide, staring eyes, the open shrieking mouth. The likenesses put him in mind of his early days in surgery. What an appalling thing it had been without anaesthesia. Walking to the operating table one had felt as the hangman must as he approaches his victim, knowing what agony one would inflict. Once started, one was inclined to rush the procedure, working far too fast for accuracy in order to curtail the dreadful screams and frenzied struggles of the patient restrained in the leather straps. On more than one occasion he had walked away when the work was completed leaving the patient half-dead from shock and had gone outside to vomit, so dreadful had been the suffering.

Of course one still saw such expressions but today one could quickly alleviate pain. Surely anaesthesia was the greatest of human inventions. To be able to relieve pain and suffering – what a blessing it was! Today the patient lay during surgery as if in a pleasant dream. Remarkable! Truly, this was a great age in which to live. Man's intellect rose ever higher, discovering, inventing, creating; why, one would soon be able to reach any part of the country in less than a day as the web of railway lines spread and it would not be long before roads would be all but redundant. So it was in every area of study – progress and improvement.

The chapter he had just read was on expressions of anxiety, grief and despair. They would perhaps always be part of the human experience but in the more just society that was now emerging, where poverty and hunger would be eradicated, surely one would not see such expressions so frequently.

Jimmy got up from the rug and turned in circles to settle himself again. Realising he was being observed, he wagged his tail and came to rest his head on his master's knee.

"There, Jimmy, you can smile as well as I! But we do not often see you like *this*."

He turned to the illustration of a hostile dog approaching another, stiff-legged and staring with hackles raised.

"That, I fear, is not unlike Mr Pollard at the last Local Board meeting."

There, he had succeeded in distracting Sophia from her book. She turned the pages to see how many remained before the chapter ended, carefully positioned the bookmark and closed the covers. Her fine features were composed, her eyes thoughtful. She still inhabited the story she had been reading. His beautiful wife! She had not yet given him any news. It was eight weeks since they had returned from Lyme; she must surely know now, one way or another. Women often preferred to be mysterious about these matters. Perhaps her silence suggested there was yet hope; he would not question her.

"I have spoken again to Mrs Hutchinson today about the possibility of taking on a Workhouse girl. She is giving the matter serious consideration but would prefer a girl of thirteen or fourteen, an orphan perhaps."

He had her attention now.

"I was afraid of that. There are several who would prefer a younger girl yet it is the older ones with children who are in most immediate need. It is, of course, those whose children have been weaned and taken from them who would be most suitable."

They had been puzzling together over the details of the plan for some weeks. He felt that it was infinitely preferable to find foster homes for the children, but this was not easy.

"I will talk to Mrs Hutchinson again. She may be persuaded to take an older girl but naturally she has concerns for her daughters if there is a history of immorality. These young women cannot all be passed off as widows. And such a girl needs a lot of direction if the plan is to succeed; we know that from our own experience."

"Has she then sufficient vigour for the task?"

He had been visiting Mrs Hutchinson daily for some months in order to treat her for mild melancholia and nervous debility associated with the change of life. He had been a little dubious of the benefits of the galvanic belt but she seemed to find it helpful and was now keen to try twice daily treatments. He told Sophia of the plan and she was somewhat alarmed at the prospect.

"How can you find time to visit Wellesbourne twice a day? And Sundays as well! William, it is too much."

"It is worth trying, my dear, if it effects a cure."

She conceded that the visits would, at least, be of great pecuniary benefit and made him promise to send in some bills soon. The school fees were due, she said, and the butcher's bill, and there was scarcely enough to manage.

"We would have no butcher's bill to pay if I could persuade you that we should all try a vegetarian diet. I am certain it would benefit our health. But very well, I shall do so soon. Cursed bills! I had rather patients pressed a coin into my hand when they shake it."

Sophia was looking thoughtful.

"Shall I one day need galvanism, I wonder?"

He looked at her quickly.

"Sophia, you do not think – "

"No, not yet."

She paused.

"But I am afraid there will not be a child, William, not this time."

He rose and sat next to her, held her in his arms. He felt unable to speak. To have eight children would have been a fine thing, a very fine thing.

Selina's hand shook a little as she poured the cocoa into the children's mugs. Dr Ackland was talking with Kingsley; she knew the conversation was about stars because that was all Kingsley talked about lately, but the names made her dizzy, Ursa Major, Virgo, Hydra. She walked around the table to Lucy and helped her with her boiled egg, then moved quickly away from the cloying, eggy smell, surreptitiously leaning against the sideboard as she stood with her hands behind her back. The faces of the family seemed to swim before her.

"Selina?"

"Yes, Ma'am?"

"Did you not hear me the first time? Some more toast please, we have very little left."

She went into the kitchen. Eliza held two toasting forks in one hand and waved the other in time to her singing, the words changing in response to Selina's arrival.

"It won't be long, long, long."

On the stove several slices of toast were keeping warm in the rack, next to the stockpot that simmered gently. The smell of the meat stock was suddenly too much, Selina turned and in a few steps was through the door and into the privy. She knelt and retched again and again, sweat breaking out coldly on her forehead. She should have eaten breakfast, she was hungry, that was all. She leaned back against the door until the spasm came over her again and she leaned forward, her stomach muscles tightening and forcing the sour liquid up into her mouth. She breathed deeply and forced herself to stand, she must go back, Mrs Ackland would ask questions.

"Come on! What are you up to? The toast'll get cold!"

Eliza stared at her, holding out the toast rack.

"I got a touch of the runs, that's all. Wait til I have a sip of water."

In the scullery she leaned her forehead against the cool wall and for a moment imagined she felt Mr Barry's arms around her, comforting her. It was no good, she must not think of him. Tomorrow she must eat breakfast, it was hunger, that was all. Now back to the kitchen, she had to keep going.

Eliza was still gawping at her.

"Don't 'ee tell Mrs Ackland, please. Her'll only make a fuss. 'Twill soon pass."

Chapter Twenty Two

Sophia patted her hair into shape and gave her head a little shake to make sure the pins were secure. She was not yet used to the style – would it really withstand the sea breeze at Westward Ho!? The day's outing was really more of a worry than a pleasure. Mr Pynsent had invited the whole family to tea at the Pebble Ridge Hotel and William had booked an open carriage so that they might arrive in style for a stroll around the resort before having a picnic on the beach and then a walk across the Burrows to the hotel in the afternoon. The carriage was then to meet them to take them back to Bideford. All this had been enthusiastically communicated to her as a 'surprise'.

He meant well of course but he did not, unfortunately, consider the practicalities. As a director of the resort, he liked to take a stroll occasionally and pass the time of day with the gentlefolk who had moved into the new villas, many of whom were involved in one way or another with the development. On this occasion, he had decided it would be pleasant to show off his family, so they would all have to be displaying their best clothes and behaviour. The clothes and behaviour also had to be on show for the visit to the Hotel, after a picnic on the beach during which both adults and children would have become sandy, dishevelled and weary. In addition, the servants had to come in order to organise the picnic and help with the children, and Jimmy, too, was to accompany them, so a sandy, boisterous dog was to be added to the equation. The day would be a trial, she was sure of it.

She took a last look in the mirror and hurried upstairs to the children's bedrooms. Annie was helping Jane arrange the younger ones' hair while Selina, having been asked to complete her morning chores earlier than usual, helped Lucy to dress. Hugh, looking very smart in his new knickerbockers and straw boater, sat on the bed next to Kingsley, who had promised to read him the book on dinosaurs if he sat still. Sophia flew around the bedroom adding hair pins and tying laces.

"The carriage will arrive in twenty minutes. Kingsley, please see that your father is ready and Selina, run down and make sure Eliza has the picnic packed. Then please carry it to the door and pack some combs and a clothes brush. And a brush for Jimmy. And see that you are presentable yourself. No, Hugh, I am sorry but there are to be no buckets and spades today. If you are good then perhaps a little paddle but no splashing."

The carriage arrived a few minutes early and by 10.30 they were bowling along the causeway. She relaxed a little. What a sight they were! Kingsley and Hugh sat proudly beside the driver, William in his best coat sat next to her with Annie on his right, and the four younger girls, looking so pretty all in white, faced each other behind with Jane and Selina.

"When we arrive in Westward Ho! I would like you, Jane and Selina, to walk together behind the family. You may need to take Hugh's hand, Jane, in which case Selina can walk alone at the back."

The horses slowed to a walk as they ascended the hill towards Northam. She wanted to ask William what it had cost to hire the carriage but was afraid the driver might overhear. It must be an extravagance. He still had not sent out many bills, she would have to speak to him about it again. He was telling her now about the plans for the pier in Westward Ho! which had been all but destroyed in last autumn's storms and was now being rebuilt.

"I call it a folly! Even the greatest example of man's ingenuity will not withstand the power of the waves that roll in from the Atlantic, and this is certainly not the greatest example; it is an insubstantial cast-iron structure with as much strength as a spider, but when we gaze on it we will admire it, will we not, children, lest the Reverend Gosset or Captain Molesworth or any of its other promoters are within earshot."

Their laughter rang out and they vied with each other to suggest creatures that the pier could be made to resemble until she had to hush them, for their noisy carriage was attracting attention from pedestrians, though she knew the glances to be chiefly of admiration for the striking party they presented.

The carriage turned off before reaching Northam village and began the gradual climb to the top of the ridge above the coastal plain. The early morning breeze had dropped a little and the light clouds had dispersed to reveal a turquoise sky. It would not, however, be too hot as there was already an intimation of autumn in the air, a sense that the pleasures of summer were drawing to a close. It would be the last day given over to pleasure before the winter came.

They reached the Upper Lodge and halted for extra brakes to be fitted for the descent to the resort. The horses fidgeted and threw their heads about as the work was done and Sophia gazed determinedly at the mullioned windows and pinnacled roof of the recently-built lodge, a little nervous of the descent with horses she did not know. When the lodge keeper opened the gate and the carriage rolled forward she clutched William's arm and reached for Annie's hand, although William had assured her that there had never yet been an accident. It was fortunate that there was the sudden view of the wide and beautiful bay to distract one. The aspect was indeed magnificent. Below them at the foot of the hill the imposing buildings of the new resort were distributed amongst level fields that ran to the shore, the edge of an immense expanse of ocean that spread from the west right around to Baggy Point. The Point formed the finger of an encircling arm of land, stretching from the twin estuaries of the Taw and the Torridge, and between the ocean and the river estuaries lay the flat green sward of Northam Burrows; further to the east the far distant hills of Exmoor gleamed as though lit from within. It was surely a view unsurpassed in north Devon and remarkable for its level nature in an area rich in hills and valleys. The huge expanse of sea was tranquil, barely a ripple disturbing its surface. So vast and so still did it seem that it calmed her nerves a little. William turned in his seat,

"There, Selina, does it not remind you of the first view of the ocean when descending to Clovelly? But it will not be so serene when the autumn storms arrive."

Sophia looked back at her younger daughters. The eyes of all four were wide with astonishment and not a little fear and she guessed she was not the only one to feel relief at their eventual arrival at the stables at the bottom of the hill.

No sooner had they descended from the carriage than a smartly dressed man emerged from the grand entrance of the Westward Ho! Hotel and strode over the road to William, shaking his hand and greeting him warmly. William introduced him as Mr Edward Willis, the hotel manager, and they quickly found themselves in the lounge of the establishment, being offered refreshments.

She began to relax a little as the morning wore on. The children behaved impeccably in the hotel and though they were a little high-spirited when released on to the street, they walked sensibly enough. Together they visited the new church, strolled past the guesthouses and took the little lane that led down to the ladies' baths. There were several visitors about and all were greeted, William enquiring quite proprietarily where they were staying and whether it met with their satisfaction.

"You see,"

he whispered after they had bid farewell to the third well-dressed family,

"There was absolutely no need for Charles to worry, for the resort is only attracting the better class of visitor and they will not defile the place with litter. Of course the prices at the hotels will ensure that it continues that way."

He felt a little uncomfortable still that, despite having suggested the title of Charles Kingsley's novel for the new resort, he had been unable to persuade the author of its worth. Sophia frequently had to listen to his doubts about the development as he veered between pride at its success and discontent that the boys who had played on its wild shores were now only welcome as golf caddies.

When they reached the beach she gave the children leave to run and she and William strolled arm in arm towards their planned picnic spot as they watched the children chasing Jimmy in ever-increasing circles, their shrieks joining his barks and the cries of seagulls. The tide was out, leaving a quarter of a mile of firm, gleaming sand. There was no need to be anxious about wet clothes and possible accidents at present. Perhaps she had worried unnecessarily.

Westward Ho! 1870's

The large pebble Selina squatted on was cold and hard. Her black buttoned boots rested in a shallow puddle of salt water, left by the tide at the base of the pebble ridge. She pushed aside a strand of hair that blew across her face. There was nothing to slow the pace of the breeze that blew fiercely across the empty sands. The beach stretched out flatly for a quarter of a mile before her, and to her left and to her right so far that she could not see the end, a dull expanse of beige interspersed with shiny silver patches where the wet sand reflected the sun. A grey haze partially obscured the distant houses they had visited and the sudden hills that rose behind. Before her in the distance were the diminishing black silhouettes of the Ackland family and, beyond them, the sea, no longer huge but a mere strip of blue edged with ribbons of white surf. She could hear the distant roar of the waves and the cries of gulls, and could smell the salt. She wrapped her arms around her knees, cold despite the warmth of the sun.

She had offered to stay here to look after the hamper. During the picnic she had tried to smile and talk to the children. She had thought it would be a relief to be alone and not to have to try so hard. But now there was nothing else to think of, and nothing else to look at, except those dreadful pictures in her head that would not go away. She must try to keep busy; she opened the hamper, rearranged the cups and the dirty plates, folded the napkins and wrapped the sandwich crusts. A large silver-grey gull with a severe yellow beak strutted in her direction. It stopped at a safe distance, eyeing the hamper, then edged slyly towards her. Its eyes were small and intent. Throw it a crust, quick. It grabbed the crust and she rose and waved her arms.

"Get out! Go on! Leave me alone!"

Then she closed the lid firmly and pushed the wicker catch into its hasp again, trying to think of something else, anything. But still the fierce memories came rushing back.

She was in the Workhouse that first time with her belly huge, impossible to hide, and mad Mary was shrieking at her, her face and her stinking breath and her flailing hands and long nails up close as Selina fought to hold her back. Then the memory switched and she was back in that bedroom, on her hands and knees on the dusty wooden floor and she could hear those heavy footsteps and the gruff voice calling out for her, that smell of hair oil coming closer. She closed her eyes tight as the footsteps got nearer but when the beach disappeared from view the bedroom was clearer than ever; his boots, muddy from the farmyard muck, shoving her, insistent, pushing her over as if she was no more than a bundle of rags.

She jumped up and walked along the damp sand, backwards and forwards, then turned and stared out at the distant sea. Why was it not more like Clovelly? There was no sand at Clovelly stretching emptily in every direction, there were things to look at, waves and boats and cliffs and walls, people repairing boats and nets and children playing and old men sitting. Here there was nothing to see, nothing to keep those fearsome memories at bay.

There were all those old fears and there was another that made her stomach lurch. She could not think of that one. It was a closed door. Part of her knew what it was and part of her didn't. If she kept busy she would not have to think about it. She was working hard, Mrs Ackland was pleased with her. She could have the situation for ever if she wanted, Mrs Ackland would not turn her out, not while she worked so well. That was all she thought of at home, her work, the next task. Fetch the slops, make the beds, scrub the floors, don't forget the windows; if she gave herself orders throughout the day it kept the other voices away. She had even told the Doctor she was too busy to visit Clovelly. It would be all right as long as she kept working. It was only here on the beach where there was nothing but the flat, empty sands and the distant hush, hush of the sea, it was only here that the nameless fear appeared and when she shut it out, the old horrors appeared in its place. She covered her mouth and stifled a cry as the images flashed before her again. Where was the Doctor? Where was Mrs Ackland? The figures were on the edge of the shore now, she could just make out the small dancing shapes of the younger children and the tall, top-hatted silhouette of the Doctor. She longed for the normality of their chatter, the deep reassuring tones of Dr Ackland's voice.

The younger children were quiet on the way home; Hugh leaning against Kingsley and Lucy resting her head in Maud's lap, her eyes half-closed, rocked by the gentle movement of the carriage. Sophia glanced at William. During the first part of the journey they had discussed the day with great enthusiasm, the various merits of the two hotels, the respectability and graciousness of the guests they had met and the impeccable behaviour of the children. Now he too was quiet. He looked tired. She put her hand on his.

"You will not have to go out again tonight, will you?"

"That depends whether there have been any urgent calls. But I have decided I shall call at Wellesbourne to see Mrs Hutchinson on our way home, it will take just a few minutes so you may all wait in the carriage."

"Perhaps, then, we may have a quiet evening at home. I told Eliza we would only need a light supper after our tea at the hotel."

She looked back again at her daughters and the servants. Lucy was now asleep and Selina, too, had her eyes closed though sitting very upright. It had been a long way for her and Jane to carry the hamper, along the beach and then over the Burrows to the hotel, but the sea air had been beneficial for them all. She herself had felt quite invigorated by the breeze and the exercise; it was not strange that those who wished to improve their health chose to take the air and bathe at Westward Ho!

The carriage carried them down the hill towards Northam. The breeze was light here, making it a warm, pleasant evening. The hedgerows were starred with the white trumpets of great bindweed, and a few late foxgloves, bramble flowers and spikes of yellow gorse were alive with butterflies, and a blackbird sang an intoxicatingly languorous melody. She could almost drift off to sleep herself, but that would hardly do when their party was so keenly observed by all those they passed. She inclined her head to a labourer who raised his hat as he trudged up the hill, a shovel on his shoulder.

William leaned towards her ear.

"Only think, just a generation or two back and my ancestors went on foot like that and carried the tools of manual labour. My father was servant to the surgeon William Smith before eventually starting his apprenticeship with him. Look at us now, in a carriage drawn by two fine horses and able to pass the time of day with some of the most highly respected people in the land! What, I wonder, may our children and our grandchildren achieve?"

"We have much to be thankful for. It is all due to your hard work, William."

She took his hand and hid from him a little shiver of apprehension. She could not be complacent about their good fortune. Had she not once lost everything she valued? One never knew what the future might hold.

Chapter Twenty Three

Selina wandered to the kitchen window, pulled up a chair and leaned her elbows on the sill. The wind was gaining strength with every hour that passed and the garden appeared to be under attack from an invisible enemy that was whipping the tendrils of honeysuckle on the trellis back and forth and tearing the last brown leaves from the lilac. A drift of leaves in the corner of the yard rose suddenly before falling again like a sigh, and one large copper-coloured leaf flew at the window and stuck to the glass just below the glazing bars. It partially obscured Selina's view but she did not trouble to move her head. A sudden flurry of raindrops spattered on to the window. Winter was coming.

Mrs Ackland had told the children it would rain and had ensured that they took their walk early. She had encouraged Selina to go out also.

"You should take some air, Selina, you are looking a little pale."

Selina had murmured that perhaps she would go out. It was not too late, even now, and she had finished her sewing, but it was warm in the kitchen and would be cosy when she lit the candles and drew the curtains. She could be alone, there was no one who might stare at her or ask difficult questions.

She was careful not to do the sewing in the evenings when Eliza and Jane were around. They were both out on a Sunday so it was all right. It wouldn't have mattered if they had seen what she was doing, of course not, but she did not want to be teased about getting fat. She was eating too much, that was all. Too much of Eliza's apple cake and apple pie. There was an apple tree in the garden and the Doctor was always bringing home bags of apples from patients; they ate apples cooked in one way or another every day, usually with cream. Even her fingers seemed to be getting fatter and the ring she had to wear was cutting into her.

Each Sunday she had let out one of her dresses and they were all done now. It was fortunate that there was plenty of material in the seams. By letting them out and tying her apron loosely she could hide how fat she was becoming. What business was it of theirs anyway?

Her thoughts turned suddenly to Mr Barry. He seemed to appear before her along with an abrupt little jolt which came from inside her and it was as if she could see his face, smell his skin, feel his arms around her, warming her and comforting her. She stood up and walking quickly across the kitchen, pulled the copper pans down from the shelf on to the table and polished them vigorously. She must keep busy. Why did the memory of him keep coming back like that? She didn't ask it to. She didn't want to see him; why should she want to see him? The memory of him that nudged at her insides stirred up such feelings of regret and longing that she could hardly bear it. She picked up a cloth and rubbed at the stove until she could see her face in it. Keep busy, that was the answer. It was easy to do during the week, it was Sundays that she did not look forward to.

He had been to the house again. Last week she had heard Eliza and Jane talking.

"He's mazed, I reckon, that man. Insisted he'd left a bottle of oil here and wanted to come in to look! As if we wouldn't have found it ourselves! He tried to push me aside but *I* wasn't going to let him in!"

"Was he a bit strange, Selina, that man who did the polishing while us was away? I wouldn't like to be alone in the house with him!"

She had said no, he wasn't strange, not really, and had turned away, not wanting to talk about him anymore, not with them. If there really had been a bottle of oil, perhaps she could have taken it to him. But she knew she mustn't even think about seeing him.

She walked back to the window and sat down. How different the garden was now that autumn was here. The seat on the lawn where she had sat in the summer was empty and would remain so now. Last Sunday the solitude had become too much for her, suddenly she had felt she *had* to go out and had decided she would visit Mary so they could talk of ordinary things, of the weather and the price of flour and little Thomas's latest tricks. She had taken her shawl from her drawer and wrapped it over her hair and loosely across her front before tying it behind. She could keep it on in Mary's house, just push it back from her head.

The weather had been dreadful last Sunday as well. The wind had howled along Mill Street carrying with it a squall of rain. There was no one else in sight and she had hurried along with head bent, glad to gain a little shelter when she turned into Coldharbour.

She had knocked at Mary's door, waited, and knocked again. The rain had come on more fiercely. After the third knock the door opened slowly and stopped when it was just ajar. Mary peered out at her. Her face was half hidden.

"Oh, Selina. 'Tis you."

"Mary? Be 'ee all right?"

Was it possible that Mary had been crying?

"You'd better come in, I suppose."

She had turned away and Selina followed her into the living room. Only then did she turn around to face Selina, but looked down, unable to meet her gaze. One eye was half closed and surrounded by a purple bruise. There was a cut on one side of her swollen lip.

"Mary! Whatever have 'ee done?"

"Thomas did it."

For a moment Selina had glanced down incredulously at baby Thomas playing contentedly on the floor.

"My husband Thomas."

Mary sat down woodenly. Her hair, normally combed into an immaculate bun was dishevelled, as if she had not arranged it since getting up. Her apron had a stain on the front.

"'Tisn't the first time."

Selina had been too shocked to know what to say. It

happened to a lot of women, of course, but Mary?

"'Tis the money, Selina. He worries. My brother has moved out so we've no help there anymore. He worries and more bills come in and then he goes out and drinks to forget it all. But when he comes home he remembers again."

Her usually bright, squirrel-like eyes were dull and empty.

"I'm doing my best though. I'm taking in some needlework, us'll get by. And he's always so sorry the next day when he sees what he's done."

They had sat in silence for a while, one each side of the fireplace with Thomas playing on the floor between them.

Mary had made a cup of tea and they had talked desultorily of people they knew in Clovelly, of the cold that baby Thomas had had and the approaching winter. Selina had known she was unable to provide any comfort for Mary, or Mary for her, so it was better to talk of things that didn't cause upset. When she left, Mary had embraced her.

"You're a good friend to me, Selina. If ever I have a daughter, I shall name her after you."

Selina shifted her weight to make herself more comfortable on her chair by the window. A wood pigeon landed in the lilac tree in the garden and tried to keep its balance as the branches bowed and swayed in the wind. Beyond the garden, smoke was torn from the chimneys in Mill Street, disappearing into the invisible gusts as soon as it left the chimney pots. Selina turned away. There was nothing out there to hold her attention.

She moved the chair to the dresser, unlocked the drawer where she kept her things and unfolded the cloth bag inside. There were the three silver crowns ready to send to her mother and there was the little lead cow and calf that she had bought for Will. She picked them up and examined them again. The colours were a little smudged but they were otherwise perfect. She placed them on the dresser so that the cow was looking down at its calf. Mrs Ackland had said to wait a few days to see whether the Doctor would be going to Clovelly again, but she had started to write a little note to Will because really there was far too much work to do for her to have a day off, it would be better to send the money and the present with the postman. If only Will could visit her here! When she pictured herself visiting Clovelly, all she could see was her mother's face and those sharp eyes examining and appraising her.

She turned back to the drawer. In a fold of paper she had a lock of Will's hair, taken during the week she had spent with him in June. She had cut it carefully from behind his ear where it would not show, making him promise not to wriggle lest she accidently hurt him. That was the last time she had seen him and it was October now. She remembered that it must be his birthday soon, or was it last week? He would be five years old. She carefully rewrapped the lock of hair and put it aside. Next in the drawer was the blue ribbon that she had worn when she had walked to Abbotsham with Mr Barry, and the cream rose, carefully dried, that he had placed in her bonnet.

The kitchen door opened suddenly and Mrs Ackland came in.

"Oh, Selina! You are still here! I'm just going to make the tea. Did Eliza make a seed cake, do you know? Oh look, are those little animals for your son? When Dr Ackland next visits Clovelly, you will be able to take them with you. It is such a shame you felt unwell last time. Now, the kettle is boiling, is it not?"

Selina got up.

"Let me make the tea, Ma'am."

She hoped Mrs Ackland would return to the drawing room, but she stood and talked while Selina arranged the tray. Within a few minutes she was back again and left a book for Selina to look at. It was a dark blue book with gold writing. She traced her finger along the embossed letters. *The Pilgrim's Progress*. Inside was a black and white engraving of a tired looking man bent double under a heavy load, walking up a long, empty road. There were few other pictures and they were all black and white and equally dull. She put it down.

Outside, the sky was growing dark; an extra strong gust of wind carried a spattering of rain on to the windowpane. She drew the curtains and lit the candles. There, the kitchen was golden in the candlelight and the little flickering flames were reflected in the gleaming surfaces that she had polished. She would finish the letter to Will so that it could be given to the postman tomorrow. She smoothed the folded sheet of paper and carefully read what she had written so far.

- *Dearest Will,*

I hope this findes you well. I am sorry that I cannot vizit you. I hope I maye vizit you agen wun day.

She stared at the candle on the table that flickered in a sudden draught, realising that she did not know when that day would come. She rose heavily and went to the cupboard for the pen and the bottle of ink.

Curse the bills! There now, Captain Richard Yeo of Cooper Street. Visits in April, July and September; it was time that was despatched. Dr Ackland took up another sheet of paper and scribbled his address at the top. The date, what was the date? 20th November 1872. He addressed the envelope and added it to the pile waiting to be collected by the postman. His desk was piled with leather-bound ledgers, diaries and casebooks, their intimidating appearance lightened by occasional children's drawings that peeped from their pages. Between them were small bottle of pills which he removed from time to time from a wall cabinet and placed on the desk as the remedies for a certain collection of symptoms occurred to him; these he would scoop up and drop into his bag before embarking on his visits. Now then, caulophyllum for the case of post-partum infection. He added the bottle to the collection. He must make that visit to Instow the priority, the Westleigh and Bideford visits could follow. From the schoolroom came the sing-song voices of his children reciting a poem and Sophia's low voice correcting and encouraging, from the kitchen the rattle of pots and Eliza's slightly off-key singing. He leafed through the pages of his casebook. Captain Richard Yeo of Cooper Street, that one could wait a little longer. Ah, here between the pages was a cheque that he had overlooked, with a note from General Hutchinson. Gracious me, well, it had only been here for a week or so. That amount would please Sophia very much indeed. Were they helping, all these visits to Mrs Hutchinson? He was being watched very keenly by Dr Cohen and Dr Thompson; they would be eager to ridicule him if they could detect the merest whiff of the charlatan. Jealousy, of course; the fees were considerable. He gazed at the skull on the shelf above his desk.

"What thinkest thou, Yorick? Am I walking a tightrope, shall I fall?"

But Mrs Hutchinson was improving, he really did believe he was effecting a cure. Yesterday she had even spoken of attempting a little golf again. Would that all patients could be visited as frequently, he would be then feted throughout the area.

Now then, there were all these visits to Mr Walter Chope's children but then there were his bills to balance against them, bills for a new gig saddle and breeching and other smaller items. Perhaps Sophia would go through those for him or he would be here all morning. He leaned back in his chair and consulted his watch. There were still letters to write and he was to visit the Workhouse at eleven o'clock before commencing his visits. Ah, here was Selina with his coffee.

"Macaroons again, excellent. Have you considered where the word comes from, Selina? I believe it is Italian and no doubt has the same derivation as macaroni. Did you know that macaroni can mean both an Italian dish and a fashionably dressed fellow? No, I don't suppose you did, but in any case please congratulate Eliza on her excellent baking."

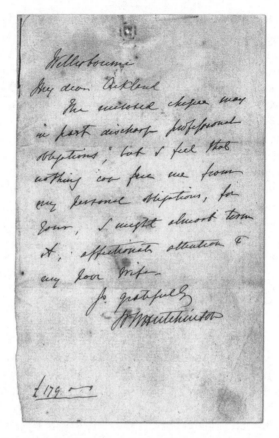

Letter, W.N. Hutchinson to Dr W.H. Ackland
(From the papers of the Ackland and Littlewood families. Reproduced by permission of the Wellcome Library, London)

Wellesbourne

My Dear Ackland

The enclosed cheque may in part discharge professional obligations; but I feel that nothing can free me from my personal obligations for your, I might almost term it, affectionate attention to my poor wife.

Yours gratefully,

W.N. Hutchinson

£179.00

Now he must write to Messrs Tilleard, Godden and Holme, solicitors to the late Mrs Elwes. Here was the list of the poor people of Bucks Mills whom he had attended during the past year. He wrote quickly, signed his name with a flourish and added the envelope to the pile. Next a quick note to Mr Bryant Ching who was now in Maidstone and again apologising for the non-payment of bills.

There, surely that would do for now. He pushed back his chair and looked out of the window to the garden where Jane was hanging out the washing. It was a sunny, blustery day and the pieces of children's clothing flapped, as if animated by unseen little ones within. Jane picked up the basket and returned through the yard to the back door. He was to visit the Workhouse to interview a young woman. Mrs Hutchinson had agreed to take a girl as had Mrs Bazeley if suitable candidates could be found. He would question the young woman and ascertain to whom she would be best suited. It was a role Sophia had hoped to fulfil but they had agreed that his profession would enable him to ask more searching and intimate questions. There had been a child who had died; he must discover the circumstances of the child's birth as the girl would be unlikely to be suitable if she felt little remorse for her downfall. There was much at stake in this venture, not least his reputation.

As he gazed at the window, seeing not the garden but the future possibilities of the scheme, Selina moved into his field of vision. He had barely heard the door. Something was awry. What he could see was not possible. This could not be Selina, not now, not here!

She was holding the tray against herself with one hand while with the other she retrieved his cup and saucer from the desk. The tray pushed against her groin, and above it her stomach swelled in a manner that was unmistakeable.

"Selina?"

"Sir?"

How could it be? His head reeled with the impossibility of the situation and still she held the tray in one hand and the cup in the other, looking at him questioningly. There was no gainsaying it. It was fact.

"Selina! You are with child!"

For several moments they stared at one another and he scarcely knew who was most alarmed, then she cried out in shrill, anguished tones that he had rarely heard outside the asylum.

"NO! No, Sir, I am not! I am not! NO!"

Then there was a crash and the day and his plans and the china all lay in pieces on the turkey carpet.

Sophia was reading aloud the story of Jesus in the temple when she heard the scream and the crash. When it was followed by the raised voice of her husband she knew this to be no ordinary kitchen accident. Mary and Emily had already risen to their feet and she quickly reassured them and requested that Mary continue the story while she went to investigate.

"Don't worry, my darlings, I'm sure it is nothing but please do not leave your seats until I return."

She hurried down the passage and as she opened the door to her husband's study, she heard him shout.

"Who was it? How has this happened in my household?"

She had never heard him speak so! She stood in the doorway and there was Selina on the floor quite distraught with William towering over her and china in pieces at his feet.

"Leave us! I will deal with this!"

She closed the door again immediately, shocked by his thunderous expression. Never had he spoken to her like that before! She could hear his voice within,

"Tell me! I *will* know!"

She could hear Selina sobbing wildly. She found she was shaking and was almost afraid to be found still at the door. She returned quickly to the door of the schoolroom and paused to collect herself. She was aware that the rest of the house was silent, listening. She took a deep breath and went in.

"There, it was nothing, Selina dropped a cup, that was all."

The four children stared at her, wide-eyed.

"Mary, I am sure you were reading beautifully. Please continue, and I shall listen."

Whatever could have happened? It was most unlike him to shout like that; if ever he raised his voice it was at some perceived injustice, never at one of his fellow human beings, certainly not at a member of his household. She tried to smile encouragement at Mary and attend to the sing-song voice.

"And Jesus went into the temple of God, and cast out all them that bought and sold in the temple, and overthrew the tables of the moneychangers, and the seats of them that sold doves."

She could hear his voice again and then suddenly a door closing loudly, almost slammed, and another. With an instinct she rose and went to the window moving slowly, so as not to disturb the children. It was a high window, too high for the children in their seats, and it looked out on to the yard. She saw William standing there, looking at the ground.

"What is it, Mother? What is happening?"

She realised that Mary had stopped reading.

"Nothing, darling. It is all right. Please continue. I won't be long."

She went out into the passage. She could hear Selina in the study, still sobbing. She tried the door but to her astonishment it was locked. The kitchen was unusually silent. She walked towards the back door and looked from the window. William still stood in the yard with his back to her but suddenly strode forward and leapt up the steps as if possessed. He continued up the garden as if driven by some urgent purpose and stopped abruptly at the end. Then he stood and stared at the high wall. A minute passed, then another. He stood very still. She wished he would turn, though at this distance it would have been hard to make out his expression. Should she go to him? His words to her still stung and she feared his reaction should she intrude again.

He had put his hand up to his face. His head was bowed and his shoulders shook a little. Surely not! Could he be weeping?

Sophia stared at the shadowy, ordered drawing room. Eliza had turned the lamps low, knowing they would not be needed for reading this evening; the dark reds and blues glowed dully from the deep folds of the damask curtains that had been drawn to shut out the cold and blustery night. She tried to draw in the shadowy composure of the room and breathed deeply to calm her aching head and her racing thoughts, but instead felt her heart start to pound again. The children were in bed and, she hoped, asleep, but their anxious faces as she had kissed them goodnight suggested that they would be awake for some time. She had done her best to reassure them. Selina was just a little unwell, she had said, but she knew that they were disturbed by the tense atmosphere in the household.

The only sounds were the ticking of the clock and the crackle of the fire. William sat opposite, his chin on his hand and his eyes quite devoid of their usual merriment. She looked at him and she saw for the first time that he was no longer young. For the last hour they had talked, desperately seeking to understand the situation, reminding each other to keep their voices low, calming and reassuring each other as each in turn became overwhelmed by the enormity of the affair. They had found no solution.

William leaned back and gazed at her.

"Whatever we decide, we must act swiftly. She must go in the morning. While she remains here she brings shame and ridicule on our household. I cannot dupe myself into believing this news can be contained. Eliza and Jane will find it impossible to keep it to themselves for even a day. Indeed, how do we not know that Selina herself has not already told others?"

"I think not. Did you not feel that she had concealed the knowledge even from herself?"

"You are right, I'm sure she did. It is not unusual in cases such as this."

He leapt to his feet, overwhelmed by his feelings once again.

"But in *my* household! In full view of *my* children! *Why* did I not see it before – all these months under my very nose! Let us see what Dr Cohen and Dr Thompson make of that! I shall be the laughing stock!"

She rose and put her arms around him, as much to comfort herself as to calm him, but his muscles were tense and he almost fought her off. She returned to her chair and clasped her hands together to stop them shaking.

"And where is she to go? Not to her parents for they will not take her in, and why should they when she is bearing a *third* illegitimate child, conceived under the roof of her benefactor and supposed protector. Would we had never gone to Lyme!"

"We do not know that it happened then."

"I am sure it is so. The dates would be right. If she would only tell us the culprit's name!"

Selina had refused to give them any information, indeed had been too distraught to understand their questions although they had both, after the first shock, been calm and kind in their manner so as not to distress her further. Sophia had taken her by the shoulders and said as calmly and firmly as she could that she *must* tell them his name, so that whether or not she had been coerced, he could be forced to make amends. She had flung herself from the chair and with her back to the study wall, had stared wildly at them both.

"I bain't going to! I bain't never going to tell you his name!"

After that she had again become incoherent until they had had to give up their questioning. Sophia had sent for some tea but she had been unable to eat or drink anything. Eventually she had been put to bed in the guest bedroom, there being nowhere else where she could be isolated from the rest of the household, and when Sophia had looked in after seeing to the children she had at last fallen into an exhausted sleep.

William had returned to his chair, his anger abated for the time being. He looked defeated.

"I could find some widow to take her in, but for how long? I cannot support her until the child is of age! Imagine what the gossips of Bideford would have to say about that; they would soon be whispering the name of the supposed father! That, more than anything, would jeopardise my reputation. At present I can see only one solution and it is the very one to which I am most averse. If she will not name the father, what can I do but return her from whence she came? But not her young son, I will not have that innocent child suffer for his mother's weakness. I will see that he remains in Clovelly. And I was to take girls *from* the Workhouse!"

She rose and sat at his feet and held his hand. She remembered the women in the able-bodied ward that she had so fearfully visited. The majority were pale ghosts creeping spiritlessly about in their dreary uniforms; a few were wild-eyed and rebellious and given to lewd outbursts; all were confined together in the sour atmosphere of the almost windowless room. It was repellent to even think of sending Selina to such a place, yet she had let them down so very badly! When they had questioned her, the sobbing had, at one time, suddenly stopped and she had gazed at them with wide, fearful eyes.

"You bain't going to send me back to the Workhouse! Not there! Please!"

Her voice had been a terrified whisper, the very memory of which made Sophia shiver. But they had reiterated that if she would only tell them her seducer's name, they would be able to make arrangements. Surely she would tell them in the morning! Whatever the outcome, their plan for the Workhouse girls would have to be abandoned now. Mrs Hutchinson and Mrs Bazeley would have to be told – the embarrassment of it! What would be whispered behind cupped hands about her abilities as a mistress and housekeeper? She leaned her head against William, hoping to draw on his strength and he began to stroke her hair absent-mindedly. She saw now that their reputations, which had seemed so assured, were in fact precarious. To have allowed gross immorality to take place in their own household alongside their young and vulnerable children! Not only that, but to have planned for other families to take on such girls from the Workhouse so that their households, also, might be corrupted!

"Sophia, I feel your pulse racing even as you lean against me."

She lifted her head. His poor, tired face, his eyes full of concern for her.

"We *will* triumph over this, I will see to it! Do you think I would allow my dear wife and little ones to suffer because of my own short-sightedness? It will be difficult but we will face it and we will see it through; to those that need to know we will say that we were too trusting, that is not so bad a fault. We wished to help and we failed to help, we have not actively committed a wrongdoing. We will walk with our heads held high and smile graciously at those who wish, at first, to laugh at us. It will soon pass, you will see. Now, now, don't cry, my darling."

He drew her up and she pressed her face into the softness of his beard as she felt the sobs rising and shuddering from her, until the warmth and comfort of his arms and his calming voice soothed her. She knew him to be as exhausted as she was herself.

Suddenly the drawing room flew open. They both looked up in surprise and some embarrassment. Eliza stood in the doorway, her eyes wide.

"It's Selina, she's gone! Gone from the bed and from the house!"

OUR CHRISTMAS MARKET.

The Bideford Christmas Market was held on Thursday, when, notwithstanding the inclemency of the weather, the show of meat, poultry, and general provisions was fully equal to that of previous years, the supply being large and the quality excellent. Our local butchers and neighbouring farmers, having faith in the disposition of the inhabitants to be true to the traditions of old Christmas, did their best to meet the demands of the season and to attract customers, and we very much question whether in any other town of an equal size there was a more profuse or primer show to be met with. Our neighbours, Mr. R. E. Holman and Mr. T. Holman, of Allhalland-street, had as usual the finest display in the meat market. Here the stalls generally were much admired, while in the pannier market the poultry, owing to the size and appearance of most of the geese, turkeys, and fowls, attracted considerable attention, as did the game, of which however, there was only a limited supply. It is unnecessary to say that for all kinds of meat and poultry there was a large demand. In the town the grocers were well provided with fruits and spices and other Christmas requisites, and the drapers, whose windows were tastefully decorated, were provided with every article of dress that could be desired for the festive season. Amongst the stock exhibited on the butchers' stalls and in the poultry market were the following:

Mr. R. E. Holman, Bideford:—3 prime fat heifers fed by Mr. J. F. Balsdon, Southcott, Mr. J. Downing, Horwood, and Mr. R. Packer, Tawstock; 10 prime fat sheep fed by Mr. G. Furze, Durpley, Mr. J. Beer, Parkham, and Mr. R. Packer, Tawstock; 2 very prime fat pigs fed by himself; also a very fine rabbit.

Mr. T. Holman, Bideford:—1 fat heifer fed by Mr. G. Davey, Plaistow Mills; 2 fat heifers fed by Mr. W. Burdens, Swymbridge; 1 very good calf fed by Mr. C. Heathcott, Northam; 12 prime sheep fed by himself; 2 good pigs fed by Mr. Warmington, Buckish; 1 prime pig fed by himself.

Mr. J. Cruse, Bideford:—1 prime ox fed by Mr. G. Lock, Instow Barton; prime heifer fed by Mr. R. Balsdon; prime mutton fed by Mr. G. Lock; dairy fed pork by Mr. T. L. Dayman, Parkham.

Mr. J. Fulford, Northam:—1 prime heifer fed by Mr. R. Packer, Tawstock; 2 prime sheep fed by Mr. Ralph, Hartland; prime mutton fed by Mr. J. Heywood, Abbotsham; 3 prime porkers, 2 of them fed by himself.

Mr. G. Cawsey, Northam:—One prime heifer fed by Mr. John Cocks, Tavern, Appledore; one ditto fed by Mr. Tucker, Arlington; two horn wethers fed by Mr. William Penhorwood, Northam; two prime ewes bred and fed by Mr. William Pickard, Bidna, Northam; prime pork fed by Mr. John Penhorwood, Northam.

Mr. J. A. Chapple, Northam:—Prime heifer fed by Mr. Packer, Tawstock; two wether sheep fed by Mr. J. Brownscombe, Huntshaw; two ditto fed by Mr. Trewin, Pillhead; two pigs fed by Mr. Ford, Langtree: one ditto fed by himself

Mr. Jones, Instow:—Fat heifer fed by Mr. Packer, Tawstock; two prime wethers fed by Mr. Tucker, Westleigh; one sheep fed by Mr. Chapple, Bideford; two small pigs fed by himself.

Mr. Wills, Westleigh:—One prime ox fed by Mr. J. B. Torr, Westleigh; one prime heifer fed by Mr. W. Widlake, Eastleigh Barton; prime wether mutton fed by Mr. T. Trewin, Pillhead Farm; prime wether mutton fed by Mr. Widlake, Eastleigh; one pig fed by Mr. S. Hookway, Westleigh.

Mr. R. Withecombe, Buckland Brewer:—1 prime heifer fed by Mr. T. Joslin, Marwood; 1 prime heifer fed by Mr. R. Balsdon, Southcott; prime wether mutton fed by himself; prime mutton fed by Mr. J. Joslin, Marwood; 1 sheep fed by Mr. T. Caddy, Parkham; large pig fed by himself; 2 prime pigs fed by Mr. J. Jenkins, Buckland Brewer.

Mr. C. Withecombe, Buckland Brewer:—One prime fat heifer fed by Mr. Balsdon, Southcott; one prime heifer fed by Mr. J. Westcott, Marwood; three prime fat sheep fed by Mr. Harris, Buckland Brewer; prime pig fed by Mr. Bailey, Buckland Brewer; two prime porkers fed by Mr. Horm, Buckland Brewer; one ditto fed by himself.

Mr W. H. Smale, Buckland Brewer:—One prime bullock fed by Mr. G. Fairchild, Alverdiscott; two prime sheep fed by Mr. Beer, of Parkham; one fat pig fed by Mr. Allen, Putford; one prime porker fed by himself.

Mr. Sanders, Lovecott:—Prime heifer fed by himself; three horn and wether sheep fed by himself.

Mr. Dennis Andrew, Parkham:—Prime ox fed by Mr. G. Lock, Instow Barton; prime mutton fed by Mr. Downing, Parkham; three dairy fed porkers by Mr. Dayman, Putford, and Mr. Seth Grigg, Parkham.

Mr. Bale, Littleham:—Prime ox fed by Mr. Packer, Tawstock; fat heifer fed by Mr. J. Balsdon, Wear Gifford; two prime sheep fed by Mr. B. Dunn, Parkham; two ditto fed by Mr. Joseph Dunn, Parkham; prime pig fed by Mr. R. Lee, Littleham; one pig fed by himself.

Mr. Hunt, Alwington:—Prime heifer fed by Mr. R. Prust, Hartland; two prime sheep fed by Mr. Sergeant, Alwington; three ditto fed by Mr. Mallett, Alwington.

Mr. John Heal, Parkham:—Prime beef fed by Mr. J. B. Reed, Shebbear; two very prime sheep bred and fed by Mr. Thomas May, East Putford; two very good sheep bred and fed by Mr. J. Beer, Parkham; a good pig bred and fed by Mr. John Beer, Parkham.

Mr. Broom, Parkham:—Two prime ewe sheep bred and fed by Mr. G. Andrew, Parkham Barton; a quantity of fine wether sheep bred and fed by Mr. Moase and Mr. Ford, Parkham; one prime pig bred by Mr. John Andrew, East Putford; one pig fed by Mr. Pearce, Parkham; a quantity of dairy bred and fed pork by Mr. S. Grigg, Parkham.

Mr. James Becalick, Parkham:—An excellent lot of wether and ewe mutton fed by Mr. Parnel, Bradworthy; 2 prime bacon pigs fed by Mr. James Jenkins Buckland Brewer; a lot of dairy fed porkers from Mr. R. Jeffrey, Parkham.

Mr. Ellis, Monkleigh:—1 prime heifer fed by Mr. J. Dennis, Sticklepath; 1 prime ox fed by Mr. J. B. Reed, Binworthy; prime mutton fed by Mr. J. Mallett, Frithelstock; prime wether sheep fed by Mr. J. B. Reed, Binworthy; one very prime pig fed by himself.

Geese, Turkeys, Dks. Fwls The Misses Powe, Bideford, a fine show of all kinds in Mill-street.
Mrs Fry, Bideford 0 0 2 0

BUDE.

Captain O. Davey, the philanthropist of this place from an attack

From the Bideford Gazette

Chapter Twenty Four

The double doors at each end of the large, high-roofed pannier market were open, allowing the frosty air and beams of wintry light to stream in. The market was thronged with men and women warmly dressed in mufflers and gloves and they jostled to get closer to the holly-decked stalls displaying geese, turkeys and fowls. Greetings were called and pleasantries exchanged with the rosy-cheeked farmers' wives who smiled and stamped their feet on the pieces of sacking thrown down as insulation on the cold stone floor. Sophia observed the scene as she stood arm in arm with her husband. He was discussing the business of the Local Board with Mr Vinson and now that she had made the expected enquiries as to the health of his family, she was free to look about, providing she occasionally inclined her head or gave an interested glance to show she was attending to the conversation. The younger women in the market had all worn their best clothes; such a very busy market was a great social occasion and it seemed that many were taking advantage of the opportunity to flirt with a range of suitors. It was the more mature shoppers she was interested in, they had no thoughts of romance to distract them. She scanned the faces, taking care to keep a gentle smile upon her face. She saw one or two observe her and turn away to remark on it to a friend. She guessed that it was not her new bonnet that was attracting attention.

It was unusual for the two of them to go out together like this and William had taken her by surprise when he had suddenly announced that his visits could wait until the afternoon.

"Come, there is no reason for you to hide away. We will go out together and prove that we can hold our heads up high."

They had walked up through the town, buying some Brazil nuts from Mrs Cooler, some sweets from Mr Coles, stopping to look in the windows decorated with rainbows of ribbons at Mr George Boyle's and admiring Mr Vinson's sewing machines a little higher up the High Street, until eventually they had reached the market. Several times she had glimpsed a slight reservation in the eyes of the shopkeepers, a barely discernible pause before they returned the greeting. She had seen it in the eyes of many since that fateful night a month ago. William had been jovial and addressed almost everyone they met on the busy streets:

"Season's greetings to you, Mrs Powe!"

"Now, enjoy Christmas with your family, Mrs Braddick, but not *too* much rich food!"

In the butchers' market every shop was hung with animals to be admired and discussed while the proprietors demonstrated the advantages of each joint in turn, confiding and persuasive in their manner until the order was placed, after which they moved rapidly on to the next customer. Sophia had already ordered their piece of beef and it had been novel to watch the proceedings without the worry of making a purchase. However, to her surprise, William had stepped forward and ordered a very large joint of beef which he asked to be sent to the Workhouse.

"They will, of course, already have donations for the Christmas meal but this will ensure there is plenty for all."

As they moved away, neither had commented on his action.

As she looked around now at the bustling market she felt her spirits lift and for the first time felt that the very difficult time they had been experiencing was drawing to a close. The shock at what had happened had caused a stir in the town and every time she went out there had been knowing looks and carefully worded comments that fell just short of disapproval, but those whose opinion she most valued had been charitable. William had gone about his business with even more enthusiasm and apparent confidence than usual but she knew that this was a calculated strategy to deflect censure; in the evenings he often looked very tired and admitted to her on several occasions that the whole sorry business could have seriously jeopardised his reputation.

Dr Thompson passed with his oldest daughter on his arm. He and William raised their hats and Sophia inclined her head a little. William moved his arm to give her hand an almost imperceptible squeeze as he continued his conversation with Mr Vinson. None of the Bideford doctors had commented openly to William on Selina's disappearance but he had heard that Dr Thompson had made some barbed comments about the appropriateness of him organising the new hospital at the Dispensary. It was merely professional jealousy, William said.

What a fearful night it had been, that night when Selina disappeared. When Eliza had burst in to tell them that she was missing, William had straightaway put on his greatcoat and gone out into the night to search for her. Sophia had sat with Jane and Eliza and they had gone over the day's extraordinary events. She had tried to calm their indignation and anxiety but, in truth, all three became more agitated as the time wore on. William returned after an hour and told them that he had walked all the streets and had enquired at Selina's cousin's house, all to no avail. He took a lantern and went out again, refusing to say where he was going. Sophia insisted that Jane and Eliza went to bed and sat up alone to wait for her husband.

It had been almost one o'clock when he returned and she had run to the door to meet him and help him off with his sodden coat and hat, for it had come on to rain and he was wet right through. He told her he had found no sign of Selina. There was no more they could do that night. In the morning he would drive to Clovelly; there was a chance she might be seen along the road, returning to the village on foot. He had been very subdued and it was almost in a whisper that he said that they should never have let her out of their sight.

It was only later that he had told her of his quest. After

searching the rest of the town he had taken the lantern to the bridge. He had leant over the parapet and had shone the light down on to the water. The river, he had said, was in spate after the recent heavy rain and rushed in muddy, swirling eddies between the arches and off towards the sea. Several times he saw an object carried fast on the tide or caught beneath the bridge and for a few moments his heart had pounded and his mouth gone dry, until he repositioned the lantern and saw that it was a branch or piece of flotsam. He had walked on and had leaned over the parapet again and again, until he had examined all the arches of the ancient bridge. He knew his task to be hopeless, but still he felt compelled to search and had walked along the Quay and questioned some fishermen preparing to go out on the tide, then had gone over the bridge again and along the wharves, shining the lantern down to illuminate the clumps of reeds growing on the muddy banks of the river. He found nothing. As he had walked home, he said, he had tried to take comfort in the knowledge that if, as he suspected, she had jumped from the bridge, her body would be carried out to sea and then, perhaps, towards Clovelly. She would be going home to her son at last.

Sophia had wept when he had told her his thoughts. He had not intended to upset her, but of course, by then, they knew the truth.

The next morning both Eliza and Jane had helped with the breakfast and although Selina's disappearance could not be discussed before the children, many meaningful looks were exchanged between the adults as the meal was served. They were still at table when the door knocker sounded and Sophia had heard a man's voice asking to see both Dr and Mrs Ackland. Eliza had prevaricated but William had risen and she had heard a quick whispered exchange before he called her into the drawing room. To her astonishment, she had seen that the man was Mr Barry, the French polisher. He stood awkwardly in the drawing room, his hat in his hand, and William closed the door.

"Sir; Ma'am; I've come to tell you Selina's with me. And she's staying with me."

They had both stared incredulously at him, until William had spoken.

"*You* are the father of her child?"

"I am, Sir, although I did not know of it until last night.*"*

At this point his emotion had burst through his efforts at being respectful.

"I *am* the father of her child and it is the greatest pleasure for me to say it. I would have married her many months ago if I had known of it, in fact I wanted to marry her, child or no child, but felt I was too old for her and then she hid herself away and I still don't understand why although she's tried to tell me! I dared not speak to you or Mrs Ackland, Sir, knowing that she would lose her job if I did, and thinking that she chose not to see me. I walked past this house so many times, Sir, I think I know every brick and every pane of glass."

He was almost overcome for a moment and William spoke out.

"It gives you *pleasure* to tell me you took advantage of a defenceless girl! In *my* house! Abusing my trust in you while my wife and my innocent children were away! How dare you jeopardise the reputation of my family and my house with your depravity!"

She had rarely seen William so angry. Mr Barry was unable to meet his gaze and fumbled with his cap.

"Sir, no harm was intended. If I did wrong, Sir, it was in thinking more of Selina than the reputation of your household. I had quite given up hope of seeing her again until she turned up on my doorstep last night. I can still scarcely believe it. And so upset, she was! Pleaded with me to take her in but had no thought of marrying. Said I could do as I wished with her, said that she preferred any life to that in the Workhouse. As if I ..., of course I'll marry her!"

"And she has agreed?"

Sophia was finding it so hard to take in the news. She felt

incapable of asking questions.

"Oh yes, Sir, she has agreed! Us've been so busy with talking, Sir, and so happy it's resolved, us've barely slept, Sir, an hour or two at most."

Sophia had turned away at that news. Selina had spent the night at his house and he seemed to feel no shame! And he was so very much older than she. He might consider the situation to be resolved, but it was far from resolved as far as she was concerned, for the news of Selina's shame and the resultant disgrace visited on the household was still to spread throughout the town.

William spoke for her.

"Have you any idea of the trouble you have caused? I was out searching for her and fearing the worst until the early hours! Why did you not let us know last night that she was with you? I am frankly astonished that someone of your mature years and with your good local reputation should act in such an irresponsible manner!"

The man apologised sincerely, stating that he had been afraid to leave her in such a distressed state, but, when William then stated that to limit the disgrace brought on his own household, she must move to a respectable house until they could be married, he responded in a most disrespectful manner, almost glaring at the Doctor and declaring that he would not let her out of his sight again.

The interview had ended soon after and there had been no contact since. After a few days, there had been the added shock of finding those stolen objects among the rubbish in Selina's drawer in the kitchen: a scrap of velvet left over from the drawing room curtains; a lost button from William's coat; an old teaspoon; a baby's sock. Worthless things, it was true, but stolen nevertheless. Well, it was over now. They had weathered the storm. And it was very nearly Christmas. The preparations were well advanced and although she had taken little pleasure in them so far, she felt that would now change. The new housemaid was settling in and learning her duties fairly quickly, although it was already apparent that she would not be such a hard worker as Selina and was rather inclined to be pert. The older children were home from school and were filling the house with excitement and noise, not to mention trunk loads of clothes to be sorted and sent out to wash. She had had to explain Selina's absence to Annie and Maud as best she could and after their initial upset they had been most sensible about it. How grown up they were becoming. And Kingsley – he was quite the young man! It gave her the greatest pleasure to see his new-found self-assurance and his enthusiasm for his studies; she and William could now feel optimistic about his future. This year would see Annie finishing at school and Mary taking her place with her aunts – the first of the little ones to leave. How quickly the years passed.

She bowed to two women patients of her husband's and wished them a happy Christmas. Their admiring gaze at their doctor suggested that they would prefer to be greeted by him personally, but he was still deep in conversation with Mr Vinson.

Suddenly she glimpsed a familiar figure across the market hall. Could it be? Her view was obscured for a few moments by the movements of the crowd, then cleared again. It was! It was Selina, standing by a poultry stall, arm in arm with Mr Barry for the whole world to see. Her condition was now quite obvious. Sophia looked around. Dr Thompson and his daughter were no longer to be seen, others whose opinion she valued were busily engaged in shopping. She did not want to be observed watching Selina.

She was wearing a new blue dress, a rather lovely colour it was true, but far too bright for someone in her advanced condition, and of cheap cotton. Her dark hair was in a small chignon topped by a little straw bonnet decorated with cream cloth roses. She and Mr Barry stood close together as they looked at the display of geese and chickens on the stall, seemingly engaged in choosing which one to have, pointing now and then and conversing. As Sophia watched, Mr Barry looked at Selina and smiled and she met his gaze and held it with a directness that was most unusual for her, leaning even closer to his side. They seemed quite unaware of the crowd around them. Sophia tried to look away and turned back to her husband. He was, she realised, making his farewells to Mr Vinson and she joined him in wishing all the family a merry Christmas. As soon as he had gone and William was about to walk on, she clutched his arm and whispered.

"Wait, Selina is there. Look!"

She was careful not to point or, indeed, to look in that direction lest it be noticed by others, so it was a moment before William saw her.

"Ah yes, there she is indeed and looking quite blooming!"

"But to be out in public, in her condition, for anyone to see!"

He looked down at her affectionately.

"And why not? They are a respectable married couple now! The ceremony was last Sunday."

He was so exasperating! Why had he not told her they were married? He told her that he had been so very busy, it had slipped his mind and besides, he had not wanted to distress her by discussing the whole sorry business again.

As she watched, a small child emerged from the crowd near Selina and took her hand.

"Who is that child?"

"Why, it is her son, of course, young Will. He has come from Clovelly and lives with them now. Selina's dreams have come true, although I fear that young man may continue to cause her anxiety."

"How did you know that he was come to live with them? You did not tell me!"

As they watched, Mr Barry picked up the child to show him the geese on the stall and the three of them stood together, a close little family group, unusual only for the age difference between husband and wife. Selina shifted her weight a little and placed her hand on an aching back; it would not be many weeks before her time came. One would never guess she had such a turbulent history.

Dr Ackland took Sophia's arm and they started to stroll through the market.

"I have visited the household twice in recent weeks. I was a little concerned for Selina's health as she had been so very distressed, but she is well and she is cheerful. Indeed, she is now delighted about the forthcoming happy event. Come, let us go and wish them a merry Christmas."

Sophia put her hand on his arm.

"No, please, I do not want to speak to her, or that dreadful man! After all the trouble they have caused us!"

But her husband was resolute and they strolled on, as if they did not have a care in the world.

Selina saw them approaching first. She gasped and turned to Mr Barry. Sophia took a deep breath.

"Good morning Selina, Mr Barry. That is a fine goose you have purchased."

Selina looked at her quickly before lowering her eyes and giving a little bob. She looked terrified, as well she might.

"And this is your son, Selina, about whom I heard so much. He is a fine boy, is he not?"

There was an awkward pause. Dr Ackland beamed at them; surely he could help her out in this difficult situation! Fortunately Mr Barry gathered his wits.

"Us have bought a goose, ma'am, but as 'tis the first time either of us have had to do so, us wasn't exactly sure about the size. Will this do, do you think Ma'am? It's for five as there's my nephews as well."

He held out the bird. Selina was still unable to look up; Sophia could only see the little straw bonnet with the cream roses.

"It looks a very good bird. I'm sure it will do nicely. And I wish you both a very happy Christmas."

There, it was said. She turned to William and started to move away.

"Ma'am."

It was Selina.

"Ma'am. I'm sorry for all the trouble I caused 'ee, and that

I let 'ee down."

Their eyes met. Selina's were clear and blue and brimming with tears. Their gaze held for what seemed an age, while shoppers bustled around them and a fruit seller called out his wares. She was so young, not many years older than Annie and Maud. And she had known such hardship. And there was a child on the way, another new life. Sophia reached out and took her hand.

"Thank you, Selina."

Dr Ackland took his wife's arm and they descended the steps from the market. He was satisfied, but he knew better than to remark on it. Sophia was quiet and he sensed that the anger that he had shaken off a week or so ago had now also left her. Below them the young pregnant woman, the small boy and the man with greying hair were crossing the road. He had thought that he understood Selina, but she had surprised him, and he was not often surprised. For a while after that night, the shock at what he had imagined to be her immorality and deceitfulness had threatened to unsteady him, and now he shook his head at his own foolishness. He should not have been surprised to find that having attained security, she wanted companionship and affection. And was it not natural that she should want the best for her child, as he and Sophia did for theirs? He had done his best; it was society, not he, that had failed. As he paused to watch, the three people stopped at the top of the steep street, hand in hand, to look at the view. The long terraces of cottages framed the vista below them; the ancient bridge arching over the now full-flowing river, the distant hills and the translucent pale blue of the sky above. Selina leaned down to her strange little son and pointed out a detail in the prospect before them and her vivid blue dress fluttered in the breeze. There was love in that little family. Please God, it would last.

He placed his other hand on Sophia's and pressed it

affectionately, and then together they turned to go their own separate way.

Marriage certificate of William Barry and Selina Burman, 15th December 1872

Birth certificate of Mary Ann Barry, 20ᵗʰ February 1873

Extract from census return, 1881, The Strand, Bideford, showing William and Selina Barry and family.
(The National Archives, RG11/2258/53)

prosecuted for their maintenance.—The magistrates reserved their decision until next meeting.

GARDEN ROBBERY.

A boy named *Wm. Burman* (Barry) was charged with stealing 4 brocoli from the garden of Mr. Caleb Friendship, in the Abbotsham road.—Wm. Hunt said he happened to be passing through Mr. Friendship's piece of ground when he saw the boy with some brocoli under his arm. Witness just afterwards asked him what he had done with them, and then found he had put them away under the hedge.—Mr. C. Friendship, owner, valued the brocoli at 6d.—On behalf of the parents, Mr. Smale asked the Bench to be lenient towards the boy, who was a little peculiar.—The Supt. put in a previous conviction against defendant, but Mr. Smale contended it should be an official certificate of conviction, if put in at all.—The Supt. then applied for a remand, but Mr. Smale asked that the case be dealt with at once.—The magistrates inflicted a fine of 6s. inclusive, or 7 days' hard labour.

BROTHERLY LOVE—SISTERLY AFFECTION.

John Bright was charged with assaulting Jemima Bright, his sister, on May 14th.—Prosecutrix stated that on the day named as she was going through Mill Street she met defendant, but did

From the Bideford Gazette, 19th May 1885
Caleb Friendship is the author's great grandfather

where luncheon was served at half-past twelve. At half-past five there was another meeting for tea. At seven o'clock the breaks left Ilfracombe, and reached home again at a quarter to eleven.

DR. W. H. ACKLAND, J.P., for many years practising in Bideford, and Medical Officer of Health for the borough, died at Compton, Plymouth, on Sunday, at the age of 72. Deceased was a Bidefordian, son of a Bideford doctor, a medical man with a very large practice himself, and succeeded by a son, Dr. Kingsley Ackland, also practising medicine here. Dr. Ackland retired some years since. He was the oldest borough magistrate, and brought a keen insight and wide knowledge of human nature to the performance of his magisterial duties. He was also a Bridge Trustee. A Churchman in religion, he was a staunch Liberal in politics. For more years than one can remember he lived in a house in Bridgland-street, which, by the irony of fate, is now a Conservative Club. A man of wide culture and many intellectual interests, Dr. Ackland was a brilliant conversationalist. His association with Canon Kingsley was for years intimate, and he had much to do with the exploiting of Northam Burrows, now termed Westward Ho. The body will be brought back to Bideford for burial to-day.

BIDEFORD BOARD OF GUARDIANS.

KENNELS !

Prebendary Dimond-Churchward presided at Bideford Board of Guardians on Tuesday.—In connection with the relief of ... ... daughters earning

From the North Devon Journal, 11th August 1898